AF060520

THIS WILL BE INTERESTING

Also by E. B. Asher

This Will Be Fun

THIS WILL BE INTERESTING

a novel

E. B. Asher

AVON

An Imprint of HarperCollins*Publishers*

Without limiting the exclusive rights of any author, contributor or the publisher of this publication, any unauthorized use of this publication to train generative artificial intelligence (AI) technologies is expressly prohibited. HarperCollins also exercise their rights under Article 4(3) of the Digital Single Market Directive 2019/790 and expressly reserve this publication from the text and data mining exception.

This is a work of fiction. Names, characters, places, and incidents are products of the author's imagination or are used fictitiously and are not to be construed as real. Any resemblance to actual events, locales, organizations, or persons, living or dead, is entirely coincidental.

THIS WILL BE INTERESTING. Copyright © 2026 by Bridget Morrissey, Emily Wibberley, and Austin Siegemund-Broka. All rights reserved. No part of this book may be used or reproduced in any manner whatsoever without written permission except in the case of brief quotations embodied in critical articles and reviews. For information, address HarperCollins Publishers, 195 Broadway, New York, NY 10007. In Europe, HarperCollins Publishers, Macken House, 39/40 Mayor Street Upper, Dublin 1, D01 C9W8, Ireland.

HarperCollins books may be purchased for educational, business, or sales promotional use. For information, please email the Special Markets Department at SPsales@harpercollins.com.

Avon, Avon & logo, and Avon Books & logo are registered trademarks of HarperCollins Publishers in the United States of America and other countries.

hc.com

FIRST EDITION

Interior text design by Diahann Sturge-Campbell

Library of Congress Cataloging-in-Publication Data has been applied for.

ISBN 978-0-06-344031-9

Printed in the United Kingdom

26 27 28 29 CPI 10 9 8 7 6 5 4 3 2

Our pets, Bronte, Forest, and Meadow, this is for you

THIS WILL BE INTERESTING

Mythria's Royal Wedding! Heroes, Hugh, Happiness (& more!) Reign in Queendom Revel!

by Celine Hazelton, *Mythria Spectator* staff reporter

Our Queen Thessia's splendid reign never showed glamour and joy more than YESTEREVE, when Mythria's most honored guests gathered for what was surely the realm's finest celebration—the queen's wedding to Sir Hugh Mavaris at the royal palace under the Queendom night!

If word has not yet reached you of the magnificent events preceding this marvelous marital development—or if you have merely forgotten, which would be well understood given the very many quests and romances scribed of these days—fear not. The *Mythria Spectator* is here to catch you up on every delightful detail and incandescent insight leading up to this point!

Among notable nuptial attendees, the revel featured the REUNION of THE FOUR, Mythria's famed heroes, including Beatrice, Clare, and Elowen, who had returned from defending the realm from dark evil once more. We'd heard whispers from Vermillion Vale of "Claretrice" getting back together . . . While what happens in the Vale *sometimes* stays in the Vale, the royal wedding offered heartwarming proof of the couple's reunion. Newly honored hero Vandra Ravenfall appeared on the arm of Miss Elowen True, each of whom, it must be said, looked enchanting in their magenta one-piece suit and green gown, respectively. Other guests included songster Sir Noah Noble, shadow play star couple Everell Smythe and Hardwicke Hunter, horseball favorite Zevan Wintersmith, starlet songstress IDOL, celebrity culinarian Jed Flame, and even Vestriyan crown prince Ezio Vestras.

Yet no revel roster could surmount the centerpiece of the wedding—the undeniably deep love the queen shares with her heroic husband. Thessia spent the evening dancing with the dashing Hugh, locked in his embrace. The looks of love they exchanged left no doubt of the couple's enduring happiness. Even the remaining Four would agree. "Thessia's happiness is enough to possibly inspire me to take another turn at matrimony. One day," Beatrice of the Four told us. It is of note that Clare Grandhart, standing nearby in glittering black, ensured this scribe had gotten Beatrice's remark on the record. Miss Beatrice—whom realm rumors inform *Mythria Spectator* is recently separated from provincial nobleman Robert de Noughton—dazzled in pale pink. Divorce suits her, if we may say!

The event featured desserts, from liqueur-filled cream cakes to fancy ice cream sculptures, prepared by competition-winning Mythrian culinary hand magicians. Musicians played popular odes, shuffled in with old favorites. "My Home Is Mythria" left no eye dry in the palace. Guests were momentarily displaced when rain fell on the dance floor, only for hand magic to change the droplets into rose petals. What royal enchantment!

Flowers and frosting weren't the only surprises guests—or the realm—experienced on the wedding eve, however. None could imagine Queendom's astonishment when, in the early hours of the morning, mysterious magic wrought the return from death itself of none other than GALWELL THE GREAT, the hero who fell in combat a decade ago. (This scribe would love to inquire with the hero what face oils he uses. He hasn't aged a day!)

Will Galwell's return complicate matters of the heart for

Queen Thessia? Is "Thesswell" in the past? This eye witness to the wedding must state her conviction: Watching the queen with her new husband, enraptured and in love, I believe "Thugh"* is here to stay! Thugh is the future!

---

* Pronounced "thew," though we of *Mythria Spectator* welcome readers' recommendations on different couple nicknames or pronunciations!

1
Galwell

Galwell felt grateful.

Very grateful. Common gratitude would not capture how he felt in the seat of honor, under the rapturous hush in the darkness of one of the finest halls in Queendom, the heat of packed spectators perfectly fending off the cool of the mountainous city's evening.

Yes, Galwell felt very grateful watching himself die.

Not literally, he corrected himself. He was watching the actor *portraying* him die onstage.

Gratitude fit the moment, Galwell the Great concluded. The chance to attend a play premiere about your life and death? Assuredly an opportunity for appreciation. Witnessing the performer exaggerating Galwell's own death gasps and gurgles in front of an audience of hundreds? How wonderful.

Galwell had become quite good at gratitude in the week since he was "brought back to life"—although from his perspective, he never really died in the first place. Instead, his dear friend Beatrice had used time-walking magic no one knew she possessed to rescue him from the moment of his killing. She had pulled him into the present, which was ten years in his future. Ten years during which Mythria had grieved his loss, only to have him appear alive and well—and decidedly youthful—again.

Oh, it was all so confusing, and Galwell was just *oh so grateful*. Galwell the Great-ful.

Under the enchanted conjuration of a lightning-racked sky in the theater, Galwell the Great-ful focused on the scene. This was, he felt, the best play he'd ever seen. It was the only play he'd ever seen. Well, no—there was the performance his younger sister Elowen put on in the dining hall when she was seven, drawing inspiration from her favorite shadow plays. Or rather, his *formerly* younger sister. Elowen was now older than him, just like the rest of his friends.

The women seated near him stifled sobs. Distracted, Galwell gazed out over the dark performance hall—the audience was weeping.

He turned to his friend Clare Grandhart to voice his bafflement. Clare, Galwell found, was wiping tears from his eyes.

Grandhart had passed the performance leaned forward, elbows on his knees, hands clasped in concentration. Galwell had seen other men watch horseball this way, as if they were participants. As if their enthusiasm or judgment could vary the physical outcomes unfolding in front of them—or, in the present case, the predetermined dramatic ending.

It could not, of course. Nonetheless, forward Clare leaned.

Gazing out over the hall of hundreds of Mythrians weeping in commiseration with the characters onstage, Galwell privately wondered whether he was the only person who did not know how the performance made him feel.

To the crowd, this pantomime, written by one of Mythria's greatest playwrights, was stirring up the grief they had felt for years. To him, it was—

No. He wouldn't let himself interrogate the feeling.

To entertain bitterness or *envy* for the version of himself dying onstage—the hero who achieved his purpose—to mourn himself the way everyone else mourned him . . .

It wouldn't be right.

Instead, Galwell the Great fixed his expression pleasantly, watching his dramatic personae perish. The performer was passable, he found. He resembled Galwell well enough. Flowing auburn wig. Strong, muscular shoulders. His eyes were presumably spelled blue to match the uncommonly piercing shade of Galwell's.

He was giving it his all, which was what mattered most, Galwell reasoned. Were Galwell himself ever to command the stage, he would give the performance his all, as well.

It was enough for Galwell to deem him the best performer of himself he'd ever seen.

The man wailed. Galwell watched.

While he could not remember his own death, he expected it involved less weeping. At least he hoped it did.

Collapsing to his knees, the actor clutched the gaping wound that Todrick van Thorn, leader of the nefarious Fraternal Order, had dealt. Imitation blood poured down the man's front. The crowd gasped.

The effect *was* marvelous. Galwell would inquire with Elowen how magic had accomplished it.

He quelled the quiet frustration this question produced in him. It was just exhausting how everything had *advanced*. He had no idea how to use the "message tapestry" Elowen had gifted him. He only vaguely understood her explanation of "spell service." He recognized none of the celebrities in the copies of *Mythria Magazine* in his friends' homes, knew none of the popular songs they hummed—of which, he gathered, a considerable number were about Grandhart.

The incompetence was not what upset him. He could learn how to use spell service. Eventually. What wounded him were the incessant reminders of the years he'd lost. The past decade of his friends' lives. His *parents'* lives. Everyone's.

"*Thessia!*"

The cry pulled Galwell from his rumination.

While he understood the writerly choice, Galwell would *not* have uttered the name of the queen of Mythria in the moments of his death. Not for lack of affection for the young regent, of course! She had been his fiancée. However, their betrothal had been the product of promises made by their noble parents. In truth, he loved Thessia like a friend.

"How tragically we have been torn apart, my love!" the performer lamented. Wistful hope flickered in the man's Galwell-blue irises. "I will wait for you, for our reunion at the Ghost's Gate! I'll love you forever."

The audience recoiled.

Galwell noticed. The weeping ceased. The reaction now was different. *Discomfort.*

He understood it well. The audience had not wished for this reminder of their queen's tragic "love triangle"—Galwell had learned the term from Elowen, who'd explained its recent coinage in *Mythria Magazine* when three shadow play characters were crossed in love.

The unfortunate coincidence of Galwell's resurrection with the royal wedding left Mythria worried. For Galwell, their hero whose former paramour wed another. For Thessia, their queen pulled to her first love. And for poor Hugh, their newly beloved soldier facing an unkind fate.

In reality, Thessia loved her groom. Hugh had nothing to fear. And Galwell was . . . Galwell.

He was *not* waiting for Thessia at the Ghost's Gate. He was here. Watching her have her fairy tale with another man.

Despite everyone in Mythria's concern, it was the one aspect of his present position for which Galwell did not need to practice gratitude. He was genuinely glad Thessia had moved on, found hope instead of heartbreak. While he'd never loved her the way she loved him in her youth, he'd only ever wanted her happiness.

Hugh was her happiness now.

Quite literally right now. Galwell could not help glancing from the stage to the box where Thessia was seated with her new husband. Hugh's arm wrapped comfortably around the queen's shoulders. She leaned into his sturdy side.

Thessia's long chestnut hair flowed over the contours of her dress, which even Galwell—no connoisseur of fashion—could see was exquisite. On the other hand, Hugh's confusingly modern doublet looked like it did not know what to do with the powerful former soldier's frame inside. The poor fit only made Galwell like Hugh more.

They were perfect. The queen, the gem of Mythria, with her new king like the shield she was set in, the work of the finest weaponeers in the realm.

Over the past week, Galwell had wrestled with whether to confess his lack of feelings for Thessia. Thessia would know she could love Hugh without reservation. The realm would release their "love triangle" discontent.

He could not, he'd decided. He didn't need to hurt her feelings ten years after the fact. Better to hope Mythria forgot and embraced Hugh.

Which seemed the way things were going, until this play, which had uncomfortably emphasized the love between Galwell and Thessia.

The Galwell actor had now perished, fortunately, ending his cries of *"Thessia!"* and their uneasy implication. No, Galwell corrected himself. The Galwell actor had *performed* his *character* perishing. The man himself had not perished!

What was important was that the performer had ceased wailing the queen's name and kissing the actress portraying her with far more tongue than Galwell would ever have used. Far more than he ever *had* used. In his experience, heroics did not leave much room for ... tongue.

The curtain fell. The enchanted stormy sky inside the hall dissipated. The audience applauded halfheartedly.

Clare—a man for whom tongues were certainly used in heroics—leaned over, unperturbed. It was one of Galwell's favorite qualities in his friend. Galwell had the courage to face fear. Clare Grandhart had the courage to never entertain it.

"Not his finest, I'm afraid," Clare whispered cheerfully.

Galwell glanced down, finding the *his* of Clare's commentary on the playbill in his hands. *Sir Cheswick Chestlewitt.*

The portraiture rendered the current favorite playwright of the realm rather dashing. In his third or early fourth decade, Chestlewitt half squinted with perspicacious scrutiny. Dark ringlets framed his sharp features. He was unsmiling, yet somehow seemed prepared to smile.

Galwell's friends shared enthusiasm for the plays of Chestlewitt, who had risen to prominence in Queendom and the realm after Galwell's death. Everyone praised his unusual skill in equal measure for writing sorrowful plays—the famous *The Weeping Widow*, *The Weeping Widow Still Weeps*, and *The Weeping Widow: She's Still Weeping*—and comedies. One could not restrain Clare's enthusiasm for *Dog Noblemen* or *The Lament of Frederick the Flatulent: It Ends in Fire*.

"I'm certain this would've gone over much more enjoyably had it come out two weeks ago," he offered in the playwright's defense.

Clare smiled as if he wished to indulge his friend's forced generosity.

The contemplative measure of Clare's expression struck Galwell. Contemplation was unfamiliar to the rambunctious, reckless Grandhart he'd once known. Such moments startled him most, like no unrecognizable song or uncomfortable play could—the realization that his friends and his sister had . . . grown up.

THIS WILL BE INTERESTING

He found himself now the youngest of the Four he used to lead. It shouldn't have made a difference, but it did. He was used to being their leader, the one with all the answers. Now he was the one confused and not sure how to use a message tapestry.

He was the one *they* had saved. Galwell was practiced in being the rescuer. He didn't know how to be the one rescued from the death he'd just watched onstage.

"Still," Clare commented. "Good to get out and experience Mythrian culture, no?"

"I'm . . ." Galwell paused, meeting the eyes of Chestlewitt's portrait. Remembering Thessia with her new husband seated overhead.

He was what? What was he?

"Grateful I had the chance," he finished.

With the crowd, they processed toward the exit under the iron chandeliers' lavender glow.

"What plans have you tomorrow?" Clare inquired gamely. "We could catch a horseball match? I think the Farmount Falcons could take the Realm Chalice this year."

Galwell paused. He knew the invitation was well-meant. It was Galwell's other favorite quality of Grandhart's. Roguish though he pretended to be, nearly everything with the former brigand was well-meant.

Why, then, did Galwell feel like the same sword dramatized onstage had just pierced his heart? Why did he feel like they were still rescuing him even now?

"Clare," he said slowly, piecing out his own emotions in words. "I'm very grateful for all the time you've spent with me, but surely you'd rather spend the day with Beatrice. She hates horseball. Unless"—he considered the illuminating, unsettling possibility—"*that* has changed since I died." Honestly, nothing would feel the same if Beatrice had embraced the fast-paced sport.

Comfortingly—discomfortingly—Clare hesitated. *Whew*. Beatrice definitely still hated horseball.

The mention of his beloved undoubtedly reminded Clare of the endless romantic and intimate pursuits he would rather get up to tomorrow. Galwell did not resent them their happiness. Just like he was happy for his parents, who had found new lives for themselves in the past decade.

The Trues had endured loss with a fortitude that even Galwell, who possessed hand magic of strength, found remarkable. The results, though, were somewhat unexpected. They'd embraced the practice of florabee cultivation, raising the hive-minded insects to produce flavored honeys in every color. On their visit home, Elowen and the perplexed Galwell had been fed new purple winterberry honey, which was, indeed, delicious.

He was happy for them. He was.

Grateful for their contentment.

They were grateful for him, he knew. Grateful he was alive. They were *overjoyed*! *Delighted!*

Everyone said it so many times. Yet Galwell knew they had . . . adjusted. They'd found comfort in their home, their new lives. In remembering his legacy fondly. In cultivating florabees. While they loved him, they didn't *need* him.

No one did.

He had slept in the guest room, his parents having converted his childhood room into the studio where his father now painted landscapes. Days into the visit, Galwell could ignore the feeling no longer: He was in the way of the routines they had made for themselves.

He did what heroism and duty demanded. He smiled and hugged his parents and promised to visit them soon. He simply *had much to do in Queendom*, he explained.

It was not untrue, strictly speaking. Galwell didn't like lying. The

THIS WILL BE INTERESTING

moment he'd returned to Queendom, he scheduled numerous visits to an esteemed hair magician in order to *avoid* lying.

Now he spent his days wrestling with questions. Not the manner of questions he knew how to confront, either, like *How will we invade this fortress?* Or, *Can our horses outrun those ogres?* Or, *What soaps will maintain the lusciousness of one's hair while on the road questing?*

Easy questions. Galwell questions.

Instead, he faced conundrums he could not resolve. What was his role now? His purpose? The realm didn't need saving. His friends had surpassed him in wisdom, not to mention skill with modern conveniences.

Said friends, of course, knew him well enough to understand his misgivings. They met the challenge by keeping him busy.

The play had been Clare's idea. The Ogre's Chess tournament yesterday, Elowen's. He'd helped Beatrice cook dinner.

He wondered whether he was to be passed from friend to friend forever, or until he figured himself out.

And so Clare was proposing horseball. Under ordinary circumstances, Galwell loved horseball. Now?

He couldn't stand the idea.

"I think not," he replied gently. "Take Beatrice out instead. Return home to Farmount. Feed your eagle. I'll visit you eventually."

Clare's conviction continued to waver, though the mention of his pet momentarily made him smile. "Are you certain?" he asked Galwell eventually. "What will you do?"

Self-sacrifice came easily to Galwell, like horse riding and wall climbing. "Oh, so much, my friend," he said honestly. "I didn't fear dying. Nor do I fear living."

"How," Clare replied, "are you *this* good at catchphrases?"

Galwell laughed.

Under the lavender lighting, he watched Clare make his decision.

The right one, Galwell knew. Clare crushed him into a hug. "I'm so proud of you, friend," he said, his voice full of emotion. "Thank you."

The words knotted Galwell up. In honesty, he dreaded being left with only his own ruminations for company. But he said nothing, following Clare outside into the pleasant chill of the Queendom night.

In the past week, Galwell found he loved the Queendom rebuilt in the decade following the Fraternal Order's destructive overthrow. The city had responded to disaster with redoubled vitality, community, and hope, creating a cosmopolitan wonder from the rubble. The polished stone castle shone in the mountaintop moonlight. In the flourishing neighborhoods, chaotic mélanges of wood and marble housed high-piled complexes of restaurants, pubs, song halls, fashionists, fortune-tellers, fortune-*changers*, featherbenders, fizz dens, glass portraitists—*everything*.

He'd expected the crowd on the wide boulevard of theaters. Nightlife dazzled in Queendom. Everyone was eagerly heading to the night markets, where one could find every manner of food, drink, and entertainment.

What Galwell had not expected, however, was a voice rising over the crowd, calling his name. Reedy yet insistent.

"Galwell. Galwell the Great."

It was Sir Cheswick Chestlewitt.

Galwell found the black-maned playwright hustling in his direction. Scribes, who'd surrounded Chestlewitt to make inquiries and notes for their scribesheet pieces, followed. They'd pursued Galwell constantly in the days since his resurrection, shouting questions like *What was it like to die? Did you hear about Thessia's wedding? Do you have a favorite shoemaker?* Galwell had struggled to answer, until Elowen explained that he didn't have to. More worldly wisdom from his famous sister.

THIS WILL BE INTERESTING

Chestlewitt looked uncomfortable, like he knew reviews would not be kind. Instant pity struck Galwell. His own complicated feelings on the play mattered not. He sympathized with Chestlewitt's professional frustration. The playwright had worked for months, even years on his piece. One resurrection later, his hopes were dashed.

"Your presence honors me. I hope my play was a fitting tribute to your great legacy." Chestlewitt's eagerness verged on desperation.

Legacy.

The word rattled in Galwell like a farthing dropped down a mineshaft.

"I'm afraid my legacy is now rather unfinished, is it not?" he mused out loud.

The next moment, he realized it was the wrong comment. The playwright's smile soured.

"Unfinished," Chestlewitt repeated. "Undone, some might say," he continued under his breath.

Galwell's brow furrowed. "Would you have preferred I died?" he inquired in genuine wonderment. He took no offense at Chestlewitt's frustration. Indeed, Galwell himself was not quite certain how to weigh legacy against a life unfinished.

"Wouldn't you?" Chestlewitt replied with more insight than Galwell had given the writer.

Galwell felt himself speechless. The answer was not simple. He didn't wish to be dead, but he also didn't wish to be . . . this. However, how could he answer with his characteristic honesty in front of his best friend?

Chestlewitt spared him, laughing suddenly like his question was mere jest. "Ghosts no," he reassured Galwell dourly. "I only mean a certain . . . rightness may be found in things remaining how they have ever been. Like my play."

"It was a wonderful ode to what was," Galwell concurred, shaken but sympathizing entirely with the poor artist. "I hope everyone sees it," he added, raising his voice.

The praise worked. Approving nods passed through the crowd.

Galwell retreated from the scene with Clare. "I fear I've ruined his play," Galwell fretted.

"He'll survive," Grandhart replied.

Though meant in irony, the words rung uncomfortably with Galwell. *He'll survive.* Then what? Galwell mustered his smile, forced himself to nod. Deep down, the idea of determining how to fill every questless day . . . exhausted him.

They proceeded down the street. Clare undoubtedly read the darkness in Galwell's contemplative quiet. "You really don't want to go watch some horseball?" he pressed.

Weariness provoked unusual irritability in Galwell. "I may not be your leader anymore, but that doesn't mean I'll have you telling me what to do," he said. "I'm fine."

Of course, his push for finality only concerned Grandhart further. Great!

"It will get easier," Clare reassured Galwell calmly. "After . . . well, after everything, we all struggled with what to do with our legacies. You'll find something," Clare promised. "You'll find yourself."

Galwell could only conjure the imitation of heroic confidence.

"Of course I will," he replied hopefully.

"Perhaps you should seek out what you never got to experience before dying," Clare offered.

Galwell forced himself to consider the suggestion. Indeed, there was much Galwell had never experienced in his twenty-seven years. Including some rather embarrassing omissions. Ones he would never hear the end of from the famous rogue he walked with were he to confess them.

Clare was . . . right, Galwell recognized with the funny feeling he'd experienced more and more often recently. What made him hesitate wasn't reasoned doubt or pedestrian laziness. It was simpler, and harder to face.

He was scared.

Galwell the Great could fight evil without flinching. This . . . was different.

"I know just where to start," Clare declared.

Despite himself, hope glimmered in Galwell. He looked to his friend.

"Let's get Harpy and Hind," Clare proposed. "They've invented a new pumpkin cream since you died."

Galwell laughed, gratitude for his friend finally coming easily. It was, he reckoned, the best idea he'd ever heard.

"Yes," he replied. "That's the perfect place to begin."

2
River

You're only as good as your next target, River Pricemark reminded herself, tucked into a narrow pocket between food stalls as she tracked a man through Queendom's bustling night market.

Whenever the spindly vines of doubt began rooting in her conscience, this mantra helped River to push forward and complete her assignment. If she didn't finish, there would always be another assassin—younger, more willing—to do what River could not. It had taken River a long while to get assigned the jobs for which an assassin could actually gain a bona fide reputation. To miss a target would be to start over at the bottom, spending years regaining the guild's trust. To pass on a target altogether would be to betray the guild completely. River would never do that. No matter how difficult this particular job was, she could not bear the thought of turning on the Deathrose Guild.

She had to kill Galwell the Great.

His legacy loomed so large over Mythria that to see him walk the streets again, River could not help but note how *ordinary* he looked. Perhaps because she had no attraction to men of his kind—the beefy, overly earnest ones who did things such as bow when a "lady" walked into a room. River didn't have an attraction to many men at all. But Galwell was not the mythical legend that all the songs and tales had made him out to be. He was just a person, chatting with his friend Clare Grandhart as they sipped brews, the foam leaving a mustache above Galwell's upper lip that he wiped off with no shortage of embarrassment.

River would not waste time reflecting on what it meant for him to be killed *again*. Regret was tedious. Unnecessary. If the guild believed Galwell to be a worthy target, then he was.

"There he is!" someone yelled.

"Hurry, before he's gone!" called out another.

The group of scribes who had been tracking Galwell all night had found him again. They'd been following Galwell for as long as River had, making it impossible for her to find a good moment to complete her assignment. They were relentless, greedy for answers about the current state of Galwell's life. His relationship with Queen Thessia. Anything. Some of the conspiracy scribes believed he'd never even died at all, and they wanted to know where he'd been hiding for the last ten years.

Galwell kept his lips pressed together in an uncomfortable smile as Clare, ever the consummate showman, dealt with the situation.

"Listen up, and listen good," Clare said, smiling with his usual roguish charm, even though he gripped his foam brew so tightly that it had started to leak onto his knuckles. "Galwell has been nothing but polite with all of you, but it's gone on long enough. I don't *ever* want to hear another person question whether he really died. *Ever.* I did not live through the pain of ten years without him to have you ask if all of us were faking." There was a raw edge to his voice, the threat of tears clear. "Surely you've got plenty to write about that play we all just saw. So why don't you go on home and do that, and let my friend have a quiet night for once?"

The scribes nodded, scattering in different directions.

Good.

With them out of the way, River could finally work. She rummaged through the satchel fixed around her waist, deciding on a poison dart as her weapon of choice. It would be quick. Galwell would barely feel it. And River could finally go home. A win for everyone, really. Except perhaps the crowd of civilians who would have to witness their beloved hero die again. Ah, well.

Life was complicated. And so was death.

But when River returned her gaze to the spot where Galwell had been set to take his last breath—his second last breath? His *last* last breath—all new faces surrounded the Harpy & Hind.

"Damn it," River said, not bothering to whisper anymore. Galwell the Great was nowhere to be found.

She slipped out of her hiding spot, pulling a hood over her chin-length brown hair and adopting a casual pace, scanning the crowd while pretending to be transfixed by the variety of stalls and shops lining the avenue. There were people everywhere. Unfortunately, not one of them was Galwell. For all River knew, she was walking in the wrong direction.

Sighing, she retreated into another dark corner.

She needed to teleport.

Her head magic gift was impressive, but it was not without its faults. River could transport herself to anywhere she wanted, so long as she had a clear mental image of the intended location. Often all she needed was the image of someone's face, and she could reach them. Thanks to a decade of looking at portraits and statues of Galwell True *everywhere*, she could practically draw the man in her sleep.

The problem with her power was, she could not control exactly where she landed when teleporting. Which is precisely how River ended up tangled in the highest branch of a tree, hovering directly above Galwell and Clare as they strolled down an empty road chatting about—of all things—the majesty of the night. River fought off the urge to shout expletives as tree bark dug into her flesh. Hanging upside down as she was, she must've looked a bit like a brushwalker—

the wily tree-dwelling animal known for wrapping its paws around a branch in order to sleep under it instead of on top.

If River let go now, she would land on top of Galwell. Everyone knew he had been born with the hand magic gift of uncanny strength. River didn't dare attack him in this way. Besides, Clare Grandhart would want to do something ridiculous, too, like joust. It would be quite the production. No, River had to stay in this uncomfortable and inconvenient location, waiting for Galwell and Clare to stop waxing poetic and move farther down the alleyway. How could two men find so much to discuss about the wonders of the realm?

Finally, after what felt like ages, Galwell and Clare parted ways, though not without several declarations of brotherly love between them. Clare traveled left down an alley as Galwell continued forward. River released her hold on the branch. She rotated three times in the air, spinning with her arms tucked tight into her chest, then pulled her feet down to land in a perfect squat, effortlessly absorbing the force of her jump.

"Ghosts! Do you fall out of trees a lot? That was flawless."

A woman stood a few paces back, her face cloaked by the very night that Clare Grandhart had just called "rich and alluring."

"Be gone!" River commanded, yanking a small dagger out of her satchel to scare the woman off.

The woman retreated into the shadows, and River continued onward. In another life, perhaps she would have entertained the compliment. If the woman was willing, and the chemistry was right, River would have even taken her out for a drink. Shown her the other things she was flawless at. But River did not live that life. She was an assassin—*only* an assassin—and right now she needed to assassinate.

Galwell turned down a side road. River quickened her pace to reach him, drawing the poison dart from her satchel once more. The closer she got, the more she realized Galwell really was exceptionally muscular. One dose might not be enough to take him down. She was using a new poison purchased for her by the guild from overseas, and she wasn't positive of its efficiency yet. No matter. River kept several darts on her person. An assassin could never be overprepared.

Thanks to years of acrobatic training, River could use both hands with equal strength and capability. It proved to be quite useful in cases such as this one, where two darts needed to be thrown at the exact same time.

Eyes narrowed on her target, River brought her weapons up near her ears, elbows bent into launching position.

"Stop!" a woman yelled.

The disruption did not shake River's focus. It wasn't the first time she'd had to complete an assignment with a protesting audience. So long as the woman didn't see River's face, it was fine. River released both darts with the exact speed and precision she intended.

The woman's interruption did, however, cause Galwell to crouch down just in time to escape being hit.

Curse his heroic instincts.

And because no one got the name Galwell the Great without running *toward* danger, Galwell turned and used his crouching position as a start to a sprint, heading in River's direction.

"Shit," River said, scrambling away, but not before making direct, unflinching eye contact with Galwell.

Galwell saw her face. She was compromised.

Frantic, River turned—and crashed right into the woman who'd interrupted her assassination attempt.

"It's *you*," the woman said.

All sense left River. Her legs, the very ones that had allowed her to leap and spin her way out of a very tall tree without any injury, turned wobbly. Of all the people, in all the realm . . .

THIS WILL BE INTERESTING

"Celine?" River asked. *Her* voice dared to tremble. How traitorous. She hadn't seen Celine Hazelton since they were teenagers. Now here they both stood, full-grown adults, and River's heart still dared to beat that same wild, erratic rhythm that always started up whenever Celine was around.

There was no time for further pleasantries. If River was going to escape Galwell's pursuit, she needed to teleport. But Celine was here, standing in her way, determined to interrupt. Galwell had seen River's face, and Celine knew River's name.

River was, to put it lightly, fucking screwed.

She did the only thing that came to mind. She wrapped her arms around Celine, trying to ignore her surprising warmth, which was nearly impossible, with their bodies pressed together as they were. River teleported them away. They landed in the front yard of what River remembered to be Celine's home.

At least, it was the home Celine had lived in as a teenager, in a small hamlet right outside of Queendom. River hadn't been able to think of somewhere better to go. More accurately, she didn't have the sense to do so. She was so overwhelmed by Celine's presence that she could not redirect her focus.

More than once, River had imagined what it would be like to see Celine again. She'd hoped to come off as cool and confident, finally knowing how to speak as eloquently as Celine always had. Instead, River could manage only the linguistic grace of a toddler, telling Celine, "Go into here now," and pointing to the house. "Forget everything you saw. Forget you know me at all."

"You were going to kill Galwell," Celine said. She had the audacity to search River's eyes for some kind of understanding, compassion bleeding out of her, as if River was being made to do this against her will.

"I was *not*," River protested. "Go inside."

Celine stepped back, scanning River from top to bottom. "You're an assassin."

"I am *not*."

"You're in all black. You're wearing a satchel around your waist that's full of weapons. You have on sensible shoes, fit for jumping out of a tree. You threw two darts at Galwell when I called out to stop you, likely full of poison. You are *obviously* an assassin."

"What if *you're* the assassin?" River fired back. She had no idea why she was entertaining this conversation. She'd failed her assignment, which was bad enough. Now here she was, chatting up the only witness.

Celine was very clearly not the assassin. For one, her flowy blouse was tucked into a skirt that went right down to her ankles. An inconvenient ensemble for assassinry. The skirt would surely get tangled. Even in her youth, Celine had possessed a chaos that bubbled out from the seams of her clothes, like all her dreams and ideas could not bother to be contained inside her, thus skewing the already messy bun atop her head, caramel-colored curls haloing her face, and untidying the tuck of her blouse. It was a lovely kind of mess, impossible to recreate. She also held a large notebook, which would make for a most impractical weapon.

Ghosts. A notebook . . .

She was a *scribe*.

"I'm not the one of us who is trained as an acrobat," Celine said. "Nor am I the one who can teleport."

"Well, you're much smarter than I am," River said. "Surely you could somehow kill people with that memory of yours."

Something curious flashed on Celine's face—regret? Embarrassment? She'd always been known for her head magic gift of perfect memory. In their teenage years, Celine was quite proud of that fact, touting it so often that some of their classmates took to calling her Miss Memory. That was obviously how Celine recalled the fact that River knew acrobatics in the first place.

"Surely you know I must report your actions to the royal guard," Celine said. "And then I will write about them."

This was already bad enough. Celine seemed determined to make it worse. If River teleported, she might end up on top of a tree again. She couldn't chance two risky jumps in one night. She was in her thirties now. Her knees could only handle so much.

What she needed to do was kill Celine. But River wasn't that kind of assassin. No member of the Deathrose Guild took out innocent people, no matter how troublesome they were.

River would be punished for this increasingly bad situation.

So much for rising in the ranks.

"I don't suppose you want to help me instead?" she asked, trying out a sly grin. She'd been told that, on occasion, she had a sort of ragged charm about her. Not that Celine Hazelton was the type to be easily charmed.

River hadn't worked with a partner since Vandra Ravenfall, and that was years ago. She found she preferred to go about this kind of job alone. There was much less distraction. Yet here she was, requesting company. It was the only way out of this that didn't involve losing her position in the guild.

"You think that I want to help you kill off our realm's greatest defender? The man who made Mythria whole again?" Celine asked.

Ghosts, Celine looked lovely like that, so full of righteous frustration.

Still, it shocked River to hear Celine admire Galwell with such vigor. Then again, he was probably the exact kind of man for whom a woman like Celine should pine. She deserved someone earnest, someone who would bow for her when she walked into a room. Someone who could earn the softness she kept hidden under her bullheaded determination.

"Are you obsessed with him or something?" River asked. "One of his worshippers? I wouldn't take you for a Galwellian."

This time, there was no missing the expression on Celine's face. She was angry, her cheeks blooming fiery red. "I am *not* a Galwellian." She paused, fidgeting with her notebook as her hand moved toward the quill she had tucked into her hair bun. "Did you make that up, though? That's actually quite good. I could use that." She shook her head. "Never mind. That's not my point. I do not worship him. I just happen to know that our lives would be significantly worse if he hadn't saved Mythria a decade ago, and the last thing he deserves is to be killed off *again*. Hasn't he suffered enough? Haven't we all? How could you *murder* him?"

"We in the assassin business don't like the word *murder*," River said. "We find it very uncouth. We'd prefer you use *kill* or *assassinate*, if you don't mind."

"So you *are* an assassin," Celine said.

River bit her lip.

"You're in the Deathrose Guild, aren't you?" Celine continued. "Isn't their sole purpose to rid Mythria of nefarious figures? Name *one* nefarious thing that Galwell True has done." She used her hands and her notebook to punctuate her points, even going so far as to nudge River with the notebook in exasperation.

Yes, this was definitely the Celine River once knew. Eerily astute. And unrelentingly ambitious in her pursuit of answers. When they were in school together, Celine often stayed after hours to read library books on subjects related to whatever they were being taught. It made sense that she'd channel all of that into being a scribe. And that she'd be the last one to go home for the night, trailing Galwell through the darkness in hopes of finding the best story possible.

"I'm not the one who decides the targets," River said, shrugging. "Why don't you find that person and annoy them with your questions?" She regretted the use of *annoy*. She wasn't annoyed at all. If anything, she could stand to be substantially *more* annoyed by all of this.

"You think I don't know that your heart is good," Celine said, low and even.

"You're wrong." River placed her dagger on Celine's throat. "I could murder you right now, in front of your childhood home." She really did hate saying that word. But she needed Celine to stop with the belief in her goodness.

River Pricemark was not a good person. Not even a little bit.

"Do it," Celine dared.

River would have. She really, truly would have. Except Celine kept *talking*, prolonging the task.

"Go ahead and murder me, a friend of yours, after failing to murder Galwell the Great. Villainize yourself for no good reason at all. It must be worth it to you."

It wasn't the villainizing bit that stopped River. She was fine with being seen as a villain, though in this case, it wasn't true. The guild must have had a good reason to want Galwell the Great dead, and River just hadn't been told of it. That wasn't her part of the job.

It was the fact that Celine had called herself a friend.

"I don't have time for this." River retracted her dagger and sulked off down the once-familiar road, a place where she'd spent a year of her life feeling like maybe, just maybe, she belonged.

She couldn't deal with the Celine of it all anymore. She needed to return to Galwell and finish her assignment. If it came to blows with him, at least River would die attempting to rid the realm of someone as dangerous as Galwell surely must be. In River's line of work, it would be as noble a death as Galwell's supposedly was ten years ago.

"If you go back to Galwell right now, I will tell everyone in Mythria what you did," Celine said, following River down the street. "As I'm sure you've already figured out, I write for the scribesheets. I can have it published as early as tomorrow morning. I'd be the first to break the news."

"Which scribesheet?" River asked, feeling like she might need to go read every piece Celine had already written. Just to see how bad this whole thing was, of course.

"*Mythria Spectator*," Celine said, chin high.

River could not swallow back her surprise. "You write for a *gossip pamphlet*? Those things are filled with nothing more than mindless lies."

River had threatened to murder Celine not one minute ago, and Celine hadn't even flinched. But this made her stop dead in her tracks.

"Oh, now you're done stalking me? But what if you get a detail of my attire wrong? In the *gossip pamphlet*," River said mockingly. Now that she knew it was a bruise, she also knew she had to press on it, if only to prove to Celine that they were not friends.

River had no friends.

"And I thought you wanted to be an acrobat in your family's troupe. How is this where you've ended up?" Celine asked. "You told me once how much you loved climbing the ladder they'd rig up in the tents, because you could jump off the highest step, flipping and spinning through the air with a harness around your waist. You said there was no feeling like it because you got to fly while knowing exactly where you'd land. You knew that no matter what, you would be safe. And that was the only place in your life where that was true."

River felt as though her head might explode, hearing Celine recite long-dead dreams River had given up on years ago. She began walking again. "Stop trying to make me feel guilt, or regret, or whatever it is you're aiming for, using your perfect memory as a weapon to pull upon heartstrings that cannot be pulled. We knew each other for a year when we were teenagers. *I* hardly remember it at all." That was not even remotely true, but River wished it was, and that was essentially the same thing.

"It isn't magic that's made your presence stay with me," Celine replied, keeping pace. "I've kept you in my memory because you're worth holding on to."

This, regrettably, made River trip, the toe of her sensible shoe getting caught on a stray rock.

"I won't stand by and let you destroy your life by taking Galwell's," Celine finished.

"What exactly do you think happens to me if I don't go through with these orders?" River asked, glossing over the whole tripping ordeal. If nothing else, she would not be embarrassed tonight. "I am as good as dead if I don't do this. The guild will never let me get away with turning down this assignment."

Celine pressed a hand onto River's forearm. Her touch was warm, and her grip was sure, even after all the trouble River had caused her. "Then I will protect you," she said. Worse, her eyes—that dangerous kind of brown, welcoming and soft—gazed at River with surefire conviction.

River laughed. One did not simply *protect* someone against the finest assassins Mythria had to offer. And certainly not a writer for one of the realm's least respected scribesheets. "And how do you think you'd pull that off?" she asked. "Checking out a library book on how to exit organized crime?"

"It's very possible they have one. The library has a book for everything."

"You're not capable of taking on an entire guild of assassins on your own," River told her.

"You have no idea what I'm capable of when I'm determined," Celine said.

Years ago, when River and Vandra would pass time together on assignments, waiting out their target, Vandra used to tell stories of Galwell's sister, Elowen True. Elowen had the heart magic gift of sensing other people's emotions. River had often thought that to be a tedious power. What good could ever come from knowing other people's feelings? But for the first time, River found herself wishing she could have such a gift. She was desperate to know why Celine cared this much.

"You're pathetic," River spit back. She didn't mean it. Not even the tiniest bit. If anything, Celine was too brave for her own good. But River needed to shake her off, so she could go kill the shit out of Galwell the Evil.

Celine folded her arms, hardening all the softness in her features. "Fine. I get it. You can't be swayed. But every scribe—even the ones who write for *gossip pamphlets*—knows you never accept a story at face value. You *dig*. And then you dig even more, until you're positive you know exactly what you're writing about. Surely you've done that in your own profession. Surely Galwell True should die. Because the River I know wouldn't kill an innocent man."

River couldn't hear another word. Or waste another second. She teleported herself away.

She'd meant to take herself to Galwell. But that's not where she ended up.

3
Thessia

"What spell did you use on your hair, Your Majesty?"

Thessia of Mythria winced. *There it was.* The question she'd known was coming.

The scribes and conjurists who packed the throne room of the Queendom royal castle watched her with undisguised scrutiny. She preferred them to Fraternal Order invaders, obviously, the cunning treasonists who had twice nearly toppled Thessia's rule with their own reign of terror. Nevertheless, their presence discomfited her.

Her fingers were cold in her new husband's hand. This was her first formal interview after her wedding to the man seated beside her, Sir—now King—Hugh Mavaris. The opportunity was meaningful, her press positioner had reminded her. The chance to establish themselves, to invite the Mythrian people into their lives, to help everyone heal after the Fraternal Order's recent resurgence.

Yet Thessia was quietly panicking.

In her mind, she dressed up the question about her hair into something interesting. *Just pretend you're fighting . . .*

What did heroes fight? She didn't know. *Pretend you're dragon riding*, she counseled herself. *Pretend the realm's most fearsome dragons won't relent unless you explain the state of your hair.*

Perhaps this was true of dragons. Thessia wouldn't know.

She mustered her most polite smile. "My facemaker did it. You would have to ask him," she replied.

When the scribe's eyes narrowed doubtfully, Thessia's stomach snaked. Oh, how she wished her body double could manage press conferences for her, the way her counterpart handled public events whenever Thessia was ill or her life was threatened. Tabitha, who had been Thessia's double since girlhood, would know what to say.

Of course, Tabitha would not have been in Thessia's unfortunate position to begin with. She'd never have done something this impulsive, this embarrassing. Thessia's facemaker had spelled the queen's hair this morning, trying to salvage what Thessia had done herself in the middle of the night.

"Your facemaker," the scribe repeated.

"Yes." Thessia nodded.

The scribe hesitated.

"Very . . . daring," he finally commented.

The queen nearly snorted. She was sure it was the first time someone had said those words—even unknowingly—of Thessia of Mythria.

Desperate to exert some control over her life, Thessia had, in the middle of the night, poorly spelled her chestnut hair in shades of unnatural yellow. She'd wanted to look like a shadow play star whom she loved—a woman who lived her life recklessly and fearlessly, whom everyone admired and desired.

Unfortunately, the queen had no skill for magic herself. None.

The irony was never, ever lost on Thessia. The woman with everything, queen of the realm, lacked the manner of magical gifts nearly every Mythrian possessed—whether heart magic in matters of emotion and intuition, head magic of vision or insight, or hand magic of physical capacity and capability.

Therefore, she'd used multiple bottles of the potion sold in the markets, which produced an uneven, streaky disaster. Her facemaker—once he'd stopped hyperventilating—remedied the damage, using

THIS WILL BE INTERESTING

his hand magic to soften the hues into the shimmering color the queen wore now.

They were calling the color "spun gold." Her press positioner recommended the "aspirational" moniker, which, she'd explained, distracted from the impulsivity of the change in ways "the queen spelled her hair blond" did not.

The scribe sat, half satisfied. Thessia could not help contemplating how many, *many* more questions like his would follow.

The sunlight dancing outside the palace window beckoned to her. Thessia knew Queendom's charms at this hour. Before she was queen, when her mornings were her own, she would often roam the streets of the city. *Her* city.

Except it wasn't truly her city. Queendom was the city of the corncake crafters who enchanted their dough with mouthwatering cinnamon sugar, filling the stone avenues with sumptuous scents. The city of the old men who played Ogre's Chess in the courtyard from morning until night. Of the brewstands from whence she'd pick up a cup of caramel honeybrew on her way home to the royal castle.

Of possibility. Of freedom.

That city felt far from her comfortable, luxurious confinement in the formal, hushed room she found herself in now.

Hugh lightly squeezed her hand, calling her back. She found expectant faces eyeing her. She realized she'd missed something.

"Pardon me," she said. One more error, she remembered instantly. The press positioner did not like the queen requesting the *pardon* of her guests. Oh well. "Would you please repeat the question?"

Fortunately, this scribe's smile was kind. Sometimes they smiled like sandwalkers scenting prey.

"What was your favorite part of the wedding, Your Majesty?"

Thessia seized on the query like it was a rope saving her from fraught waters. "Dancing with my husband," she replied.

She felt Hugh's adoring gaze on her. He was perfect. Utterly perfect. Of course, he charmed every scribe just like he'd charmed her.

"She's the best dance partner a person could have," he replied. "I'm lucky she's mine forever."

The whole room swooned. Thessia herself swooned a little, too.

She smiled, finally genuine in her gladness. If she could not have freedom, she could have the sweet memories of dancing under the rose-petaled sky with the man seated next to her—

"King Hugh." A scribe's voice rose eagerly from the crowd. "How did you feel when you faced the dastardly Myke Lycroft in battle?"

Thessia fought to keep her smile while Hugh recounted the duel in Vermillion Vale where he—alongside the members of the Four, Mythria's grandest heroes and some of Thessia's dearest friends—slew the Fraternal Order's dangerous second-in-command.

The scribes listened, enraptured. Hugh *was* a hero. He deserved the recognition. She just could not help noticing how he received questions about his heroism while she received questions about their wedding. Her hair.

She knew why. Queen Thessia had no heroism to speak of. While she'd been rescued—several times—she'd never ventured on quests of her own.

Indeed, she did not even do much ruling. The innumerable councils who gathered in the Queendom castle governed the realm. The Economic Council, the Magistration Council, the Magizoology Council, the Interrealm Council, the War Council. Oh, the councils. Thessia knew their functions yet received no invitations to participate in them.

Instead, Thessia served in the role of Mythria's figurehead. The lovely, loving queen who embodied the realm. Who sometimes needed rescuing. Mythria's favorite damsel in distress.

Always the damsel, never the hero. Excitement for Thessia looked like spelling the shit out of her hair, for Ghosts' sake.

She did not resent Hugh for his heroism. No, the root of her new identity crisis, like the drop of Deathrose poison in the cunning potions her spymasters used, was elsewhere.

It was—

The next scribe spoke, still to Hugh. "It must be somewhat a relief," she ventured, "to find yourself a hero in your own right on the eve of the return of Galwell the Great."

It was that.

Galwell.

Her smile slipped, finally bested.

Hugh's, fortunately, did not. When the press positioner chastened Thessia later for the reaction, she reckoned Hugh would receive praise for his *heroic* composure in response to the uncomfortable question.

"Well, of course," he replied confidently. His deft showmanship really was something, Thessia could concede. "It should be no surprise it takes a great man to be worthy of our queen."

The inquisitive scribe looked to Thessia. "We must ask, Your Majesty. Is your heart . . . rent in half?" she inquired. "To have your first love return right when you'd married someone new? How are you coping with it all?"

What a question.

Thessia nearly replied with unvarnished honesty. She nearly confessed that Galwell's return, though joyous, had ripped Thessia's story from her own hands. She was no longer a young and driven ruler. She was a girl in a tragic love triangle. Nothing she could say or do would ever surmount the power of such a story.

"By going blond, obviously," she blurted.

Everyone laughed.

Thessia smiled. She hadn't been joking. However, she recognized it was preferable if everyone thought she was. Much, *much* preferable to the realm learning the queen was struggling.

"I am very happily married," she went on. "Galwell, Hugh, and I only wish to move on with our lives. The past is in the past."

"Not to Galwell," the scribe pointed out. "It was only a week ago to him that you were betrothed."

"What a nice observation," Thessia retorted.

Hearing the strain in her voice, the scribe had the grace to look regretful. Other scribes frowned in disapproval of their colleague's pressure. For this, Thessia thanked her cherished reputation. The press did respect their queen's heart and discretion, mostly.

The next scribe to speak redirected the discussion gently. "What of your honeymoon, Your Majesty? What plans have you?"

Despite the well-meant question, Thessia found she could not recover her composure. The mention of Galwell—the reminder of their eternal interconnection—unsettled her in ways she hated to reveal.

The response should've come easily, for the honeymoon had occupied much of Thessia's week. The planned voyage was political opportunity and marital occasion in one, with Thessia and Hugh to tour Mythria's picturesque countryside.

Thessia needed only to describe the public receptions her domestic councilors had planned, where the couple would wave to village visitors from their country inn windows.

She found she could not. Nervousness mounted in her. Undoubtedly every villager would look at her and speculate about her tragic love triangle.

It would be torture.

Her poet-rhapsodized eyes fled to the window. Heart pounding in her chest, she felt suddenly she needed to be somewhere else. Somewhere far away . . .

Past the window. Past Queendom. Past the very border of Mythria itself.

She thought of the Sweetwater Sea. Of Vestriya.

In the waning days of her mother's illness, the former queen recounted to Thessia stories of the most wondrous voyage in her four-decade reign. The way she described the distant land had enchanted the twenty-two-year-old Thessia—distracting her, if only momentarily, from the pain of her mother's frailty.

Thessia had never journeyed there herself. She had only her mother's stories of her diplomatic voyages to negotiate trades and treaties. Relations were so peaceful between the two lands, the Vestriyan crown prince, Ezio, had voyaged to Mythria several times, including to Thessia's recent wedding. Given Thessia's proneness to being kidnapped, she'd never had the opportunity to return the visit.

She went there now, in her mind. Imagining cities thousands of years old, wrought in stunning stonework using arcane hand magic. Of sleepless streets where powerful drink flowed without end. Of masquerades and fashionists' balls, where magic gave fascinating life to the couture.

Of shadow-kissed promises spoken in darkness. Of unimaginable possibility.

Of freedom.

Hugh seemed to notice her contemplation. He gave her hand a gentle squeeze. When it did not prompt her response, Hugh, once more the hero, spoke up.

"We plan to—"

The queen interrupted him. Going blond wasn't enough, she decided.

She needed more.

"We are going," she announced, "to Vestriya."

Gasps rustled through the room.

Thessia understood the reaction. The original honeymoon would offer scribes plenty of pleasant conjuration opportunities and charming stories of local visits. A royal honeymoon tour of *Vestriya*, however? She would be far away from the Mythrian press.

Few Mythrian scribes would follow them on the expensive, weeklong voyage crossing the Sweetwater Sea. Her retinue of guards could be reduced. Mythria had only peaceful relations with the neighboring continent to the west, and former foot soldier Hugh could protect Mythria's favorite damsel. While she wished she did not need protecting, she knew wishing alone would not convince the Interrealm Council or the Queenship Council.

Yes, she had her own council. They never consulted her.

At her declaration, Hugh's head whipped in her direction. *Change of plans, husband*, she could not say out loud.

Despite his surprise, Hugh did not contradict her whim. There were *some* benefits to being queen.

"But who will rule?" a scribe called out over the commotion. "What of Mythria?"

The councils. Oh, the councils, Thessia wished she could say. She'd been directed, however, to uphold the image of her own leadership, which Mythria—she'd been told—found comforting.

She thought quickly. She would give them something equally comforting, she decided. "Beatrice and Clare of the Four will fill in for me on official queenly matters," she stated.

Beatrice will hate this, she thought remorsefully. Clare, on the other hand, would probably spend the remainder of the year calling himself "Good King Clare" or some Ghosts-damned nonsense.

"What of Galwell?" one courageous scribe ventured. "Won't he miss you greatly?"

Thessia smiled. In Vestriya, she wouldn't be asked that question. It would be perfect, she knew.

"Thank you for coming," she said. She felt confident now, enough to project finality. Queenly. "My husband and I have much to do before our trip. We leave"—*what was one more impulsive decision?*—"at this week's end."

With frantic whispering and quills scribbling, the scribes complied. Each of them rushed from the room to wherever they could summarize the conference's events in uninterrupted longhand, then magic the contents over to their editors—Thessia had witnessed the ritual often.

Finally, only the wedded pair were left.

Hugh broke the silence.

"We're honeymooning in Vestriya now?" he inquired politely.

He released her hand. Thessia released her regal performance. "Will it be a problem?" she replied wearily.

"Of course not, my love," Hugh said without hesitation.

My love.

The words grated. She faced her husband fully.

His calm, clear gaze remained on her. Hugh was classically handsome, with inviting rugged flourishes, like the dark stubble now coloring his prominent chin after he'd shaved his wedding beard. His black hair looked ever windswept. His brown eyes were warm and framed with laugh lines. He was rather remarkably handsome, in fact. It was her second-favorite quality of her husband's.

The first was the sturdiness she found in everything he did, in every expression his perfect features formed. Not humorlessness—she'd known of Hugh's unpretentious wit since the day she met him. Just . . . calm.

My love. She echoed the words in her head. From the moment she first saw Hugh Mavaris, she knew he was exactly what she needed. Sometimes, in her weakest moments, she even let herself believe the royal fairy tale.

"You don't need to do that when no one is around," she informed him.

"I don't mind it."

"I do," Thessia said.

Other men might have resented the rejection. Instead, her husband's dashing features showed something worse. *Relief.* Hugh was a wonderful actor, which was why he was here. Nevertheless, Thessia knew how their charade wore on him. Like it wore on her, but differently.

She pretended it did not sting.

Hugh rose from his throne, stretching his six-irons-one frame. "Is there anything else you need from me today?" he asked.

The words were polite, formal. The tone the rest of Mythria never heard him use with her. Not the councils. Not the Four. Not their families, for they had none. Nobody.

"No," Thessia replied. "Do whatever you wish, but put together a list of what you would like packed, and the servants will make sure it's done."

Hugh nodded.

With nothing more keeping him, he strode down from the dais to the doorway, where he paused.

"I meant it, you know," he said from the far end of the echoing room. "When I said you're a wonderful dance partner."

Thessia smiled past the pain of his kindness. Some gifts she preferred not to receive. "Me too," she replied, grasping onto honesty where she could. "You're very skilled."

She did not expect the quick delight in Hugh's expression. "I have a gift for music," he shared.

"Do you? Are you a hand magician?" *What a question to ask one's husband*. Entire diplomatic crises would commence were someone to overhear their unfamiliarity with each other.

"No, a heart magician, Your Majesty. Through singing I can inspire emotions in the listener," Hugh replied. "I learned harp and many other instruments to accompany myself."

"I've never heard you sing," Thessia replied, momentarily letting herself imagine Hugh on a stage, a harp in his hands. It would suit him. Yes, it would suit him very well.

Somberness flickered in Hugh's features. "I haven't sung since . . . I haven't sung in years." As if to close off the topic, he continued. "Do you have magic?"

"Royalty has no need." The words fell without thought from her lips, the press positioner's prepared response for whenever Thessia received this question. Hugh's eyes dimmed further. Promptly, she felt guilty. She'd ended the pleasant genuineness of their conversation. "Thank you for sharing, though," she continued weakly, hoping to salvage the connection.

It worked, for Hugh was kind. "I do hope we will develop a friendship," he offered.

Thessia smiled. "I know we will, Hugh."

He nodded once more. Something seemed to hold him momentarily, a hesitation in which Thessia felt the glimmer of inexplicable hope.

Then he walked from the room.

Her gaze returned to the window.

The view looked different after her conversation with Hugh. Queendom lay in the peace of ignorance. Mythria surrounded them in the contentment of deception.

For the past week, the realm had thought Thessia was wrestling with the impossible love triangle now detailed in literally hundreds of scribesheet stories. Thessia, Galwell, Hugh.

The truth was much, much worse.

Galwell the Great never loved her. Yes, Thessia was young when they were betrothed, but she knew enough to understand Galwell felt only duty for his fiancée. Had he survived the Four's quest, he would have married her out of obligation, to fulfill the promises his family had made hers.

For the princess, it would have been enough. She'd loved Galwell in the manner of many young women—dreaming of the realm's greatest hero coming home to *her*. She would have settled for whatever he would have given her and hoped one day he would feel for her the way she felt for him.

When he died, her one-sided love had haunted her for the next decade. She took the throne and began her reign, and Mythria never, ever forgot her doomed engagement. So how could Thessia?

Until one day, she decided she needed to move on.

Which she could not do unless *everyone* moved on. Her love story was Mythria's infatuation. She could not release the ghost of Galwell from her heart until Mythria saw more in the queen's future than the pain of the past.

She needed someone to distract them.

Hence, Hugh. Their arrangement.

No one knew. Not even the Four. Not even the councils.

It was perfect. Until Galwell was resurrected. Suddenly, the morning after Thessia's wedding, instead of the queen who'd moved on with her handsome fake husband, Thessia was now the most envied woman in the realm—with *two* handsome heroes pining for her.

If only!

No, Thessia was entangled in no tragic love triangle. The tragedy was the opposite. A *loveless* triangle. Neither man loved Thessia. She could not get two heroes to love her—couldn't get *one* hero to love her, couldn't get one *person* to love her.

Oh, everyone in Mythria loved the queen, of course. It was *Thessia* no one held dear.

She was a figure. Replaceable with a character from a drama, a mention in a song, a body double. She was reminded of it in every scribesheet story and Cheswick Chestlewitt play and gossip-filled whisper. Yes, no dulcet countryside honeymoon with Hugh would do.

She needed to escape.

4
River

River had spent a full day observing the only person she'd ever known to successfully leave the Deathrose Guild—her former partner, Vandra Ravenfall. River had been trailing her on and off, waiting for the perfect opportunity to speak. By nightfall, she realized there would be none. Vandra never spent a moment away from her girlfriend, the famous Elowen True.

So from a neighboring rooftop, chewing on a mint leaf, River watched the two of them.

Vandra was wearing knee-high heeled boots and a shimmering maroon bodice, while Elowen was in her coziest nightclothes, both of them nestled atop a mountain of pillows and blankets they'd constructed into some kind of backyard fort. As long as River had known Vandra, she'd never dressed practically for anything. They'd once spent days together casing Archibald the Limb-Cleaver. Days in which Vandra insisted on wearing a rotating collection of velvet capes in bright jewel tones.

"Just because I'm an assassin doesn't mean I have to look frumpy," she'd explained, plucking a hemalia flower in the same shade of purple as her cape, then tucking it behind her ear.

The comment was probably a note for River, or maybe even an insult, but River didn't take it personally. River and Vandra cared about different things. Vandra had an eye for aesthetics. She noticed the tarnish of a villain's jewelry or what exact shade they'd had their nails charmed. River was an expert at examining a room for good hiding spots. Years of teleporting to inconvenient locations had made her keenly aware of what could hold her weight and what couldn't, which in turn allowed her to be distinctly adept at figuring out where someone else might have stowed themselves away. Their different focuses were what had made River and Vandra a good assassin team. They'd helped each other rise through the ranks of the Deathrose Guild.

Until one day, sitting side by side atop a roof not unlike the one River was perched on now, Vandra had announced she was leaving the guild altogether.

She must have made the right choice, because there she was, grinning ear to ear as she plopped Sizzle Crystals into Elowen's mouth.

"That's enough," Elowen said, then did something River had never seen from the famously grumpy Mythrian hero before— smiled. "*Desires* is about to begin."

Ghosts alive. Was River watching an . . . intimate moment between them? She closed her eyes, prepared to teleport to . . . absolutely anywhere else. This was a bad idea anyway, coming to Vandra. As if River would ever follow in her footsteps. The guild was all River had.

She shouldn't have let Celine's words get into her head. River's job wasn't to research her targets. Her job was to kill them.

This situation was such a mess. News had surely already reached the guild about her failed attempt at killing Galwell yesterday. They'd trusted her with the biggest job of her career, and she'd completely botched it. They'd be waiting for a good explanation. And River didn't yet have one to give.

"How dare you start without me!" another woman's voice called out, startling River out of her planned teleportation.

She opened her eyes to see Beatrice of the Four, also in nightclothes, walk into the backyard carrying a bowl of popped corn.

"Please tell me you have dollpeppers I can put on top of that," Vandra said.

Beatrice tipped the bowl toward Vandra. "Already on there. Unlike the two of you, I consider my fellow sleep-outside party guests when I make decisions."

"If you'd looked at the conjuration for more than a second, you'd know it hasn't actually begun yet," Elowen told her. "They're still summarizing yesterday's performance. I figured you'd be fine with missing that part."

Beatrice plopped down onto a blanket beside the two women, no other word said on the matter.

Now it made sense. They were gathered together to watch *Desires of the Night*, a popular shadow play. But Beatrice had called what they were doing a sleep-outside party. River thought sleep-outside parties were only for young girls. Not that she'd ever been invited to one as a child. Still, she'd never heard of adults partaking in the activity.

For a while, River attempted to understand. Vandra, Elowen, and Beatrice were giggling and gasping in equal measure, reacting to every shadow play reveal as if it personally affected them. How childish it was, these women sitting atop bedding they'd dragged into the yard, eating candy and popped corn, watching a made-up story in which villains and heroes kissed and fought and died and came back to life, sometimes in the same performance.

And still, a hollow ache settled into the pit of River's stomach. What was it like, to be a part of a group where the only collective goal seemed to be to delight one another?

River could not take another minute of this. She couldn't watch Vandra forever.

She spit out her mint leaf, then whistled, long and low. When she'd worked with Vandra, they'd used this code whenever they needed to announce their presence without startling the other.

Vandra perked up. Her eyes scanned her surroundings until she found River on the rooftop. Her expression morphed into a deliberate, hardened frown.

"Good to see you, too," River called out. There was a lingering bitterness in her words, something she thought she'd long ago resolved.

Beatrice and Elowen flung themselves off the blankets to assume the fighting stances River recognized from the countless statues and tributes that had been rendered in their honor. How silly they looked, poised to attack while wearing their nightclothes. Another reason adults should not have sleep-outside parties. You never knew when an assassin might ambush your hangout. Especially when you were two of the realm's most famous heroes.

Vandra still did not move.

Jumping down would have been the appropriate move for River to make, but she really did fear the impact it would have on her knees. She needed to start wearing supportive braces.

She settled on climbing down the building's overgrown trellis, suffering all manner of cuts along the way. By the time she reached the ground, Beatrice and Elowen had dropped their protective positions. Elowen folded her arms across her chest instead. Beatrice arched an eyebrow as she leaned against the back door.

Vandra lounged even harder than before. She had her hands behind her head and a smile back on her face, though this one looked more threatening than friendly.

"Hello," River said.

The air hung heavy with silence. River wished her embarrassment was only at the level of wearing nightclothes during an ambush. This was worse somehow, arriving during the middle of someone else's party and having no one care enough to ask why.

She cleared her throat, determined to appear unaffected. "I was wondering if I could discuss something with you," she said to Vandra. There was no way River could explain her situation in front of Galwell's sister, so she added, "In private. It's related to *the business*."

Vandra faked a yawn. "Sorry, Riv. I'm quite comfortable right here."

She wasn't making this easy, and River could understand that. But River did not know why she was making it so difficult, either. They'd spoken a few times since Vandra left the guild. Nothing too serious, but nothing this strained. When they'd parted ways, Vandra promised they would remain on good terms.

Perhaps River's fatal error was referencing *the business*. Vandra had left because she felt defined by the guild. She thought no one cared about her as a person there. She believed they only cared about her accomplishments.

Vandra had grouped River in with the rest of her colleagues, as if River didn't care about her as a person. As if River only cared about her accomplishments.

On second thought, River had no regrets about her current approach.

"Not a problem at all," she said to Vandra, grinning in return. "Happy to discuss this in front of everyone."

It was a lie, but River had to keep some semblance of dignity. Explaining this in front of Elowen and Beatrice was not just inconvenient—it was dangerous. They had taken down the Fraternal Order—the realm's most evil organization—not once, but *twice*. Beatrice had personally brought Galwell back from the dead. And again, Elowen was Galwell's sister. According to all accounts, they were the kind of family who actually loved one another. To tell them about the target on Galwell would be to put a target on River, too.

"I was just wondering if you'd ever had a target whose devious deeds you did not know of when you were given the assignment," River said.

"Never," Vandra replied.

"Really? Not even once?"

This got Vandra to sit up. "No. I never once completed an assignment without knowing my mark's misdeeds ahead of time."

"I didn't say I completed anything," River told her. "All of this is hypothetical."

"Who is your target?" Beatrice asked.

"She won't tell us that. The guild has strict rules," Elowen answered on River's behalf. "But I sense a great deal of fear from her. And also, beneath it, some hurt."

River was seeing Elowen's famous heart magic in action. And she did not like it. Not one bit.

"I have no target," River said. "I was just inquiring."

Elowen scowled. "You interrupted us in the middle of *Desires of the Night* to run a scenario past your former colleague who no longer works in assassinry and would therefore have the kind of moral compass one might need when faced with an assassin-related existential crisis, and you expect us to believe it's hypothetical?"

It did not previously seem possible, but River had found a way to make the situation worse.

"Forgive me for having a complex imagination!" River protested.

Vandra finally stood. She placed a hand on River's shoulder as she said, "If you've come here for help, I have none to give you right now, aside from this—come clean to the guild. About all of it. Ask them every question you've just asked me and see what their answer is. And maybe, after that, ask the guild what your favorite color is. What your best non-assassin quality is. Ask them where in Mythria you grew up. And when you find the answers to be unsatisfactory, just *leave*."

It was such a change in tone, all Vandra's posturing replaced with a sincerity that made tears threaten to well up in River's eyes. She bit the inside of her cheek to stop the sensation from taking hold.

What terrible advice. Insulting, even. River did not bother to teleport away. No. She stormed off instead. The situation demanded it.

What was she thinking, coming to Vandra Ravenfall? Vandra had let the time away turn her soft. She no longer remembered all the good that the Deathrose Guild did.

River would find Galwell the Great again. She would watch him obsessively until she figured out the reason the guild wanted him dead.

Then she would kill him.

5
Galwell

*B*runch. Galwell turned the unwieldy portmanteau over in his head. It reminded him of biting into something delectable, which, he ventured to guess, was quite the point.

When Galwell the Great last lived, there were two meals in the early day. Breakfast welcomed the morning with savory good cheer. Then, hours later, lunch held the honor of supporting the eater into the early evening.

Now there was, Galwell had learned, a third morning meal.

Brunch.

He did not understand brunch.

On days like this one, should he simply skip breakfast entirely and wait for this confounding "brunch"? Or was he expected to eat three early-day meals on brunch days? He wished he knew the right custom.

He'd opted for the second plan, protecting himself from the possibility of hunger and the impatience that occasionally followed mid-morning malnourishment. With a half-full stomach, he walked down one of the flourishing streets in Queendom's artisan district.

Not even his need to check every shadowy corner for lurking assassins dispelled Galwell's admiration for the neighborhood. From upstairs shop windows, weavers hung hand-magicked quilts enchanted for children with moving scenes of dragons and fairies. Glass magicians occupied stalls of glittering, shining sculptures.

And everywhere—the scent of food. The smells of nutty, milky sweetened drinks drifted from the palatial Harpy & Hind on one corner. Silky, salty noodles foamed in restaurant pots. Dough whirlers whipped glazed, puffy patties from streetside ovens.

Indeed, had Galwell not eaten earlier, he *definitely* would have succumbed to stomach-growling exasperation this morn.

Instead, he entered his destination with, he proudly determined, the perfect level of hunger.

The Brunch Belblossom's sign hung above the white-stone entryway, festooned in flowers. Over every column of hand-painted white and blue tiles, winding vines popped with wide chartreuse and purple petals. Grandhart had invested in the restaurant, he'd boasted. From the vibrant crowds occupying the contiguous indoor patios past the entryway, Galwell suspected the venture had proven lucrative.

He spotted his friends instantly. In the center of the nearest patio sat Clare, Beatrice, Elowen, and Vandra. Flowers like the ones over the entrance floated in their drinks, multicolored liqueurs marbling the sweet juice in which they swirled.

From where Galwell watched, Grandhart said something. Vandra laughed uproariously. Even Elowen could not help grinning.

They looked happy. Unworried.

They looked . . . whole.

Galwell strode to their table. "Good sir!" Clare greeted him, and new cheer sprung into his companions' faces.

Nevertheless, while Galwell offered his hellos and seated himself next to Elowen, he recognized the familiar feeling of intruding. Just a little. While the emotion might have preoccupied him on other days, he found he could not dwell on it right then. Almost being assassinated had distracted him from his malaise.

Clare leaned on his elbows on the table. "Secret identical twins," he marveled. "Wow, they really got me on that one. Fantastic stuff."

Galwell smiled, understanding he'd interrupted an enthusiastic discussion of *Desires of the Night*.

"It was expertly foreshadowed," Elowen replied.

"Yes, with that reference in the episode with the fire," Clare rejoined contemplatively. Elowen nodded, looking pleased he'd remembered.

Since his resurrection, Galwell had watched one or two *Desires* episodes with his sister, whose heart magic had promptly discerned he was not enjoying himself. He'd wrestled with which characters one was intended to find virtuous or villainous. Elowen had gently reassured him he did not need to follow the shadow play.

"You really don't watch the show, Grandhart? You seem to know it as well as these two," Vandra remarked.

Galwell smiled. "He prefers for Beatrice to tell him the details herself," he said.

"That's not true," Beatrice replied. "Is it?" Incredulity mixed with flattered shyness in her voice like liqueur in marbled juice. She looked to her beloved.

Unabashed in his devotion, Clare lifted her hand to his lips.

"You just get so impassioned," he explained.

Right then, Elowen coughed into her drink. Galwell found the utterance sounded like the word *slime*.

Clare caught his eye. "Not everything has changed in ten years, has it?" he inquired.

Galwell reached for the menu scroll in front of him. "Not everything," he conceded. "But *brunch*?" He examined the options. The Brunch Belblossom's offerings were, intuitively, floral-themed, varying from jasrose-syrupped corn cakes to limonella-petal-zested crunchy egg sandwiches. "It really is just a later breakfast, isn't it? Fascinating. Why did this catch on? Why not just meet at a proper hour for this meal?"

Beatrice looked glad for the distraction, though she couldn't stop the pleased pink flush invading her cheeks. "Because, dear Galwell, some of us like to sleep in."

He looked up from his perusal of the menu. "But then you would miss the sunrise!"

"Quite intentionally, yes."

Gently Clare plucked the menu from Galwell's hands. "I've already ordered. Meal's on me because we're celebrating today."

Elowen's eyes shot to her friend's ring finger.

"No," Beatrice preempted. "Not that. This is better."

"I think I must take offense," Clare protested.

Beatrice rolled her eyes. Galwell smiled. He knew delicate discussions passed privately between them on the subject of marriage, and he felt inquiring further would surpass rightness, even if he did genuinely look forward to being Clare's Man of Honor. His sister, he'd found, did not share his scruples. She pressed Beatrice on the matter incessantly.

"Thessia and Hugh are going abroad for their honeymoon," Beatrice continued, "and they've left Clare and me to fill in on all royal duties."

The pronouncement widened Vandra's eyes. "Oh, Ghosts, please tell me Clare isn't getting a crown."

"I think Clare would look nice in a crown," Elowen ventured. Whether to playfully rile her paramour or because of her longstanding soft spot for Grandhart, Galwell did not know.

"Exactly," Vandra returned. "Are we prepared for what the image will do to the scribesheets? We'll never escape it."

Clare swirled his liqueur, the purple-petaled flower whirlpooling in the glass. "I do think I could make a run for a seventh Mythria's Sexiest Man title."

"Sorry, dear," Beatrice returned sweetly. "I'm sure Galwell will have that honor this year."

THIS WILL BE INTERESTING

Galwell could only *hmph* in response. Hers was not the first reference Galwell the Great had heard related to his desirability. He'd received other indications from the unabashed maidens whose stares followed him on the streets, and from scribes intent on populating scribesheets with his dating preferences. *Would he desire long walks on the Sweetwater seashore, or dining in the finest fillet restaurant? Opera or dragon jousting? What heart magic would he wish in a partner?*

Galwell knew his merits—his flowing auburn hair, his enormous shoulders and chiseled chin. He did not, however, know his dating preferences, having done very little dating while defending the realm from evil and being betrothed to the princess.

In honesty, the ever-present recognition discomforted him. He'd never resented heroism's inevitable fame in his first life. Now, however, he struggled with how everyone felt they knew who he was. *Galwell the Great. Hero of Mythria.*

How could they know him when he did not know himself?

"Careful, you," Clare warned Beatrice. "Pretend you aren't completely smitten with me one more time and I'll have no choice but to propose to you on the spot. Publicly. With a shower of rose petals."

Beatrice locked eyes with him, dauntless.

The sight was familiar to Galwell, who'd caught the expression countless times on their quests. No different from when she fended off vicious pursuing grasswalkers or ran out of stoneflour provisions.

Then Beatrice leaned forward and kissed Clare swiftly on the cheek. That *wasn't* familiar to Galwell. Such open, honest affection. Such maturity in his companions.

Suddenly, he felt once more like the dead man in their midst.

"You're not the least bit worried about the responsibility that comes with filling in as regent?" Elowen inquired.

Clare shrugged. Galwell knew not to read any Ghosts-may-care selfishness into the gesture. Grandhart had grown into a shrewd strategist and considerate leader. "Ever since Galwell's return, violence in Mythria is at an all-time low," he replied. "So . . . no, not really."

"I'm sure that has nothing to do with me," Galwell interjected. He could use one of those colorful liqueurs right now. "Perhaps you four have inspired the queendom. Or Hugh has—he's very inspirational."

"Galwell, don't discount the joy and relief your return has given everyone," Vandra said. "When you died for us, it was very heroic, but it also made everyone feel keenly the costs and risks of heroism. Now that you live . . . Well, speaking as a reformed villain myself, it's a reminder that being good isn't just right—it's rewarded."

Galwell shifted in his cushioned leather seat. Hearing how he'd inspired people with something for which he was not responsible felt . . .

Irritating.

Like he'd neglected his morning meal.

Galwell the Great should not feel irritated, he chastened himself. He forced himself to focus on more important matters. Assassins! Peril! These were his strong suits!

"That's lovely," he remarked hastily. "Anyway, quick query. What's the current landscape when it comes to assassins in Mythria? Are they . . . also peaceful?"

Once more, every eye in his party found him.

"I assume," Vandra said, "this is not idle brunch chatter."

"Completely idle brunch chatter. No worries at all," Galwell reassured her. While the disingenuity in his voice dismayed him, he found it preferable to frightening his friends. "I'm just a little curious because I believe I met an assassin recently."

Very well said, Galwell, he lauded himself. *Very nonchalantly done.*

Elowen's face went rigid with fear.

"What do you mean you *met* an assassin, brother?" she asked.

Clare grimaced in confusion. "When?"

"No need to worry, friends. It was fine," he persisted.

He could convince his companions of the encounter's harmlessness, he counseled himself. Indeed, he had to. The duty of friendship demanded he not over-worry them.

"She barely tried to kill me," he explained.

At that opportune moment, the day's mystery meal—*brunch*—finally arrived. Huzzah! Galwell found himself suddenly very supportive of brunch.

The Brunch Belblossom had earned his welcoming conclusion. The food looked wondrous. The egg-crisp bouquets, papery sheets of fine eggy dough wrapped into floral-shaped cones, surrounded purple lushberries piled in the center, with their dark juice coloring the crispy "petals." Miniature sandwiches of thick bread with crunchy fried hroxen-flank strips sat four to a plate. Thin cornmeal squares proudly showed off puffs of sweet cream decorated with—what else?—bright blue belblossoms.

"This really does look delicious, I must say," Galwell enthused.

Everyone ignored the food.

"How does one *barely* try to kill someone, pray tell?" Beatrice pressed.

Galwell seized one of the sandwiches. He rammed the delicacy into his mouth. "She disappeared into thin air after just one unsuccessful attempt," he offered, the "she" sounding like *fhe* and "just" like *juft*.

Following his explanation, glances he could not decipher were exchanged. "Do you think—" Elowen finally started.

"Yes," Vandra preempted. She sighed. "Of course. That's why Riv wouldn't tell us who her target was."

Noticing Galwell's incomprehension, Elowen looked solemnly to her brother.

"River Pricemark," she elaborated. "She was an associate of Vandra's. She came to see us last night. She had failed to kill her target. Which we're realizing was . . . you."

"That must have been awkward for her," Galwell replied. "Do you think she's likely to try again? I'm not afraid. Just curious." He reached for his next sandwich. Diversionary efforts had compelled his first venture into brunch. Deliciousness compelled his second.

Vandra shook her head slowly. "River failed. Worse, you spotted her and would recognize her in the future. The Deathrose Guild is a venerated order of assassins. She'll be cast out."

"Poor fhing," Galwell sympathized past his sandwich. "This hroxen flank really is great. Why isn't anyone else eating?"

Nervousness on Clare Grandhart, Galwell found, looked like a nightwalker playing a harp. Entirely unlikely and painfully out of place.

"Galwell," his friend started seriously, "if the Deathrose Guild sent River to kill you, that means someone has requested your assassination, and the guild has found you deserving. More assassins will come for you. You're in grave danger." Clare's eyes swept the crowded restaurant.

"Why would anyone want to kill me?" Galwell asked honestly.

"I'm sure many of your enemies wish you dead," Beatrice mused. "But why would the guild *agree*? They hold themselves to a strict code of honor. Something is not right."

"I will try to speak to some of my old contacts. See what I can learn," Vandra offered. Galwell noticed Elowen clutch the other woman's hand on the tabletop.

"In the meantime, we must get Galwell somewhere safe," Elowen said.

"Oh, that's not necessary. I'm fine," Galwell offered. "Death doesn't scare me." He laughed, hoping to raise spirits with his insouciant confidence.

"Yes, well," Clare said, "it scares us."

He held Galwell's gaze. While the rest of the restaurant innocently chattered on, his companions descended into heavy silence.

He faced them, their hero once. Their former champion. Now the innocent, inconvenient charge under their protection. Yet in the noisy quiet of their collective concern, Galwell found he was starting to understand something of who he was. *Theirs*. He was theirs.

"If the guild is hunting you, nowhere in Mythria is safe," Clare concluded.

Everyone was silent—until Beatrice's gaze rose from the cornmeal squares cooling under her dismayed stare.

"Nowhere in Mythria is safe," she repeated. "Then you shouldn't stay *in Mythria*. And lucky for us, there happens to be one very protected boat about to leave the harbor."

"The one taking Thessia and Hugh to Vestriya," Elowen exhaled. "Yes, of course! Vandra and I will accompany him."

He imagined it. They'd shepherd him from the realm, guard him from threats, make yet more noble sacrifices. He wouldn't be the hero. He'd be the damsel.

"No," Galwell uttered. He set down his half-eaten sandwich. It was not the notion of leaving Mythria to which he objected. Indeed, venturing out of the realm where every statue wore his face, reminding him of his unfinished legacy, sounded somewhat pleasant. No, something much more Galwellian compelled his obstinacy.

"What do you mean, no?" Elowen said.

"I will not put you in danger," he declared. "I've done quite enough of that. If you tell me I must flee my homeland, so be it, but I will do so alone."

"But—"

"No but," Galwell said firmly.

Elowen's eyes widened. Clearly she hadn't been reading his emotions with her magic. She'd never really needed to before—he had never been in the habit of concealing them.

Galwell did not regret his harshness. *Theirs* he may be, but he was Galwell the Great nonetheless. *One could take the man out of the quest*, he found himself thinking, *but one could not take the hero out of the man.*

"While I am . . . glad to be alive, the truth is, I was not consulted when I was spared my death. Nor have I chosen anything since my return, not even this meal. In fact," he went on, "the last choice *I* made was to sacrifice myself and be remembered forever for my heroism."

No one could meet his eyes then. Beatrice went ghostly white.

Guilt finally panged in his enormous chest. He'd hurt them, he knew. One could use one's words like one's sword—to menace or to cut. He'd only intended the former. He wished he could withdraw his error.

But, he reminded himself, he'd spoken only the truth. Galwell the Great did not lie. Even in matters of death and destiny.

"If he wishes to go alone, we must let him," Beatrice relented, her voice strained.

"Thank you, Beatrice." He spoke to her gently. Forgiveness lived in honesty, too.

"But," Beatrice went on, "you will need someone to shelter you once you reach your destination. So . . . who do we know in Vestriya?"

When the words left her lips, two things happened. Inspiration lit Grandhart's eyes immediately. In the same moment, Beatrice's face fell, horror plummeting over her features.

"No," Beatrice said firmly. "I didn't mean *her.*"

Elowen leaned forward. She eyed Beatrice and Clare like they were drama-charged *Desires of the Night* characters. "Who? Both of your emotions are very confusing right now. Clare, you look pleased, but your feeling is . . . dread."

"Exactly right," Grandhart confirmed. "I do know someone in Vestriya. Someone who would certainly have the resources to keep Galwell safe."

He inhaled while everyone waited raptly. Galwell suspected Clare was enjoying indulging in drama.

"My sister," Grandhart stated.

Galwell faltered. *Had yet more time-walking magic jumbled his whereabouts? Was he living in some . . . parallel realm of Mythria?* "I did not know you had a sister," he ventured. "Did everyone know you have a sister?"

"Not a clue," Vandra said, bewildered. Elowen shook her head, likewise stunned.

Whew. No Multi-Mythria, then.

"Only Beatrice knew," Clare confirmed. "My sister, Mona Grandhart, is not someone I am proud to claim. She is—well, to put it simply, she is the worst."

"I find that hard to believe," Elowen interjected.

Clare's smile did not reach his cerulean eyes. "As you all know, before I was a hero, I was a bandit. I'm not proud of my past. But given how I was raised, *who* raised me, I didn't have many options in life—until I met you."

His eyes flashed to Galwell. Their hero once. Their inspiration once. He was a man made of *once. Once upon a hero.*

"Mona," Clare continued heavily, "didn't have friends to pull her from villainy. She let it become her. She runs a small but thriving criminal empire in Vestriya today, and she is absolutely terrible in every imaginable way. I do not just say this because she is my younger sister, I promise you."

Vandra straightened. She'd forked one of the belblossom cream puffs but now paused with the delicacy halfway to her rouged lips. "You don't mean . . . Mona the Merciless?"

"I'm afraid I do," Clare rejoined.

"If she's so awful, why exactly should we trust her to help Galwell?" Elowen demanded.

Clare reached for his menu scroll. Galwell planned to protest, unable to contemplate eating *more* delectable midmorning victuals, when Clare produced from his pocket his ever-present autographing quill.

He scrawled something on the menu, then folded the scroll and, using the candle in the center of the table, poured hot wax onto the parchment's edges. With his ring, he pressed his seal into the soft wax.

Finished, he extended the parchment missive to Galwell.

"Give Mona this and she will help you," he promised. "We will seek to discover the plot against you, and when we have, we will call you home."

Galwell grasped the letter, though he had no intention of seeking out this Mona for protection.

He did not need or want sheltering. He was the hero.

But . . . if Mona the Merciless was renowned in criminal circles, maybe she would know something about the people who sought to kill him. He could use her to root out evil in the realm.

"Now," Clare said, ushering the moment forth. He reached for the plate in the center of their table. "Who wants Hangover Corn-Toast? I invented them myself."

While Hangover Corn-Toast did earnestly interest Galwell, discomfort clung to him. If he needed—for the moment—to remain his companions' obligation to protect, he would. He would not, however, leave them with one ounce of unnecessary concern.

"I'll be fine," he reassured them. "You forget, but I dodged assassins my whole life before I had you lot protecting me. I can do this."

Weak smiles met his pronouncement, and he knew—they did not believe him. His death had made him human to them. Galwell the ... guy named Galwell.

This would not stand. If only for his companions' easy rest, he needed to prove he was still the hero they remembered.

He would be Galwell the Great once more.

6
Thessia

Seawings wheeled overhead, spinning specks in the gorgeous sunlight. The water lapping against the boat was only a gentle whisper in the salt air. From the white stands where Mythrians waited to send off their queen, cheers echoed into the harbor.

The *Sapphire Palace* prepared to set sail. Thessia stepped onto the polished deck, feeling... unlike herself.

She loved it.

With the wind whipping her blond hair, the salt drying her skin, the queen of Mythria smiled.

She peered over her nearest railing, gasping when she found the huge wooden hull descending far down into the water. They were hundreds of irons above the ocean! She'd never sailed on the *Sapphire Palace*, the finest seaworthy vessel ever constructed in Mythria, but she'd waved the enormous passenger ship off on her maiden voyage. Enhanced by hand magic from a hundred hand magicians, the ship's size rivaled Queendom's castle—hence her impressive name.

When Thessia leaned forward, Hugh grasped her elbow, halting her. Half protection, half restraint.

"Careful, my love," he murmured.

Thessia withdrew from the deck's edge.

She rejoined her royal entourage, who'd ensconced her on the short walk from their carriages in the seaport onto the decorated wooden walkway that led high up and onto the *Sapphire Palace*.

Her press positioner was there, of course. Her fashionists. Her schedulers. Tabitha, her body double, had boarded earlier. Thessia would have liked to have given her the vacation off, but her team *insisted* that she may need a decoy for protection in a foreign realm.

The *Sapphire Palace* usually played host to Mythria's wealthiest travelers, including now, on the queen's honeymoon voyage. Despite Thessia's objections, a few scribes had also been invited, for "necessary" honeymoon coverage, ensuring Mythrians felt connected to her.

Yet Vestriya waited. The realm had fascinated Thessia since girlhood. In centuries long past, explorers from Vestriya had founded Mythria, and the vestiges of Vestriyan culture had grown into something unpredictable on the shores Thessia now ruled. Vestriya's older roots had flourished into an illustrious land at once familiar and entirely remarkable. For every commonality—language, government—Vestriya was enchanted with rich details entirely her own.

After the walkway had been pulled up, the boat's crew sprang into action. Vast sails dropped from wooden masts. Suspended on midair perches and secured with complicated interconnected ropes, hand magicians conjured wind and parted the waves.

With the first enormous, coordinated gust, the *Sapphire Palace* lurched powerfully out of port and onto the open ocean, commencing her swift journey toward the horizon.

Thessia could not help herself. She let out a small whoop.

The sound made Hugh's eyes shoot to her. Past her self-consciousness, she saw curiosity flash in the king's expression for an instant, before portcullises dropped once more over his gaze.

"Welcome, Your Highness," Captain Norcross greeted her as he descended from the helm. Weather had roughened the captain's skin, but kindness, Thessia suspected, had crinkled his eyes. "I hope you find everything of your palace in ours."

"I thank you, Captain," Thessia replied earnestly.

But I hope I don't, she wanted to say.

Her entourage dispersed to attend to out-of-sight preparations while Thessia and Hugh toured the ship with Captain Norcross. Only one guard followed.

Only one! Thessia marveled. This voyage was looking up, and that was *before* Norcross revealed the ship's stunning features. They were led down to the lower decks, past stackjack tables with magical views of the ocean, open-roofed gardens where pinroses grew under flourishing high cloudflowers, and liquermasters who hand-magicked effervescent cocktails into shapely glasses on shining silver counters. A small theater played medleys of Sir Cheswick Chestlewitt's comedic plays.

One entire lower deck consisted of restaurant-style dining, with chefs who could net pestleshells right from the ocean floor and bake them into honey-dough pockets on the spot, or sweep up sealeaves and fry them into crispy pancakes. There was even a small Harpy & Hind outlet.

Thessia could easily enough imagine herself here with Hugh on a real honeymoon. Happy, honest, and in love. Hugh, in the dashing gold-threaded doublet he wore now, would share cracklecandies with her while they watched the waves. She would pretend to need instruction in disctoss, then trounce him easily while he laughed, her gullible mark. They would . . .

Never mind it, Thessia comforted herself. Who fretted over loveless royal marriages when one had fresh sealeaf pancakes?

Not she!

Captain Norcross smiled. "Would you like to see your suite now?" he asked.

"Yes," Thessia replied instantly. The suite would perfect the honeymoon experience, providing what Queendom could not—privacy.

While Norcross escorted them down the ship's corridors, Thessia envisioned indulging in solitude, the sweetest of luxuries for ever-public royals. Outside the hallway's grandest entryway, Norcross presented Thessia with a key. She eagerly unlocked the door—

In hindsight, she should have expected what would come with privacy.

Pinrose petals carpeted the floor. Conjurated pink miniature clouds hung in heart shapes everywhere. Cherry wine flowed in a small fountain on a wrought-gold table in the corner, with rougeberries floating in the sweetened drink. The bed—heart-shaped like the clouds—invited the occupants to enjoy hours of passion upon the crimson silk sheets.

Reminders, reminders, reminders.

Her face fell. The captain noticed.

"We are honored you would join us for the beginning of your honeymoon. We did our best, but I see we have fallen short," he said with earnest dismay. "My deepest apologies. We will fix it. Swans would improve it, yes? And—"

"No, this is . . . everything," Thessia managed hastily. "Isn't it, my love?"

She winced, hearing her own mangled delivery. Desperate, she looked to Hugh. He was the performer, not she. He could pretend to this happiness like she never could. She, someone who'd never experienced it.

Of course, Hugh rose to the occasion.

He swept Thessia up, hooking his powerful grip under her back and beneath her thighs while her arms fell to rest around her husband's neck.

Her eyes found his. Surprise dropped her defenses, forcing her to face just how handsome her husband really was. With his stubbled chin inches from hers, his gaze held depths to rival the ocean underneath them.

"May I carry you into our bedchamber, my queen?" he asked.

His voice was velvet even while his grip was stone. Oh, he really could perform, couldn't he?

Mouth dry, Thessia nodded.

As if she were featherlight, he strode over the threshold. Then, gently, he spun her while he set her down, sending the rose petals and conjurated clouds whirling with them, wrapping them in pink and red.

The movement disoriented Thessia, and she couldn't find her footing. With no other choice, she kept her arms locked around Hugh's neck, pressing them close. When she finally righted herself, she dizzily recognized the cleverness of Hugh's maneuver. Their noses were close, their chests pressed together, their lips a breath away from kissing.

Captain Norcross applauded. "We shall leave you alone for many, *many* hours now," the captain promised, relief profound in his voice. "Enjoy, Your Highnesses!"

The moment he closed the suite's door, Thessia let go of her husband.

"I think I don't like being carried," she said.

Hugh blinked. "Oh," he uttered. "Of course. My apologies."

"It's fine," she replied. "I'm sure other women enjoy it. But it's not for me."

"Noted." Hugh strode to the cherry-wine fountain. "For the record," he continued, plucking one of the rougeberries from the fountain, passing the round fruit past his lips, "they do. Enjoy it, that is."

Thessia watched the cherry wine drip down his fingertips. "Yes," she replied, her voice stately. "Yes, you're very skilled at it. It just does nothing for me," she insisted.

Hugh scrutinized her. "I wasn't aware I was trying to do . . . something for you."

Thessia reddened.

"No. Of course not," she hastened to say. "You're right. The captain loved it. That's what matters."

Hugh kissed the final errant drop of wine from his thumb.

"Although," he said.

He strode forward. Were they entering uneven ocean waters? Why, if not, did Thessia feel slightly uneven on her feet?

"You would be more convincing if you *did* enjoy our playacting," he commented.

"You're saying I was deficient," she returned, grasping her chin as she mentally replayed their exchange.

"I'm saying I often carry the horseball team on my back in our performances. No offense," he added with a wry smile.

Thessia felt herself deflate. He was not wrong. "It's difficult for me," she conceded with a sigh. "I've never had . . . the real version of this."

Hugh frowned, understandably uncomprehending. "You and Galwell were engaged and loved each other."

Thessia did not bother to correct her fake husband.

"We were very young. Very innocent," she said, proud of the honesty in her evasion. Galwell, she reckoned with mirthless humor, would not have wanted her to lie.

"I see." Hugh clasped his hands behind his back. While Thessia was tall—indeed, she'd noticed how the half iron she stood over most women made her fashionist and press positioner purse their lips ruefully—her husband's high, muscular frame imposed on hers easily.

"I'm not like you," Thessia went on. Her unselfconscious explanation had unlocked something in her—a jealousy she was ashamed of. She cast her gaze to the floor. "You experienced it in every way. Love. You know how it should feel. How it should look."

Everything I don't, she stopped short of confessing. Like she would never know how it felt to use magic. The queen of wanting.

"It's nothing like this," Hugh said.

His pained conviction startled Thessia.

When she looked up, Hugh turned from her. He went to the wall, spelled transparent to reveal the shining sea outside their suite. She could not see his face.

"The real thing is . . . easy. Joyous." His voice was everything but.

Thessia cursed her clumsiness. Of course the memory still hurt him.

"Frightening, even," Hugh went on. "A wanting both wonderful and terrible at once."

Her mouth opened, yet Thessia knew not what to say. The Hugh she'd wed was charismatic, quick to smile, even quicker to joke.

He had been . . . performing, she was realizing. The whole time, even for her, in ways she didn't notice. He'd mastered the conjurated cheer Thessia sought for herself.

She should have known. It was why she'd chosen him, wasn't it?

Chosen him, with her royal request, to pretend to the love he'd once known for real. When she was younger, she'd hoped to find genuine love, of course, before she'd learned that any man who courted her was courting the queen. Not Thessia. Any relationship she began would be . . . empty. Fake.

Why not control the farce? Embark on a relationship that was only ever *intended* to be fake? She'd never be guilelessly swept away into a one-sided romance again.

She'd gone on secretive dates with a number of eligible men. All of them had sought to flatter or impress her. Hugh was pleasant, as was his nature. She'd decided he was not the one for her before they'd even gotten to dessert, thinking that someone so happy and affable would never make a good match for a frustrated queen.

But then on the carriage ride home he'd suddenly begun to weep.

Guilt knifed into her. "If this is too hard for you, I would understand," she hastened to say.

When Hugh faced her once more, his easygoing charm had returned. His mask, gorgeously flawless, like enchanted Vestriyan workmanship. "No. I'm fine," he reassured her. The queen very nearly found herself convinced.

"I'm sorry I never knew her," she said instead.

He'd told her only her name, gasping out the syllables between sobs in the carriage. *Zaralie.* They'd fallen in love as teenagers and pledged their lives to each other. She was a soldier, and he'd volunteered to fight in the war against the Fraternal Order to be with her. Hugh had come home from the Queendom campaign. Zaralie had not.

Hugh's expression faltered. This time, Thessia fought off the guilt. She owed him this. If they were to lie to the realm, she wished her fake husband to know he could speak honestly with her.

"She was very dour upon first impression," Hugh said. His eyes went distant. "But when you made her laugh, her whole face lit up. She loved to dance."

"Then she must have loved to hear you sing," Thessia offered.

Hugh smiled. His real smile, as if the compliment had illuminated some long-covered light in him.

Then his expression closed up again. The fragile magic of their connection disappeared. King Hugh, formidable and composed, stood once more in the grieving, kind man's place. "I find very little reason to sing these days." He smiled once more, though Thessia could tell it was forced. "No, it is not too hard," he said, still pondering Thessia's question. "I can never see myself wanting any of this for real." He gestured to the honeymoon suite. "Not without her. It is best that I only be asked to pretend."

Thessia nodded with perfunctory haste. Did the reminder of how he would never desire her in earnest sting? Indeed.

Despite Hugh's handsomeness, Thessia had stopped herself from developing real feelings for her fake husband. But his dismissal reminded Thessia that *nobody* desired her.

Not even the queen could withstand this notion with an uninjured heart. In her feigned marriage, Thessia would never feel the passion, the yearning, the companionship of which Hugh spoke.

A wanting both wonderful and terrible at once.

In the end, her husband's painful history was exactly why she'd chosen him. She was not stealing a future from this man. It would not have been fair to form her fake marriage with someone whom she might have held back from real love. Hugh, however... Heartbroken forever over the death of his beloved, Hugh would never love again.

He was interested in elevating his station, in giving up soldiering for good. She was interested in removing herself from *The Tragedy of Galwell and Thessia*.

He was safe. He was perfect.

Perfectly unreachable.

"There is only one bed here," Thessia observed loudly. "Obviously. We shall sleep in shifts."

She wondered whether her husband looked pleased to move the conversation on to logistics or whether she was merely projecting. "I'll take the first shift," he offered. "You enjoy the boat."

His selflessness softened her. "That is kind," she conceded. "Thank you."

Hugh nodded once.

Eager to escape the conversation, Thessia pulled her cloak's hood over her head. While everyone knew of her presence on the *Sapphire Palace*, she wished to move in privacy when she could.

This meant steering clear of populous places. No Chestlewitt theater or seafood spread for her this evening, unfortunately.

Instead, she decided to walk the crew deck. Like in Queendom,

THIS WILL BE INTERESTING

when she found unassuming city streets the elegant equal of the finest castle corridors, the undecorated deck captivated her. From the humble wooden railings, she watched the sun set over the ocean.

Or—she would have.

But Captain Norcross was descending from the helm to the deck, and Thessia knew only moments separated her from an unwelcome interrogation on why she was not indulging in her honeymoon suite.

Desperate, she scuttled to the nearest hatch.

The ladder deposited her in a quaint crew compartment, small, with one bunk. The cabin—

Wasn't empty, Thessia realized.

"Sorry!" she exclaimed. "Oh, Ghosts, I meant no—"

The explanation died on Thessia's lips, for she *recognized* the other person in this compartment.

"*Galwell?*"

The enormous man hunched in the corner, hands raised in contrition. His remarkable rust-colored hair hung over half his face.

"What in the Ghost's tombs are you doing here?" Thessia hissed.

"I—I'm so sorry. I had hoped to stay out of your way on the voyage," the regretful hero promised. "I have no desire to interrupt your honeymoon."

"And yet you have," Thessia replied.

Galwell straightened, some of his heroic self-possession returning. "In fairness, you stumbled in *my* way," he pointed out gently.

Thessia rubbed her forehead in exasperation. Was nowhere on this damnable ship free from her present or former romantic partners? She wouldn't run into the foreign prince with whom she'd shared her first kiss next, would she? Would she find the shadow play star on whom she'd had her second-ever crush hiding under the dinner spread? If she was forced to walk the decks of her heart for the entire voyage, she would not mind the ship sinking.

"Why are you here? I literally boarded this ship to escape you," she complained.

Galwell cocked his head in surprise. "You did? Why?"

Thessia immediately wished she could rescind the confession.

Straightening, she pretended to possess regal confidence, meanwhile searching for an explanation that would be preferable to honesty. She couldn't very well describe how incessant questions about her loveless love triangle were simply depressing, could she?

She settled on dishonesty. "It's my honeymoon, Galwell. I wanted to be alone with my husband," she said primly.

Guilt fell heavily over Galwell's statuesque features. "Yes. Yes, of course you did. I promise you won't see me at all. I'll stay in this room the whole voyage," he vowed, rambling in his urgency. "And when we disembark, you won't even know I'm in Vestriya. No one will. That's the point."

Thessia frowned. *The point?* "What do you mean? Why?"

Despite herself, she could not fight curiosity when Galwell's eyes darted past her, scouring the room. "It's—nothing. Enjoy your honeymoon, Thessia."

Oh, he expected her to simply accept his words like some pitiable princess, did he? Thessia crossed her arms. No, she would not be brushed aside. "Funny," she challenged him, "how in another life, I would be on this honeymoon cruise with *you*."

Galwell shifted his feet. While she did not welcome his discomfort, Thessia was proud of herself. *She* could confront their hollow romantic history, even if he—the dauntless hero!—could not.

"You would have put on such a brave face," she went on. "But of course, it's what you're best at. Nobly sacrificing yourself."

His eyes widened, and Thessia realized he'd never suspected she knew his heart was not in their engagement. For a moment, she felt in control of her life. She was *not* innocent or helpless. She was clever and brave. She did not fear the truth.

"How did you—" Galwell started.

The cabin door flew open.

With dismay, Thessia welcomed their intruder. "Captain Norcross," she greeted the old seaman.

She was on the verge of pretending she did indeed urgently need swans for her room when the captain drew a long, shining knife.

He made no reply to her greeting. His eyes were unrecognizable. Venomous, hateful, instead of his earlier weathered kindness.

"Assassin!" Galwell shouted. "Run, Thessia!"

It was no use. One very important question held Thessia in place. *Why does Captain Norcross want to kill me?*

Then she was shoved out of the way. The captain didn't lunge for her—he lunged for Galwell.

7
River

River moved fast, but the Deathrose Guild moved faster.

She'd secretly boarded this disgrace of a ship—a gigantic abomination that housed more amenities in one single place than she'd experienced in her entire lifetime—to trail Galwell, find something that merited his assassination, and then complete the task.

Following him down countless corridors as he took himself to his stowaway chambers, she'd seen nothing suspicious from him. In fact, he'd been comically good. Dressed in a poor excuse for a disguise, he'd passed an old woman struggling to carry her luggage and wordlessly hoisted it over his shoulder to bring to her room. He'd spotted a large spill and used his own cloak to mop it up.

Perhaps the guild didn't yet know River had failed, she'd thought. Because for all the ways Galwell thought he was being discreet, he may as well have painted an actual target on the back of his absurdly large shoulders. Even with the disguise—which amounted to nothing more than a cap pulled over his long curls and an unusually cumbersome cloak—and the cabin tucked deep inside the ship, anyone he passed on his way into hiding could confirm he was alive and well, including the young child he'd scooped up and dropped off near her parents after she'd gotten lost.

But the Deathrose Guild was already one step ahead of her and Galwell both. They'd sent Dougal, one of the guild's most esteemed assassins, to finish River's job. River had spotted him in his captain disguise, hurrying in the same direction as Galwell's cabin.

Hearing commotion below, and not wanting Galwell to die before she figured out why he'd been targeted in the first place, River teleported herself to where Dougal was. She'd expected a rational conversation would take place, where she could explain what went wrong earlier in the week and all the steps she was currently taking to resolve it. Maybe Dougal would even be impressed by River's initiative.

Instead, River landed atop Dougal in the small crew cabin where Galwell had set up camp. Literally atop him, her legs straddled around Dougal's shoulders as he swung a long knife with reckless abandon.

"What are you doing? Stop at once!" a woman shouted.

River nearly lost her focus. Queen Thessia was in the cabin, too, backed into a corner, mouth agape in horror. Not only was Dougal attempting to kill Galwell, but he was doing it in front of the *queen of Mythria*.

"River! Get off me!" Dougal yelled, spinning so as to dislodge her. She wanted to ask how he knew who'd landed atop him, but appearing unexpectedly inside a room from some place other than the door was a rather unforgettable skill.

To keep her purchase, River gripped what little remained of Dougal's hair. "Hold on! Let's talk about this!"

"There is nothing to discuss! Let go of my hair!"

River knew she needed to respect Dougal's request. He outranked her in every way—the kind of member who might even be able to restore her sullied position within the guild. But he was being so . . . unwieldy. Sometimes assignments took place in public, but the assassin was required to remain unidentifiable to any innocent witnesses. Queen Thessia could have counted Dougal's nose hairs, she was getting such a good, unobscured look at him.

"Stop at once!" Galwell boomed. "State your intentions!"

River didn't know if the prompt was for her or Dougal. Galwell's voice made both of them pause anyway. She hated to say it, but up close, Galwell really did have an energy about him. As if at any given moment, he needed to have wind blowing through his hair, an artful rip in his tunic, and sweeping, orchestral music to score his actions.

If only Celine could see this . . . River thought as Galwell stepped protectively in front of Thessia. *The gossip pamphlets would be fed for months.*

She shook her head. Enough thinking about Celine.

"I'm here to kill you," Dougal told him. "Since *she* failed to get the job done."

At that, Dougal whipped sideways as hard as he could, flinging a distracted River off his shoulders. The cabin was so small that she clunked her skull against the bunk bed on the way to the floor.

River scrambled to her feet, dizzy but determined. "You cannot kill Galwell in front of our queen." She dug her fingernails into Dougal's forearm to stop him from wielding his knife. He'd taken a reckless swipe that had nicked Queen Thessia on the arm. River turned as much as she could, keeping pressure on Dougal as she attempted to curtsy. "Your Majesty."

"That's really not necessary right now," Queen Thessia told her. "But I do command that Captain Norcross state why he is attempting to kill Galwell at all."

"We are on water," he said. "You do not govern me here."

"And when we reach land, what do you expect will happen then?" the queen asked.

"I won't be here to find out. And neither will you."

Perhaps the guild's code did not matter to Dougal on water. But it mattered to River everywhere. So she did the only thing she could think of to stop him.

She kneed Dougal in the groin.

He doubled over, and River bent down to meet him, hissing out, "What are you thinking? Innocent witnesses aren't meant to be collateral damage. It's a part of our honor code."

"Forget the honor code," he told her, face purpled in agony.

The guild *also* forbade members from killing each other without just cause, which was the only reason River did not take Dougal's knife and plunge it into his heart right then and there. Because how dare he say such a thing when he'd been in the guild for as long as River had been alive?

She settled for ripping the knife from his hand and placing a boot on his neck. She needed time to think.

Something was wrong. Very, very wrong. The code was life. No member of the Deathrose Guild would ever wish to do away with it.

"I know I'm not the first person you'd want to do a favor for," River said, looking to Galwell, chancing a half-grin his way. "But could I trouble you to grab that rope behind you, so I can tie him up?"

Galwell nodded. "Of course. I'm happy to do the tying, if that's easier."

"*Galwell*," Queen Thessia warned. "She's an assassin, too. What if this is all part of an elaborate plot between the two of them?"

"It's not," River and Galwell said in unison.

Ghosts. Even his faith in her was good.

"Prove it," Queen Thessia challenged.

River had to take a risk. Desperate times called for desperate measures.

"This is not Captain Norcross," she said. "This is Dougal Farkenstomp, supposedly esteemed member of the Deathrose Guild. A man who should know that the guild forbids him from completing an assignment when a witness can plainly identify his face or share his real name. And a man who certainly knows he cannot kill *the queen of Mythria*."

She'd never betrayed another guild member before. It would be yet another offense in the eyes of the guild—but what was one more infraction on top of her already growing list? Surely if she got the chance to plead her case to whoever it was at the very top of the guild—a name no one at River's level was allowed to learn, for purposes of safety—she'd explain all the rules Dougal himself had broken first, and everyone would understand.

Assassins—notoriously understanding!

River kept her foot on the side of Dougal's neck as Galwell secured the rope around the man's hands and feet. Once done, they propped him up in a seated position, his back resting against the wall behind the door. Looking at him—a man who up until three minutes ago River had thought she someday wanted to be—disgust overwhelmed her.

Why would he do this?

"Who gave you this assignment?" River asked. There was no use in skirting around it in front of Galwell and Queen Thessia. They'd already heard too much anyway.

Dougal said nothing.

"You're really embracing the protection of water," she continued. "But we will reach land soon enough. And you will have to come clean then. The Deathrose Guild doesn't operate in Vestriya as it is. Both of us will need to stop."

He almost smiled as he said, "And who will captain the ship in my absence?"

"Even *I* know that your position on the *Sapphire Palace* is mostly for appearances," Queen Thessia interjected. "There are hand magicians here who have spent their whole lives on water. We will be fine."

"And what is *your* position on the ship, exactly?" Dougal asked. "Shouldn't you be bedding your new husband instead of stowing yourself away in the quarters of your ex-lover?"

River couldn't help but notice hurt on Thessia's face as the queen said, "You were so kind to me earlier."

"All a part of the job," Dougal told her coldly.

"You know that the penalty for breaking the code more than once is death." River pointed Dougal's knife at his chest. Finally, she saw something other than mockery on his face. He feared her.

As he should.

She did not plan to kill him. Not yet, at least. She only wanted to give him a good scare, in case that rattled out a piece of real information. But something stopped her.

Someone, more accurately. Galwell the Great used his hand magic strength to prevent River from hurting the very man who had come here to kill him.

"We don't know enough about his heart," Galwell said, snatching the spine of the knife out of River's hands and sheathing the blade. "What if he's driven by desperate financial circumstances?"

"Yes!" Dougal cried out. "What do you know about me beyond my name and job? That cannot possibly be all that defines a life!"

"Exactly," Galwell said. "Perhaps he's never known true companionship or joy."

"Never," Dougal agreed. "Oh, how I've yearned to be seen for who I really am!"

"Please. His job is to be whoever you need him to be," River said. She almost rolled her eyes, but she didn't want to insult Galwell too much. "You could suggest that Dougal might accidentally empty his bowels forty times a day, and he would agree with you if he thought it would keep him alive."

"I would never let people believe I lived my life with permanently soiled undergarments," Dougal protested.

"Look at that. I've already found his limit," River said, oddly proud of herself.

"We need more time," Galwell insisted.

River looked to Queen Thessia. How strange it was to be in such a small room with the literal ruler of her realm. If only River's parents could see her, discussing soiled undergarments with royalty. And they said River would never amount to anything!

"You're the queen," River said. "What do you think we should do?"

"Set him off to sea," Queen Thessia instructed.

River wanted to pump her fist in celebration, but she suspected it would be uncouth. "That works for me," she said instead, squeezing her lips together to fight back a smile.

"We will load his boat with food and supplies," Queen Thessia added. River's fist of joy loosened. "But we will keep him tied up."

The fist tightened again.

"We will do this during the dead of night," the queen continued. "Until then, he can remain tied up here under Galwell's supervision. He won't escape, but we know Galwell will not prematurely harm him, either. And perhaps, Mr. Farkenstomp, you will be able to convince Galwell that you do not soil your undergarments forty times a day. But you will never convince me."

Much was made of Queen Thessia's friendly disposition and the benevolence of her rule. Even in the face of not one but two assassins *and* her ex-lover—which, why was she in Galwell's cabin, again?—she had stayed levelheaded. Everyone knew the queen to be kind, but River never would have expected that Queen Thessia would be so . . . fun.

However, the queen was also a bit naive if she believed a man at the skill level of Dougal Farkenstomp would perish under these circumstances. This survival challenge was the exact kind of thing a Deathrose Guild member would find enjoyable.

The queen excused herself, climbing up the ladder and leaving River, Galwell, and Dougal alone in the cabin.

Galwell looked at River with such a surprising generosity of spirit, his eyes friendly instead of angry. His smile honest instead of cold. In that moment, River realized she couldn't do it. She could not kill Galwell, no matter how much it ruined her reputation. He was too nice, too sincere. He'd helped her without reason.

He didn't deserve it.

The problem was the solution, River realized. If she found out who in the guild was giving out these bad orders, poisoning the minds of members who'd been around as long as Dougal had, perhaps it would be enough to not just get back in their good graces but to take over Dougal's position altogether. Surely the leader of the Deathrose Guild would be horrified by the way he was behaving. He didn't deserve to do elaborate jobs such as this one, going deep undercover and captaining a ship. It was the kind of job that would be perfect for a woman like River, who had never been tied down to one place for very long. Let her go live someone else's life for months at a time. The Ghosts knew she didn't have her own to live.

She needed to figure out what the ever-living *fuck* was going on with the Deathrose Guild, and she needed to do it quickly, so that no more innocent people were harmed.

"In the interest of full transparency, I did board this ship to see about killing you. But I don't think I'll be doing that anymore," River said to Galwell.

He pressed a hand to his heart. "That means a lot."

"I don't suppose you have room down here for one more, then?" she asked him.

"As much as I would love to provide you with lodgings, I'm afraid that Dougal will already take up what little space I have to offer in this cabin."

River burned with embarrassment. Why did she make such an ask in the first place? It wasn't like her. None of this was like her.

She'd slept in countless supply closets before, her head resting on an overturned mop bucket or a stack of discarded rags. She could do it again. Perhaps the discomfort would set her mind straight.

River climbed up the same ladder Thessia had just used, ignoring all of the kind suggestions Galwell called out regarding alternative sleeping arrangements. When she made it to the crew deck, she breathed a sigh of relief so deep that she could almost taste the Sweetwater Sea on her tongue. If only she could rest here, surrounded by nothing but the cool air and the gentle mist of rocking water. Maybe she'd finally sleep through the night.

She headed toward the ship's railing, prepared to spend her evening watching the pink-tinged sky transform to inky black. As long as she was on this ship, she was safe from the consequences of her actions. That gave her more peace than any good night's rest ever would.

"My queen, you're *injured*."

River whipped her head around, searching for the source of the voice. It couldn't belong to whom she thought it did. Surely not.

She saw Queen Thessia first, her spelled-blond hair shining bright against the last dregs of sunlight. "Oh, no, it's nothing really," the queen said, placing a protective hand over where Dougal had nicked her.

"Who did this?" asked another voice. It was King Hugh, though none of his well-known cheeriness colored his tone. "You're bleeding."

"It's fine," Queen Thessia said to him, curt. Then she pasted on her most queenly expression as she told the other person, "Let's keep this off the record, shall we?"

Thessia grabbed King Hugh's arm and stepped to the side, revealing what River already knew in her bones to be true.

Celine Hazelton was on this Ghosts-damned ship. She had her notebook in her hand, and she was putting back the quill she seemed to always keep tucked into her bun, no longer allowed to turn Thessia's injury into the *Mythria Spectator*'s next great scandal.

Unfortunately, when Thessia and Hugh walked off, they chose to walk *toward* River. Which meant Celine looked right at her.

Celine gasped, tossing her body in front of her queen. "You're in grave danger! That woman is an assassin!" She pointed at River, who was in the middle of resting her forearms on the ship's railing as she gazed thoughtfully at the water.

Thessia patted Celine's hand. "I know. Now if you'll excuse me, we really must be going."

River overheard pieces of their low, impassioned conversation as the king and queen exited, King Hugh gently pressing Queen Thessia for more explanation, and Queen Thessia refusing to give it.

To Celine, River let out a low chuckle. "Sold me out that quickly, huh?"

"Pathetic, right?" Celine said back, a biting reference to their conversation from the other night.

River squeezed her hands together so tightly her knuckles turned white. An apology formed in her mind. One she'd never give. She'd done what was necessary. She couldn't have attachments. Not in her line of work. It was far better to have Celine hate her than to have Celine think she was someone capable of being saved.

Celine came up beside her, mimicking River's posture by slinging her arms onto the ship's railing, her notebook dangling precariously over the rocking waves.

"Do you plan to interview me now?" River asked. "Not sure the readers of the *Mythria Spectator* will be very interested in what I have to say, unless they want my opinion on our realm's obsession with domesticating wild animals."

Celine pulled that damned quill from her hair. "Are you for it or against it?" she asked, hand hovering over an empty notebook page.

"Against it," River said. "Their nature can't be changed."

Celine let out a low *hmm*, sounding more like a heart healer than a scribe with all the implications she managed to layer into the noise. She jotted something down. When River peered over, making no effort to disguise the fact that she was attempting to read whatever Celine had written, Celine snapped her notebook shut.

"Are you aware that the Deathrose Guild's last three targets have been people with no known criminal record?" she asked.

"And here I thought I was finally getting my chance to advocate for lyricats." River staged a yawn, if only to stop herself from looking at Celine's face for too long. She had her brows furrowed in concentration, and River quite liked when she got serious in that way. Really, she liked every expression Celine made. On a purely objective level, Celine had a face made for emoting. "You shouldn't be poking around in the business of the Deathrose Guild. It's dangerous."

"I know you know that Galwell is on this ship," Celine said, ignoring the comment.

"I think everyone knows Galwell is on this ship."

"If you have no doubts about the validity of your assignment to kill him, why haven't you done it yet?" Celine asked.

"Who says I haven't?"

"Have you?"

They held eye contact for far longer than River should have allowed. It was just—the sunset was doing such wonderful things with the planes of Celine's face, bouncing light off her rosy cheeks, adding an extra sparkle to the warmth of the brown in her eyes. It felt so risky to be near her, heart-stopping in the exact way River had gotten addicted to long ago. But this was far better than walking across a tightrope or flipping through the air. Those moments were fleeting. Celine was steady. For as long as they made eye contact, the sensation sustained itself.

"No," River admitted. "And I don't plan to."

Celine broke their gaze to open her notebook again. Curse River's honesty. She should have kept lying, kept forcing Celine to probe her with questions, staring deeper and deeper into the limitless well of her eyes.

"Tell me what you know about the Deathrose Guild and how it operates," Celine said. With one sentence, she'd shifted into full scribe mode. Her voice even hit a different register.

"How about this? You let me stay in your room, and I tell you a little bit about the guild," River bargained. She would not share much. But she wanted a pillow to sleep on, if nothing else. It had been an exceptionally terrible few days.

River knew what she was asking was . . . loaded, calling back to their long-ago history and all the things they'd never said to each other.

Celine's quill fell from her hand. She dropped onto all fours to retrieve it. "Of course not. You're . . . you're . . ."

"Dangerous?" River guessed, stopping Celine's fumbling hand by squatting down and placing hers atop it. She waited until Celine looked up. Waited until their eyes were locked on each other again. "You're right. I am."

"Is that meant to help?"

River picked up the quill and handed it over. "You tell me."

"Fine," Celine said, much faster than River expected. "But you'll be sleeping on the floor."

River made protests she didn't actually mean. Because deep in her heart, underneath the layers of protection she wore as armor, she suspected she would sleep dangling over a pit of vissharks if it meant getting to be closer to Celine.

* * *

Celine's sleeping chambers were smaller than River anticipated. The floor might as well have been the bed, for the pinrose scent Celine had used in her bath was so close, so sweet, that River felt as though she had her nose pressed into Celine's neck. At least from the ground, River didn't have to continue learning all the ways time had been kind to Celine's face, or catch the way her nightclothes clung to the glorious fullness of her.

River closed her eyes, fully aware she'd find no sleep. How could she, when everything had gone to such shit? And really, how could she even *think* with a woman like Celine once again so near?

In River's childhood, there had been many nights when her family's troupe stayed up late to drink and dance, and all River had wanted was a peaceful night's rest. For so many years, there was nothing River could do about the constant noise. She never rested well. But one of the first things Celine had ever told River was that River was always welcome at Celine's house.

On one particular night, when every muscle in River's body ached from practicing her tumbling, and her head felt like it might split open from the beat of the music, she'd politely asked her parents if they could quiet down. Instead of obliging, they'd screamed at River, then continued their revels.

So River walked to Celine's house.

She'd told herself she could knock once on Celine's bedroom window, and if Celine didn't answer, she would find a comfortable spot on the ground to rest. It would be no less comfortable than the worn old cot she slept on at the circus. And at least it would be quiet.

Celine *did* answer. She was groggy, only half awake, but she opened the window to let River into her room, where River slept on the floor, much like she was doing now.

As teens, Celine must have understood how vulnerable that moment was, because she didn't press River on why she'd come. She actually said nothing at all, wordlessly inviting River into her room. Her life.

And every night thereafter, Celine had left her window cracked. Eventually, they *did* talk, only not about the circumstances that brought River to Celine's window. River did not want to dwell on those bad things. She didn't want to waste her time with Celine in such a way.

They talked instead of their hopes and dreams, with the kind of unbridled optimism only the young possess. Optimism River had long since discarded.

"Hey now!" Celine called out.

A crumpled piece of parchment plunked onto River's face.

She opened her eyes to see Celine peering over the edge of her bed. Celine had let down her curls during her bath, and they dangled toward River in loose, damp spirals, dripping pinrose-scented water onto River's cheek.

"You promised me answers," she said, a far cry from the silent understanding they'd had as teens.

River rubbed her eyes. "Right now? I'm quite exhausted . . ."

"Yes, right now! I don't harbor assassins for free." Celine made a big show of opening her notebook to a fresh page as she sat with her legs crisscrossed on the bed. "When did you join the guild?"

"Not long after you knew me, actually," River admitted. "Pretty soon after I turned seventeen, my parents told me they could no longer keep me in the caravan, and they wouldn't let any other circus performers house me."

Celine dropped her scribely pretense. "*What?* How could they do such a thing?"

River hesitated. She hadn't talked about this in a long time. Ever, more accurately. She'd never discussed her Deathrose beginnings with anyone, not even Vandra. This was even stranger, though, because Celine knew River's parents. Not very closely, of course. Not even River knew her own parents very closely. But River had brought Celine around the troupe enough that Celine had a familiarity with the players, and combined with the many nights River had snuck in to sleep on her floor, Celine could surely deduce that they weren't the kindest of folk.

She knew she needed to be careful. And frankly, so did Celine. Meddling in the guild's business was dangerous. While everyone in Mythria knew of their existence, the guild relied on mystery to keep its assassins protected. Perhaps if River distracted Celine with the personal side of things, it would keep her from probing too far into the guild itself. Surely no *Mythria Spectator* reader would be interested in the sad beginnings of a random assassin who'd recently fallen from grace.

"It all started when I'd finally mastered my standing backflip," River said. "I'd been working on it for years. I was quite excited."

"I remember you working on it," Celine interjected. "We used to bring pillows into my yard and stack them up, and you'd flip down from them to practice. You had a ritual before each attempt, where you'd hold your arms out straight to the side and take a quick, deep breath. You were always so serious about it. I liked seeing you that way."

"Yes. Miss Memory. Of course." River cleared her throat. It was strange to be remembered. Her entire profession was about slipping in and out of the shadows. She'd long since forgotten the ways she used to chase the light. "Anyway, I'd teleported to my father to show him, and I caught him kissing another performer. *Not* my mother. Horrified, I teleported to her to share what I saw. But she wasn't mad at him. She was mad at me."

River hated how her voice had quieted. None of this bothered her anymore. It was just something that happened a long, long time ago.

"Now, look, you know better than anyone that my parents were never the nicest people in the realm anyway, but up to that point, they'd mostly tolerated me," River continued. "After that incident, everything changed. They told me my powers were too much of a problem. No one felt safe around me, because they didn't know when or where I might show up. They couldn't be sure I wasn't spying on everyone for fun. Or breaking into locked rooms to steal things. They said—and this is a direct quote, so make sure to get this right for the pamphlet—*You're not a person. You're a weapon.*"

"Surely you know that's not true," Celine said, her brown eyes bright with sincerity.

"But it is," River said. "I can go anywhere, so long as someone describes it to me well enough. I can find anyone, so long as I know what they look like. Even if you hadn't let me stay in this room with you, I could've done it anyway."

A shadow of concern fell across Celine's face.

"See?" River said. "It's frightening. My power is dangerous. And I think what made it even more horrifying for my parents was that because of the circus, they'd contributed to the problem. Early on, I wasn't very good at teleporting. I didn't like to do it, and I used to wish every night that I could get rid of my gift. It was scary to suddenly be thirty irons high when all I'd meant to do was find my mom. But my parents thought it might be a useful trick to put into the circus show, so they forced me to practice. They let the acrobats start teaching me how to tumble at a very young age. That way, wherever I landed, I'd know how to flip my way down. By making me safer, they put everyone else in danger."

Celine's mouth hung open in a delicate O shape.

"I'd heard of the Deathrose Guild the same way everyone else does," River continued. "Whispered rumors. Our circus traveled to so many places throughout Mythria that when my parents kicked me out, I decided to go where the whispers had been the loudest, and I started asking around."

Celine had been scribbling furiously, but now she paused, her quill pressed to the bow of her lips. "Is it really that simple? To join?"

"No," River said. "Most people get recruited into the guild. They're sought out because they've already adopted a vigilante lifestyle, or rumors of their gift have reached other members. They didn't know about me, probably because I hadn't yet been put into the circus show, and I'd never teleported anywhere interesting up to that point. But I knew what I could do was valuable, and I liked the idea of using my dangerous gift for some . . . backward kind of good. So I sought the Deathrose Guild out myself, and I asked them to let me join. I *wanted* this life. And I'll do anything to protect it, because they are the only group that's ever protected me."

A single, traitorous tear slid down River's cheek. She swiped it away before Celine could make a comment about it.

"They don't seem to be protecting you now," Celine very unkindly pointed out.

"Something is amiss," River snapped. "This is not how the guild normally operates."

"You should just leave them," Celine whispered. "You don't have to live like this. You're capable of so much. We can find you a new life in Vestriya."

We. As if Celine and River were a unit. A team.

"That's enough," River said, her patience thinned. "I've fulfilled my promise to you. You know a little bit about how the guild operates. I have a place to sleep. Now do me a favor—don't write about any of this just yet, okay? I need to figure out what's going on within the guild. Until I do, we shouldn't call more attention to ourselves by putting this information in the scribesheets."

Celine snapped her notebook closed. "You're right. It's time for us to sleep. We can pick this up tomorrow." She rolled onto her side, blowing out the candle that illuminated the room.

In the dark, the rocking of the ship took on an ominous quality, like the Ghosts themselves were humming. It was almost enough to dull the horror of all that River had confessed. She should have lied, made up a story. But part of her wanted Celine to understand that even though she hadn't killed Galwell, she was still an assassin. Just like the lyricat, River's nature could not be changed.

This would be good, she decided, pushing away her anxieties. She could use Celine's excellent investigative skills to uncover what was happening within the guild, and in turn, she could ensure they both remained safe while doing so. And she could keep Galwell safe, too, which mattered to her more than she expected. She'd almost killed him, and he seemed to be a genuinely wonderful guy.

"I'm sorry your parents didn't protect you," Celine suddenly whispered.

It was River's turn to be speechless. Yes, she'd certainly shared far too much. The last thing she needed was Celine's apologies or, worse, her pity.

"Don't be," River said.

The past was just that—past.

River would rather focus on the future.

Sea-lebrity Sightings on Sweetwater Set Sail!

by Celine Hazelton, *Mythria Spectator* staff reporter

Yesterday's sunlit send-off of Queen Thessia and her handsome husband, Hugh (Ghosts save Thugh!), on luxury ship extraordinaire the *Sapphire Palace*, commencing our gentle queen's honeymoon in Vestriya, offered much more than royal relaxation. Yes, dear readers, *Mythria Spectator*'s own reporter on board will join the royal honeymoon for every spectacular event, bringing YOU unparalleled insights into the wondrous voyage!

Just how many sensational Mythrians could one scribesheet reporter spot sailing the Sweetwater Sea? Not enough to exhaust this writer's use of words starting with "S"! (It was close, though.) Here's several more for your vicarious enjoyment of this Vestriyan voyage:

- Stellan Whitehall, shadow play star, rumored for the realm's hottest role of portraying Clare Grandhart in the upcoming dramatic re-enactment of the venerable deeds of the Four! Whoever wins the part, the conjuration will certainly celebrate Mythria's well-loved heroes.

- Venturia Smythe, celebrity entrepreneur, seeking some space from Mythria following the Deathrose Guild's murder of her brother Elmumd. Which was strange, in this reporter's opinion, given the Deathrose Guild's stand-up reputation for slaying those who deeply deserve it. Yet Elmumd Smythe was known for revolutionizing crop cultivation in Devostos, ensuring

THIS WILL BE INTERESTING

no one went hungry this past winter. Not the manner of man deserving sudden separation from his head! While this inquiry is unusual for the *Spectator*, this reporter feels it worth our readers' consideration. *Sea*-spicious!

- Standish Chobb, whose entry into the upcoming Vestriya Now competition promises to be one of the showcase's most comedic. At the time of this reporting, Chobb was five and one-quarter sweetbuns into "practicing" his famous feat of consuming a dozen of the sandwiches uninterrupted.

When not gazing from the vast decks of the *Sapphire Palace* over the shimmering Sweetwater Sea, guests can indulge in every entertainment and delicacy imaginable. We're hearing hand magicians will present the most marvelous entertainment in the form of never-before-seen water sculptures enacting detailed scenes upon the stage of the waves themselves, while restaurants will offer culinary creations innovated in the queen's honor, and Sir Grandhart's own Hero's Reward libations will flow from every on-board tavern.

The only complaints of some guests were the exceedingly cramped and scarce cabins for common voyagers, requiring some to share lodgings with persons unexpected, vexatious, or otherwise very distracting.

Don't miss this column for more Thugh honeymoon coverage! For now, *sea* you later!

8
Galwell

Vestriya.

Galwell slipped down to the docks, eager for his first glimpse of sunlight in days. He'd received next to none the entire voyage, only venturing out of his cabin when he worked with River in the dead of night to heft Captain Norcross—Dougal—overboard on a wooden dinghy loaded with a week's provisions. They'd told the first mate he'd tumbled into the Sweetwater. No rescue mission was launched, for it turned out he was not well-liked by the crew.

Setting foot onto the creaking, waterlogged dock, Galwell breathed deep. He loathed hiding. He'd felt in danger of losing his mind, shut up in his concealed cabin.

Now with every step, he felt himself returning.

The Vestriyan dock's clamor embraced him, sailors' shoulders rubbing easily with his while accented chatter surrounded him. He found everything unfamiliar, yet he minded not. Even Mythria felt unfamiliar to him now, since his return into his own future. Unlike home, foreign shores were *supposed* to feel foreign.

Vestriya—he could nearly hear the realm's promises whispered in his ears when he gazed up. If he was honest, the capital city's grandeur surpassed Queendom's. The streets rose high with columned facades of cream-colored stone. Stunning sculptures loomed from street corners. Lively brewshops and bars spilled out into the streets on wide patios. Galwell had heard of how, past sunset, the Vestriyan sky hued deep purple. Even now, wisps of lavender and pink were streaking the cloudless sky.

Onto the waterfront the *Sapphire Palace* poured tourists who shared Galwell's wonderment. He saw fingers pointed in rapture, heard gasps of excitement, and noticed many passengers wearing imitation jerseys of professional horseball players.

The latter quickened his heart. Once he'd dealt with his assassin problem, Galwell himself looked forward to the horseball Realm Chalice championship, which would be held in Vestriya later this week. Posters flapped everywhere advertising the match. Indeed, he rather wished he'd remembered the jersey Clare had gifted him with the name of Zevan Wintersmith, the young Farmount Falcons striker whose gameplay exhilarated the realm. On the run from hired killers, Galwell had unfortunately not had much chance to pack with care.

For now, he fixed his focus on his mission. He could not concentrate on horseball until he'd located Mona Grandhart.

Luckily, harbors oft lent themselves to seedier folk. If he wished to find the local crime lord, he likely needed only ask.

He strode from the sea-slickened street down the first dark alleyway he could find. It was narrow, crookedly leading deeper into the city. Decidedly villainous, Galwell determined.

He cleared his throat. He straightened. He ventured to look guileless, an easy mark for malcontents and miscreants. Villains would come to him.

Instead, in a magical jolt of energy, two figures dropped in a heap in front of Galwell.

River was one. Galwell recognized the other, too. Celine . . . Hazelton, he remembered. Compared to other scribes who'd followed him lately, he'd noticed the questions Miss Hazelton called out to him were uncommonly incisive. Not, respectfully, what Galwell expected from the *Mythria Spectator*.

Celine was presently splayed out on top of River, looking startled. Not *just* startled. The women's cheeks reddened. Their locked eyes said this was the last place they wanted to find themselves.

"Wonderful," Galwell stated dryly. "*Romance.*"

Celine scrambled off River instantly. River spoke first, flustered. "There's no—romance," she protested.

"We're just friends," Celine corroborated.

"Childhood friends," River concurred. "We hardly know each other now."

Galwell glared. He was wasting valuable moments for heroism here. "I may have been recently dead, but I'm not daft," he declared. "Why are you here?"

Celine smoothed her skirt. "You're in danger, Galwell," she stated, matching him for heroic solemnity. "River is here to protect you until we may determine why."

Galwell commended her valiance. However, he couldn't welcome her intrusion. He turned skeptically to River. "I do not need protecting."

"Too bad," River replied. The dark-haired woman's voice held no emotion.

Galwell frowned. "And you?" he inquired wearily of Celine. "What will you do?"

"I," Celine returned proudly, "am going to find out who is behind the plot to kill you."

Galwell opened his mouth to speak, but River interjected. "You should accept our help," she said, and Galwell realized he'd overlooked the quiet conviction under her detached demeanor. "Celine is an excellent investigative scribe."

Celine went Vestriyan-dusk pink. "Thank you. You're an excellent, um, killer."

"That's very kind," River replied quickly.

Neither would meet the other's eyes. Galwell narrowed his.

"I can teleport anywhere," River reminded him, ushering the moment on. "You can't get rid of us."

Yes—she had him there. The hero of Mythria ground his jaw, permitting himself one flash of very unheroic exasperation. "Fine," he conceded, throwing his hands up. "But just once," he went on, starting off past them, "I would like to lead a party of people who aren't sorting out any sexual tension or unspoken longing."

"Not sure I agreed to you being the leader of—ow!" River exclaimed.

Galwell glanced over his shoulder and determined Celine had elbowed her companion.

He strode on. Sexual tension or not, he liked the feeling of leading. If Vestriya was welcomely unfamiliar, leadership felt like home for Galwell the Great.

"Clare has arranged a meeting with someone who can help us," he informed them. Well-established objectives were essential for successful questing. "Someone I believe can introduce us to parties with information about this dastardly plot. You may come with, on one condition," he declared. *"No romance."*

His new cohort replied in unison.

"None."

Very well, then. Leadership felt good indeed.

Galwell continued forth, grinning to himself. The dark passageway widened, the stonework overhead playing host to domestic flourishes—clotheslines strung from narrow windows, horseball mascot flags hung from rooftops.

"Who exactly is it we're meeting?" River inquired.

"She is called Mona. Mona the Merciless," Galwell replied. He felt somewhat silly using Clare's sister's ominous moniker.

"Interesting," Celine interjected eagerly. Galwell was quickly

coming to understand that earnest, insatiable curiosity drove her journalistic pursuits. "Mona the Merciless is well-known in underground circles," she explained. "Young, though reports vary whether she is twenty-five or thirty. Princess of her own criminal empire, focused on stealing luxury goods from royal ports, with some intimidation and protection racketeering thrown in."

"Celine has head magic of everlasting memory," River informed Galwell, who was listening with interest while Celine divulged this dossier fit for the queen's spymasters.

"Mona often leaves roselia flowers where she strikes—" Celine went on contentedly.

Eyes fixed forward, Galwell slowed. He quite regretted interrupting Celine, but unfortunately—"We're being followed," he murmured.

River did not hesitate. In a warping jolt of magic, she disappeared. Moments later, she reemerged, holding their pursuer—

"Thessia," Galwell observed, dismayed. What did a hero need to do to get followed by real bad guys in this realm?

Neither her seizure by River nor the perplexing uneven goldenness he'd noticed in her hair could quell Thessia's regal confidence. "I listened to your entire conversation and I'm joining the party, too," she informed him. "My body double will pose as me on the gondola tour Hugh and I are supposed to be on—no one will notice I'm gone."

"Not even your husband?" River asked.

"He'll be fine," Thessia said. She continued, offering no opportunity for the others to interrogate this intriguing response. "You cannot kick me out, because I'm your queen."

"But your honeymoon," Galwell insisted.

"I can honeymoon and foil evil plans at the same time, Galwell. In fact, I would prefer it," Thessia retorted. She drew herself up, rising nearly to Galwell's eyes. "I'm not the teenager you used to know."

THIS WILL BE INTERESTING

Galwell's shoulders slumped. No, she was not. Thessia of Mythria had found her stubbornness while Galwell was dead. "Is there anyone else wishing to join my party?" he queried, unamused. "Perhaps the captain we heaved overboard? Oh, or the entire visiting Farmount horseball team?"

River snorted. "I'd like to see them keep up, the way they've been moving the ball this season . . ."

Galwell did not indulge this remark. Relenting, he continued on, his entire new questing party with him.

Unconventional, unnecessary questmates or not, Galwell needed to find some vagabonds. *Well-established objectives*, he reminded himself.

"Hello. You look of ill repute," he greeted the first Vestriyan he found who fit the parameters. "Could you point me to Mona the Merciless?"

The man, his features grease-streaked, was picking his teeth with whittled volshark ribs. His eyes shot up when Galwell uttered Mona's name. Without reply, he skittered off.

"Might not be wise to speak so openly," River suggested.

"I'm not afraid," Galwell replied. "This is more efficient." He elevated his voice, catapulting his words down a dark alleyway. "I'm seeking the notorious crime lord Mona the Merciless!"

Galwell congratulated himself when a limber, skeletal wraith of a man vestmented in night-shade leather slunk up to them. He was, frankly, scary. Galwell's companions stepped back instinctively.

Not Galwell.

"You want to be careful shouting a name like that in a place like this," the skeleton man hissed.

"He meant no harm," River interceded, urgency in the forced calm of her voice. "He died recently, so he doesn't always know how to behave."

The man scrutinized Galwell with crimson irises. "Not surprising he died," he remarked reproachfully.

"You mean to insult my honor, sir," Galwell replied.

"Not your honor. Your intelligence," the wraith returned. "Looks like you mean to die a second time."

Galwell held the man's glare. "I don't fear death. Do you?"

Quiet descended over the group like violet Vestriyan dusk. From the hush, Galwell felt it—the power of his presence. No heart or head magic summoned his heroic self-possession. It just *was*. He felt the spark of his old self—inspiring. Leading. *Great*.

The man broke eye contact first.

"Not one of Ario's men, are ye?" he demanded.

Thessia's brow's furrowed. Galwell had no idea what the man meant. "No," he replied sincerely.

"No," the man concurred, half to himself. "Shit spy you'd make, shouting Miss Mona's name in the streets. I'll take you to her," he muttered, spiteful. "I want to watch her gut you."

Galwell gestured to the darkening street. "Lead the way, good sir."

As they followed their disreputable escort, Galwell positioned himself close to Thessia, wary.

He was not expecting the glare he received from the queen. "I'm protecting you," she insisted witheringly. "You're not protecting me."

Galwell humphed. This was, he reckoned, not his finest questing party. His ex-fiancée, the assassin who sought to kill him earlier this week, and a gossip scribesheet reporter. *Have fun saving the realm*.

The skeletal man led them from the loud Vestriyan street corner to—well, the cutest crumbiello shop he'd ever seen. Fit seamlessly within the majestic, sculpted streets, the white-and-black checkered stone of the storefront complemented the vines spilling from flowerpots hung on golden hooks. And inside the front window, rows and rows of soft crumbiellos.

Galwell loved the Vestriyan delicacies, which his family would import on special occasions. The crumbly cake—hence the name—wrapped over molten cream was hand-magicked for eternal warmth. Pastry culinarists crafted every imaginable combination of cake and filling. Honey-rougeberry crumbiellos. Whitecake-citronelle crumbiellos. Dark-brew-whipped-milk crumbiellos. And Galwell's favorite, classic dark chocolate, sweet-cream crumbiellos.

Clare had clearly exaggerated. If Mona knew the value of delicious crumbiellos, she couldn't be so bad. They would get on just fine.

Their guide led them into the shop. The scent of sweetened dough overwhelmed Galwell. His stomach growled.

Then the man led them past the counter. Then into a shabby back room. Then they descended a rickety staircase, Galwell's hopes of crumbiellos and civilized conversation descending with them.

Reaching the bottom, whatever magic enveloped the shop lifted, for Galwell was suddenly nearly crushed under the loud beat of thrumming music. They rounded a corner, and Galwell found himself in some sort of secret criminal clubhouse.

There were no crumbiellos here. Instead, dramatic, sharp shafts of light cut up the pitch-darkness of the subterranean room, where bodies writhed provocatively to the punishing music. Scantily clad men thrusted to the beat in enormous dark-metal cages. The whole room smelled of strange magic. From shadowy corners, sounds crept over the music that made Galwell blush. In his twenty-seven years, give or take one resurrection, he'd never seen—never even imagined—so much debauchery.

"This is a secret criminal hideout," Celine hissed, sounding less scandalized than fascinated. "Illegal deals are made here. Illegal magics practiced. If I wrote about this, it would be front page—"

"You will not," River ordered. Celine scowled.

"Galwell is right," Thessia said more gently. "If we want to lure his enemies out, this is the perfect cover for it. We ought not ruin the opportunity."

Their escort spoke to some hulking doorway guards. "Found this one outside hollering Mona's name. Not working for the spymaster, but still, figure it might be *worth something* to the boss lady to keep him quiet?"

One of the guards, rolling his eyes disdainfully, deposited some Vestriyan sterling coins in their disreputable escort's hand. "Good luck," the man said menacingly to Galwell on his way out, rubbing the silver between his fingers.

The guards grasped Galwell. As they hauled him toward the dance floor, Galwell prepared himself to resist, feeling the hand-magical strength coursing through his muscles.

"Gentlemen, though your establishment is lively, I do not wish to dance," he said. He produced Clare's letter from his tunic. "I wish to confer with Mona the Merciless."

One of Galwell's escorts nodded toward the dance floor.

"Miss Grandhart," the man replied, "is over there."

Galwell turned just in time for the most striking woman he'd ever seen to lock eyes with him.

Mona Grandhart was dancing right in front of him. Her dress was very sheer, with nothing underneath. He could see every line of her body, more of a woman than he'd ever seen in his twenty-seven years—give or take one resurrection—and it stunned him speechless.

She sashayed forth, sweat shining on her shoulders, her chest. Her hair was dark brown, falling in glistening waves past her collarbone. Dazed, Galwell couldn't help but note that she didn't much resemble her brother except for her eyes. Cerulean like his, but cold. Where Clare's glittered like the ocean, Mona's glittered like a knife.

She stopped in front of them, smirking, her dagger eyes never leaving Galwell.

He did not speak. He could not. When River coughed something sounding like "so much for no romance," he hardly heard her over the pounding in his head, his chest, his—

"You were shouting my name in the streets," Mona said. "Yet now it seems you've nothing to say."

Galwell started to suspect he'd made a profound miscalculation. He could not compel his concentration away from Mona's curves. She was a demon sculpted by the hands of the Ghosts themselves. She was a dirty dream from which he suspected he would never wake up. When Vestriya whispered promises in his ears, they were in her voice.

River stepped in. "Clare sent us," she announced. "We have a letter."

Unceremoniously, she swiped the page from Galwell's stiff hand and presented the sealed parchment to Mona.

Mona unstuck the seal. She read the contents. Then she grimaced and promptly tore the letter up.

"Lock this man in a cage," Mona ordered. Her voice held no smirk whatsoever now. Galwell felt hands on him once more and knew—the letter's contents had failed. "The rest of you can enjoy the club if you wish, but know that there is magic in this place. Speak its name to anyone or seek to destroy it and you will receive a curse of my choosing," Mona went on. "I'm fond of changing people into grumblefrogs this week."

The guards clapped hands on Galwell. Too stunned, too distracted by Mona, he didn't resist as they heaved him roughly into one of the dance floor's metal cages.

This was unfortunate. The metallic-purple-haired gyrating man in the neighboring cage winked when he caught Galwell's eye. Winked! First his odds-and-ends questing party, now sexy dance-cage confinement? Oh, this was not the heroism the legend of Mythria expected.

He wrestled with the closed lock, which he found magic held shut. Not even his uncommon strength would permit him to rend metal from metal. No, Galwell the Great was left to watch the dance floor from his confinement.

Watch Mona, more precisely. She stepped right in front of him. *Mona the Malevolent*, Galwell deemed her, for he knew the way she danced was half intended for him.

Her movements captivated him, her hips as much a prison as his cage. The music punished him, for with every pounding pulse, Mona's supple form flexed, sweat running ecstasies down her skin.

Oh, Ghosts, give me back my ordinary, uncomplicated heroism.

She flung smirks over her shoulder at him like poisoned darts while Galwell looked on helplessly. When he searched the room for his questing party, he couldn't find them amid the crush of dancers.

With swaying movements following the rhythm, Mona slunk right up to his bars. "My brother should have warned you about me," she said.

"He did," Galwell replied.

He fought for composure while Mona smiled pityingly. "Not well enough, it seems."

Well-established objectives. Well-established objectives! "I seek—I seek an alliance with you," Galwell managed.

Mona cocked her head, indulgent. Patronizing him. "And what," she asked, "can you give me, Galwell the *Gorgeous*?"

Her eyes sparkled dangerously. *Good*. Galwell had little experience with sexy dancing women. He had *lots* of experience with danger. He stepped closer to his bars. "Release me and find out," he returned. "I'm certain your brother wouldn't wish me confined."

Mona's smile sharpened. "Quite the contrary," she chided. "My brother has merely asked me to keep you safe in exchange for something I have wanted for a *very* long time. Would you agree that you are perfectly safe in your cage?"

Squaring his shoulders, Galwell held her gaze. "I do not seek safety from you," he replied.

He'd hoped to intrigue Mona or impress upon her his fearlessness. Instead, she slipped her hand into his cage to stroke his chest.

"Do you seek danger, then?" Her voice stole over him, low and sultry. "I didn't take you for someone who likes it rough, but I'd love to find a man who can surprise me."

He did seek danger, in fact, he wanted to say. Just not like this!

Regrettably, the physical contact damned his powers of speech. Startled, he withdrew sharply, stumbling—*stumbling!*—into the back of the cage.

Mona laughed, louder now. Victorious.

"On second thought, perhaps not," she crowed. "Enjoy the club, Galwell. It's more fun if you dance."

She returned to the dance floor. Galwell looked on, quelling his frustration with more heroic strength. He was *not* enjoying the club. He wished to be questing, in fresh sunlight, with resolute companions and *well-defined objectives*. Not here, confined, with nothing to do except watch Mona, who maintained her position quite resolutely on the dance floor in front of him. While Galwell looked on, helpless, she writhed to the pummeling music, no doubt inventing for Galwell's own torture entirely new ways of moving her voluptuous body.

Yet . . . with every passing, punishing moment in his dance prison, Galwell the Great began to second-guess his resistance. Yes, perhaps his circumstances demanded innovation. New, unforeseeable measures of heroism. Perhaps his imprisonment was opportunity in disguise.

Perhaps . . . yes, if he just . . . *stayed* in here, *observing* Mona, immersing himself in the world of her club, he could find some leverage, or discover some hidden secrets of the Vestriyan criminal underworld, which would surely help them—

"You all right, G?"

Galwell blinked, finding River at his side with a green drink in hand.

He cleared his throat, hastening to rationalize his surveillance of Mona the Merciless. He had just come into his new questing party. The last thing he needed was for them to find him useless. Weak. Needing more damnable *help*. "Yes," he managed. "Yes, I'm very well. I'm—gathering intelligence."

River grinned. "Is that what you're calling it?" She appraised his very real, very honorable intelligence gathering. "Looks to me like you're"—her eyes went to Mona's rear end—"*held captive*."

Galwell grunted. *Galwell the Grunting*. Oh, this was wondrous. He could hear Mona's mockery in his head now.

River sipped her emerald drink, looking perfectly content to leave Galwell to his "intelligence gathering." While he hesitated to demand help, if forced to choose, he would rather his questmates find him ineffective than distractible.

"You're quite right," he grumbled. "We must be on our way. Please—get me out."

River said no more. She disappeared, instantly reappearing inside Galwell's cage. She clasped the hero's enormous biceps forcefully.

In the same moment, Mona's head jerked up—her eyes met Galwell's—

Crack.

Galwell found himself, stomach-churningly, dizzyingly, instantly on the dance floor outside his cage.

For the first time, real fury—not something coy—flickered darkly in Mona's exquisite features. *Ghosts, even her anger is alluring*, Galwell heard himself think.

He locked the errant observation up in a little cage that he then cast into the darkest corner of his mind. "It was our pleasure meeting you, Mona the Merciless," he said. "My questing party and I shall be on our way. We seek your alliance in exposing and defeating nefarious forces. While Clare wishes me kept only out of harm's way, I do not want to be kept safe if safety requires confinement—and as you've seen, my companion here can teleport me out of your clutches instantly. Unless you plan to help us, *I* cannot help *you* in your well-intentioned if ultimately self-serving aim of securing my safety."

He waited, proud of his compelling speech. He always was the speech giver in his quests.

When Mona said nothing, he nodded once in farewell, fighting down a strange disappointment. He moved toward the club's clandestine entry, fearing no guards—

"*Wait*," he heard over the music.

Suppressing his smile, Galwell looked back. While he held his breath, something passed over Mona's features. A question, he discerned, and a decision.

"Very well, *Galwell the Guileful*," Mona conceded, her voice like poison-laced crumbiello cream. "What do you have in mind?"

9
Thessia

Dance clubs, the queen of Mythria concluded, were *incredible*. Especially underground magical criminal dance clubs.

Mona's lair made Thessia's ears hurt. The smoky, leathery, noxious scent of magic and powerful liquor stung her nose. People who had no idea who the queen was pushed past her and compressed her unceremoniously against the shining blackwood bar where she stood.

It was wonderful.

She appointed herself sentry, watching Galwell—poor Galwell—from her vantage point. After River magicked Galwell out of his dance-cage door, Mona led him past enchanted ebony curtains into the club's private seating, which—oh, this was not good—

"Grab my hand."

Thessia startled. River had just snapped into visibility next to her, clutching the palm of a nauseated-looking Celine. "What?" Thessia managed.

River humphed. "Not used to following orders, are you?" she muttered while she seized Thessia's hand.

The world spun in a dizzying *crack* flash. Everything changed in an instant. *Whew*—while River's power was freeing, the stomach-warping effects were less than desirable.

They found themselves next to Galwell in Mona's private enclave. Mona, Thessia noticed, looked curiously unsurprised to have Galwell's three guests magically appear out of nowhere.

Head magic, Thessia realized. What power did Mona possess? Seeing the future, or sensing what magics others had?

The club pulsated right outside the dark, dramatically furnished room. Yet, due to the enchanted curtains, only a distantly muffled pounding pervaded the space.

"Lovely. The motley gang's all here," Mona remarked. "Now, why can't you make this easy for me, Galwell?"

She spoke his name like she found the syllables ridiculous.

"I do not wish to make . . . things . . . hard for you," Galwell replied. He seemed to have some difficulty with the words. "I seek your help. We"—Galwell glanced to his questmates, resolve sharpening his noble features—"seek your help."

Mona scrutinized him. Lounging on one of the room's crimson couches, she looked spilled onto the furniture.

"Very well," she said. "I want what Clare's offering me. Even if you go Galwell-the-Gallivanting on your obnoxious quest, you shall have my protection. I will have my finest sentries, heavies, and intimidators accompany and surveil you wherever you go."

"No," Galwell replied.

Thessia's gaze shot to him. *No?*

Mona glared. Galwell met her glower.

"I came here with clear intentions," he went on. "I request your collaboration, not your protection. The surest way to keep me safe is to help us thwart those who would do me harm."

"Who might that be?" Mona returned.

"I am a target of the Deathrose Guild," Galwell announced.

While he'd delivered the information the same way he would pronounce his favorite color or crumbiello flavor, Mona's eyes widened.

"The guild has long targeted my colleagues. The crown has kept them out of Vestriya, mostly. Now you want me to cross them?" She shook her head, incredulous. "No. None survive when the Deathrose has marked them for assassination. But you," she mused, studying Galwell, "you're . . . not their type. So noble and boring. How did you manage to get their attention?" She sounded half impressed.

"That's what we want to find out," River interjected. "Something isn't right here. Galwell isn't a villain. I fear the guild has been infiltrated by dark forces."

Mona's eyes swiveled to River. "I see. So you seek my help . . . rooting out evil and saving the day? Have you looked around my club at all?" She splayed her hands, smiling an indulgent smile. "I actually *am* a villain."

"Which makes you our best chance to make contact with whoever has requested Galwell's murder," Celine returned. "Lure them in. Whoever it is will surely grow frustrated with the guild's failure to kill him. They will seek . . . alternate options."

The suggestion seemed to intrigue Mona. Thessia saw the moment she went from languid to interested, her posture sharpening, her hand ceasing its careless stroking of the velvet pillow closest her.

"A meeting," Mona proposed, considering the possibility.

Galwell nodded.

It would have been easier in Mythria, Thessia could not help thinking, where the realm's strong magic would permit conjurations or message tapestries to facilitate the contact. But Vestriya's magic was less developed, according to Thessia's diplomatic dossiers. Spell service, Mythria's network of interconnected magic, was nowhere to be found here.

"And what if," Mona challenged, "I invite them here, and they offer me untold riches to kill Galwell myself?"

"Then I would prevail upon your honor not to," Galwell replied.

Mona laughed—a long, delighted, trilling sound. "You'll find I have none," she promised Galwell.

"Then I'll prevail upon your greed."

THIS WILL BE INTERESTING 113

The words sprung from Thessia without foresight or preparation. They drew every eye in the room to her.

I, who command my realm, she reminded herself. Who'd endured unendurable grief. Who'd held an entire Ghosts-forsaken press conference with hair she'd badly spelled blond. What was one little crime lord to Thessia of Mythria?

"No one can outbid me," she promised, holding herself regally.

Mona blinked in doubtful recognition. "I thought you looked familiar," she finally said. "A queen in my humble club."

Mona rose slowly, taking in the room with her gemstone gaze.

"Unfortunately," she went on, "you're out of luck. You want me to challenge the Deathrose Guild while proclaiming my willingness to assassinate a well-known hero? I'd have half the spymaster's men on me, to say nothing of the fucking guild. No," she went on. "Clare's letter required I provide you *protection*. Which I have extended. I'll grant you nothing more. Not for every farthing in the Mythrian coffers."

"What if I offered more than farthings?"

Ghosts, was Thessia's mouth simply working on its own this evening? She managed to maintain her composure despite her own impulsive proposal.

Even more unexpectedly, her involuntary gambit seemed to work. Mona fixed her cunning stare on Thessia. "What do you mean?"

"Name your price," Thessia managed.

Mona paced. The entire room seemed to freeze, only the faint murmur of the music pulsing under the quiet. Thessia pretended her stomach wasn't knotting. What would the manipulative Mona demand? Thessia's tiara? Galwell, in one of her cages—

"Immunity," Mona said. "In Mythria."

Thessia hesitated. Mona had evidently amassed a flourishing criminal empire in Vestriya. What manner of queen would Thessia be if she were to freely permit Mona to spread her evil enterprises in Mythria?

On the other hand...

Who would she be if she rejected someone who could help her dear friend? The man who inspired their realm, no less?

"Thessia—" Galwell started.

"No. But I can extend a total pardon for all your crimes," Thessia said, conjuring authority in her voice. "All warrants for your arrest in Mythria will be suspended and you'll be welcome to come home. Until you commit new crimes, of course."

Mona's eyebrow quirked. She seemed... impressed? "If you catch me, of course. Deal."

Thessia could not quite conceal her flash of surprise. The speed with which Mona agreed to her counteroffer was unnerving to say the least.

Mona grinned widely. "I'm a villain of my word. You'll have your murderous meeting." She stepped past Galwell, sliding a finger down his shoulder. "Until then, your dance cage awaits any time you wish to put yourself in my restraints. Galwell the... Gargantuan, was it?" Her eyes slid down his body.

Galwell went ramrod straight.

Mona passed through the curtains, her svelte figure letting crushing music in for one vibrating moment. Then the curtains swung closed, leaving Thessia and the party in the quiet of their complicated victory.

"I'm sort of obsessed with her," River confessed.

"Me too," Thessia said. Mona was... inspiring. Probably not something the cherished queen of her realm should admit out loud. Yet Mona's self-possession and confidence were captivating.

"A fascinating figure," Celine said. "I'd love to write a profile on her."

THIS WILL BE INTERESTING

The group's focus gradually found Galwell. Everyone waited.

"I didn't like her," he finally declared.

Thessia concealed her laugh. Galwell had, she suspected, just told his very first lie.

"Now what?" River prompted. "We just wait for her to find whoever wants Galwell slain?"

Thessia straightened. "We don't need to wait," she announced. "We have a lead. If we want to investigate in the meantime ourselves, I know who we need to find."

She'd noticed the passing mentions that Mona, as well as their gaunt, menacing escort, had made. *Shit spy you'd make* and a name she recognized.

"Prince Ario," she said. "He's second in line to the throne, and apparently the spymaster of Vestriya. Who better to help us catch and interrogate our enemies?"

* * *

The Vestriyan palazzo was in every way the opposite of Mona's lair. In the heart of the capital, the palazzo's stone curves, soaring domes, and spiraling spires stood majestically in the purple night.

Thessia had no time to concentrate on the palazzo's splendor, however. She was running late. Really, *really* late.

Her first night in Vestriya would be commemorated with a masquerade ball, a noble custom in the realm. While Thessia had never attended one herself, she'd heard that magic cast over the entire room permitted ornate metal or ceramic masks to mold to and move with the face of every wearer.

She walked briskly through the shadowy interior hallway of the palazzo toward the sweetened swells of enchanting music escaping the grand salon's wide entryway.

Past the entryway, the Vestriyan royal masquerade waited.

This was *not* the pleasantly grand, courtly party Thessia was used to. Darkness seemed to shroud the room, closing conspiratorially over the dim glow emanating from the ornate chandelier. The music held the entire salon under a spell while crimson candles glowed and Vestriya's noble and notable danced.

Masks decorated every face. The rumors were no exaggeration. Metal and gemstone moved like skin, glimmering under the low light, depicting the faces of monsters, animals, and other novelties. Thessia saw wolverlings dancing with plume-hens, fearsome wraiths flirting with firebirds. Frills of lace and gaudy stripes of leather decorated bright gowns and dashing doublets.

The sight momentarily stole Thessia's breath. *This* was what her mother had recounted in rapturous sighs.

It was stunning . . . and yet Thessia could not shake the memory of the ramshackle and dangerous alleyways she had just come from. She wondered whether Vestriya's people knew how much wealth and enchantment filled the palazzo. She suspected they did.

She spied Hugh dancing with Tabitha, who imitated Thessia perfectly. Her "spun gold" hair swished over her shoulder with every whirling step of the dance. Her fashionist had chosen a masquerade mask in the visage of a lyricat, the svelte features of the feline predator ornamented in glittering purple gems.

Pausing in the entryway, Thessia pressed her thumb to the gemstone on her bracelet.

She watched the identical gemstone on Tabitha's necklace illuminate. She knew the pendant would hum, intensifying until it was near Thessia's.

Tabitha politely excused herself from Hugh's embrace. Thessia meanwhile retraced her steps to the hallway and stole into the first washroom she found.

THIS WILL BE INTERESTING 117

Moments later, the door opened, revealing—herself.

"Your Highness," Tabitha greeted Thessia in Thessia's own voice. She curtsied, which Thessia found unnecessary, especially in the small confines of the washroom.

"Love the mask," Thessia replied. "It suits us."

With the compliment, Tabitha dropped her supplicant demeanor. She broke into a smile. "Doesn't it?" She removed the enchanted metal from her—Thessia's—face. "The masquerade is wondrous," she gushed.

Thessia returned her smile. If she was honest, sometimes the other woman's enthusiasm for royal goings-on could inspire excitement for the parade of frivolities in Thessia herself. "It looks it," Thessia said sincerely.

Tabitha reached for her gown's fasteners.

Thessia reached for her own.

"I spoke with the king and queen on your behalf," Tabitha reported. Her nose scrunched. "Figured you'd not enjoy that conversation. Very dour, judgmental people with nothing interesting to say."

Thessia grinned, shrugging out of her gown. Even more than she welcomed Tabitha's zeal for the royal life, she rather enjoyed the girl's freely offered, wide-ranging commentary.

"Chatted with nobles from the East Vestriyan Isles," Tabitha continued, passing the gem-stone mask to Thessia. "Oddly judgmental on the subject of Prince Ezio. Said he was 'too kingly' or some such."

Interesting. Thessia's councilors had informed her that the crown prince was very popular in his homeland. "What of the other prince?" she prompted. "Ario?"

Tabitha frowned. "Not here, I don't think. So many nobles, so little time. Oh, and that handsome horseballer," she went on, blushing faintly. "Nevo Yrillis. He said he's very excited to host Vestriya Now with you."

At this, Thessia nearly dropped her mask onto the stone tile. "*What?*"

With Thessia's exclamation, Tabitha's gaze flew up in surprise.

"Vestriya Now," Tabitha repeated. "The . . . talent competition?"

"I know what it is," Thessia replied.

Everyone knew what it was. Conjurated across Mythria and other realms, Vestriya Now assembled the very finest performers in every art form and stunt imaginable, hosting them in the finest theater in Vestriya. When Mythrian musician Noah Noble had won, Thessia had knighted him herself.

"I didn't know I was *hosting* it," she went on.

Did I? She racked her memory. Her royal schedule featured this masquerade, canal sightseeing, and dinners with nobles—which Tabitha could handle—the Realm Chalice horseball cup, meetings with olivera farmers, and wine tasting in the rustic countryside . . . Yes, Thessia was quite certain an obligation to host the realms' preeminent talent revue would have lingered in her mind.

Tabitha's mouth worked. "Nevo mentioned the enormous honor of the king and queen inviting you personally. I—I said you were looking forward to it," she got out.

Thessia knew her double felt guilty for the miscommunication. "It's quite all right, Tabitha," she replied gently. "I'll . . . have my councilors confirm my willingness to the royal family."

Tabitha nodded, clearly relieved. Reoutfitted in Thessia's nightclub clothes, she moved to the doorway, where she hesitated.

"For what it's worth," she said, "I think you'll be a marvelous host."

Thessia's smile did not reach her eyes this time.

She returned to the grand salon, where the music continued and revelers followed the revolving steps of a Vestriyan dance in a carousel of silk and laughter and motion.

THIS WILL BE INTERESTING

As Thessia entered, Hugh moved from the wall to clasp her hands and sweep her into the dancing crowd. To every observer, the queen would seem simply to have returned from a moment's intermission from the dance floor.

Effortlessly, Hugh led Thessia into the dance. Distracted, the queen let her husband's footwork guide them. "Did you know I was hosting Vestriya Now?" she asked.

Hugh cleared his throat sharply. "Hm," he responded noncommittally.

He sounded—impatient. Angry, even? Thessia shot her eyes to her husband. His mask decorated his handsome features in the image of a wild goat, which Thessia found inexplicably fitting.

"You're upset," she ventured.

Hugh grimaced under his mask. "You don't have to sneak around behind my back, you know," he said.

Thessia's pulse quickened. "I wasn't sneaking," she insisted. "I was helping Galwell. There is a plot against his life, and I wish to save him."

Even saying the words in indignation, she found the declaration quietly thrilling. She was *helping*. Instead of just being helped.

Hugh swung them in the dance's next steps, sending the dance floor whirling. "Of course. Of course you must save him. Galwell is . . . here in Vestriya?" he clarified.

"He traveled with us on the *Sapphire Palace*," Thessia confirmed.

While the music lilted on, Hugh contemplated this development.

"Thessia, my queen," he said slowly, "I know we made our arrangement before Galwell returned. Now that he has . . . I think the Queendom would fully understand if we were to announce an annulment."

Thessia very nearly stumbled over her own feet.

"You . . . wish to annul our marriage?" she choked out.

"Don't you?" Hugh inquired. "If my Zaralie came back to life, I'd want to be with her. I completely understand if . . . this marriage is no longer of interest to you. Given we never . . . consummated it, annulment should be simple enough."

Thessia found her heart rate slowing. Hugh thought she still loved Galwell. Of course he did. Everyone did. He was merely misunderstanding her, not rejecting her.

"Hugh, I . . ." She mustered her words, her composure. "It's true that as a young girl I loved Galwell. But that was many years ago. I've changed," she said. "I'm . . . well, I hope very much I'm not the girl I used to be. I don't love Galwell now. That's not why I want to save him. I want to save him because . . ."

Oh, how to say it? Thessia remembered how she felt in Mona's club. She fought past every regal instinct for understatement and pleasantry and spoke her heart.

"I . . . want to *do* something. I'm always watching heroes rescue the day for me," she finished. "I want to be the hero this time."

She found this oddly freeing—sharing her thoughts and feelings for maybe the first time ever. Her confessions continued to pave their own road from her heart to her lips.

"And—and Galwell never loved me," she said.

Hugh's brow furrowed. "I'm sure that's not—"

Thessia cut him off. "No, it is. I . . . No one has ever felt that way about me," she admitted. "I'd know if they did."

Hugh regarded her, recognizing her honesty. She'd spoken one of her very deepest secrets—one of Queendom's deepest secrets—for the first time.

She looked down, not wanting to meet Hugh's eyes, scared of what she would find in them. Pity? She forbade it, by private royal decree. She would not be the deprived queen once more. The woman who had everything—except magic, or love.

Then Hugh entwined his fingers with hers. His calloused caress was impossibly gentle.

"How can I help?" he murmured. "I may not be your lover, but I am your husband. Your goals are my goals. How can I help you be the hero you're certainly capable of being?"

Now Thessia looked up. She started to smile—

"May I cut in?"

The voice was velvet confidence. Thessia looked over her shoulder.

Even masked, Prince Ezio of Vestriya was unmistakable. Thessia remembered the young man's shimmering white-gold hair from their formal introduction during Thessia's wedding.

Hugh hesitated but released Thessia into the prince's deft embrace, where Thessia could closer examine her new partner.

His fine, effete handsomeness was nothing like Hugh's. His mask depicted the Vestriyan starjay, the realm's luminous emblem bird. His irises were unmistakably golden in color.

"Pardon my interruption," he said. "But I wouldn't want the night to pass without stealing some moments with the jewel of Mythria."

"Is that what they call me—" Thessia started.

"Good prince," someone interjected.

The dance offered guests the chance to converse when their paths momentarily crossed. *Every* guest, in Ezio's case. Thessia could not get a word in edgewise with the constant chatter of eager, ever-changing company. *"Our gratitude for the marvelous portrait!" "Going to the Realm Chalice?" "Fine work restoring the Skyshade Canal!"*

"We'll see you tomorrow eve, then?" exhorted one bearded man whose visshark mask sparkled silver.

"Wouldn't miss it," Ezio replied.

Thessia watched, intrigued. "Planning tomorrow's revel while this one's still on?"

Ezio laughed gracefully. "No, no, it's—that man is the head

of the Fishers' Guild," he explained. "Last year, I commissioned public works to improve the stonework under the city's docks. Unfortunately, the enhancements ended up elevating the water level of the entire harbor. This led the large, low-dwelling fish to move deeper relative to the fishers' surface level, which challenges their livelihood, given they need the larger fish to—" No doubt noticing Thessia's expression, the prince paused. "I'm boring you," he guessed.

Thessia found his modesty even more charming than his princely smile. "Not in the slightest," she replied honestly.

Indeed, what had fluttered under Thessia's expression wasn't impatience. It was envy. Inspiration. Ezio, dashing and caddish, had molded himself into an experienced and knowledgeable governor.

"You're well-liked," she ventured.

Ezio demurred. "I have my moments."

Something stiff in his voice led Thessia to continue. "*Too* well-liked, some might say."

Ezio watched her closely. They spun under the chandelier. "Spoken with our nobles, have you?"

"*Kingly* was the word they used," Thessia confirmed.

Ezio frowned as if the compliment unnerved him. "I care very deeply for my realm," he explained slowly. "Our people care for me in return. This has led certain proponents of my parents to fear I may . . . challenge their reign. It is a risk I consider worth taking."

Challenge. Thessia heard the unspoken synonym. *Coup.* Curiosity and concern for the young prince made her lean closer.

"What do you think?" she murmured. "Would you consider yourself kingly?"

Ezio smiled, understanding the concealed question. But when he winked rakishly, Thessia knew she would receive no straightforward information. Only spinning sidesteps like those of this dance.

"If I'm kingly, I'll need a queen to share my dances with," Ezio returned.

"I'm married," Thessia reminded him. "You forget yourself."

"Never," Ezio replied.

"May I cut in?"

The dance had returned them to Hugh. Obligingly, Ezio released her into Hugh's embrace, then whirled away with his new partner, whose dress seemed to change swirling patterns on its own.

"We were speaking of your lead on Galwell?" Hugh prompted. Thessia caught her husband's eyes following Ezio with something like...

No. Only Thessia envied the prince this evening, surely.

"There is a royal spymaster," she informed Hugh. "The younger prince, Ario. If anyone knows of evildoers working with the Deathrose Guild in Vestriya, the *royal spymaster* would be the man. Unfortunately," Thessia continued, "he's not here this evening."

Hugh nodded. When the dance changed direction, he led them gracefully while the chandelier cast indigo over the masked crowd. The illumination's color changed, and suddenly, in the golden glow, shimmering apparitions of enormous eagles soared overhead, luminous wings outstretched. Dancers gasped in delight.

Hugh held her close. "I can help," he said, his voice low. "I planned on getting drinks with palazzo guardsmen and foot soldiers later tonight. They're likely to know where the spymaster could be found."

"Hugh," Thessia exhaled. "That's perfect. Thank you." When he only smiled with modest pride, guilt found Thessia. "I'm sorry," she went on. "Sincerely. For leaving you here earlier this evening without explanation."

Hugh dipped her with gentle grace. "It's fine, Thess. Tabitha was pleasant company. I do worry for her, though," he said with what

Thessia considered entirely charming concern. "Does she ever wish for . . . her own life?"

"Tabitha has been with me since we were five years old. Never has she been confined to my retinue," she reassured Hugh. "She's the daughter of a minor noble. Unkind, manipulative man. He gets his daughter close to the throne, Tabitha gets to leave her cruel home. Everyone wins," she concluded. "She imitates me perfectly, does she not?"

Hugh frowned in contemplation. "Well enough," he said. "But the flecks in her eyes do not sparkle the way yours do. She is not prone to raising her chin when she asks questions, like you do. Nor does she do this thing where, when you find something sincerely humorous, you smile with one side of your mouth."

Thessia found herself disarmed. "I—"

"I must cut in once more."

Hugh stiffened, but propriety demanded he and Ezio exchange dance partners again.

Thessia was surprised to find no debonair flirtation on the prince's half-masked expression. Ezio looked grave. "I could not help but overhear you discussing our royal spymaster."

Thessia faltered. "We—how could you—" *Did the prince have magically enhanced hearing? Or merely loyal listeners everywhere?*

"I must warn you," Ezio went on, "my brother is not . . . like me. Do not seek him out. Our spymaster is our realm's most dangerous man, his cunning and mercilessness unrivaled. Except by Benjamin, of course."

"Who," Thessia asked, "is Benjamin?"

"His enforcer."

Thessia gulped. Though new to heroics, Thessia knew confronting people with "enforcers" was not recommended. *Galwell would do it for me*, she reminded herself. Summoning her friend's courage,

THIS WILL BE INTERESTING

she straightened her shoulders under the prince's grasp. "I must. My companion's safety may depend upon information your sibling possesses. Surely you understand"—she met his golden eyes—"some risks are worth taking."

Ezio regarded her. Overhead, the chandelier changed once more to deep red. Scarlet light engulfed Ezio's face as conjured windsnakes erupted from the chandelier's limbs overhead.

"Please return me to my husband," Thessia ordered him.

The prince did not protest. In swift, sweeping strides, they crossed the chaotic salon, and Ezio passed Thessia wordlessly to Hugh.

"Nice mask," Ezio remarked.

"Thank you," Hugh replied. "I'm a goat."

Thessia smiled with one side of her mouth.

10
River

"I'll see you later," Celine said, almost tripping over a stack of materials she'd checked out from the nearest library. Celine had procured everyone rooms in a sprawling Vestriyan villa, paid for by Queen Thessia, and River and Celine had spent the better part of the day and early evening in the study together.

River abandoned her copy of *How to Know When It's Time: The Ultimate Guide to Leaving Organized Crime Behind*. Celine had been right. There really was a book for everything.

Not that River was reading it in earnest. She'd come to understand that Celine was not going to let up on the whole redemption thing. The only way to stop her incessant questioning was to pretend her relentlessness was somewhat working. If River had to look at the words inside a book every once in a while, it was worth the price of access to Celine's mind.

"And where exactly do you think you're going?" she asked as she grabbed Celine's arm. It wasn't necessary. But any excuse to be nearer—to smell the muddy ink mingling with the sweat and salt of Celine's skin—River had to take. They'd spent entirely too much time sleeping in the same room on the ship. River had started to memorize the way Celine breathed, and she was very aware of the quick, hasty inhale Celine had taken when River touched her.

"I've found a lead on a Deathrose Guild member who might be stationed here in Vestriya. I'm going to investigate," Celine told her.

"Stationed in Vestriya? Our operations don't leave the realm of Mythria," River said. She hesitated. "Except for special assignments. But those are always done undercover."

"*Aha*. You've given me another piece of information." Celine winked.

This was an accidental game they'd been playing now for days. River kept slipping up, offering up small bits of guild information she didn't mean to share. And Celine, being the ever-observant memory master she was, noticed each time.

River tightened her grip, enjoying the way the pads of her fingers pressed into Celine's soft skin. This was another game they'd been playing. How many ways could they touch each other? "You think you can just get up in the middle of this study session that *you* requested, so you can investigate?"

"Yes. I will try to pick up supper on my way back. What do you think of braised hroxen? It's quite good here."

If she wasn't so smart, so obviously meant to use her sharp mind for writing and observing, Celine might've made a good assassin. *That* was a bit of information River hoped to never slip up and share. Everywhere she went, she was supposed to be looking for recruits. Assassinry was a dangerous, deadly business, and the guild always needed new members. River was to observe the people around her. See if any of them were assassin material.

And it troubled River to admit it, but Celine met the criteria. For all her smarts, she was also alarmingly fearless.

"You must be joking," River said.

"Does it seem like a laughing matter to you?"

"Am I to believe you found a lead . . . inside a book?"

Celine held her chin up. "You can find anything you need inside a book," she said. "But this particular piece of information happened to come from the scribesheet I grabbed on our way out of the library."

She wriggled out of River's hold and departed, apparently believing there was no other discussion needed on the matter.

River shoved her feet into her shoes and hurried to follow.

It was a balmy evening. A gentle sea breeze whipped through the reckless curls that always managed to escape the bun atop Celine's head. She hurried down weathered sandstone paths, moving like she knew exactly where she was headed without needing to consult a map or ask a local for assistance.

Celine didn't bother to turn around when she called out, "Will you be joining me, or do you plan to silently follow the whole way?"

"Silently follow," River answered. "Until I must rescue you. Which is inevitable, since you're storming toward some sort of hideout for a trained assassin with nothing but a notebook and quill to defend yourself."

"You know what they say about words," Celine retorted. "They're the most powerful weapon of all."

Ghosts. Was Celine . . . teasing her?

River couldn't help herself. She quickened her pace until they were walking side by side. There was a mischievous smile still carved into the delicate, swooping planes of Celine's profile.

"You really believe you can kill a Deathrose Guild assassin on your own?" River asked.

"Why does it always go straight to murder with you?" Celine said. "There are other ways to go about things, you know. And what information could I gain from a corpse?"

"Quite a bit, depending on what you're looking for."

The farther they walked, the more confused River became. She imagined they'd be cutting down dark alleyways until they ended up somewhere similar to Mona's place—an inconspicuous front that housed something quite different in its depths. But Celine seemed to be heading toward the cluster of large, colorful tents pitched in the middle of a wide-open patch of grass. The tents were surrounded by gigantic orbs of light, magicked to be bright enough to make you squint if you looked at them directly. It wasn't that Deathrose Guild assassins needed to hide in the shadows at all times. The whole point was often to hide in plain sight. But this looked like . . .

Well, it looked like a circus.

"*No*," River whispered. It was an unconscious declaration of surprise that she wished she hadn't made, because Celine looked at her in that way she was so fond of—the cutting gaze, determined to continue unwrapping River's psyche like a gift. That first night on the ship had been an anomaly. River would not share any more about herself.

"There is no lead," Celine admitted. "But there *was* a full-page advertisement for the Vestriyan Caravaners in the scribesheet. The realm's premier traveling circus. Actually, the advertisement called them the best of every realm. That's right. *Every* realm. Not just Vestriya. I found that to be a rather bold claim. I remember seeing your family's show. And I remember seeing *this* show once, a long, long time ago. I don't feel qualified to say which is more impressive, so I want an expert's take on the matter, in case I ever do a write-up. You know, scribely integrity and all."

"You . . . tricked me," River managed to get out. She did not know whether to feel betrayed or impressed. Yes, Celine would make a very fine assassin indeed.

"I knew you wouldn't go if I asked. But I really want you to see this," Celine said. Her eyes did that puddly, hopeful thing that made River's knees go weak. "Will you please come with me?"

River could hear the circus music now, waltzing and repetitive. It wasn't the same tune that her family's troupe played, but it had the same spirit to it—a relentless, looping brightness that was so cheerful it bordered on eerie.

She formed her lips around the word *no*. Of course she would not see the Vestriyan Caravaners. She'd go back to paging through that damned crime book, fighting off a sigh as she read passages like, "The first step to leaving crime is admitting you're a criminal."

Instead, River found herself saying, "Fine."

Fine! None of this is fine! And yet, it was exactly what she told Celine, trudging beside her as they walked up to the ticket booth.

"Two front-row seats," Celine said.

"Back row," River corrected. Anticipating Celine's disapproval, she leaned in to whisper, "It's the best way to get a full sense of the staging. Plus, we can decide if they play all the way to the nosebleeds like they should. You know, scribely integrity."

Celine's smile lit up her whole face, and oh, was it dangerous, the way Celine's visible pleasure made River want to give her more of it. Worse, Celine seemed to recognize River's enjoyment. Perhaps something in River's own expression gave her away. Instead of dropping her smile, Celine deepened it, her lovely brown eyes twinkling, her gaze full of determination. For what, River did not exactly know, but she felt it in her bones.

"Let's take our seats," she said, breaking the tension.

As they entered the main tent, Celine let out another yelp of delight as she took in the spectacle of it all. "This looks marvelous!"

"It's . . . sufficient," River replied, trying hard not to look too impressed herself.

"I'm going to get us something to eat. Would you like sweet or savory?" Before River could answer, Celine tapped her forehead and said, "Savory. I remember, of course. I'll be right back."

Alone, River couldn't help but admit that the whole stage did look rather spectacular. The Caravaners must have had a hand magician in their troupe who specialized in decoration, because the inside of

THIS WILL BE INTERESTING

the tent was draped with layers upon layers of sky-blue curtains. Some sort of effect shone onto them to give the appearance of moving clouds. The performance floor was a vibrant sea-foam green instead of the practical black River had expected. Waves of light burst up from beneath it to warble like water. Put all together, it gave the illusion that the acrobatic troupe would be performing over sea and through sky, though not any sea or sky River had ever seen in real life. It was a perfectly heightened exaggeration, as sumptuous as it was deceptively simple. The troupe had plenty of wide-open space to dance and tumble and play.

River could already imagine what kind of moves they had planned. The fabric curtains would likely be climbed up and spun down. The floor had a fine net over it, with rope that would get raised for tightrope walking. Any troupe worth their farthings would have a trapeze, too. Sure enough, when River gazed up, she saw it secured to one side of the tent, pinned up until it was time for that part of the show.

River could almost feel the way the air would whoosh through her hair if she swung from it—a breeze created not by the elements, but by the force of her own movements. It really was like flying, especially when you let go of the bar and swung only from your knees, for a moment suspended, waiting to grasp your partner's forearms.

A smile must have crept up River's face, because when Celine returned with food, she said, "I knew you would enjoy this."

"Me? No. This is just what I look like when no one's watching."

"You have a resting smile face?"

"Don't forget to include that in your write-up. *River Pricemark, known for her permanently delightful expressions, says the show was satisfactory at best.*"

"I suspect you may switch from satisfactory to swept away when you taste this," Celine said, handing River a salt-covered twist bun.

The bun was easily the size of River's face, and so buttery that it glistened even in the dimness of the tent's elevated back row. River took a hearty bite, and rivulets of a rich, orange cheese sauce oozed out, dripping down the side of her mouth.

"Oh dear. You don't like it," Celine said. She reached over to take the twist bun back. When River elbowed her away, faking a growl, Celine clapped her hands together as she laughed.

"This may be the best thing I've ever eaten in my life," River conceded.

"Finally, I've found your weakness!" she said.

"I have no weakness," River told her.

"That can't be true." Celine had another twist bun on her plate, and she took her own bite, letting out a sigh of pleasure so deep that River had to squeeze her thighs together.

"It is. The guild even tests you on it." River didn't know what possessed her to admit this. Compared to Dougal's crimes on the ship, it was a far milder transgression, but it was still the most specific piece of knowledge she'd shared so far. Celine was winning this information game far too easily.

"What do they do? Dump stingbugs on you to see if you'll scream? Trap you in a room that shrinks in size until it becomes an airless coffin? Show you renderings of your loved ones and explain the ways they might be ripped limb from limb?"

Celine was almost exactly right, but River gave her a look that said, *You know I can't tell you that much*. Instead, River used the pad of her thumb to swipe cheese from the corner of Celine's mouth.

It was as if other patrons had vanished in a puff of smoke, leaving only River, Celine, and their salt-covered twist buns. River could not help but indulge this feeling, letting her thumb linger on Celine's lower lip, pulling it down until Celine's bottom teeth were bared. Even still, she did not pull away. She wasn't sure she could. She might have to live the rest of her life right there, with her thumb against Celine's mouth.

It was Celine who interrupted, letting out a soft, "Sorry," moving so that River put down her hand.

"I'll tell you this much," River said, fighting to regain her composure, looking everywhere but at Celine's lips. "Some of the guild members *do* have weaknesses. And they're a lot funnier than you'd expect."

Celine grinned in delight, sending another shimmering thrill down River's spine.

"For one, Vandra Ravenfall believes she can tame brushwalkers," River continued. "Anytime the guild sent the two of us near a cursed forest, she'd stop in to find one and try to pet it. Her hands are covered in scars from all the bite marks, but she gets them charmed away so you can't tell."

"No way," Celine said, sufficiently scandalized. "Brushwalkers are so unpredictable! Why would she ever believe she could tame one?"

"That's her nature." River tapped her finger on her chin, trying to think of another guild member's weakness that Celine would find amusing. Vandra had left the guild and become a Mythrian hero in her own right, so her desire to love a brushwalker would not compromise her. River combed through her knowledge of her colleagues until she landed on another weakness she felt would be safe to share. "There are these twins, Gary and Mary. They work as a team, and they're very good."

"Twin assassins? How does that happen? Did one join before the other? Do they love it equally?"

"Hush, love, let me finish," River said.

Shit. The endearment had just slipped out, no effort or thought.

She tried to continue as if she'd said nothing out of the ordinary, not allowing herself to examine Celine's face for any clues that she'd caught it, too. "Gary is incredibly ticklish in his left elbow. To the point that he collapses to the ground. Only the left side, though. It's quite odd."

"Very peculiar indeed," Celine said. "How did they even discover this?"

River gave her the same look as before, the one that said she'd already shared too much. But how could she resist a woman like Celine, whose curiosity needed to be sated somehow? This was a far better option than what River *really* wanted to do.

"Well, these twist buns would be a good weakness, if you ever need to give one," Celine told her, accepting that River had already gone far beyond the limits of what was allowed.

"I'll keep it in mind."

"I had them the last time I visited, and they're even better than I remember. Then again, I was young when we came the first time. Well, not *that* young, I suppose. It was the summer before I met you, which feels like a lifetime ago, but also feels like just yesterday now that we're around each other again."

"You know, it's occurring to me that you never told me back then that you'd seen another circus troupe perform," River said.

"I must have forgotten to mention it," Celine replied.

"I find it hard to believe Miss Memory would forget to bring up seeing a traveling circus to the girl from a traveling circus. Just yesterday you mentioned the time I accidentally wore two different color socks to school."

"It was funny," Celine said.

"They were two different shades of black!" River protested.

"Yes, but it was still memorable."

River wished she had Celine's gift of perfect memory, so she could accurately recall her earliest weeks stationed in the outskirts of Queendom with the Pricemark Family Circus. All she remembered was her first impression of Celine—she was kind and welcoming to River when no one else had been, but she also seemed withdrawn. A little shy, even. Then River had shown up to school with flecks of bright blue shimmering hair powder still lingering on her scalp—remnants of standing too close as her mother had gotten ready for a performance—and suddenly, Celine bloomed like a flower, asking River a dozen questions about why her hair was that color, then even more inquiries about what it was like to travel with a circus. She was neither shy nor withdrawn. River always assumed she'd misjudged her, projecting her own initial teenage self-consciousness onto Celine.

But watching her now, she saw that same shyness bloom again, thinly disguised by a lifted chin and clear-eyed stare.

"We came here once on our annual family voyage. And you know how family voyages can be," Celine said. "I often wished I could forget them, so I always tried my best to do so."

Celine was withholding something, that was clear. As much as River wanted to know what that might be, she knew it would do her no good to uncover it. When this time in Vestriya was done, and River had restored order in the Deathrose Guild, she'd go back to her nomadic life of assassinry—hopefully after being promoted to a position like Dougal's—and Celine would return to the hamlet outside Queendom. They need not forge any closer bond than the one they already had.

So River truly didn't know what possessed her to say, "My family never went on voyages. Although some might think moving to a new place every nine months qualified as a constant voyage. I got to see almost all of Mythria in those years. But I never had a place to call my own. No real home. Just a temporary tent. And in the end, I didn't have any people to call my own, either." Finally aware of herself and her words, River threw on a casual smile as she added, "Ah, well. Who needs other people anyway?"

The tent lights flickered, allowing River to fix her face forward and ignore Celine's probing gaze.

A man dressed in a black bodysuit with a sequined jacket atop it sauntered to the center of the floor. "Welcome, welcome! The show will begin shortly. All we ask is that you cheer loudly, watch closely, and believe *everything* you see. The realms are full of magic, but none more potent than ours. Let us enchant you tonight!"

He threw his arms open, and a dove flew out of each jacket sleeve, growing larger and larger the farther away they flew, until suddenly, each bird puffed out into a cloud of sparkling nothing.

The crowd gasped. Not River. She knew the birds were an illusion, though she couldn't quite figure out how the man had done it. Perhaps it was his hand magic. Or just a well-timed stunt. It made sense that these kinds of shows would have gotten more elaborate. Everything about the realms had improved in the years since River had traveled with her family's troupe, and though Vestriya had not progressed in ways such as spell service, they'd evidently put their effort into more practical improvements.

As the show progressed, River found herself incapable of keeping her critical eye at the forefront. The Vestriyan Caravaners were *good*.

They could flip and fly just as well as they could make jokes and entertain, and their stage was ever-evolving, curtains shifting from sky blue to midnight black as troupe members twisted, spun, and swung from the fabric like animals in trees. The sea-foam floor held real water beneath it, and at one point the water rose, suspended in the air by a magical barrier that was as wide as the stage and as tall as the tent. Troupe members dove into the water and swam, performing synchronized stunts while fully submerged. Then the water lowered until it was back under the floor. Somehow everyone on the stage was dry, as if they'd never been swimming at all.

"*Wow*," River couldn't help but utter.

"Just incredible," Celine confirmed. She reached for River's hand and squeezed.

The hope and possibility bubbling up inside River spilled over, and she grinned so wide she could feel the air on her teeth.

If they were different people, living different lives, this would've been something like a date. And River hated how much she liked that idea.

On the stage, acrobats started tumbling in rows, running from opposite directions and flipping toward each other. They were so precisely placed that they landed shoulder to shoulder, facing different directions before running off diagonally to do it all again.

From the top of the tent, trapeze artists began swinging.

Along the walls, troupe members hung from ribbons of silk, spinning and climbing in dazzling synchronicity. The conjurated music swelled. River could feel the tune pulsing inside her chest. She tried to savor the moment by making note of every single troupe member's contribution to this grand finale.

At the peak of the tent, high above the spectacle, she noticed something peculiar. A troupe member hung upside down by her ankles. Her costuming indicated her importance—a tight-fitting bodysuit covered head to toe in crystals. Ones that would surely dazzle once the light caught them. But she was above the light. Above the action. And she didn't begin artfully spinning from the harness around her ankles like River would have expected. She looked instead like she was flailing.

River squinted, trying to focus on the performer's mouth. Was she saying *Hall plea*?

No.

Help me.

River looked around, all her wonder replaced with worry. Surely there was another troupe member who'd noticed this. But River could find no one on the stage paying attention to the woman strung up at the peak of the tent. Everyone else had their own role in the performance to complete, and they were fully committed to doing just that.

Even if she's stuck, at least she's safe, River convinced herself.

The woman was probably supposed to plunge straight down into the heart of the action, stopped only by the tie around her ankles, but the mechanism wasn't working right. That kind of thing happened during shows all the time. More than anyone would ever guess.

The woman was a professional. She'd know what to do.

Still, River couldn't stop watching her.

That was how she noticed that the harness around the performer's ankles was not only stuck, but it was *fraying*. And with every flail, the twine unraveled farther.

River didn't remember teleporting. She only knew that one moment she was in her seat in the last row, and the next she had her arms around the crystal-covered troupe member, holding her tightly as both of them flipped through the air together, neither of them tied to any harness at all.

When they landed, River was faintly aware of the audience's confused quiet. She was significantly more aware of the perilous stinging in her legs from the impact of hitting the ground and of the stunned glances from the troupe members who had narrowly dodged being squished by the two women.

All that mattered was River was on her feet, and she wasn't hurt. More important, neither was the performer.

"What are you doing?" The performer faked a grin as she burned holes into River's face through her crystal-covered eyelashes. "Let me *go*!"

"I . . . You were going to fall," River said.

The performer was still smiling, ever the professional. "Of

course I was going to fall! It's called a performance! And you've just ruined our grand finale! What is wrong with you? How did you even reach me?"

"No, no. You don't understand. It wasn't going to be your normal trick. Your rope was fraying," River told her. "You couldn't see that, but I could. If you'd stayed up there any longer, you would not have fallen down the way you planned. You'd have crashed headfirst into the stage."

The performer's anger was not quelled by this truth. Instead, she got even more upset, calling out to other troupe members to have River removed from the stage. "You know nothing of what you speak!" the performer screamed. "You ruined my performance!"

River had nothing to say. No explanation to give. She'd let the spectacle of the night get to her head, believing for a moment that she could be a hero.

The other members of the troupe closed in. Through hollow, angry smiles, they bombarded River with questions. *Who are you? How did you do that? Who sent you? Was it the Clover Circus? The Illustrian Illusionists?*

River closed her eyes and teleported away, thinking of the back row.

Naturally, she landed atop the last of Celine's twist bun. Cheese sauce squirted into her eyes.

"You saved her," Celine squealed, eyes alight as she grabbed River's hand to help her up. "And you made it look so artful, too! Everyone back here was a bit confused about what happened. I told them you were a part of the show. They couldn't believe a beautiful woman appeared out of thin air! But I could. What was that stage name you always wanted to use for acrobatics? Fearless Flyer? It still suits you quite nicely. *This* is what you're made for!"

"I didn't save her at all. I ruined the show." River swiped the cheese from her eyes, frustrated to find her tears mixed with the sauce. What a fucking embarrassment. "Listen, do yourself a favor and stop trying to convince me that I'm good."

Celine flinched, her mouth hanging open in unguarded shock. "I only thought—"

River cut her off. "Exactly. You and your *thoughts*. You *thought* that you could treat me like one of your scribesheet investigations, trying to force your preferred narrative onto my story. But there is no number of library books I could read or acrobatic shows I could attend that will ever change what's true. I don't care what I told you when I was sixteen. I'm not sixteen anymore. I know the truth. I was born with an unpredictable magic. I am meant for an unpredictable life."

It stung to say it, more than River anticipated it would. She knew it to be true. She'd just lived through more proof that her magic would only ever cause trouble. But there was still a reckless hope in her that refused to die without a fight—a hope that Celine had instilled in River when they were teens and they'd whisper their dreams to each other in the dark.

"That's not true," Celine replied, her gaze intent. "River, you could have any life. You could have this one." She gestured to the tent. "I know it's what you really want. That's why I brought you here. There's more for you than the guild."

River put her face as close to Celine's as she could handle. "You know nothing. I am an assassin, and I always will be."

It was then that River registered what Celine had said. She'd called her beautiful. But River took no pleasure in it. She'd made the mistake of believing this kind of fantasy once, when she'd hoped to become an actual member of her family's troupe. All that had brought her was pain.

Watching the Vestriyan Caravaners, River had made the same

mistake again. She'd bought into the illusion. Up until a few days ago, River Pricemark never made the same mistake twice.

There would be no more entertaining Celine's whims. River was not here to be a hero. She was here to restore order to the guild. Nothing more.

"I'll still be publishing a piece on the guild," Celine said before River could teleport away. "I'm not stopping my story for you."

"*Fine*," River said. "You already snuck information into your last piece. Don't think I didn't notice. So go and keep doing it. See what happens when you continue. I certainly don't care."

11
Thessia

Hugh's hand in hers, Thessia departed the Vestriyan palazzo late the next morning with the excuse of wanting to walk along the river running through the city's heart in romantic seclusion.

The Skyshade River flowed powerfully within constructed stone channels. Thessia understood the name—in the Vestriyan morning, the reflection on the water made it seem as if the sky itself flowed through the metropolis.

When they reached the riverbank, she dropped Hugh's hand.

Not far from the palace, the serene statues and white-flowered trees changed to outlandishly sculpted facades of clubs and bars from which dance music hummed, even in the early day. Vendors of questionable commodities lingered on street corners. Couples who'd clearly passed a sleepless night lounged in each other's company.

Thessia and Hugh knew exactly where they were going. When they located the tavern, they slipped inside.

The queen of Mythria had not often ventured into her homeland's establishments for the casual purveyance of liqueurs. However, she had experienced enough to notice the differences in Vestriya's. Mythrian pubs were homey places, wood-paneled and warm, intended to welcome the lonely or weary.

Not here. Small windows set in stone let in only enough light to leave plenty of shadow. Over the ebony surface of the bar were stacked shelves of dark, glassy liqueurs. The room's rectangular proportions and high ceiling indicated it once was a warehouse or craftwork facility. The place was sparsely populated, as if no one wanted to be there unless they were seeking sanctuary for elicit dealings or a *very* strong drink.

Thessia moved swiftly to Galwell, who occupied one of the few booths, clearly visible with his perfect posture and memorable auburn hair. Celine sat with him. Neither had touched their drinks.

"Where's River?" Thessia asked as she slid onto the seat next to Celine.

"She wished to come separately," Celine replied quickly.

Thessia caught the new stiffness in her voice. *Should I inquire further? What is the etiquette with questmates?*

She looked to Galwell for guidance. Before either of them could speak, however, a thud in the rafters drew their gazes up.

River had magicked suddenly onto a long beam. In surprise, she wobbled until, with fast, spider-like movements, she righted herself. Gracefully, she flipped down onto the floor in front of her compatriots.

"I wouldn't think an assassin would be so fond of making an entrance," Thessia remarked when River seated herself next to Galwell—the farthest seat from Celine.

"I can choose where I go," River explained. "I just can't control where I *land*."

Hugh, who'd watched her entrance in silent interest, climbed into the booth, looking boyishly fascinated. "What happens if you're twenty irons in the air?" he inquired.

"I've gotten very good at landing on my feet," River replied.

Grabbing Galwell's drink, she sipped deeply from the sparkling green foam. Then she eyed Thessia.

"By the way," she returned, "why is the king here?"

Now this, Thessia had plenty of etiquette and experience in.

Assembling questing parties was something of her royal specialty. "Everyone, my husband, Hugh, is joining the quest," she informed them.

Hugh straightened up, having evidently forgotten his own novelty. Squaring his doublet with proud propriety, he grinned.

"Very glad to be here, folks. It is an honor. Love your mission, and I can tell that you all are a formidable party," he started. "I'm thrilled to offer my own humble skills. I've actually been rather a ringer for questing parties, if I do say so myself. Joined late on my previous one, too, but proved myself in the end. Would love to be the horseball player drafted in the first round one day instead of the last member to join. But either way, I'll certainly give it my all!"

His pronouncement left everyone perplexed, if amused. Even River and Celine, hiding smiles, seemed momentarily to have forgotten their discord.

"Hugh, we're delighted to have you," Galwell welcomed him. "And what a weight off my chest that this quest won't be taking Thessia away from you on your honeymoon."

"I thought you said this was a no-romance-allowed questing party," River grumbled with what sounded like wishful wondering.

"They're married," Galwell replied. "That's different from romance."

"I think romance can only get stronger in marriage, actually," Celine ventured primly.

River scoffed.

Uncomfortable with the discussion's direction for several reasons, Thessia interjected. "Hugh and I won't derail any of this quest with romance, worry not," she promised. "We'll have *plenty* of time outside the quest for that."

At this pronouncement, Hugh caught her eye in surprise. A glint of accusation shone in his gaze. *You don't wish to tell your own questing party the truth?*

Thessia didn't.

"Hugh is proving himself to be Most Valuable Questmate of our team," she hastened to say. "Tell them, Hugh."

She nudged him proudly. The judgment vanished from her husband's eyes. He beamed, facing the party.

"Being only recently a member of this commendable crew, my background is probably unknown to many of you," he said. "We haven't had the chance to swap stories around the campfire yet."

"Hugh Mavaris," Celine cut in, with gentle incredulity. "You're one of the most famous men in Mythria. Everyone knows how you survived a sledgeling bite when you were younger under mysterious circumstances. You prefer to play first defender in pickup horseball matches. In your *Mythria Magazine* coronation cover story, you described the rocky shores of your Paramar Bay hometown to be the 'closest place to the Ghost's Gate in the realm itself,'" she rattled off. "You were a foot soldier in the queen's army who has risen to the rank of king and the hero who slayed Myke Lycroft alongside Elowen, Vandra, Beatrice, and Clare in Vermillion Vale."

Commonplace knowledge or not, the recognition flattered Hugh. "Thank you, Celine," he replied earnestly. "That's very nice. Your memory is exceptional."

"I have a head magic gift. Perfect memory," Celine replied.

"That must be marvelously useful. Especially for a scribe. Yes"—Hugh nodded vigorously—"I was a foot soldier. Which means whenever I go somewhere new, the routine that brings me comfort is meeting other foot soldiers and guards. I've gotten pretty close with some here already. Delightful fellows. Impressive Drinking Swords competitors."

His smile went mischievous, and Thessia could not help mirroring his expression.

"Impressive," Hugh went on, "but no match for your king. With enough games of Drinking Swords, one can get men to divulge their closest guarded secrets. Like," he elaborated slowly, "which tavern the royal spymaster frequents midday."

Galwell, whose eyes had wandered to the few other patrons as if he feared confrontation, snapped his gaze forward. "Midday is in mere moments," he pointed out.

"What does the spymaster do here?" River inquired. "Meet informants? Clandestine intimidation tactics?"

"Shall we find out?" Thessia rejoined. "Perhaps he's outside?"

No further invitation needed, everyone stood eagerly.

Especially Thessia. Exhilaration danced in her chest, her fingers practically itching with excitement. She was really doing this! Part of her own quest. The scribe of her own story.

And she was in possession of a lead that could spell their victory— one she'd procured! Well, Hugh had helped.

What should we call ourselves? she nearly asked her questing party. *The New Five?* No, that sounded like a musical group. *Thess and the Best?* Rhymes were chancy. She needed to consult with one of the Grandharts, she concluded. They were good with self-promotion.

Their unnamed cohort spilled onto the street corner outside and scoured the Vestriyan scene. Thessia searched for someone who looked—well, spymasterly. Cloak? Dagger? She remembered Ezio's grim warning. *The realm's most dangerous man.* No one stood out, however. Until—

While Thessia watched, a handsome yet inconspicuous carriage stopped near the stone curb. A man stepped out purposefully, hood drawn, while guards, similarly hooded, fanned out to observe from peripheral posts.

The hooded man continued to the street corner and cleared his throat.

"May I, with poems most *florid*," he declared in an enthusiastic oratorical mode, "deliver thee from daily dullness most horrid!"

He whipped off his hood. Dashing off an expensive hat that he, for some reason, wore underneath, he revealed perfect silver locks and sparkling gray eyes.

Thessia recognized him instantly. Or recognized the description he matched, for they had never met.

Into his hat he dropped several silver coins, like he expected tips. Instead, instant furor greeted his revealed identity. People jeered and shook their fists.

"We told ya never to recite your loathsome stanzas on our block again! Find another corner to torment," a passerby hollered.

"I'll give you a poem for free, good sir!" the dauntless poet offered. "Merely render me a word to compose around!"

"You're awful," the passerby muttered.

"*Awful*! Very good!" the poet cheered. "As struck with awe, I seek to rend you *awe-ful*. The poems I dare to gift will leave your *jaw full*"—he winked upon the rhyme—"of idioms indulgent in verse. Perhaps it'll inspire ye to donate a coin from your purse."

Thessia winced.

"What's he doing?" an onlooker wondered loudly.

"He's just rhymed *awful* with *jaw full*," his friend replied gravely.

"Horrid!" the other man protested, then vomited profusely onto the street corner. In its mother's arms, a baby wailed.

"I'm taking money out of your hat for that one," the indignant mother chastened the poet, who watched cheerfully while she extracted the coins he'd dropped in.

"You can't abuse alliteration this way," exclaimed a sweaty man lying in the gutter. "Poetical devices should serve only to enhance the speaker's meaning, never to lend unearned substance to lines lacking imperative!"

"Yeah!" the first man concurred.

"I appreciate the constructive criticism!" the poet promised.

He endured his condemnation impressively, Thessia could concede. Unfortunately, it was the only compliment she could offer the spymaster prince of Vestriya, who was presently making a fool of himself on the street corner of his own capital city.

She could not quite believe her eyes. "Prince Ario?" she murmured. What in the realms was the royal spymaster doing playing street-corner poet? Weren't spies supposed to be more . . . secretive?

"Perhaps this is like a shadow play storyline and he has a secret twin," Galwell speculated. "I've heard of those."

"He doesn't," Celine confirmed.

"*This* is the man whose reputation has scared the guild out of Vestriya? I don't understand," River said.

"Perhaps the guild hates poetry?" Hugh offered.

They watched hopelessly as the prince continued to happily rhyme *iridescent fire* with *my tumescent desire*. How could a man this ridiculous help them face down grave evil?

"Compatriots, cheer up," Hugh ordered them. "Every quest has its setbacks. When I was captured by the Fraternal Order, I feared for my life, but here I am. We must persevere. No one would think we would make a formidable team, and yet we do."

Thessia looked up.

No one would think we would make a formidable team.

"Hugh," she said, realizing. "You're right. On a first impression, any of us might seem to be someone we are not. What if our spymaster's no different? It would make sense, wouldn't it? Concealment of his cunning under this . . . this . . ." She gestured toward the poet.

On the corner, the prince compared the constancy of his heart to the endurance of fossilized insects found in Vestriyan caves.

"Thessia is right," Galwell declared despite the discouraging display. "Can we speak with him?"

Hugh nodded. "I'll approach. Why don't you all return to the tavern and find a private corner?"

They went inside while Hugh spoke with the prince. Summarily, Hugh led their silver-haired objective to their table.

Prince Ario dropped into an open seat. He wasted no time. "I hear you're admirers of my work," he announced, gazing loftily over them.

"Yes," Thessia eagerly confirmed. "We are in desperate need of valuable intelligence. We hear you're the most cunning spymaster your realm has ever had."

With the compliment, however, Ario visibly slouched. Disappointment flattened his expression.

"Oh," he replied. "*That* work."

Thessia exchanged a glance with Hugh. Hadn't Prince Ezio promised a menacing master of espionage? Ario was performing foolish foppery perfectly. Wasn't he? Or perhaps his frivolity was *part* of the menace, Thessia reasoned, like a fearsome clown. She hated clowns.

"*And* your poetry, of course," Celine courageously chimed in. "You have . . . such a way with words," she managed.

"We couldn't look away," River concurred with clear honesty.

It was Thessia's turn now. "How ever did you learn such a large vocabulary?"

When Galwell shifted uncomfortably, Thessia realized their persuasive fibbing sat poorly with the honest hero. "I don't know much about poetry," he finally said.

Hugh frowned. Ario seemed pleased. "I've had to practice *in secret*, you know," he shared exuberantly. "Entirely self-taught, because my family doesn't approve." He caught himself, clearing his throat like he regretted the reference to his prominent parentage. "That is, they don't approve, because they'd rather I spend my time on something practical like the family trade of torture and intimidation."

Thessia winced, realizing her hopes of torture and intimidation were as slim as this man's grasp of effective alliteration. "You're wondrous," she promised him hastily. "Now," she went on, "we are given to understand you serve as royal spymaster. We seek your covert intelligence in determining what villains—"

"Oh! Villains!" Ario interjected. He shivered. "I hate villains."

Thessia paused. "Right," she patiently concurred. "Yes, so do we. Villainous forces have infiltrated the Deathrose Guild, and now our—"

"The *Deathrose Guild*," Ario repeated in wonderment. "What's *that*? Oh, what a marvelous name. Death-rose."

Thessia faltered. She was starting to find Prince Ario's persona unnervingly . . . convincing.

"I'm sorry," she restarted with the height of regal politesse. "You *are* the spymaster, are you not? Vestriya's royal spymaster?" When Ario nodded pleasantly, she went on. "It's just . . . the crown prince promised us you were very intimidating. Very dangerous. He warned us not to—"

"Oh, Ezio's always exaggerating my dangerousness," he replied fondly. "It's his way of keeping me safe. My parents wanted me to become a spymaster because . . . they think me suited to it and thought it would toughen me up, but Ezio knows me better. Why would I ever seek to be toughened up? Ezio keeps me safe by building up my reputation so that people leave me undisturbed to pursue my passions. Truly, he is a wonderful brother."

It was Thessia's turn to slump in her seat. "Yes. Yes, he is."

Shame consumed her now. Of course *she*, inexperienced and guileless and vainly hopeful, had led her group into this humiliating waste of time.

"I'm sorry," she said dizzily. "We must be going. Thank you for your time." She stood. Starting for the door, she decided she would leave courage to Galwell, and intrigues to Mona, and—

"Wait. Don't."

Hope sprung in Thessia at Ario's exhortation. Perhaps *now* he would reveal his flawless pretense!

Except when she rounded with more damnable hope, she found no smug spymaster. Only the pleading poet.

"You . . ." Ario managed. "You're the only people who've ever complimented my poetry. I . . . I wish to . . . Please, perhaps you'd hear more of it?" he pleaded. "I can help you, too! While I'm not a spy of evil, I'm still a spy. A spy of humanity! Nature! The magic of this existence! I spy loads of excellent things every day. I've spied starjays nesting in the eaves of ancient cathedrals, and the serene turquoise water of the Grotto where the harpies enhance magical gifts, and—and the twin brothers downtown who've invented this delightful snack where flattened dough is slathered in sumptuous sauces—"

"What?"

Thessia looked inquisitively at River, who'd just interrupted the prince.

"What did you just say?" River demanded.

"Sauces," Ario repeated. "Oh, you simply must sample a slice—"

"No. Not the—sauces," River interjected. "The Grotto thing."

Excitedly, Ario nodded. "Yes, yes. The Grotto outside the city where harpies dwell. Rare, wondrous spirits capable of enhancing one's magical gifts if they deem one worthy in soul. Testy little creatures. Hearts in the right place, though. Pray, do they have hearts?" he mused to himself now. "Oh, how I wish to know."

"Take us there," River commanded the prince. She faced the questing party, each of whom wore uncomprehending looks—

Thessia included. "If my magic is amplified, perhaps I can teleport us to *anyone*. Even someone whose identity I don't know," she said.

Thessia chewed her lip. Could it truly work? Could River simply think about who wanted Galwell dead and then use her amplified magic to bring her to them? It was worth trying, in any case.

"Delightful!" Ario concluded. "We'll go at dawn tomorrow. I'd dearly welcome the chance to share some rhymes with you, if you wouldn't mind."

"Yes," Thessia agreed uncertainly. She looked to River, who nodded. "Yes, of course. Just take us to these—harpies."

"Grand." Ario grinned. "Let me just get Benjamin . . ."

Benjamin.

Thessia went still, remembering the name. *His enforcer.* Was *this* the other shoe? Had the prince set them up, sussed out their intentions, only now to sic his *enforcer* on them? Oh, he *was* good. Desperation clutched her nervous heart—

Until onto Ario's shoulder inched a horseball-sized, deep chartreuse *snail*.

Everyone startled except Ario himself. Grinning radiantly, he gestured with flourish to the gastropod. The snail extended globular eyes on supple stalks, examining the group with calm intelligence.

"My new friends," Ario went on, "meet Benjamin."

"Benjamin!" Celine repeated exuberantly. "Oh, hello!"

Thessia blinked.

"*This*," she replied, "is Benjamin?"

"Yes." Ario beamed. "Isn't he darling?"

12
Galwell

Galwell the Great could lift hulking hroxen over his head with ease. In his hometown, craftspeople would rely on him to haul slabs of quarry stone to their workshops. When he was nine years old, he witnessed a team of horses stumble and overturn the wagon they drew. The young Galwell dashed over and righted the cart with one hand.

Unfortunately, however, his power extended only to *physical* strength. Not emotional fortitude or the peculiar endurance politeness demanded.

Which meant that one hour of listening to Prince Ario of Vestriya rhapsodizing in verse over the beauty of the fried plum blossom they'd ordered had left Galwell *exhausted*.

Hugh, impossibly, welcomed the silver-haired, lead-tongued royal with ceaseless encouragement, praising his poetical choices while lounging in the booth, drinking dark rum.

Watching him, Galwell knew why Thessia loved her husband. He understood the other man's virtues. If not of Galwell's size, Hugh was still muscular. He was rakishly handsome, undeniably. Yet it was when Hugh encouraged Ario most vigorously, or laughed with real joy in quick, loud thunderclaps—when the seemingly effortless magic of kindness radiated from him—that something leapt into Thessia's eyes, like lightwings dancing on prairie nights.

It made Galwell smile.

The prince, however, had made him weary. Not to mention the prince's pet snail, which had commenced introducing itself—himself, Galwell supposed—to the party. One of Galwell's whole shirtsleeves had become slime-slickened by the time Galwell managed to coax the creature to return to the tabletop.

He was very grateful when Hugh clapped his arm around the royal's shoulders and accompanied him home to the palace along with Thessia, leaving Galwell, River, and Celine in peace. They soon went their separate ways, having no means to further their efforts with the Deathrose Guild for the moment.

Galwell wandered the streets, lingering in the hardscrabble neighborhood. Wishing, perhaps, for the opportunity for some good, honest heroism. People to save, disasters to divert. Even one overturned horse cart would do.

He found none. Discouraged, he turned toward home as Vestriya's purple dusk descended over the stonework skyline.

Home was the villa Celine had procured for them in the city's heart, on Thessia's purse, of course. Old Illustria, the neighborhood was called, where stone steps led up to graceful, elevated manor houses. The estates were enchanting, figuratively speaking. Their columned entries, high windows, and expansive, sloping green grounds masterfully represented the oldest of Vestriyan architectural styles.

One could not find such homes in Mythria. While the realms shared a language, their histories were unique. Vestriya, far older, had generations more cultural riches and colloquial wisdom, and thus little patience for Mythria's upstart idealism. Vestriya held no reverence for the Ghosts, whose legends had grown only on Mythria's shores. Heroism, it seemed, was not remembered long in this land.

Mounting the final stone stair, Galwell continued into the entryway, past the statue on the dusk-shaded grass of the grounds.

THIS WILL BE INTERESTING

The statue seemed to smile when he passed. This feature of Vestriyan stonework rather unnerved Galwell, if he was honest. Which he was.

Inside the front hallway, rich red walls and sumptuous rugs welcomed him. Heading to his chamber, Galwell passed the expansive common lounge, where maps of the realms overlooked soft leather furniture.

Galwell waved to River, who was reading there, upside down, her legs draped over the back of a large armchair, her head dangling down toward the floor. She looked perfectly comfortable. Celine, who often retired earlier, was nowhere to be found.

He entered his bedchamber, not ready to relax, yet knowing he must. While the lack of opportunities for heroism earlier disappointed him, quiet contemplation and dreamless sleep would suffice. His richly furnished room and its cream-colored walls hardly made the prospect uninviting.

He changed out of his clothes and pulled on—*yes, wondrous*—the yellow silk sleep set decorated with blue eagles that Clare had packed for him. The stitches were magicked to keep out heat. If Galwell could not enjoy good, vigorous heroism, he would enjoy his always-cool silken sleep clothes.

While perhaps not the stoic warrior garments he was used to, this sleep set was the most comfortable he'd ever worn. He also quite liked the little eagles. They cheered him when he caught his reflection in the mirror as he applied the many facial lotions Clare likewise insisted he pack. Remembering Grandhart's urgent recommendation, Galwell smiled. *You're young enough you could start now and make a real difference. It was already too late for me when I commenced my skincare journey. I must save you from my own mistakes!*

Galwell was less certain about this particular insistence of Clare's. However, he was happy to humor his friend, and the oils smelled nice.

He started with the Vesper cream, following Clare's recommended routine.

He'd just reached for the honeyjade oil when a fearsome scream split the night.

Praise the Ghosts! Galwell's heart sang. *How perfect! Someone is in peril!*

Not that Galwell wished fear on innocent people. But this presented a chance for him to be the hero once more! Finally!

He abandoned the honeyjade oil and leapt from his window, down from the villa's stately elevation and out into the city. He hit the ground powerfully, with one knee and the opposite hand planted perfectly on the flagstone. While he'd never wished that statues be made of him, he could concede that his heroic pose would make for an inspiring sculpture.

He stood, feeling his magical strength coursing within him—

"*Please! No!*"

Another scream shattered the quiet. Galwell ran toward the sound, not caring he was barefoot and in his golden sleep clothes. Heroes cared nothing for appearances when someone needed help.

He rounded the corner and found the calamitous scene. A carriage had lost a wheel, and the horses, still attached to the heavy wagon, were panicking.

In front of the window, a hooded figure menaced the carriage's occupants with a crossbow.

The woman inside was crying out for help. Passersby offered none, fleeing past the carriage in selfish desperation. There really was no heroism here! When no one honored the heroes of old, no one felt inspired to be like them!

Until now.

Galwell strode unhesitatingly in front of the crossbow-wielding figure.

"Put that down and let these innocents go," he demanded.

Very well done, he commended himself. His resonant, low voice carried convincing confidence.

The hooded figure did not lower the crossbow. Not even a little. Not even one millionth of an iron.

Instead, the figure made no reply. Slowly, the crossbow moved to point at Galwell.

Very well, Galwell reckoned. Keeping his gaze trained on the tip of the crossbow, he called out to the carriage passengers. "Run! Now's your chance!"

He heard the clamor of their exit—and then the crossbow fired.

The bolt slammed into Galwell's shoulder, the pain shocking him for a moment.

"You . . . shot me," he exclaimed.

He hadn't been shot since before his death. It didn't hurt overmuch. Just a sting, really. But past the pain, he observed blood seeping from his shoulder, from the ragged hole in his . . .

"You ruined my eagle sleep clothes!" he cried.

This would not stand! His only set! He lunged for the villain.

The crossbow wielder was fast, however. Not just fast—impossibly reactive. They leapt nimbly out of Galwell's reach. When Galwell swung out his leg, trying to sweep the villain off their feet, the villain jumped away with precision. Galwell punched—the villain feinted easily to dodge the strike.

Was he losing his touch? No, Galwell consoled himself. This evildoer must have head magic of some kind. Perhaps they could glimpse the future.

While Galwell contemplated how to fight someone who could predict his moves, the villain loaded another bolt.

"Don't you even think—" warned Galwell.

His adversary fired.

The second bolt pierced Galwell's thigh. With the painful puncture, blood spurted on yellow silk, swallowing blue eagle heads.

Now his pants were ruined!

"You," Galwell gasped, righting himself, "shall pay for that."

The desecration of the finest fabric he had ever known unleashed an unexpected rage in Galwell. He lashed out, landing one heavy punch on the surprised villain's shoulder, then hurling himself to the side before they could fire their next crossbow bolt. Roaring in fury, Galwell leapt forward, managing to slam the other fighter to the ground. Sitting astride their torso, he had the villain good and truly pinned.

While they thrashed uselessly, Galwell wrested control of his emotions. The blood from his wounds ran down his skin, and sweat beaded his brow. He heaved calming breaths.

He felt good, though. *Heroism*, he marveled, *is a hell of a healer.*

His restrained opponent seemed to be shaking with fear beneath him. *Good.* He glanced down at their hooded form. Wait—were they shaking in fear or . . .

Laughter?

Galwell felt suddenly insulted. This villain had shot him twice, had tarnished his eagle sleepies ruthlessly, and now they were *laughing*?

No, Galwell realized . . .

Not *they*. She.

"I didn't think you had it in you, Galwell the Glistening," she crowed.

In the same moment the figure's hood fell, Galwell recognized her lithe proportions. None other than Vestriya's princess of crime was smirking underneath him.

"*Mona*," Galwell exhaled.

"Ooh." She pretended to shiver gleefully. "I love it when you say my name that way." She propped herself up on her elbows, her face perilously close to his—nearly nose to nose—while he straddled her, still pinning her to the ground with his enormous form.

Was he dizzy? If he was, the cause was surely sanguinary.

Meaning his wounds. Blood loss. Sanguinary of that nature only. Nothing to do with blood flowing . . . elsewhere.

"So this is what Mythria's hero wears to bed," she remarked. "How . . . cute."

She slid one finger down the stained silk. Indeed, Galwell *did* find his patterned eagles cute. However, this was precisely the problem. His sleep clothes were shredded.

"You . . ." Galwell struggled to speak. "You shot me."

"You let my prey escape," Mona returned.

Galwell frowned. Despite finding their unintended closeness inconvenient, he could not risk releasing her or opening himself up to her cunning combat style. "You cannot just go around robbing people," he chastised her sternly.

Mona rolled her eyes. "I'm a crime lord. That is literally exactly what I do," she retorted. "Why should I let my underlings have all the fun?"

Galwell found himself distracted. Their combat had left Mona breathing hard. Hood off, her robe had descended halfway down her shoulders, revealing the corset she wore underneath. The constricting garment compressed her chest, the tops of her breasts heaving evenly under Galwell's effortful consideration.

No! He could not succumb to her cleavage! He would focus on . . . evil! Yes, evil!

"That's not honorable," he declared. "Or virtuous."

He was speaking half to himself, of what the sight of Mona beneath him produced in his heart.

He hastily leapt off her. She could shoot him with her crossbow if she wanted. Nonetheless, he offered her his hand gallantly to help her up.

Mona eyed him, seeming puzzled, then laughed. Hesitantly, she placed her hand in his.

"No. It's not honorable or virtuous," she concurred. She stood, hand in Galwell's. "Neither were the nobles in that carriage. In Vestriya, no one is. Live here long enough and you'll see what's under the veneer. My pitiful, defenseless marks," she emphasized mockingly, "employ desperate children in their gem mine and don't even pay them an honorable wage. As you prepared to sacrifice yourself for them, they spared not a single thought for your life."

She looked like she expected her revelation would stun him. She hoped to chasten him with her hardened, shrewd worldliness.

Instead, Galwell considered her. He remembered how unsurprised she seemed when his friends magically materialized in her club's private room. How often she'd seemed to read people, including them, with uncanny intuition.

He remembered how she'd predicted his every punch—until he'd stopped *thinking*, giving himself over to instinct.

They spared not a single thought for your life . . .

"You're a mind reader," he murmured.

Mona smiled humorlessly. She pulled her cloak back up over her shoulders. When she retied the ebony fabric, she left the hood down, her hair spilling around her like night itself.

"If that were true," she replied slowly, "then I would know every dirty thought you've had about me, now, wouldn't I?"

Her hand lingered on her corset's fringe, fingers playing with the top stays, as if she might unbutton just one.

Galwell the Great did not have the magic for this sort of strength, either.

When he was silent, his knees weakening with what he knew was *not* exsanguination, Mona laughed, and he realized what she'd done.

"You pretend to be all virtue," she drawled, her words heavy with seduction, "but there's more to you, I think."

Galwell recovered himself, for on matters of honor, he feared not Mona's mind reading. He knew his own heart. He *was* virtuous and good. His thoughts about Mona or anything else didn't change that. Thoughts did not make a hero. Actions did.

"There's more to you, too," he returned levelly. "You pretend to enjoy crime, yet you target those who deserve punishment."

Now she pantomimed gagging. "I didn't *target* them. I stumbled upon nobles with a broken carriage and I took my opportunity. Yes, their thoughts revealed their crimes. But make no mistake, Galwell. Everyone is guilty of something. Which means everyone deserves what I might choose to do to them."

"Perhaps Vestriya merely needs more heroes to inspire her," Galwell protested, hearing how naive he sounded despite his own conviction.

He expected Mona to laugh at his earnestness. Instead, something shadowy descended over her face.

"There are no heroes here or anywhere, Galwell the Guileless," she replied. "Only villains."

Galwell possessed not his sister's heart magic nor Mona's penetrative powers. But he didn't need them to feel the sadness in Mona's words.

"That's not true," he insisted. She was welcome to roam his mind—she would find only sincerity.

"If you had my head magic, you would know," Mona said. "You wouldn't be so heroic if you heard the very worst things every seemingly poor victim has done."

She sounded weary. What had she seen in others' souls? he wondered. What horrors had she known?

He saw Mona differently, suddenly. Huddled on the corner, her cloak drawn. She wrapped herself in night for protection, not intimidation. Surround yourself in darkness—let it embrace you—so it never surprised you. This conviction, Galwell knew, was the only consolation her horrible power left her. What a lonely life she led.

"Stop that," she snapped.

Galwell's focus sharpened, and he realized what she meant.

"I demand you stop pitying me," she insisted. "I'm evil. Don't overthink it."

"Who has hurt you, Mona?"

She faltered.

"Not used to having someone read you, are you?" he asked.

When Mona said nothing, her face tightening, Galwell smiled, smug. He knew people sometimes suspected his hroxen-like strength meant Galwell shared the herd animals' intelligence. Not so.

"I know a little of your childhood," he went on. "Clare told me how you were raised in a band of thieves, by people who did some pretty terrible things for coin. How they would involve you. That must have made you feel—"

"Don't," she warned, motionless. He remembered how she'd characterized her noble marks—*my prey*. Yes, she looked poised with the patience of a fearsome cave-dwelling nightwalker now.

"But you must not have wanted to live like them," he went on recklessly. "You left your family. You left Mythria. You escaped."

"I escaped *nothing*."

"Clare—"

She cut him off. "Clare was lucky. He always is. He stayed behind. He got rich on *heroism*. I tried to start fresh. I found a new family—people my age who were striking out on their own. We settled in a small village in Vestriya, trying to live better than we were raised. You know what happened to them?"

Galwell knew. He could see it in her eyes. Tragedy. Pain.

"I learned something when I lost them. You're only as good as the worst thing you've ever done. And everyone has done something horrible. There's no redemption. No change. No hope. There's only those who can admit it and those who lie." She turned toward the moonlight, letting it cast her face in cold silver.

She knew every horrible part of humanity, Galwell realized. But surely she knew its goodness, too. Surely her magic showed her the light along with the dark. Perhaps if he could bring her back to Mythria with him, bring her to Clare . . . maybe he could save her.

Mona's expression shuttered with damning immediacy. She snatched her crossbow from the flagstone and threw the weapon over her shoulder.

"Stay out of it," she hissed. "You won't be saving me from anything."

Now Galwell startled, for Mona's menacing was no longer playful. She seethed with the stung fury of the unsuspecting.

"You're not the hero you pretend to be," she spat. "In fact, you're no one. The greatest thing you ever did was die, and you didn't even do that right."

Galwell said nothing.

"Now you're only"—her eyes locked with his—"a burden."

He clenched his jaw. He knew she'd read his thoughts, collected his insecurities to fire at him with more accuracy than even her arrows. She wasn't saying this because she believed the words. She was saying it because *he* did.

When she walked defiantly past him, he let her. As she did, she knocked her shoulder into his injured one—a final reminder of how much she could hurt him.

Oh, he knew.

13

River

Galwell was late.

They'd all gathered in one of the villa's stately dining halls, morning sun spilling in through limestone-framed windows that stretched over ten irons high, dining on colorful Vestriyan breakfast cakes as they talked around his absence. Galwell was not a man who made people wait. And since he'd already died once, it was hard for most of the people in their party not to immediately assume the worst.

Searching for a lighthearted distraction, River focused her attention on Prince Ario. "Your choice of wardrobe today is not what I imagined a spymaster would wear," she said. "But you know what they say . . . Never assume."

"Why's that?" Prince Ario asked, a glop of pastel frosting lingering in the corner of his mouth.

"Because to assume makes an ass out of you and me," Celine interjected, even though River had been striking up a conversation with Prince Ario in an attempt to avoid Celine and her unflinching gaze.

"Your surprise at my attire is not uncommon," Prince Ario said, missing the clever play on words. "It's because I choose to dress like a poet instead of a spymaster." He looked around the room for someone to validate his claim. When no one met his eye, he glanced down at his outfit. He was in a dark tunic with exaggeratedly puffed-out sleeves. There were gold fabric stripes running down each arm, matching his puffy golden hat. With the intricate golden brocade pattern on his puffy pants, he looked like a tapestry meant to adorn a wall. And he had that damned snail, Benjamin, perched atop his shoulder.

River did not know much about the Vestriyan royals, but she had been under the impression that Prince Ario would be like Thessia. Someone elegant. Refined. His status visible in the very way he moved. She'd seen conjurated portraits of him and assumed his silver hair and mischievous smirk hinted at an edginess lurking beneath the surface of his royal facade.

While he was by no means meek—no meek person would ever wear so many puffy items at once—he did not seem interested in presenting himself as someone powerful, and certainly not as someone edgy.

River felt a strange urge to help him. Prince Ario had a good heart and a clear vision for himself, but the execution wasn't very sharp. It reminded River of all the times her family's troupe had begun assembling a new routine to incorporate into their circus performance. In the early stages, all the moving parts were incoherent, like an unsolved puzzle with pieces that had been spread out upside down. Even through the mess, River could always spot the bones, knowing exactly which parts to pull forward and which parts to cut.

She'd forgotten this about herself, discarded this ability the day she'd been kicked out of the troupe. Yet here it was, waking up within her as if it had been hibernating.

"I am no fashionist myself, but there's something to be said for an entirely black ensemble," she told Prince Ario. "Could work for both spymaster *and* poet."

"Very elegant and mysterious," Queen Thessia chimed in, nodding in approval.

Prince Ario tugged the golden hat off his head. "All right, then," he said, surprisingly amenable. "I have no plain black garments with me, though."

King Hugh lit up, excited for the opportunity to provide further distraction from Galwell's absence. Or maybe also in agreement that Prince Ario needed a makeover. "My good fellow, come with me!" he said. "We can find something dark and mysterious in my apparel."

Not long after their exit, Galwell finally appeared. Queen Thessia, Celine, and even River let out soft exhales of relief. He entered with great haste, yet River noticed there was a slight hitch in his walk that he could not mask, not to mention a large bandage over his shoulder.

"My lateness is inexcusable, but I apologize all the same," he said, kneeling gingerly on one knee as he placed a hand over his heart. "It was an eventful eve, and I rested far longer than I intended to. I will do whatever is necessary to make up for my absence."

Queen Thessia gasped. "You're injured!"

"Yes," Galwell confirmed. "But it is no need for concern. I have extremely large muscles, and they stopped the crossbow bolts from penetrating too deeply. The wounds only bled for two or three hours last night."

"Crossbow?" Queen Thessia shrieked. Her eyes darted around the room as if anticipating the reappearance of whoever had attacked Galwell. River did the same, her back straightening as she moved herself toward a corner so that she could have the best vantage point.

"Two or three hours?" River could not help but ask.

Galwell sat down as delicately as possible. "Worry not. There is no risk of me being harmed again."

"What happened?" Celine asked. She was already jotting something down in her notebook, probably spinning this incident into the kind of scribesheet story that would fly off the stands at every Mythrian magazine shop.

"I ran into Mona last night. She shot arrows at me, but we resolved it. As I said, no need to worry." He stuffed his mouth full of an entire breakfast cake.

Galwell was raised as a noble. Even River knew that nobles didn't stuff their faces with food. Certainly not in the middle of a conversation. Whatever Mona Grandhart had done to Galwell last night had left him panicked in a way no one, including himself, knew how to deal with.

There was no time to probe him further, because King Hugh had returned. "Galwell!" he said with naked relief. "It's wonderful to see you. You're just in time for the grand reveal. Allow me to present Prince Ario of Vestriya, poet-spymaster extraordinaire."

Prince Ario stepped out from behind the door to reveal his new ensemble, a sleek black tunic with matching leggings. Not a puffy sleeve in sight. He looked mischievous and unpredictable, even with Benjamin the snail. He looked good.

Yes, River thought. *There you are.*

The group exploded into applause, and Prince Ario took a bow, his cheeks warming at the generous reaction. "Thank you, thank you! Now let's go impress some harpies!"

* * *

River had never teleported so many people at once. Six, to be exact—plus Benjamin. To get it done, she'd asked them all to hug one another like a horseball team huddling on the field. She didn't know if she'd be successful, since she was working off Prince Ario's impassioned description of their destination, but she figured admitting that would dampen the mood.

They arrived in a giant pile. Of course River landed atop Celine, their legs entwined and their chests smashed together. Celine's heart was beating fast, her cheeks pink with exhilaration. River wanted to stay mad at her, but she found it hard to do so when Celine got such visible pleasure from River's gift.

Once the group untangled themselves, River looked to Prince Ario. "We're here!" he confirmed. "Welcome to the Grotto!"

The outside was made of jagged, mossy rocks that jutted up toward the sky in peculiar shapes. Prismatic hemalia flowers bloomed in cracks like iridescent orbs. There was an opening that looked exactly as Prince Ario had described it—like a large, yawning mouth, within which a vast water cave was barely visible, its greenish-blue water like a tongue.

"The harpies are in there!" Prince Ario told the group excitedly, pointing to the entrance.

All the other people outside the cave were dressed in black from head to toe. Some sat at slab tables locked fist to fist, challenging each other to thumb wars. Others were practicing their sword fighting or wrestling in patches of muddy grass.

"And these people are here to impress said harpies?" Celine inquired. Harpies were capricious beings made of pure magic, capable of amplifying the magical gifts of anyone they deemed worthy.

"Indeed," Prince Ario told her. He waved at a gruff man nearby, who had large, muscular arms inked with renderings of dragons, nightwalkers, sledgelings, and wights. Any fearsome creature one could think of, this man wore on his skin like a badge of honor.

The man did not acknowledge him.

"Should we be concerned about our fellow visitors?" Queen Thessia asked.

"We're all very familiar with each other," Prince Ario assured her. "I come here often in my spymaster dealings. I blend right in."

Dressed in his current attire, he did look right at home. But River thought of the puffy ensemble, and his penchant for performing poetry off the cuff, and River suspected Prince Ario had been the source of more than one cruel joke around these parts.

"I think you could blend in even further," she said, still feeling that tug inside her, the urge to complete the puzzle that was Prince Ario, shaping him into the version of himself he believed he already was. "Notice how everyone here holds their head up? Walks like they have a purpose? Let's try it."

"All right, then," Prince Ario said. He strode ahead, his chin up so high it looked like he smelled something rancid and was trying to identify a source.

"Good start," River told him, wincing when she knew he couldn't see her. "Lead with the pelvis a little more, though. Like, say, a king would?" Only after she suggested it did it occur to her that Ario's father was an actual king and his brother would someday be one, too. She had not yet adjusted to this strange adventure she was on, assisting the rulers of two different realms.

"My father walks like this," Prince Ario said. He arched his back as he took strangely wide steps, almost as if his thighs had begun chafing.

"*Mmm*," River said. She couldn't offer words. Only sounds.

"Is it my arms? Perhaps they need more purpose," Prince Ario suggested. "Everyone here has very prominent arms." He put his hands on his hips, doing his wide jutting walk with his nose to the sky.

River's head was starting to ache. "Do you really not have a single edgy bone in your body?"

Prince Ario shuddered. "Please don't say bone."

"Don't say . . . bone?" As she said the word again, the prince turned pale. "What is it about that you can't handle?"

"It's my power." He pinched the bridge of his nose and squeezed his eyes shut.

"Your power is—" Celine started.

"*Don't*," he warned. "I have a hand magic gift of manipulating . . . the b-word. I can break them. Rearrange them. Make them shake. Whatever, really. It's foul."

"Foul? That's the edgiest thing I've heard about you since we met. It might be the most impressive power I've ever heard of in general," River said.

"There's nothing impressive about making someone's spine crack." He shuddered again, visibly upset. "That's enough on the topic. I cannot say more. I will be sick."

"Very well, then," said Queen Thessia. "Perhaps we should go in?"

Inside the Grotto, there were no lights that River could see, but the foamy, gurgling pool of water that wove all throughout the winding caverns seemed to glow from within, turning everything a shimmering greenish-blue. There were only a few other people inside, and they'd waded into the water, letting the harpies sense their magical gift, hoping to be blessed with amplification.

"The harpies are a tough crowd. Nobody's impressing them today!" Ario said cheerfully. "But you'll turn it around." He patted River on the shoulder.

River gulped. Her fear was an urgent, unfamiliar sensation, causing her limbs to tremble. She did not want to fail this group. She tried to reason with herself about it, noting that she owed them nothing.

She thought of her parents. They hadn't trusted River, and they were the ones who'd raised her. They'd known her mind, her heart, her beliefs, and they'd still turned their backs on her. But this group, a mix of royalty, nobility, and whatever Celine was—friend from the past, object of her affection, source of all her frustrations—*did* trust her. They all believed in River's capability while knowing exactly how dangerous she could be.

This was why she liked to work alone.

"What's wrong?" Celine asked, whispering in River's ear.

She hated how Celine could read her like a book. Hated even more that some sick part of her *liked* it.

"Nothing," River said, shrugging her off to walk into the pool.

The water was surprisingly warm. River found herself melting into it, her nerves dissipating. She swam out until she could no longer feel the rocks beneath her feet and started treading water, inviting the harpies to sense her presence.

She waited.

And waited.

"Think of your gift," Prince Ario urged. "Perhaps the harpies' senses are clouded by all the other people vying for their attention, and they haven't yet noticed you."

River closed her eyes. She found it strange to only *think* of teleporting, but she attempted it all the same, creating what she hoped to be a convincing mental presentation for the harpies.

A gurgling began beneath her feet, gentle and encouraging. River's face relaxed into a smile. *Finally*, she thought. *You've noticed me.*

A soft breeze blew past River's head. She opened her eyes, expecting to be greeted by the harpies themselves, ready to bless her. Instead she found an arrow floating in the water beside her. The source of the breeze.

River looked up to see Gary and Mary, the twin assassins, rushing into the caves. Mary had a crossbow pointed at her face, with another arrow loaded up. Gary had a crossbow pointed at Galwell.

The Deathrose Guild was *here*.

"Nice work at the circus the other night," said Mary with a sickly smile.

"Made it much easier for us to find you," said Gary. "Which led us straight to *him*."

River jerked in the water, scrambling to swim ashore.

"Ah-ah," said Mary, striding closer. "You know we can't let a teleporter get near our target. You'll take him away from us and ruin all the fun."

"Run!" she shouted to Galwell.

It was bad enough that River had led the guild here. It was worse that she did not have the time or the resources to stop them.

This is how it all ends, isn't it? She squeezed her eyes shut once more. What a coward she was. She could not bear to witness this catastrophe.

The silence stretched on, no sounds of arrows whizzing through the air or the agonized cries of death.

River chanced a look. What she found made her gasp—the rest of her group had surrounded Galwell, forming a barricade between him and the twin assassins.

Gary lowered his crossbow. "We'll come back with more assassins next time."

"You'll run out of friends to hide behind eventually," Mary said with a sneer.

This was River's opportunity to take them out or die trying. If she succeeded, her actions would go against the guild's code, but did any of that even matter anymore? If she failed, well, at least the Grotto was beautiful.

"Don't you *dare*," Celine said, catching River's movement out of the corner of her eye. She leapt into the water, throwing her body atop River as they both plunged into the depths of the pool.

Underwater, they were once again tangled up with each other. Wherever they went, they always found themselves like this in some way, as if their bodies had been made to be entwined. River wished they could just keep going down, down, down, capable of living underwater, knotted together as one.

But they shot back up to the surface, gasping and heaving.

Gary and Mary were out of sight.

"Shit," River said. She started to swim, hoping that Celine's stunt hadn't cost her too much time.

The gurgling started again, much stronger than it had been before. River could no longer swim through it. She could hardly move at all. It took all the energy she had just to turn back and check on Celine, scared the swell might pull her under.

Celine was fine. More than fine. All around her, glowing figures floated in the air.

Harpies.

They were dressed in long gowns and emanated a starlike light. They had the face and hair of humans—long and black and wavy—but their skin was the same bluish-green as the water, and they had wide, feathery wings instead of arms.

Celine had begun to glow, too.

"They've chosen *her*?" questioned Prince Ario, voicing the very confusion River also felt. Celine's gift for everlasting memory was certainly impressive, but what was there to amplify?

Only the harpies knew, and they dove back into the pool once their magic was complete, disappearing far beneath the surface.

The gurgling stopped, and River climbed out of the water.

Celine, as if released from a trance, began to shout. She no longer glowed bluish-green, and all the calm that had washed over her was replaced with frantic tears.

"No!" Celine cried, searching the water for signs of the harpies. "Take it back! Take it back! I don't want this!"

Everyone gawked at her as she treaded water in her crooked blouse and sopping wet, mussed bun, looking as though she'd fallen in by accident and had not just summoned powerful, mercurial creatures and wordlessly gotten them to amplify her powers.

"Isn't her gift everlasting memory?" asked Queen Thessia.

"Yes," River said, but it came out more like a question.

"And why is that bad?" Queen Thessia inquired.

Celine swam to the edge, silencing everyone's questions with a single, firm statement. "Once she teleports us out of here, I want to be left alone."

River had been so busy trying to hide information about the guild from Celine, not to mention hide her own feelings, she'd missed that Celine had been hiding something in return.

Why *was* it bad? And how did River not know the answer?

The Guild-ed Cage: A Peek Inside the Questionable Deeds and Stifling Demands of Mythria's Deadliest Organization

by Celine Hazelton, *Mythria Spectator* staff reporter

Many in Mythria have heard whispers about the Deathrose Guild, a famed league of elite assassins said to rid our realm of its most nefarious figures, but few know how the lethal institution actually operates. The guild itself has never substantiated claims of its existence, though assassins both past and present who've worked for the organization confirm that the Deathrose Guild remains active in Mythria to this very day, operating under a strict honor code that prohibits members from speaking openly about their work. The failed assassination attempt of beloved Mythrian hero Galwell True is the first in a recent string of suspicious behavior tied to the once-lauded league, leading to questions about the true nature of the Deathrose Guild's motivations.

Inside sources confirm the guild alleges their work is limited to Mythria, yet according to several eyewitnesses, a violent disturbance at legendary Vestriyan hotspot the Grotto involved two high-profile guild members targeting an innocent mark and fleeing the scene upon failure to execute! These same sources share that the Deathrose Guild ejects any assassin who betrays the guild's complicated, often oppressive honor code, yet the assassins have no knowledge of who leads their organization or why the guild's agenda has changed, recently targeting marks with no known penchant for villainy. Not so honorable now, is it?

With our realm fresh off a failed resurgence of the Fraternal Order, the nefarious organization that sought to overthrow Queendom, this unexplained change in behavior has many in Mythria feeling utterly confused! These assassins, once known for their vigilante good, have now stoked the flames of unease across two different realms, leaving a messy trail of reckless behavior.

Will the leaders of the Deathrose Guild come forward and explain their behavior, or are we on the precipice of another dark age full of fear and confusion? Or is it possible the guild has entered a new era of humiliating missteps and we are soon to see an end to their days of moving in deadly secrecy? Either way, *Mythria Spectator* pledges to remain your premiere source for this unfolding saga!

14
Thessia

Thessia could feel herself glowing with pride as she read Celine's story proclaiming their cunning victory. *A new era of humiliating missteps!* Oh, her reportage positively shone with incisive condemnation. Exactly the way the Quintessential Questers—*no, Ghosts damn it, it still isn't right*—intended. Sure, it was a setback that River's plan to amplify her teleportation hadn't come to pass. But the guild's sloppy attack was a new opportunity in their quest. Undoubtedly, Mona's connections would soon lure out whoever sought harm to Galwell as the nefarious parties grew desperate for alternative means of assassination.

Satisfied, Thessia tucked the scribesheet proudly into the box of keepsakes she'd packed for her Vestriyan voyage.

In the quiet of her quarters, she sighed. The cream-colored stone echoed her discontent as she turned to the rest of what waited on her crestoak desk. Her "royal duties" that her councilors had provided to her to review.

Reading, Thessia found her resentment mounting. The scrolls were designed to convince the queen of her own importance, to impart grave imperative upon her entirely ceremonial and frankly frivolous duties. Line upon elegantly calligraphed line detailed her "responsibilities" for the upcoming Realm Chalice horseball match in two days.

Oh, her councilors were good. Stomach-churningly so. They made her obligations sound oh so important. Like kissing the Farmount Falcons' horseball would be the difference between war and peace between the realms, like greeting the starting horses was tantamount to draining the Sword of Souls. Like eating a shankfry was the equivalent of stealing the Orb of Grimauld.

Thessia could imagine herself enjoying the game were she not scheduled to the hilt with queenly duties. On empty nights in her palace, she would sometimes throw on conjurated matches magically projected from stadiums throughout the realm, studying with interest the strategies the players refined every year—though she had neither the courage nor the cruelty to tell Clare she rooted for the Northwood Knights.

Unfortunately, Thessia the erstwhile horseball fan was not who the Realm Chalice called for. They wanted only the image of Thessia the diplomatic queen.

She would watch the match's play from the Notable Persons box, where she would cheer for the Falcons. Later, she would spend the Fifth-Chunk Squat, the sport's tradition before the penultimate period of play in which attendees stretched sore muscles in a comically relaxed pose, on the private balcony of Vestriya's king and queen.

It was silly, useless work designed to prop up Thessia's image. Without intention or individuality, without personality or philosophy—without *her*. Thessia herself was utterly replaceable in the prescribed role.

The only consolation she found in the correspondence came in the very final scroll, placed there, no doubt, by councilors who wished her to prioritize her very important horse-greeting obligations. With some renewed vigor, she opened the missive from sitting King Clare.

Thessia dearest,

The realm flourishes exceedingly well under Beatrice's and my excellent reign. Ha. Beatrice insisted you would not find this notion funny, but she is not the only one who knows you well.

Thessia smiled.

I have occupied myself with reading and contemplating your wonderfully fair tax legislation. Beatrice expected you would find this funny, for my legal scholarship for much of my life consisted of having local magistrates dictating my sentencings to me. But going from petty bandit to king has shown me I need not only be the Clare I once was.

Enough on my scholarly pursuits—I write to you with one simple request. May we commission a tapestry of my eagle, Wiglaf, for the throne room? He is the most handsome bird in the realm. For obvious reasons, I request your reply forthwith.

Sincerely, with much love,
Clare Grandhart

Every person in Mythria would recognize the grand signature that concluded the scroll.

Thessia scrawled her reply hastily. *Why the Ghosts not?*

Indeed, contributing a portrait of Wiglaf the eagle to the Hall of Queens was damn near the full extent of her governing powers.

As Thessia sealed her response with dropped wax embossed with her royal seal—enjoying the ceremonial flourish of the process, one she'd had no occasion to undertake since the invention of the message tapestry in Mythria—knocking sounded on her door. "Come in," Thessia said.

Tabitha entered. The girl's uncanny resemblance to Thessia never failed to startle the queen.

"Do you need me tonight, Your Highness?" she inquired.

Thessia put on a smile. She supposed she saw herself in Tabitha's selfless diligence no less than in their physical resemblance. "No, Tabitha, you may live your own life tonight," she replied.

"It's no burden," Tabitha insisted. She played nervously with the ends of her spelled-blond hair. "My father never would have permitted me to travel so far. I'm grateful for the chance."

Her kind words comforted Thessia. The queen hated to imagine that the young noble felt imprisoned by her role. *Yes, one woman imprisoned within the identity of Queen Thessia is quite enough*, she thought resentfully.

"Enjoy the city tonight," Thessia replied. "I mean it."

Finally, real excitement illuminated Tabitha's features. She darted for the door, then doubled back, looking like she was mustering her courage.

"You . . . should, too, Your Highness," she ventured, placing a tentative hand on Thessia's shoulder. "I know how constricting your life is. It must be its own challenge to never have a break from it, the way I have."

Her surprising words touched Thessia. Tabitha smiled gently, perhaps understanding the queen was not used to—well, understanding.

"I know King Hugh is at the Wandering Raven tavern downtown. Perhaps you should join him?" she suggested with what could not pass for an innocent suggestion, her cheeks pink. She withdrew her hand self-consciously. "He talks about you a lot when I'm working with him. It's very sweet. I wish I had a lad as smitten with me."

Thessia managed to keep her smile unchanged, pretending the expression was carved into her face like the visages on famous Vestriyan statues. She nodded, giving Tabitha the encouragement the other woman needed to consider herself relieved for the night.

When Tabitha left for whatever Vestriyan revelry she wished, Thessia let her stony smile slip. Yes, she wished she had a lad smitten with her as well, not one performing his role to perfection at all hours.

Still . . .

Tabitha's words rattled cages within her. Why shouldn't Thessia enjoy herself for the night? Why should Hugh have fun while Thessia had scrolls of horse-related nonsense? Why shouldn't she go out drinking with the soldiers?

Who's to say what was and was not queenly, if not her?

She'd managed to stir herself into vigor now! Her heart crackling like the hearth in her cozy marble chambers, Thessia seized her cloak. Without second-guessing herself, she climbed out her window into the lovely Vestriyan evening.

She was going to have *fun*, Ghosts damn it.

On the short climb from her window to the ground, she pretended she was River Pricemark, assassin at large! Or she was Celine Hazelton, daring in her pursuit of the truth, following a mysterious lead in a story. Or even Mona Grandhart, out to seduce and claim her city.

Anyone except Thessia.

Her cloak's hood hiding her recognizable "spun gold" mane, Thessia followed the canals until the cool quiet of the capital city's labyrinthine corridors gave way to the raucous downtown, where the inebriated lay in the streets, where music pounded and slithered from the taverns, where lovers embraced in shadowy archways, where hand magic conjurated light shows from the fingertips of street performers to simulate sprites or harpies or miniature dragons dancing in color over the cobblestones. This, Thessia knew, was the Vestriya of her mother's stories.

Her heart pounding with eagerness, Thessia continued until she found the Wandering Raven, its marquee magically decorated with crows who flapped their wings into dissolving shadows, only to reform. The place was packed, lovelier and livelier than the pub where they'd encountered Ario. A musician played the lute onstage, their tuning leaving something to be desired.

Thessia couldn't see Hugh in the crowded space. No matter, she reassured herself. She didn't need Hugh to enjoy a tavern! She walked confidently to the bar, only to find a wall of burly soldiers blocking her from the barkeep. She hopped on each leg, hoping to catch the eye of anyone willing to make room for her.

Instead she caught an elbow to the ribs. She wheezed with shock. Then laughed. No one noticed her. Her face wasn't on the coins here. There were no tapestries or murals or statues of her. No one expected the queen of Mythria to be at a seedy tavern.

It was . . . freeing.

She giggled. She didn't need a drink, although she'd very much like one—she could get drunk on this feeling alone! Beside her, soldiers were complaining with vulgarities that Thessia had never before heard. Delightful! A man burped behind her. Less delightful but still exciting!

When the soldier in front of her slumped onto the bar, passed out from too much drink, Thessia gingerly stepped around him.

"What'll you have?" the barkeep asked without even looking at her.

"Ale, please," Thessia shouted over shouting that had broken out seemingly in regards to the out-of-tune lute.

The man poured with exceptional skill. "Six sterling."

Thessia paused. She . . . had no coin. She'd forgotten she'd need it—she never did at home.

The barkeep sensed her hesitation and held her almost-won ale away. "No. Not doing that tonight. Not the weekend of the Realm Chalice. Every soldier in the city is here before their shifts. Never seen anything like this. It's too busy for negotiation."

Thessia realized she'd be getting no ale tonight. She turned to go, then halted. Perhaps something better than ale was on tap.

"Why are so many soldiers working the Realm Chalice?" she inquired lightly.

The barkeep glared at her question, like she owed him seven sterling now for his time. He turned to the next *paying* customer.

Thessia wilted.

"We're all expected to work the entire day. They gave us the night off to drink as apology," the man slumped beside Thessia said, seeming much more sober than she'd given him credit for. "Lots of unrest in the city. Prince Ezio and the spymaster worry the Deathrose Guild might be plotting something during the distraction of the match. Then there's rowdy revolutionaries chanting 'King Ezio, King Ezio' in the streets, cinderflower poison killing folk left and right . . ." He grunted. "You know how it is."

Thessia straightened. "Yes," she said distractedly, for while she had never heard of cinderflower poison and certainly did not *know how it was*, the man had unintentionally offered her sudden inspiration. *The guild might plan to attack Galwell during the match when the city is distracted.* Thessia and her companions could keep him safe by keeping him inside, or . . .

Or they could lure their enemies out into the open.

More shouting suddenly broke through her scheming. The horrible lute player was pulled offstage to much applause. When the crowd heard mellifluous strains of a harp, they instantly calmed.

Thessia turned, drawn to the powerful melody.

She was not the only one. Every Vestriyan within was transfixed, drinks undrunk in their hands, eyes on the stage.

She must see this musician, Thessia felt, moved by the beauty in every note.

She nudged her way through the crowd of muscular soldiers, finding—

Her husband.

Onstage, Hugh handled his harp like a lover. He sat on a simple stool, coaxing music from his instrument.

Looking like he did, Thessia imagined he could have coaxed harmony from rusty pots and pans.

He was . . . unreasonably sexy. Inordinately, inhumanly, inhumanely, incredibly sexy. His linen shirt half open, dark curls cascading over his forehead, he looked like the music stars who could fill whole Mythrian stadiums with hyperventilating fans, like Noah Noble or the Brethren's charismatic frontmen. Ghosts, he looked fit for the Vestriya Now stage. From foot soldier to king to song star. Thessia could easily imagine the scribesheet exultations.

She would definitely snatch up those headlines.

Every barmaid and several barmen had paused in their work to drool over him. While Thessia could not blame them, she had the errant urge to jump onstage and tell everyone he was *her* husband.

Even though he wasn't really, her cruelest impulses reminded her. Not like that. She had his ring but not his heart.

Nevertheless . . . with the music sweeping over her, Thessia permitted herself to pretend. She pretended she'd enchanted this extraordinary man like he'd enchanted her. Pretended his calloused hands, moving expertly over the harp, had moved with the same devoted finesse over the curves of her body. Pretended she had the sole right to let her gaze linger on every movement of muscle in his neck, to stare in indulgence at the way he thoughtlessly tapped one foot against his stool. He was magnificent.

In her reverie, he was hers.

Hugh played, expanding the melody, taking the crowd with him—

Until, at the height of the refrain, his eyes locked with Thessia's.

His surprise strangled the high note on his harp. Everyone noticed. Hugh recovered quickly, descending into the chorus's resolve, but the damage was done. Everyone followed the startled gaze of the performer to Thessia.

At last she was recognized. Soldiers first. Then the common folk enjoying the raucous night out. Suddenly, everyone was bowing deeply to the queen in their midst. On cue, Hugh paused in his song.

Thessia wanted to wither into nothing. She hated that she'd disrupted the simple fun of their evening. Was she cursed? Would the status, the face, the name she carried pursue her everywhere, ruining every uncomplicated joy? Was there nowhere she could hide from herself?

On the verge of running from the room, however, Thessia remembered her courage. Would River run from embarrassment? Would Mona flee recognition?

No. What did Thessia really want? She forced herself to consider. She did not want to stop the revelers.

She wanted to join them.

She composed herself. Coolly confident, she strode over to the nearest bowed soldier. She was not, she decided, with impulsiveness running wild in her, the queen in this moment. This wondrous Vestriyan night, she was whoever she wanted to be.

She reached down, like she intended to grant the soldier her royal favor with the touch of her hand on his forehead.

Instead, she took his drink from his fingers.

Her eyes meeting Hugh's, Thessia lifted the mead for the entire crowd to see. Her husband held her gaze. She brought the drink to her lips wordlessly. While everyone watched, Thessia drained the entire flagon.

Stunned silence followed the feat for half a moment, and then the Wandering Raven erupted in cheers.

Thessia knew not where her next drink came from. The shot glass was thrust into her hands. Gamely, with the hot magic of courage raging in her, she downed the glass. More cheering followed. More shots came forth.

Liquor spilled on Thessia's sleeves when the crowd suddenly lifted the queen up. The movement of the enthusiastic throng deposited her onstage, in front of her husband.

Hugh watched her with nothing simple like humor in his eyes. No, Thessia found his gaze very complicated. Or was the drink overcomplicating everything? No matter. Underneath Hugh's warmth and roguish good nature, Thessia found . . . intrigue? Desire? The kind of pleasant surprise that hit like a stiff drink in a foreign pub.

No. Not for her. Not from him. Ghosts no.

Thessia stumbled over her feet for a moment. Dizzy from drink, surely. She chastened herself. Hugh was probably upset with her. He probably wanted just one night free of the obligations Thessia presented, like Tabitha did. He probably found her drinking un-queenly. Well, it was un-queenly. What of it?

These thoughts, combined with potent drink, made Thessia's stomach lurch. She could stumble on this rough stage, yes. She refused, however, to be sick in public. Regaining her balance, she moved to flee.

Hugh's grasp on her elbow—she immediately knew it was his hand from the musician's callouses on his fingers—stopped her.

Hesitant, Thessia turned, finding his same complicated gaze on her.

Holding her in place, he removed the drink from her hand. The gesture wasn't one of frustrated condemnation of her un-queenly drinking. Instead, Hugh seemed . . . tender. Even welcoming.

With one hand remaining on her, Hugh lifted the glass. The room went silent, permitting the king's warm words to ring out.

"To my queen."

Heat flooded Thessia in the happiest way, heat she knew had nothing to do with her own semi-drunkenness. She could not meet Hugh's eyes—not when he promptly downed the entire shot in her honor.

Everyone cheered, unsurprisingly. Thessia herself felt like cheering, except she could not contemplate the possibility when her heart suddenly felt as unsteady as her stomach.

"Give us a duet!" one of the more inebriated soldiers hollered out.

The crowd embraced this suggestion, whistling and repeating the syllables until "duet" merged with "do it!" Nervous excitement wound through Thessia. Her councilors would never approve of this.

Hugh raised his eyebrow in invitation.

"I don't know any songs," Thessia whispered to him.

The excuse was flimsy, and she knew it. Fortunately, so did Hugh. He turned to his instrument without reply, smiling rakishly. Under the spotlight, he started to play, shooting Thessia a wink with his harp's opening notes.

When he hummed the melody, Thessia felt courage flame through her. His heart magic, she knew. She was grateful he was using his gentle power on her. Even his hum was powerful, and beautiful. She could only imagine what it sounded like when he sang. She hoped one day he would.

She recognized his song instantly. Not caring that her voice was untrained, Thessia sang the words, her heartstrings coming to life under Hugh's musicianship.

"My home is Mythria, my love is here . . ." she sang out. "My home is Mythria, I hold her dear."

The Mythrian tourists in the tavern sang with them, lending Thessia support. The rest of the crowd swayed in contentment, and in their embrace, Thessia learned how foreign shores could feel like home.

Her gaze remained locked on Hugh's. His hold on her—wrapped in music, magic, and perhaps, she wondered, more—was absolute, and she had the strangest sensation that no one had ever looked at her so fully in her entire life.

In front of everyone, she looked right back.

* * *

The night passed in a carnival of drink and song. It was, Thessia determined halfway through her fourth flagon, the very best night of her royal, restrictive life.

The tavern expected no ceremonious comportment from her. They minded not when she spilled her drink or burped. Their laugher was friendly, not forced. When Hugh ceded the stage to other musicians, Vestriyan folk songs filled the room. Thessia danced until the night grew late.

When everyone started to empty out of the Wandering Raven, Thessia felt herself move with the crowd and was deposited outside on the dark stone street. With mere hours until dawn, Thessia was not certain she was steady enough on her feet to manage her way home. Nevertheless, she ventured forward.

Until she felt the same calloused hand on her arm.

"You should ride in my carriage, wife," Hugh murmured.

He held her, and his firm grasp unsteadied her knees even more than the alcohol. When Hugh gently drew her closer, toward his waiting carriage, the onlooking foot soldiers wolverling whistled. Thessia blushed, but found, unexpectedly, she rather enjoyed this manner of embarrassment.

Hugh helped her inside and sat opposite her, then closed the carriage door. Silence roared in Thessia's ears. The night of carousing made her much more conscious of their closeness, their privacy. The intimacy of the gilded compartment. Worse—or was it?—Hugh idly outstretched his hands on his seat, the movement tugging open the collar of his tunic.

Thessia had to pull her eyes to his face. Which, Ghosts, wasn't much more helpful. "You play wonderfully," she managed.

Hugh grinned. "It's the magic," he deferred. "I make everyone feel relaxed and happy when I hum."

"You made me courageous."

"Only a little," Hugh replied. "You didn't need much in the way of courage, Thess."

His compliment—and his casual use of her name, her real name—warmed her like no drink could. She was herself tonight.

She could be herself with him.

"I hope I hear you sing one day," she said quietly.

Hugh startled. "I—"

Thessia winced. "Forget I said it. I don't mean to overstep, just to say . . . I don't know, really."

She wished she had more drink to erase this mortifying moment forever from her mind.

"I . . . I could sing. Just—only for you," Hugh replied, his voice serious. Thessia stilled, not wanting to do or say anything wrong. Everything in her yearned to hear him.

Hugh breathed deeply. Unaccompanied, with only the rolling rhythm of carriage wheels on stone driving forth his melody, he started to sing softly. Thessia did not know the language of his lyrics.

She did know the music was romantic and melodic. His voice was sublime, as if from the Ghost's Gate itself.

She felt herself melting in contentment. Desire stirred in her sharply. She gasped. "You don't need to put that into your music, you know," she chastened him.

Hugh stopped. "I don't know what you're referring to," he said. Damn him, the innocence in his dark eyes was convincing.

Thessia swallowed. "You're already . . . I already . . . Even without the music, I already want . . ."

Oh, this explanation was not going to plan.

Hugh seemed neither amused nor confused, however. His gaze consumed hers.

"You already want what?" he asked.

Thessia supposed she would have withdrawn from the inquiry on other nights. She would have retreated into qualities fit for queenhood—propriety, politeness, poise.

On this night, stubborn passion took over.

She leaned forward and kissed her husband.

Hugh kissed her back, hard.

Then he was moving forward, hand on her side, cradling her like she was his harp and her delight his sweetest melody. His other hand rose to her cheek, delicate. Thessia lost herself, the kiss crescendoing while the carriage's pounding rhythm entwined with her heartbeat. She was kissing her husband, and it was everything.

The carriage hit an uneven stone, and Hugh fell back, their embrace broken. His chest heaved. His eyes burned. Thessia feared he'd retake his seat. That with his senses recovered, he'd end what'd only just begun.

Instead, he remained on his knees before her, eyes fixed on hers with desperate supplication. While the carriage swayed, Hugh did not move. Slowly, deliberately, she pulled his hands to her thighs, feeling the hot flush of his skin. Fingers calloused from harp strings and sword hilts caressed her legs, sending shivers through her.

It was irresistible. *He* was irresistible.

Thessia could rule her composure, could even command her heart. She could not surmount her desire. Not now.

When his hands moved lower, to the undersides of her thighs, Thessia parted her legs to let him come closer.

Hugh welcomed his queen's summons. He moved forward, so she could wrap her legs around his impressive frame. His rough hands clenched her soft skin—Thessia reacted on instinct, crossing her heels to pull him to her, passion roaring in her pounding heart.

Locked in their embrace, Hugh didn't hesitate. His lips met Thessia's, reprising his song of rogue devotion and unconquerable need.

While she kissed him deeper, moving with the rhythm of the carriage, Thessia wished the palace would never come. She only wished this ride would never end.

With Hugh pressing her into the seat, the queen let his music swell within her.

15
Galwell

Galwell had fond memories of the Realm Chalice. Revels in the village square with his school friends, watching the conjuration with a basket of shankfries. Hearing stories of decade-old matches from his grandfather, who'd played one season with the Devostos Dragons. Galwell's father proudly presenting Galwell with field-side passes for the two of them when Elgin hosted the match, then pulling some local strings for one more ticket when Elowen—who'd never showed the least interest in horseball but sought to follow Galwell everywhere—insisted on coming with them.

Ordinary memories, uncomplicated memories.

Not like now, on the eve of the Vestriya-hosted match. Now Galwell found himself useless once more as they headed into the next important part of their quest. *Bait*, he thought miserably. Heroes weren't bait.

While recuperating from some undisclosed illness, Thessia had a letter delivered via Vestriyan guard—the parchment was scented with the smell of fresh brew, so whatever malady had affected the queen evidently required fortification in the form of the spicy liquid. She thought the Chalice could be a chance to draw the guild out. Galwell needed only attend the game, safe in the royal box in view of everyone in the realm. Then, accompanied by Hugh, he could lure the guild assassins to a tavern nearby, where they would think him vulnerable—but where River would be waiting.

Celine, for her part, had published precisely the story they needed in the press, proclaiming the Deathrose Guild outmaneuvered. They would be desperate.

Everyone was doing something heroic.

While Galwell would do . . . nothing. Except get shot at and find himself the damsel everyone else was protecting.

He was miserable. He hated how Ghosts-damned *restless* he felt, spending the early morning rearranging the part in his rust-colored hair in his mirror because he literally had nothing else to do. He felt vain and vaguely irrelevant.

Except worse, for Galwell the Great was also homesick. Not for Mythria—Galwell was homesick for his past. When the villains were evil men who owned their villainy. Not beautiful women with whom one was forced to work, who . . .

No, he would not venture there.

Except . . . he had, quite literally, physically ventured there. Leaving his chambers and his mirror in the late afternoon, he had wandered the streets with motives he refused to let fully coalesce in his mind, until he found himself camped outside Mona's hideout.

When she emerged, he followed.

Though he left some cunning distance between them, Mona promptly paused, then looked over her shoulder, smirking. Not meeting Galwell's concealed watchful gaze but subtly indicating she knew he was there. *Of course she does*, he reminded himself. She was a mind reader.

It mattered not. Mona herself was not Galwell's objective.

No, he was determined to undo every stroke of villainy she'd wrought on Vestriya's capital this lavender-skied evening.

This he could manage. Villains might look like voluptuous, charming shadow play stars, but the raw materials of heroism—courage, generosity, consideration—wouldn't change. *Couldn't* change.

Or he hoped they couldn't.

He watched Mona closely. First, she pickpocketed a man longingly eyeing the enormous flanks of fire-dusted hroxen roasting on spits in a roaster's stall. Shameless! Nevertheless, Galwell was there, heroically, offering to purchase the man the fattest sandwich on the menu when he found his pockets empty.

Leaving the stand, Galwell caught Mona's eye. In the shade of a street corner, he found her watching him, scowling.

He nodded to her cheerfully. *Game on*, he sought to say. He knew she could hear him even with the words unspoken.

Mona rushed from his sight. Galwell pursued. The winding stone street she led him down held numerous carriages, all jostling for position on the chaotic road. Galwell momentarily wondered whether he should revise his view of the sorry state of heroism in Vestriya, for mere pedestrianism here required great courage. Folks took their lives into their own hands crossing the road to get from the silk spinner's stall to the brewshop.

Yet whether heroism could be found here or not, villainy definitely could. Galwell spotted Mona down the path, confidently slashing the harness of a carriage with her dagger. No doubt to steal the fine horses!

"Good sir!" Galwell called out, hailing the coachman directly. At Galwell's urgent waving, the sleepy-eyed man straightened up from his slump. "Your harness," Galwell explained, coming closer. "Inspect your carriage's harness."

"I'll be," the coachman muttered, leaning down to look. When he clambered down from his post to rectify the damage, Galwell noticed the man shivering in the cool evening.

Readily, Galwell shrugged out of his coat.

"Here," he said, offering it to the coachman, who knew a good deed when he saw one. Wordlessly, meeting Galwell's insistent gaze, the coachman pulled on the comforting fur-lined leather.

Galwell grinned. *He probably thinks me one of the Ghosts themselves*, he thought proudly.

Mona slunk into the shadows, glaring.

Now this, Galwell could concede, *is fun*. Good, clean heroism. If it delighted him in some modest measure to vex the woman who'd kept him in a cage while dancing provocatively in front of him and who'd shot him in the leg and shoulder while he was wearing his favorite sleep clothes, well . . .

He was a hero, not a monk.

Pursuing Mona from street to street, he spied her ducking into a shabby inn crammed between nearly identical brewshops with wide patios spilling out into the street. Looking for tourists as easy marks, Galwell guessed.

He entered the close-quarters lobby, where conjurated miniature musicians played pipe whistle tunes on the marble check-in counter, just in time to watch Mona sell counterfeit Realm Chalice tickets to some gullible guests. When she headed for the stairs, her con complete, Galwell strode neatly forth, noting he felt the family's new tickets looked "outdated."

Fortunately for them, Galwell had his very own Realm Chalice tickets on him. He'd kept them in his farthing pouch. Without hesitation, he implored the visitors to use his instead.

Mona was close enough for Galwell to overhear the scream she restrained in her throat with a frustrated sound. He smiled to himself.

When she dashed upstairs, he gamely followed. In the upper hallway, he glimpsed her picking the lock on a grand door at the end of the corridor.

Galwell flew downstairs. "The room at the end of the hall," he half inquired, half demanded of the innkeeper—pleasantly, of course. Heroically. "Is it occupied?"

"Why, no," the innkeeper—Lanzelo, his nameplate informed Galwell—replied. "Our Regent's Suite is our loveliest room. Rarely occupied except by our most esteemed guests."

"I'll check in now," Galwell declared, depositing his entire coin purse on the counter.

Though clearly surprised, the innkeeper did not question the high-paying hero. He handed over the indulgently curlicued metal key immediately.

Galwell grasped the object, started for the stairs, then doubled back.

"You've been very helpful, Lanzelo," he remarked. "I shall— leave you a warm review on Mythria's most frequented travel message tapestry."

Lanzelo raised a hand in perplexed parting.

Galwell rushed upstairs. If the room was unoccupied, Mona couldn't do much damage in the way of purloining valuables. Perhaps, however, she intended to use the balconies or side doors for ingress and egress of other rooms? He wished he had her mind-reading power, but even without magic, he knew one thing. She meant no meager mischief with her dastardly presence here.

He reached the upstairs hallway—

The door to the Regent's Suite was half open.

Curious. Galwell strode closer, cautious now, the way he would venture into enemy fortresses . . .

When he neared, he glimpsed through the open door—Mona. Smiling, on the coverlet of the enormous burgundy bed inside. Propped up on her elbows, waiting.

For him.

Well played, he thought to himself.

Mona smiled, hearing him perfectly.

He slowed his pace, eased open the door, and stopped in the doorway, going no farther. "You should lock your doors in places like these," he said. "You never know what sort of unsavory sort might be engaged in crime or villainy here."

Mona smiled. She shifted to lie on her side, head resting on one elbow. "I take it," she drawled, "this room has been let to one Galwell the Grating?"

Pleased with himself, Galwell the Grating held up the curlicued key. Mona's eyes landed on it with a mixture of amusement and annoyance.

"Would you like me to lock it for you?" Galwell gestured to the door, moving as if he planned to depart. "It's yours for the night."

Mona's eyebrows rose. "You don't intend to come inside?"

"I've not been invited," Galwell replied.

Rolling her eyes, Mona stretched—the contours of her body curving and coursing under the ever-impeccable crimson fabric she wore. "You mustn't always wait for an invitation to the things you want."

Galwell shrugged. He felt on firm footing now—how often had opponents taunted or sought to confuse him with intimidating word games? "I wasn't aware there was something I wanted in this room," he returned. "I'll admit the furnishings are quite handsome, though, and the view of the canals rather marvelous."

This was true. Past Mona, the window framing the evening revealed the reason this room was the Regent's Suite—the view of the Vestriyan capital's widest waterway, where gondolas and skiffs maneuvered in the dazzling sunset.

In damning contrast, Mona's expression darkened imperiously.

"Not"—she stood, her movements poised and fluid, her hair falling loose over her shoulders—"what I was referring to."

She walked—no, *slunk* over to him, then plucked the key without hesitation from his fingers. As she reached past him for the door, she pulled herself chest to chest with him, leaving Galwell certain she could hear the blood pounding in his veins. With her gaze fixed on him, she tugged the door closed, drawing him inside, even closer to her, then turned the lock decisively with her free hand.

Galwell held his posture rigid. When he'd engaged with his other opponents, they'd never sparred with him quite like *this*.

He kept his eyes on the very large wardrobe in the corner. Was it crafted of crestoak? Indeed not. It looked more like northern white nettlewood.

"Stop that," Mona snapped. "It won't work."

Galwell swallowed. "Stop what?" he inquired.

"Focusing on innocuous thoughts to try to bore me into not reading your mind."

"Why would I presume you were interested in my mind at all?" Galwell asked, fighting for the upper hand.

Mona glared. With her rage lighting up her every sharp feature, her gorgeous hair descending over the sculpted shoulders her dress exposed, Galwell could fend off his mind no longer. She was fire in a storm. Disaster upon disaster, and stunning in her destruction.

Her eyes went half-lidded. Like she could feel his concession.

"You shouldn't have given your coat away," she chastised him. "Now you need someone to warm you up." Her hand rose to his tunic.

Galwell heard himself echoing her. "Stop that. It won't work."

The selfless part of him felt guilty when Mona's expression slipped, just a little. Nevertheless, he continued.

"You want to disarm me with flirtations you don't mean just to make me uncomfortable around you," he explained. "Shooting me didn't work. Hurting my feelings didn't work. This won't, either."

Mona eyed him, then stormed back to the bed. Recognizing he'd pierced her defenses, Galwell permitted himself a bit of rueful pride.

Mona was a dangerous compatriot, he reminded himself. He needed to know how to penetrate—so to speak—her disingenuous facade.

"I put the word out in the underworld that I have a close connection with Galwell the Great, and if anyone was interested in hiring someone competent to assassinate him following the Deathrose Guild's failure, I'd be more than happy to provide such services," she stated.

Pivoting to business, then. "Thank you." Galwell met her formality with politeness.

"I'm coming to the match tomorrow. Need to keep an eye on my investment," she announced.

The thought of watching his favorite sport with this . . . this . . . *villain* sounded . . . fun? "I look forward to your company," Galwell said honestly. "I'll buy you a shankfry."

"I'd like to get a better sense of your allies, too. I don't trust that scribe of yours. Her thoughts are guarded. Compartmentalized in a way I've not seen."

Galwell knew she sought to sow distrust among the heroes. To prove that everyone had a villain inside them. Galwell wouldn't fall for it. "She has head magic," he replied. "Perhaps she's protected from your intrusions. Or perhaps she's merely smarter than everyone else."

"Perhaps." Mona shrugged, examining her nails. "Of course, I could always take the job for real."

Galwell nodded, considering her words. "I wouldn't," he returned.

She went silent. Though she did not look up, Galwell sensed she was reading his mind.

He did not interrupt her. Let her see just how much he did not fear her. Indeed, he practically wished *more* villains possessed this power. He'd probably save himself plenty of needless fights if every henchman or regional operative knew that *he* knew that fisticuffs with Galwell the Great would not end well for them.

"You think because you foiled my petty crimes today that I can't do it?" Mona uttered.

He heard the menace she sought to summon into her voice. He cared not.

"I think you can't do it because you know I don't deserve it," he replied simply.

When Mona scoffed, Galwell credited himself, for he felt he was improving at figuring out when Vestriya's princess of lies was representing herself falsely. "You certainly do after making me watch all those good deeds you did today." She grimaced, as if witnessing goodness made her feel like a child who'd been served sledgeling egg jelly with dinner. She rounded on him, confrontational. "Those people didn't deserve your help, you know."

"I know. I helped them anyway," Galwell replied. "What are you going to do about it?"

He stared her down. She wasn't the sort of villain he was used to, not in the least. But he *was* still a hero. He knew that much.

Finally, Mona huffed, infuriated.

Galwell smirked. He'd never smirked before. He didn't know he possessed the skill until just then.

"I need to shower off your . . . goodness," Mona declared, cringing. She stalked to the corner of the room, where she pressed a rune marked on the wall. Cream-colored fizzy wine sparkled to life in thin glasses on the minibar. "Better yet, I need a palate cleanser."

Galwell nodded to the crystalline glass she sipped from. "That sparklina looks rich enough for the job."

"It's a start," Mona replied. She faced him. "My tongue craves something . . . stiffer."

When her eyes raked down his form, Galwell recognized the desirous look in them. Yet combined with her words, the sensation left him feeling only confusion. *Her . . . tongue? What could her tongue want down there?*

Mona straightened, startled. "Why are you confused?" she demanded, now sounding utterly confounded herself.

Galwell felt himself start to sweat. "I'm not—confused," he protested.

Nervousness mounted in him when he confronted the inevitable. This was a *sex* thing, wasn't it? While he wished to interrogate the possibilities further, even this would reveal to Mona truths he did not wish revealed. It was just—he thought tongues went in mouths. That was the only source of his confusion. Quite reasonable. Perhaps she wanted to press delicate kisses to his legs? That sounded pleasant. He could understand why people wished to engage in that during lovemaking—

"Oh, Ghosts, please don't call it that. And no, I don't want to kiss your thighs, you *gryphon*," Mona said.

"I assure you, they are clean and muscular," Galwell managed.

Offering no reply, Mona examined him. On the upside, the fury seemed to have fled Mona's striking features. Only her inquisitiveness remained.

However, Galwell concluded ruefully, *the inquisitiveness might be worse.*

Fervently, he sought distraction in his own mind. The wooden furniture in the room! Yes, certainly. Now, was it northern white nettlewood or western? Northern, he was certain—difficult to work with because of how firm and rigid the wood is, just like his own—

Fuck. He corrected himself. Despite Mona's doubtfulness, Galwell knew exactly what to do with *his* wood. He'd done . . . woodworking many times on his own terms, to great success.

Unfortunately, this made Mona gasp.

"No," she stated.

Galwell sweated. He knew he was in *perilous* danger. He wished he were facing her with his crossbow instead of this.

"Galwell," Mona asked calmly, "are you a virgin?"

He said nothing.

The hero of Mythria refused to be embarrassed. There was no shame to be found in this simple reality. He was a questing hero in his youth. Then he was *dead* for ten years. Everyone in his position—or rather lack thereof—had valid reasons that should not be interrogated. Especially by the likes of wily, unfairly hot ladies of crime.

Mona started to laugh. In the sound, Galwell heard incredulity, yes, but curiously enough, not judgment. Or perhaps he was only deluding himself. Imputing too much *good* to her, like she insisted he did with the commonfolk he helped without question.

"Of course. Of *course*. Too busy being good to have any real fun," she commented. "No wonder you're strung so tight."

Galwell cleared his throat. "I don't know what that means, but I'm sure I'm strung an adequate amount."

Impossibly, Mona only softened. "Baby, you can't take your eyes off me. Your thoughts—they're persistent but indistinct, which now I'm realizing is because you want me, but you don't know what you want to *do* with me."

Even Galwell's magical strength could not withstand much more of this. The cooing. The unhurried exploration into his sexual history. The sound of Mona—*his best friend's sister, for Ghosts' sake*—saying *you want me*.

He held on to his heroism. "Mock me all you want, Mona. It was a sword that killed me once, not embarrassment," he returned.

Mona came closer to him. She walked slowly, like a predator. *Why, then, do I so wish to be prey?*

With her voice low, coming from deep within her throat, she spoke softly to him.

"I don't want to mock you."

She moved her hand slowly down his chest. Lower. Lower—Galwell hardly perceived her passing the waistband of his trousers—until, with the most devastating combination of confidence and care, she grasped his firmness in her hand. He exhaled hard, fighting to keep his eyes open.

"Would you," Mona asked, "like to do something a little bad?"

Ghosts, yes, Galwell heard himself think. Oh, fuck it if she heard him. What she held in her hand spoke the same message without word or thought.

He needed to say something, though. He fought through the haze of her intoxicating touch. "I won't pretend I don't desperately want whatever it is you're proposing," he conceded. "You can hear my thoughts. You know I do."

Then, with more strength than Galwell the Great had perhaps ever needed to command, he opened his eyes fully and found Mona's, his stare piercing.

"But let's not pretend this is a palate cleanser, Mona," he ordered. "I think watching me do all those good deeds hasn't made you need to be bad. It's made you want me. You *liked* it." He gazed down, victorious in defeat. "You're—strung as tight as I am."

Mona's touch released just slightly. For the second time this evening, surprise flooded her face.

Surprise that changed, like deep night into pale lavender Vestriyan morn, into approval. She *liked* that he'd knocked her off-kilter. He'd expected she might.

Slowly, with that smug, impressed satisfaction on her features, she sank to her knees in front of him.

Her hand never left where it rested. "What—" Galwell struggled. "What do I do?"

Mona smiled. "Fight those heroic urges, Galwell," she ordered him softly, "and surrender. Surrender to me completely."

He swallowed hard, nodding.

She undid the lacing of his pants fully, exposing his very stiff wood. Then, with smoldering eyes upturned to his, she drew him into her mouth.

Galwell's knees went weak. He stumbled backward into the closed door, earning a chuckle from Mona, who did not cease in her efforts.

It was . . . it was no kiss on the thighs, that was for certain. Mona was experienced, obviously, and she did *everything* with complete, commanding commitment. Over and over, deeper and deeper, she pulled him into her throat, tortured him with her tongue, and ripped every shred of strength from him with each consuming stroke.

For he didn't know how long, he surrendered.

16
Thessia

The queen of Mythria did not know hangovers could last this long.

Is this how Beatrice quested? Thessia wondered, marveling at the possibility. When her friends had set off to rescue Hugh in Vermillion Vale, was *this* how the former Lady de Noughton's head had pounded, how her stomach had lurched? Impossible.

Fucking heroic.

Thessia had even requested that the royal kitchen prepare Clare's famous—"Famous," Grandhart had insisted, repeating the recipe so often Thessia could remember it readily—Hangover Corn-Toast. However, either the Vestriyan kitchens did not prepare them correctly or Clare had oversold his invention, for Thessia remained miserable despite the plateful she'd consumed.

By the morning of the Realm Chalice, she was just beginning to feel like a person again, instead of like a bilious sledgeling on the floor of her bathing chamber.

If she was honest with herself, heavy drinking had not entirely been to blame for her inability to roust herself from the—wonderfully cool, comforting—marble floor yesterday. Mortification had kept her plenty self-confined.

She'd kissed her husband. Passionately, without restraint! The man who'd made no illusions or misrepresentations concerning the entirely formal pretenses of their relationship! She'd kissed him like they were shadow play characters, he her long-lost love and she the wildhearted ingenue!

Had it been the best kiss of her life? Obviously. Not that she'd much to compare the kiss to, but kisses could not possibly get much better. If they could, nothing in the realm would ever get done.

Which only made this worse.

Thessia forced the memory from her painfully pounding head. She'd been avoiding Hugh ever since. The hangover was her convenient excuse. When Hugh's carriage returned them to the palace, Thessia realized in full what she'd done, and fled his company using faked illness . . . which wound up being very *not*-faked illness.

Hugh, for his part, had intuited her discomfort—emotional, digestive, both. Either out of gentlemanliness or horror at her impropriety, he'd found other lodging. Thessia was left entirely on her own, without company other than the enterprising palace chefs and the toilet in her bathing chamber.

The Realm Chalice, however, demanded Hugh and she reunite.

Hungover was *not*, put generously, the ideal conditions for one to experience the horseball Realm Chalice. Each year, the match united fans from every city, every realm, every class as they filled landmark stadiums with cheering, food, drink, carousing, and general merriment. The event was utterly enormous.

Vestriya's capital stadium, the queen could concede, surpassed most and rivaled Mythria's grandest sporting halls. The marble coliseum rose sky-high out of the western commercial district's stone streets. Crowds dressed in team jerseys streamed in from every direction, and the scents of liquor and fried goods pervaded the sun-seared day.

Protected by royal escort, Thessia had processed through the stadium to the Notable Persons box. Of course, celebrities from each realm spectated the epic match, congregating in the field-side gilded compartment with cushioned leather seating and endless mead on tap.

Thessia sat next to Hugh, each of them forcing smiles for the players to whom they were introduced.

It was . . . tense. When Thessia bumped Hugh's arm accidentally while reaching for the spice-salted potatoes, Hugh practically leapt from his seat. When they were requested to pose for a conjuration with Zevan Wintersmith and his husband, Nevo Yrillis, players on opposing squads today, Hugh was suddenly uniquely ungainly. He placed his hand much too high on Thessia's back—nearly on the queen's shoulders!—like he feared touching her waist or lower.

Thessia was certain the conjuration would capture her pained smile. *Wonderful.*

It was ironic. They'd pretended this whole time to be besotted husband and wife, but now, after *actually* kissing for the first time, they suddenly did not seem married at all. How grand.

Zevan and Nevo were ushered forward to conjurations with Ezio in the front row. The Vestriyan crown prince looked impressively regal, his white-gold hair impossibly straight, his generous smile illuminating every conjuration. There were rumors he'd used royal funds to pay for all the city orphanage's children to watch the Realm Chalice from their own box.

Honestly, could he offer lessons in effortless royalty? Thessia would count herself interested.

Instead, Thessia found herself effort*ful*, when she was finally without publicity obligations to distract her from Hugh's presence.

She could bear it no longer. If Beatrice could confront hungover questing, Thessia could confront the uncomfortable matter of her own husband. She turned to him and opened her mouth—

Not knowing what to say, she promptly closed it. The silence—oh, the silence—was horrible. Hugh winced. Composing his expression with evident force, he faced her in turn, but seemed to know no more than she how to commence this conversation.

"*Nine horses with nine riders take the field! Where courage and good sportsmanship shall not yield.*"

The voice that ended their stalemate was neither Hugh's nor Thessia's. Ario leaned down, close to them, sharing his horseball poem with evident pride.

Here as the elusive and dangerous spymaster, he was dressed once more entirely in shades of black. His snail, Benjamin, was nowhere to be found.

Hugh grasped the interruption with relief. "Bravo!" he replied overenthusiastically to their interloper.

Ario straightened in delight. "You think so? Ezio told me I was to get all my rhymes out before the guests arrive, but maybe this one—"

"Ario, you promised. No rhyming relapsing," Ezio cautioned, pausing on his way to the front of the box. "I fear sinister evil today. You need to focus your energies on spycraft."

Pouting, Ario withdrew to his seat. "I wish Benjamin were here. He would like it."

"I'm sorry," Hugh murmured to her when Ario had receded.

Relief coursed through Thessia. Finally, they were talking about it. Her gratitude for Hugh's plainspoken courage was immense. "*I'm sorry,*" she replied. "I never should have . . . I was very drunk. Let's just—forget it."

Hugh cleared his throat.

"I meant about Ario," he explained. "I could have endangered his reputation."

Embarrassment hit the queen hot and mercilessly. She felt her cheeks flame. Could she leap onto one of the horseball horses and ride right out of the stadium? Could she consult River on how to disappear from public life entirely?

"Thessia," Hugh said.

She determinedly faced the field. Perhaps if she pretended with queenly conviction that the conversation was concluded—

"Thess," he insisted.

Now Thessia could not fight the memories of him calling her "Thess" in his carriage. She wished she had head magic of memory erasure. Her own, specifically.

"No, really. It's—" she managed.

Hugh interrupted her. "I wasn't using my magic on you in the carriage. I want you to know that. I would never—do that. It wouldn't be right."

"Oh," Thessia said, quietly crushed. Deep down, this was the only possibility she'd held on to. The only opalicyte lining on the dark clouds of her mortifying memories. That perhaps he'd wanted her, even a little, enough to want to conjure melodic, magical desire in her. "Of course you weren't. Why would you want me to do what I did?" she continued.

She immediately wished she hadn't spoken out loud. When Hugh's eyes found hers in puzzlement, Thessia knew she'd earned what she wanted least—the prolongment of this discussion.

"That's what you think?" Hugh inquired. "Thessia, I—I mean, anyone would want—anyone would be lucky—"

He was fumbling his words. Uncomfortable, like her. Oh, where were Ario's horrible rhymes when you needed them? Thessia sought to put Hugh out of his misery.

"Yes, because I'm the queen," she said, looking away. "But they don't really feel those things for *me*. It was the same with Galwell, wasn't it? He couldn't break his promise to me, and neither can you."

Hugh grasped her hand fiercely. The urgency of the movement was enough to pull her eyes back to him.

"You must not think that," he demanded, his tone half desire, half determination. "What we did the other night was a mistake, but it was one I wanted. One I . . . enjoyed. Too much. My regret has nothing to do with you, and is only because I know I cannot give my heart to another," he explained. "I have always made it a rule not to act on physical desires when I know I cannot give more of myself. Last night, I succumbed. Because you were . . . irresistible. But I should have been better," he concluded. "Nobler."

His voice was rough and low. Yet for Thessia, his words sounded like music—lovelier than the sweetest melody, for one word resonated in her heart. *Irresistible.*

She dared hold his gaze. In his eyes she found—hope.

Irresistible. No one had ever thought of her that way.

She was opening her mouth, starting to formulate how she would venture to inquire more, when they were interrupted. Mona entered their Notable Persons compartment with Galwell. She was here to help protect him, like Hugh, until Galwell was in River's care. He would be safe from assassins.

Whether he was safe from Mona was another matter, Thessia realized.

The crime princess was dressed in lush purple, her dress shimmering in the sun. She looked over the emerald horseball field, the clamoring spectators, the preening players and celebrities with enviable control. Like everyone, everywhere, was one grand mark for her endless cunning.

Following her, Galwell tried chivalrously to help her to her seat. Mona ignored him, cheerfully seating her herself right next to Ario.

Galwell frowned.

Odd, Thessia noted to herself. "Prince Ario, yes? Mona Grandhart," she introduced herself, voice like silk. "I've long been a fan of yours."

Ario looked to the gorgeous woman sitting next to him.

THIS WILL BE INTERESTING 211

"You flatter me," Ario pronounced elegantly. "It's so rare to find a fan of my pursuits."

Mona did not seem to understand he meant poetry. "I agree. The realm could use more fans of interesting people, couldn't it?"

"Yes," Ario concurred, eagerly now. "Tell me, Mona. Do you like snails?"

When Mona laughed, the sound sparkling like the finest crystals from Mythria's famous caves, Thessia heard Galwell grunt. In . . . displeasure. Glancing the hero's way, Thessia found Galwell *glaring* at Ario. *What has gotten into him?* she wondered.

Interrupting Mona's flirtation with the young royal, guards approached Ario. With them, the crowd's fervor swelled. Thessia heard cries of *I love you!* and *Sign my horseball!*—not to mention exhortations for signatures of a more intimate nature.

When the phalanx parted, Thessia understood why. Prince Ezio stood in the soldiers' midst.

"Brother!" he called out. "We must pose for conjurations— Yes, thank you, you're very kind," Ezio replied to a woman holding forth her infant for him to kiss and saying he made her feel proud to be Vestriyan.

Ario slouched. "Must I?"

"Yes, you must," Ezio replied patiently. "I know you would prefer to be socializing or . . . spying or some such, but posing for conjurations with donors will help fund my efforts to remove toxic sludge from our canals. Don't you want the children of Vestriya to be able to swim again, brother?" He caught Thessia's eye, his golden irises gleaming in the midday sun. "While it would certainly be pleasant to stay and pass the game with such a lovely Mythrian royal—"

He gestured to the clamor surrounding him. "*Eẓio! Eẓio! Eẓio!*" the people had commenced chanting, as if they were here to see him and not the Realm Chalice at all.

"So many causes," Ezio said. "So little time."

Thessia smiled. "Of course," she replied. It was . . . heartening. Thessia had seen enough of Vestriya's dark corners to comprehend that Ezio meant more to Vestriya than personality or public service. To these people, he was hope.

Ario rose reluctantly. "I'll return shortly, and we can discuss our mutual pursuits," he promised Mona, who nodded.

While the princes headed to the other end of the Notable Persons box, Mona turned to their questing party.

Mona's gaze followed her silver-haired suitor. "I must admit, there's a unique sexiness to a debauched poet, isn't there?"

"You knew the spymaster was a harmless poet all along?" Thessia asked.

Mona grinned, looking much more like a spymaster than Ario, even as he was dressed in all black. "I heard you had fun with the harpies," she cooed.

Galwell grunted in displeasure again.

Thessia whirled to face him. Hugh eyed their friend more inconspicuously. "Are you quite all right?" he inquired.

"I'm going to get some shankfry," Galwell grumbled.

"Take Hugh or Mona with you," Thessia commanded.

Galwell's face hardened. "I can manage the concession line on my own. I'm not a child."

"Let him," Mona said quietly, watching him rise from his seat. "I'll keep listening to his thoughts to keep him safe. It's better if he's seen alone for a moment anyway."

Thessia didn't like the suggestion, but Galwell was already fleeing the Notable Persons section in such a hurry that he collided with the usher come to replenish everyone's mead.

"Pardon—pardon me," Galwell said, clasping the man's forearm to steady them.

"It's no problem, noble sir," the usher replied. "I bumped into you."

Now Thessia knew for certain something was wrong. Galwell was *never* clumsy. Though she guessed his quest for shankfry was in earnest—Galwell loved the peasant delicacy of gryphon shank fried in sizzling batter on a wooden stick—she doubted stadium concessions had driven him from their company.

"Why's he so upset?" she wondered out loud.

"Oh, I expect he's jealous," Mona replied genially. "We had some fun last night, and I guess he thought it was some commitment it wasn't."

Thessia exchanged glances with Hugh, their eyes widening in unison. Galwell and *Mona?*

"What . . . sort of fun?" Hugh got out.

Mona smirked. "In horseball terms, we reached second horse arch," she confirmed.

Now Thessia laughed. It was just—it was ridiculous, and ridiculously delightful. She'd known, obviously, of the limited romantic history Galwell possessed. If he wanted to have some second-horse-arch fun with Mona, he was more than entitled.

Hugh met the queen's eyes, and then he was laughing with her. She hadn't expected her jubilation to charm him, yet there they were, charming each other.

Without prologue, rhythmic pounding filled the stadium.

Thessia knew the source. With excitement fluttering in her secret-horseball-fan heart, she looked to the field, where the field guard had commenced the pregame introduction. Custom in every major horseball match was for the finest percussionists in the city to kick off play by drumming crestoak staves on stone slabs. They were magicked to echo their rhythms stadium-wide.

"*Vestriyans! Visitors! Spectators young and old!*"

The announcer's amplified voice boomed throughout the stadium. Thessia leaned forward.

"To commence our sport, we are pleased to invite an honored guest to pitch the first chuck-up!" the announcer declared.

Where was Galwell? Thessia wondered. He would miss the opening minutes!

"He hails from Mythria," the announcer continued, "he's a supporter of the Farmount Falcons, and he once saved his realm! Please put your hands together for . . ."

Thessia straightened, startled. No, it couldn't be—

"*Galwell the Great!*" cried the announcer.

Hugh and Mona looked perplexed, just like Thessia. This, the queen knew with certainty, was *not* the plan. Although it wasn't a bad idea—perhaps Galwell took this upon himself to organize. To make sure all his enemies knew exactly where he was.

The hero strode onto the eye-wateringly green grass of the horseball pitch under the perfect midmorning sun. He smiled grandly, waving to the crowds with none of his recent unpleasantness. Honestly, Thessia felt he was doing a passable impression of Clare.

"Did you know about this?" Hugh inquired.

"No," Thessia replied. "Not at all. Perhaps it was scheming from my press positioners." *Oh, if this was the case, they were so fired*, she noted to herself.

The questing party watched Galwell receive from the referee the hard, duramelon-sized horseball. He waved once more to the crowd. Everyone cheered. The horses lined up on the pitch's chalked center divider, ready to scrum for the ball Galwell would hurl into their midst. The hero positioned the horseball in his powerful hands, wound up—

And at the last moment, he pivoted. With deadly intensity, he threw the horseball *directly at the Notable Persons box*.

Given Galwell's powerful strength, the projectile flew impossibly, lethally fast. The impact was nearly instantaneous, the *crack* echoing in the stadium when the horseball struck Crown Prince Ezio in the head.

Chaos unfolded. Everyone screamed. Thessia's heart leapt into her throat. Over the clamor of thousands of frantic spectators, she could still hear the sound of the bone-breaking strike resounding in her ears.

People were jumping up and fleeing the stadium. But Thessia could not move. The whole pitch seemed to wobble and slant in her vision, dizziness descending over her. Struggling for composure, she saw Ario. He'd caught his brother and was shaking the elder prince's form like he sought to wake him.

Ezio slumped in Ario's grasp, unmoving. Crimson streaked his forehead, starting to stain Ario's hands and the silver of his hair. There would be no recovering from the impossibly hard throw.

A throw, Thessia knew with damning conviction, that could have only been made with Galwell's hand-magical gift of strength.

On the field, the horses stomped and whinnied, hearing the crowd's panic. Guards rushed forth into the box, shoving Notable Persons out of the way as they moved to conceal the princes from view. Galwell—where was Galwell? Dizzy with fear, Thessia realized she was clutching Hugh's hand with white knuckles.

She could not let go. "Surely it was . . . a mistake," she got out.

"He doesn't make mistakes," Hugh returned gravely.

Mona stood behind them. Thessia was distantly surprised to find even the criminal mastermind's face shockingly pale. "Yes, but he'd also never do this. He'd never kill someone unless he had to. He's too . . . good," she insisted, struggling with the word.

When the guards parted, Ezio was gone. She watched as Ario followed them out, his face twisted in concern, tears in his eyes.

Thessia was profoundly shaken. The a-word was not one political leaders liked to contemplate, but Thessia had when her military commanders had given her imperative instructions on her public safety.

She considered it now. They'd witnessed the successful assassination of Vestriya's crown prince.

And their friend—their good, kind, noble friend—had done the deed.

"Maybe the injury wasn't as bad as it looked?" Thessia managed.

"It was worse," Mona replied. Her color had not returned. Her voice wavered.

Thessia shivered involuntarily.

While clamor and fear unfolded around them, Thessia reminded herself that she was no idle spectator. She was the queen of Mythria. She needed to remain collected in crisis.

River had seen people die, many people. Vandra Ravenfall, Beatrice, Clare—they'd witnessed horrific things. Reminding herself of how they'd carried on, Thessia rose from her seat, refusing to let her fear stop her.

"Come," she ordered Hugh, grasping his arm. "We must find Galwell *right now*."

They fled the box, only for Thessia to realize—this was easier declared than done.

Chaos continued to unfold on the field. Guards rushed in from every direction. While some guests remained, looking unnerved, most sought to flee the stadium. Horses continued to wheel and whinny on the horseball pitch.

In the midst of it all, Galwell was nowhere to be found.

17
River

River had been at the pub they'd designated as the planned meeting spot. She was nursing an ale, only half paying attention to the Realm Chalice. All the stadium's surrounding pubs were conjurating the match for viewing, so she couldn't escape it fully, but the truth was, she didn't much care for horseball. She kept up with it because it was an easy shorthand to reach for, something that often let her converse with people she needed a connection with—people with whom she'd usually have nothing to discuss. Today, she'd had much bigger things on her mind. Celine had indeed published her piece on the Deathrose Guild. She cared more about her scribely integrity than she did about River's personal feelings. So what if River had told her to go ahead and do it? She'd obviously not meant it. It was just something she'd said.

Damned words. Damned feelings.

River had entirely too many of them, and she'd wanted a chance to sort through them in peace. Here she was in Vestriya, knee-deep in the business of royals from both realms, fighting feelings for a woman she could never have—a woman with secrets she wouldn't share—when all River had ever intended to do was her job. A job that no longer existed, for a guild she no longer seemed to understand.

Then Galwell threw that ball at Prince Ezio.

Considering her line of business, River often thought it was impossible to shock her. That had done it.

Was it finally proof that the guild had been right all along? Was Galwell an evil, murderous man?

River teleported to Celine, landing squarely in front of her in the press box beside the playing field. It was getting to be a bit tedious the way they kept ending up with their bodies smashed together, as if River's magic were playing an extended cruel joke.

"Sorry," River said, creating immediate distance. "I just . . . I figured you knew more about what was going on."

"The match won't be happening. They'll be announcing it soon. They think Ezio is dead," Celine whispered, her face pale. "And suddenly the scribes down here are saying Ario was harmed, too?"

"*What?*" River could not hide her shock. Not that snail-loving, terrible poet of a prince.

"We need to find Galwell," they both said in unison.

It felt good to have a task to share, something that didn't involve their personal drama. Feelings only ever complicated matters, made secrets feel like weapons. River worked best when she didn't have to focus on any of that.

Celine grabbed hold of River's arm as River visualized Galwell's billowing hair and immense, muscular frame. She tried her best to not let her emotions cloud the image, but it was difficult. She'd really believed Galwell was good to his core. But he'd fooled her. Fooled everyone, really.

Yet again, River had been wrong to place her faith in someone. It bothered her in ways she hardly knew how to express. She figured she'd try all the same. Perhaps she'd use her fists. Even though Galwell had magicked strength, she would be fueled by betrayal, which she felt to be more powerful in the end.

They teleported to the very top of the stadium, where wide, empty walkways surrounded the nosebleeds—the seats were so high above the action that the horseball players looked more like

THIS WILL BE INTERESTING 219

bugs than people, and the spectators often wore special glasses to see the action.

Galwell stood with one foot propped up on a bench and his lips wrapped around a gryphon shankfry. A glop of oil was dripping down the corner of his mouth, and he didn't even seem to notice, for he was too busy contemplating the expansive Vestriyan hillside.

River had imagined they'd be teleported to the tunnels under the field. That was where she presumed he'd have run to, considering the location of his actions. Finding Galwell alone at the highest point in the stadium threw all her previous plans into question. Had he already eliminated an entire team of people tasked with keeping him from causing more harm? Was he up here basking in his evil glory?

"What have you done?" River cried out.

"Forgive me!" Galwell said, startled. "I did not hear you arrive." He looked down at his tunic, where the oil had dripped a trail that traveled all the way to his shoes. "I believe I took too large a bite."

"You've just killed Prince Ezio," Celine said. Her composure soothed River, who typically reacted to dangerous figures with violence. When in doubt, knock the person unconscious until you have a clearer picture of the situation.

Then again, considering what had happened at the Grotto, Celine clearly had her own secrets. Perhaps River was being deceived everywhere she went.

Galwell looked to his gryphon shank in horror. "Has . . . has Ezio shape-shifted into my food? I swear I did not know that was his magical gift." He threw the last of the fry onto the ground, then fell to his knees with his hands clasped together. "Ghosts forgive me. I never meant for this to happen."

His brand of evil was not one River had ever encountered before. For him to openly mock Prince Ezio like this . . . It actually scared her. This was the kind of villain she did not know how to fight, because his intentions were so well disguised by his performance of sincerity that she couldn't figure out how to play to his sensibilities enough to get the truth out of him.

"He is not in your fried gryphon," Celine said calmly. "It happened on the field. You threw a ball at his head with such force it knocked him out. All the scribes believe he is now dead, and that Ario has been grievously harmed as well."

Galwell rose up, holding out his hands to show he had no weapons on him.

"That does us no good," River said. "You have the gift of strength. We just watched you use it to deadly effect. *You* are the weapon."

She exchanged a look with Celine. The very line her parents had once said to her—the one that had driven her to the guild—she'd just spoken to *Galwell* of all people.

"I swear to you on the honor of Mythria that I know nothing of what you speak. I heard uproar and assumed it was because the game had begun." He kneeled. "I have been up here completely alone, reflecting upon the events of my personal life."

"Everyone in Vestriya watched you do it. This could very well be the start of a war between our realms, and you mean to tell us we all suffered a collective hallucination?" Celine probed.

"I mean to tell you nothing except that I would never cause harm to Prince Ezio, and I wouldn't hurt Ario, either," Galwell said. "If I were to suggest how this could have happened, I might point toward an impersonator. It's a popular custom in Mythria. Clare has an entire annual convention in his honor. Perhaps some Galwells have traveled to Vestriya."

"But no one has strength like you in any realm. It's a very famous part of your legend," Celine said.

"That is true." Galwell was still kneeling. The man absolutely

THIS WILL BE INTERESTING

loved to kneel, and he looked good doing it. River had to give him that.

"Even if it *wasn't* you, everyone else thinks it was," River said, though she had no idea why. Perhaps the kneeling had done it. Perhaps she was playing right into his hands. But there was a part of her that needed to believe in his goodness. She desperately wanted one thing in her life to be exactly what it was, no catches involved.

"They will still paint you as a villain," Celine said. "I already heard the other scribes discussing it. They are preparing their stories as we speak."

"And they will publish them, no matter who resists," River added, chancing a look at Celine.

"Because the people deserve to know the truth," Celine replied.

"Even when that truth could cost you your life?" River asked. "And speaking of truths, there's something you're very clearly keeping from me. Something that's made you avoid me ever since the harpies chose you in the Grotto."

"Aren't you the one who said you were dangerous? Who made a big point about how I shouldn't trust you?"

"Pardon me, but I believe we've strayed from the original point," Galwell interjected. "I'd love it if we could revisit the possibility that my life's honor has very recently been compromised." The devastation on his face was plain. If it was indeed a performance, then he'd chosen the wrong calling. He could've been a star of shadow plays.

"*If* what you say is true, I will teleport to the impersonator and handle this myself." River closed her eyes and thought of the terrifying focus she'd seen in Galwell's expression before he'd thrown the pitch.

When she opened them again, she *had* teleported. Only she'd gone about three irons west of where she'd already been standing.

"Not a very compelling case for this being the work of someone other than you," she said.

"I swear not just on the honor of Mythria but on the life of my sister and my parents that I did not kill Prince Ezio," Galwell told her.

River tried again to teleport. This time, she landed on the railing that surrounded the top of the stadium. Thank Ghosts she had good balance. She hopped down, arching an eyebrow at Galwell, who was—unbelievably—*still* kneeling.

"Galwell, I cannot find an impersonator anywhere in this stadium. If there really is a duplicate of you running around and tarnishing your legacy, you'll need to go into hiding until this is resolved, because his work is so convincing that even my magic cannot differentiate between the two of you. Wherever you go, keep it a secret from Celine, or she's sure to write about it."

"River, please," Celine said. "It needed to be written. The public must know about what the guild is doing, especially now that they're targeting innocent people."

"The public also deserves to know what you're hiding from us," River replied. It didn't *quite* work, so she did her best to revise the sentiment on the fly. "The public being our group. All of us who are working together. We can't keep things from each other."

"Once again, I must beg we stay upon this current task, though I admit I too have noticed you've been less than forthcoming," Galwell said. He rose up, and the wind caught his hair *just right* as he strode past River and Celine toward a stairwell, his cape billowing behind him. "I will never hide. I will find this impostor myself and battle him for my honor. You said this happened on the field? Then I imagine he will be somewhere below it. If this may be my end, please let my family know I am sorry for dying again. I doubt they will forgive me, but please ask them to try."

Sighing, River followed him. "At least let me provide backup."

THIS WILL BE INTERESTING 223

"Me too," Celine chimed in.

"What do you have to offer?" River asked. "Your quill?"

It was mean, and not even the true kind of mean. Celine had proven herself quite a capable companion on more than one occasion.

"You're the one who came to get me," Celine reminded her.

River wanted to take it all back. Start everything over. Return to her childhood and prevent the acrobats from teaching her how to swing and flip. Choose a different life altogether. But there was no time. There was never enough time. Galwell was already running at a pace that required all her energy to match, and she feared what would happen if she lost him.

The stairwell took them down to the field level. Galwell used his strength to open a secured door that led to the inner workings of the stadium.

"Galwell!" Galwell yelled. "Come out at once!"

River was comforted by his dogged insistence that he was innocent. She was not, however, comforted by his reckless pursuit of justice. "If we are to find him, we should consider being quiet, for one. We should also seek the nearest washroom, where he's likely disguising himself for escape."

"That's very clever," Galwell said, turning to offer River a smile of approval.

"What can I say? The guild doesn't pay me the moderate farthings for nothing," River replied.

"Here," Celine whispered. "A washroom."

Galwell wasted no time punching through the locked door, where they found a security guard sitting atop the toilet with his pants around his ankles and a pained expression on his face.

"No! Please!" the guard yelled. "My stomach fell ill while pursuing you! I promise I will bring you no harm! I have a family! Please!"

River knew this kind of groveling well. She'd heard more than one plaintive cry from both the innocent and the guilty. Nearly everyone begged in the end, mentioning loved ones or cherished animals or whatever else they valued too much to leave behind. The times River had faced a dagger at her throat or an arrow pointed at her heart, she'd never had anything to say. There was no one who would miss her. She only knew that she would miss herself. That was how she kept her composure. She reminded herself that she'd miss her thoughts. They were entertaining. And no one else in the realm could handle her power the way she did. But there was no explaining that to someone who wanted her dead. So she'd squeeze her lips tight and stare her attacker in the eye, waiting until the very last moment to teleport herself out of the way.

Just beyond the washroom, shouting began in the tunnels.

"We've found him!" someone yelled. Another guard, River figured. "But we need backup! His strength cannot be matched!"

"Let me look first," River said. She did not know who she said it for—Galwell or Celine. Both, she supposed. They were equally likely to charge toward this situation without any forethought.

In fact, that's precisely what they did, leaving River to scramble after them.

Around the corner, a group of guards had Galwell pinned against a wall. It was a brain-aching sight, because the *real* Galwell was only a few paces to River's right. Glancing between the two, River could spot no obvious difference. The only thing this impersonator lacked was the glop of oil on his tunic.

"Well, now you've ruined it," the impersonator said in a bored voice, locking eyes with the real Galwell. "They can't know there are two of us." With unnerving ease, the impersonator shook off the guards who'd pinned him to the wall, punching them with such force that their necks cracked at unnatural angles.

Each guard crumpled to the ground.

For a brief moment, relief flooded River's system. Galwell had been telling the truth. He was still good. Rage quickly followed. For the violence this impersonator was inflicting. For his attempt to harm the real Galwell's reputation. This was the exact evil that the guild was supposed to fight against. This was what she'd been trained to stop.

River charged toward him. She had no time to reach into her satchel for the poison dart she'd intended to use on the real Galwell all those days ago. She would use her fists. It would have to be enough.

"No!" Celine screamed. "You cannot fight him! He will kill you!"

It was only when River slammed into the impersonator with the entire force of her body that she noticed he'd made no effort to resist. He was standing so still it was almost like he *wanted* River to do this.

Up close, she could see the very faint sheen of charm that coated him. Villains were fond of employing hand magic transformations to avoid detection, so River had gotten good at identifying the way the charm shimmered ever so slightly. She could see it all over this man. Even atop his clothing.

He was no Galwell the Great. Yet somehow, he had not just Galwell the Great's appearance, but also his legendary strength.

"Thank you," the impersonator said, squeezing River's shoulders so tightly it hurt.

Then he vanished into thin air.

Stunned, River looked back to a dazed Galwell. Celine had already begun checking the guards' bodies for a pulse.

"They're all dead," River said gravely. She didn't need to get up close to know. "And now he's disappeared."

A new urgency dawned on Galwell's face. "Earlier, in the Notable Persons compartment, a man grabbed my shoulders as I was leaving. It struck me then as odd, the way he'd gripped me. He'd gone out of his way to bump into me, but I was too distracted by my own inner turmoil to think about it further."

"What are you suggesting?" River asked.

"That perhaps . . . perhaps he was able to copy my power when he did that," Galwell said.

"And someone else charmed his entire appearance, even his clothing?" Celine was still checking the guards, even though they were all as dead as River had told her they were.

"It's a common practice among villains," River told her.

"Interesting," she said, reaching for the quill in her hair, then remembering herself. "So he copied Galwell's powers. And just now he copied yours?"

River knew of only one man with that kind of power. A member of the Deathrose Guild she'd never met, only heard tell of his work at various guild events.

"Yes," River said. "He's a mimic."

She almost laughed. If it was true, and he hadn't vanished, but *teleported*, then this situation was far less dire than it currently seemed. The mimic surely thought he had an advantage, borrowing her power for escape. But River had seen him up close. She could tell him and the real Galwell apart. Which meant she could successfully teleport to him, no matter where he went. And she'd had years of practice in the delicate, dangerous art of her magic.

This mimic knew nothing.

Closing her eyes, River imagined the charmed shimmer that covered him—a phony, hollow Galwell indeed.

She landed atop a snowy mountain peak.

"*Really?*" she said, her teeth already chattering as frigid winds whipped her hair every which way. "Here?"

"What?" The mimic was sitting with his knees pulled into his chest, gazing out above the clouds. "I've never seen the view from atop the Evriel Mountains."

"Who do you work for?" she asked.

"You know the answer."

"The guild would never do what you did to those guards."

"Sweetheart," the mimic cooed. The charm that disguised him was beginning to wear off. His hair was no longer red and flowing. It was short and brown, with a round patch of baldness at the crown. "The guild has new directives now."

His tunic, which had been charmed green to match Galwell's, began to fade into black. She gripped it in her hands, swirling the changing fabric around her fists. Wrinkles had begun to etch themselves into the mimic's long, sharp face.

"What does that mean?" she asked.

The mimic shoved River off him. "Ugh, fine. I'll take in the majesty of this scenery later."

He vanished.

River followed.

She would be the one to find out what had really happened to the guild. Not Celine. This was River's story to learn.

She landed in a field of sweet-smelling jasrose flowers, with florabees buzzing about, collecting nectar.

"For my girlfriend," the mimic said, arranging a makeshift bouquet. "She loves gifts."

River yanked the flowers from his hands and tossed them to the ground. "What do you mean the guild has new directives? Who is in charge? And who in the guild charmed you to look like Galwell?"

Unbothered, the mimic gathered up fresh jasroses. He didn't even have the dignity to look River in the eye as he said, "You'll never be welcomed back into the guild." He squashed a florabee beneath his boot. "You're on our list, too."

He vanished again.

The next place they landed was somewhere precarious. The mimic dangled by his fingertips from a tree branch that hung over the edge of a roaring, majestic waterfall. His jasrose bouquet had already plummeted into the raging water, and by the looks of it, the mimic was soon to follow.

The charm that disguised him had faded completely. He wore the monogrammed clothing of a stadium usher, and the haunted expression of a man staring down certain death.

River hung beside him on the branch, relishing the terrified glint in his eyes and his desperate, white-knuckle grip. She could do this all day. "Sightseeing not going like you imagined?"

"Help!" he begged. "Help!"

River pulled herself up and over the branch until she was in a front support atop it. "This is what happens when you use a power you don't understand. You end up in danger."

His fingers began to slip. His pleading intensified as he mentioned his new girlfriend, his recent promotion. The venomous sledgeling he'd captured that he hoped to keep as a pet.

"I don't care who you love or all you haven't accomplished. We're done playing teleportation tourist. *I* decide where we go next."

River hooked her leg around his torso, closing her eyes and sending them away from the waterfall. But the mimic, in his infinite ignorance, intercepted this attempt, trying to teleport in the middle of River's teleportation.

The result of the double teleportation placed them firmly in the sky, right below the clouds and falling *fast*. All River could make out below them was the uniform grass of the horseball field and the tiniest moving specks in the surrounding seats—the exiting audience.

"Tell me who runs the guild now!" River shouted. She stretched out her arms, attempting to grab hold of his shirt.

"I would rather die!" he shouted back as the wind pulled his cheeks up into his eyes.

"Farewell, then!" River said, teleporting out of the sky right as the man crashed at full speed into the horseball field.

River landed back in the tunnels, where the Farmount Falcons were making their way to their changing room, expressing their shock at what Galwell had done. Judging by their chatter, they had no idea Galwell himself was somewhere within these same tunnels, so River tiptoed past them and farther into the bowels of the stadium, until she found him and Celine.

She was dismayed to see that they had been apprehended by two security guards.

The guards were laughing, exchanging jokes as one restrained Galwell and the other had his arm wrapped around Celine's torso. Celine thrashed about, her face purple with barely contained anger.

River fought the urge to charge. With two princes potentially dead from his actions on the horseball pitch, a handful of guards dead in the tunnels, and the mimic dropped to his death on the field, carnage currently followed Galwell, and they needed to be very careful not to make him look any guiltier.

River had to do what Celine would, under normal circumstances—be the calm, collected scribe, here to gather information.

"What's happened?" she asked, stepping into view.

The guard who held Galwell looked over, smacking on a chewing leaf with loud, aggressive thwacks. "What's it to you?"

River straightened her spine. "I'm a ... member of Queen Thessia's undercover guard. She's sent me here on her behalf."

"Your queen knows perfectly well what this monster did," said the leaf-chewing guard. "He killed our prince. And he's killed these other guards, too."

"Not us, though," the second guard said. "We're too smart for him. He doesn't stand a chance. And this pretty lady—" He put his mouth right up to Celine's ear. "She was down here with him, looting their bodies for coins."

"I was *checking* their *pulses*," Celine said. Ill-concealed venom coated her tongue.

"I think I'd like to check *your* pulse." The guard licked Celine's cheek. "Maybe we will keep you for ourselves."

"Wouldn't be the first time," said the other guard.

"Apologize!" Galwell commanded. "Or I will report your disgraceful conduct to your superior."

River clenched her jaw to keep from turning feral. She hated seeing these grimy men touch Celine like that, and if she didn't need to preserve Galwell's reputation, she was quite sure she would rip them limb from limb. "Unhand them both at once!" she commanded. "On the order of the queen of Mythria!"

The guards laughed.

"*Please*. As if your queen means anything to us," said the leaf-chewing one. "Nice body, though," he told Galwell. "I could see why you'd come back from the dead for that."

River wanted to strangle both these men with her bare hands. Charging forward, she looked to Galwell, who gave her a nod, seeming to agree. Forget the consequences. Forget civility. Together, they could do away with these disgusting, hapless guards without breaking a sweat.

River threw herself atop the guard who held Celine. The leaf-chewing guard let go of Galwell, and before Galwell could get a hand on him, the guard rushed over to throw aimless punches at River and Celine.

These guards were disastrous at combat, but their reckless, chaotic swings made it impossible for her or Galwell to get a steady hand on the fight. It was a tangled, writhing mess of bodies. If River wasn't so angry, she'd have been horrified by the sloppiness of it all.

Suddenly, Celine *screamed*—a guttural, consuming sound, like a flock of carcass hawks collectively attacking their prey. Her boot connected with River's stomach, knocking all the air out of her chest.

River flopped back on her rear, dazed, gasping for breath. Galwell, stunned by the sound, backed up, too. Was Celine turning on them?

Was *Celine* the evil one?

The veins in Celine's neck had stretched so taut they looked like ropes. At once, she stopped screaming, and her face calmed into a perfect portrait of peace. River was so transfixed by this shift, she almost missed the flames.

Orange-red fire shot out of Celine's hands the same as it flowed from a welder's torch, fast and powerful, scorching a clean hole through each guard's chest.

But Celine's magical gift was everlasting memory.

So what in the Ghosts was *that*?

River tried to stand but fell over twice before she regained her footing, unable to reconnect her mind to her body. She looked around for something—a respite, an answer, a sense of understanding. All she saw were more guards rounding the corner.

All three of them were utterly *fucked*.

River rushed over to Galwell.

"We need to get you out of here," she said, her hands shaking so terribly she could barely grab hold of him to teleport.

"*No*," Galwell told her. "Take Celine. Not me. I need to clear my name."

River started to protest. Celine was not who anyone thought she was. She'd been lying to them all in more ways than River had even imagined. But an image flashed in her mind—Celine alone with more guards, taunting her and touching her and doing whatever they pleased.

She rushed over to Celine, who'd crumpled into a ball on the ground, shaking and crying.

"Leave me be!" Celine cried.

"I'm afraid I won't be doing that." River placed a hand on Celine's arm and teleported them away.

18
Galwell

What the fuck just happened?

Galwell the Great did not like profanity. He did not condone rough language where eloquence could combine clarity with courtesy. Yet in his present situation, Galwell could not help the desperate question pounding in his head.

What the ever-loving, Ghosts-damned fuck just happened?

The corpses of the guards smoldered grotesquely. This was no illusion. No, this was gruesome, and real, and . . . Celine's doing.

She'd somehow summoned fire, killing the pair of men instantly. *How?* What was more, how could she have concealed this power from everyone? He considered her his companion, his friend, though he'd not known her long. It unnerved him, witnessing what devastation waited entirely concealed under her skin.

What else was she hiding? How many other secrets were his "friends" withholding?

He felt desperately disoriented. Homesick for the realm that *made sense.*

While he stood stunned, unmoving, over the charred men, more guards rounded the corner. When they saw the man they hunted for the murder of their prince standing over more viciously slain bodies, they came to the reasonable conclusion. Crossbows flew to the ready in their hands, pointing straight at Galwell.

For the second time today, it very much looked like Galwell had killed someone. This was the worst Realm Chalice of his life, the hero thought darkly. Even worse than when the Paramar Pirates had utterly routed the Falcons, seven horse arches to zero.

He would not allow appearance to become reality. No one would die facing the genuine Galwell the Great in this stadium.

He raised his hands in surrender.

"I know it looks like I am guilty of horrible crimes today," he said, speaking slowly and clearly. "I assure you I am not, but I trust justice to prevail, and I understand you must arrest me. It is your job. I do not wish for further bloodshed."

The guards exchanged looks. Admittedly, the smoking corpses in front of Galwell offered little corroboration of his peaceable intentions. The men reluctantly closed in, crossbows raised warily.

Galwell would clear his name. He knew he would. He would submit himself to the king and queen's justice. Honorable judicial thoroughness would prevail.

None of it would change how carnage and chaos had reigned this day. Sadness settled over him slowly.

He knelt, compliantly putting his hands behind his back, hoping this would help matters.

When the guards descended on him, wrestling him into restraints despite his lack of resistance, he caught—in the shadows—a flash of shimmering purple.

Mona watched, unseen by the guards. In her gaze he found . . . concern.

Would this day never cease to surprise him?

While he was not in the fondest spirits regarding his relationship with Mona, right now was *not* for irritating, incomprehensible romantic jealousies. Mona was . . . Damn it, Mona was his friend, too, or something like it. Something close enough that he did not wish for the guards to spot her, too.

As the men hauled him to his feet, Galwell thought very intently, *I'll be fine. We will sort this out.*

Mona looked to him, hearing his thought.

She chewed the inside of her cheek, lingering on the edge of the shadows. As if she wanted to come forth and defend him.

She didn't, for which Galwell could not fault her. She was still Mona the Merciless, her reputation preceding her. Criminal notoriety did not exactly lend itself to leaping into the midst of law enforcement proceedings. She started to withdraw into the darkness.

Tell the others I'm being taken into custody, Galwell thought loudly.

Mona nodded. Then she vanished into the shadows.

Without resistance, Galwell permitted the guards to lead him through the hallways and out of the stadium. Sunlight stabbed his eyes.

He moved slowly, keeping his head bowed, trying his very best to reassure the very nervous guards.

They were reaching the city streets when he heard the first shout.

Not of horror or rage. The sound was one of disgust.

Passersby had glimpsed him emerging from the stadium in custody. The cacophony grew—gasps, now of horror, conjoined with jeering, snarling, and insults Galwell had never heard in his life. *For him.*

As he and the guards continued forth, Vestriyans started hurling trash at him. Shankfries and spice-salted potatoes and spat sizzle crystals from the Realm Chalice poured down on Galwell and the guards. When they'd nearly reached the prison cart, someone's half-full flagon of mead struck him directly in the chest, dousing him.

He understood the people's ire. They were hurting, frightened. Looking for someone to pin their pain on. They thought he'd murdered their beloved future king.

But he'd never had people react to him with such loathing. Never. He was their villain.

He hated it.

Though he sympathized with his tormentors, Galwell still found himself quietly furious. None of this was his fault. Try though he might—his entire life was out of his control these days. He felt foolish, possessed of gargantuan strength yet unable to exert control where it counted. What good was hefting hroxen when he couldn't defend his own destiny?

The guards stowed him inside the barred carriage while the venomous crowd continued their tirade. Finally, the horses took off down the royal boulevard and Galwell realized where they were escorting him.

The palazzo. Where the king and queen of Vestriya waited.

Attendees from the match ran behind the carriage, eager to hear the crown's judgment. Eager for his downfall. Galwell did his best to hold himself up straight in his shackles. When the carriage halted outside the palace, Galwell lifted his head high. The king and queen were mourning, he reminded himself. Their suffering was far greater than his own. He would help them get justice for their loss. Honor would prevail.

Soldiers held the crowd back as they escorted Galwell from the carriage into the castle. When the heavy iron doors closed behind him, the sounds of jeering faded into an angry echo, replaced by his footsteps and the clanking of his chained wrists.

Upon reaching the throne room, Galwell knelt. Neither the king nor queen stood. The deadliest hush Galwell had ever heard descended over the gilded room.

"Galwell True," the king pronounced. "You were welcomed into our realm as a guest. We have always shared strong ties with your homeland. The fact you would attack us is . . . a grave disappointment."

Galwell cleared his throat, eyes downcast in respect. Heroism de-

THIS WILL BE INTERESTING

manded honesty. He wished the king and queen no further grief, but he would not honor falsehoods.

"Your Highness, I did no such thing," he replied. "It was an assassin. He was magicked to look like me and possessed his own hand magic to mimic others' powers. This is a plot—a conspiracy against us both."

The king's expression did not change. The queen shifted in her seat with what looked like impatience.

Galwell felt his cheeks flame. Yes, he heard how his protestation sounded. Like Elowen when she'd shattered their mother's precious glass vase playing horseball on broomsticks indoors and blamed wood sprites for the misdeed.

"And the guards beneath the coliseum?" the king returned. "Was there yet another assassin wearing your face standing over them?"

"No," Galwell replied miserably. "But it wasn't me. I didn't kill anyone."

The king leaned forward quickly. "Who did, then?" he snapped.

The sudden viciousness on the man's soft features, his skin like fine suede, startled Galwell, but the hero held his tongue hesitantly. He was experiencing ignominy for the first time and very much disliking it. But to betray his companions, his crew? Then he would be a villain even to himself. He knew not what had happened with Celine, but he would not disavow his friend.

He shut his mouth. He hung his head.

The king withdrew, frowning—

"Galwell!"

A door behind the thrones flew open.

"Galwell, are you all right?" Thessia cried out, breathless from rushing there.

"I'm sorry." The king spoke to Galwell despite Thessia's interruption. "You leave me with no choice. You have killed the heir to

Vestriya, our son, and gravely wounded our second son and the only future we have now."

"What?" Thessia interjected, her gaze whipping to the king and queen. "Prince Ario is—"

Vestriya's queen cut Thessia off coldly. "He was injured in the attack as well," she insisted. "Our healers have fought to preserve his life, but he sleeps. We don't know if he will wake."

Yet Thessia, Galwell found, only looked wary. Her confusion changed into guarded poise. *Odd.*

"That doesn't make sense," she replied.

"Stand over the lifeless body of your first son," the queen hissed, "and then you may lecture me on what *makes sense.*"

Thessia's mouth worked, like she wanted to refute the queen's point but knew not how. Galwell's hurting heart went out to her, too.

"Galwell, we charge you with conspiracy and violence against the crown," the king of Vestriya declared.

The hero hardly heard him, so preoccupied was he with everyone else—yes, he might be the one in custody, but Ario was wounded, his friends were separated, who knew what was happening with Celine.

"For these crimes, we sentence you to be executed. Immediately."

At last, Galwell looked up.

Thessia's face had gone utterly pale, her fine features horror stricken. It was the first thing he noted. Not the king's and queen's uncompromising expressions, nor even . . . whatever he felt, hearing his death sentence be handed down.

He was . . . numb. His blood pounded in his ears. Thessia's distress commanded his focus. What did it mean that even now, his first feeling was for her? The desire to spare her the pain of the royal judgment, not his own sense of self-preservation?

Was it ironic? Was it just . . . Galwell?

Is it the same stupid noblesse that got me here? whispered something from shadowy corners of his thoughts.

Fear descended over him. He'd died once, he reminded himself. This should not scare him.

The reason it did, he knew, were the circumstances. Galwell would *not* reprise his first death, defeating villainy, sparing his friends. He would die in dishonor. In disrepute, with dishonest sentences hung on him. He would die unjustly impugned for ignominious crimes.

He'd hoped he would *inspire* hope. The Vestriyan judgment would not only kill a man—it would rewrite a legacy.

That was what Galwell feared.

"You cannot," Thessia struggled to get out. "He's Mythrian. He's under my rule."

"On our land," the king returned. "Where he slew our prince. We have the utmost respect for Mythria and the long-standing friendship of our realms. But Galwell's crimes are too grave to go unpunished. There must be consequences," he pronounced. "Even you must consent to let your subjects face punishment when within our borders."

Thessia looked shattered. Galwell knew the king's judgment made horrible sense. He was on the verge of interjecting when Thessia seemed to collect her shattered pieces. Her spine straightened. She faced the Vestriyan couple like fucking royalty.

"Galwell is *not* my subject," she returned. Imperiousness flickered like magic fire in her forceful syllables.

She turned, meeting his gaze. Galwell saw something there, some significance, but he could not understand it. Thessia's expression wavered, then went calm with carefully controlled panic. She looked back to the king and queen.

"He is my betrothed," she stated.

Gasps came from the guards, the queen—from everyone. Galwell heard one come from himself. He stared in wordless wonder at Thessia.

Incredibly, she now looked perfectly composed. Courageous, even, in her solemn pronouncement. She continued. "Sentencing him to death without fair trial would be an act of war against our realm."

"Your—betrothed?" the king sputtered. "You do realize you're here on your honeymoon with another?"

Thessia looked past Galwell, her expression somehow serene. Glancing over his shoulder where he knelt captive, Galwell realized Hugh had entered the throne room from the direction the guards had led Galwell.

Hugh held his wife's gaze with fraught emotion that Galwell had never witnessed on his rugged features.

"My queen doesn't lie," he said. "Our marriage was a sham."

He walked into the room with quick, even strides, looking at once entirely certain and yet somehow fragile.

"As everyone in our realm knows, Thessia was betrothed to Galwell True in her youth. When we learned he had returned to life on the night of our wedding, we never consummated our marriage," he went on, voice stiff—nothing like the charming man whose honest goodness made charisma come easily. "We knew it would not be right," he explained. "Thessia always wanted to honor the promises of her youth. But more than her promises, her feelings for this hero have never faded."

Galwell was dizzy now.

Her—her feelings? Nothing Hugh said made sense, yet it . . . sounded impossibly plausible. Galwell could not understand how Hugh and Thessia could have made this plan so quickly, entirely unspoken.

Still, they *must* have consummated their marriage. They were in love. He was certain of it.

"We were waiting for the right time to tell my people," Thessia rejoined quietly, "while still respecting the other hero my realm loves—Sir Hugh."

She looked like her heart was splitting right down the middle. Galwell had to force himself to watch.

She fought past the pain to face the king and queen, whose eyes were rounded, their complexions peculiar shades of pinkish white.

"You cannot execute the future king of Mythria," Thessia concluded. "Not without—what was it you said?"

She fixed her unflinching stare on the king.

"*Consequences*," she repeated.

The king stared Thessia down. Galwell fought to remain compliantly on his knees when everything in him revolted.

He hated this. Not just the part where he'd received his sentence of execution. He hated the helplessness—the *consequences* his hapless presence wrought on everyone else. He was meant to protect his loved ones, not the reverse. Especially not when it cost Thessia and Hugh the unimaginable declaration they'd just made. He was the *hero*, damn it.

But everything had changed since his death. He knew not how to be a hero in this time. He knew not if they even existed.

"You say he is the future king and yet you remain married to another. Your realm knows nothing of your so-called plans," the king said. "If you *were* married, of course we would *never* open such hostilities." He exaggerated his words, his mocking implications clear. "However, you are not yet."

"I'll marry him tonight. Just give me time to dissolve my marriage to Hugh," Thessia offered quickly, her eyes darting to Hugh's with what Galwell knew to be regret.

"I do not think that would be wise," the queen warned. "We must wonder at the intentions of any ally of ours marrying a man accused of murdering our son."

"I wonder at any ally of *mine* questioning my judgment or my honesty," Thessia returned stonily.

The king's stare didn't waver, holding Thessia's mercilessly.

"Very well, then," he finally said. "Let us have your consequences." He nodded to his men.

"Transport this criminal to the Black Keep. We execute him tonight."

Galwell watched rage warp Thessia's features. He could not hear her furious protests, not over the devastating rush that consumed his thoughts.

It is really happening. Galwell the Great's improbable second life would end on the meaningless point of a misguided sword. Or meaningless drop of poison. Or meaningless obsidian glint axe. He did not know how they handled executions in Vestriya.

The point was, it was horribly, hilariously, wretchedly *worthless*. He had returned to life only to destroy his own legacy.

The men hauled him through the palace, then outside, where onlookers continued to jeer. It started to rain. Galwell felt like he'd stepped into some time-slowing fog, some warping dark magic. Every moment seemed to stretch forever. Galwell could see every grimace, every foul gesture, every word of condemnation forming on the mouths of everyone he passed.

Hugh's words echoed in his head. *Our marriage was a sham. Our marriage was a sham.*

Galwell had admired Hugh for his honesty. He considered the man's genuineness equal to Galwell's own—except when Hugh was praising Ario's verses. Hugh would not lie to escape danger this way.

Yet the king of Mythria's voice had sounded impossibly steady. Frighteningly earnest. *Our marriage was a sham.*

How?

THIS WILL BE INTERESTING

Either Hugh had lied to the king of Vestriya just now . . . or he'd lied to *everyone*, the entire realm, for months.

First Celine. Now possibly Hugh and Thessia. Galwell's head spun. Was no one, even those closest to him, honest in themselves? What was next? Would River reveal she could change into a wolverling under the full moon's light?

The rain plastered his hair to his face. The sky warped with ugly contours of ominous gray. He trudged over uneven flagstones, over the black water puddling in the cracks. When he reached the prison cart, shackles were locked onto his feet.

The sound of the clamping chains returned him to himself.

If he stepped into the waiting prison carriage, he would be executed. He, Galwell the Once-Great. Thessia could not save him. She could not marry him while he was in custody. Not that he'd ever welcomed the notion of needing rescue. The real villains had vanished, out of his reach.

Galwell gazed up into the stormy sky.

He was no hero. Not here. No longer. What had heroism earned him in this shadowland? His party shattered. His feet shackled. What was the point? Why cling to honor and virtue?

When one of the guards tried to push him forward, Galwell didn't move.

The man's elbow struck his enormous back without effect. The men redoubled their efforts, but Galwell the Great was strong. These men did not know how strong he was. How much they were never in control.

He stood, statuesque, motionless in the rain. His guards did not realize they'd only managed to constrain him due to his oh-so-Ghosts-damned noble cooperation. Only his honor held him in chains.

Well, *fuck* that.

With one powerful stomp, Galwell shattered the Vestriyan metal around his ankles. He pivoted, pummeling one of his guards with enough force to send the man flying.

More guards descended on him—Galwell flung them off easily, hurling them ten irons with flicks of his hands. With rain whipping from his drenched red locks and the swift, sweeping movement of his fists, he was a one-man maelstrom.

When his captors were subdued, Galwell let the storm pound down on him. Turning his back on the prison carriage, he did something he'd never done before.

He ran.

With the rain coming heavier, Galwell fled through the city, knowing he'd destroyed the final pieces of his reputation. He did not slow down. He ran past shadowy street corners, past shrieking pedestrians, into the crumbiello shop he remembered. Down the inconspicuous stairs, where he pounded on the secret door.

Please. Please, he thought loudly. *Please. I need you.*

He was reaching up to redouble his pounding when the door opened from within.

Mona for once looked shocked, beholding Galwell dripping wet, his heroic head hung low. She did not gloat or smirk.

He spoke now. "Please, Mona," he implored. "I need you. I need—I need you to hide me."

With her stare on him, Galwell felt her reading his thoughts, learning what had happened. Upon the conclusion of her examination, something like sympathy settled over Mona the Merciless. She opened the door wider.

"Come inside," she said. "Fugitives are always welcome with me."

Realm Chalice Chaos: Prince Slain, Other Prince Gravely Wounded, Mythrian "Hero" on Run

by Rocklin Thorpe, *Voice of Vestriya* staff reporter

What do you get when you invite Mythrians to the Realm Chalice? Utter chaos.

The *Voice of Vestriya* had uncommonly low hopes for the Realm Chalice entering the year's seminal match for one reason: The sluggish gameplay of the Farmount Falcons, led by provocateur striker Zevan Wintersmith, whose gameplay is all style and no substance. The *Voice* was, we dare say, looking forward to critiquing the sloppy form of Wintersmith's team on the pitch as they contended with the superb horsemanship of our own Cascara Cleavers.

Unfortunately, neither inexpert ballhandling nor lugubrious passing plays were the worst of what this scribe, not to mention the entire realm, witnessed on the Realm Chalice pitch. Our crown prince was assassinated. Worse, Mythrians were responsible. Yes, while this scribe could hardly imagine leaving the stadium holding one of Zevan Wintersmith's realmsmen in *lower* esteem than the pompous player himself, none other than Mythrian so-called hero Galwell the so-called Great murdered in cold royal blood our Prince Ezio, hurling a horseball at the head of the unsuspecting prince. (Nice form, notably. Were Sir Galwell not prone to political violence, he could have found honest wages on the horseball pitch.)

Reports directly from the crown confirm the younger prince, Ario, was also attacked. How could this happen? In our realm?

I don't know. I'm a sports scribe, for Ghost's sake.

What we know for certain comes directly from the Vestriyan crown: Prince Ezio is dead. His brother, Prince Ario, was severely wounded and is recuperating in his chambers and unresponsive.

In this dark time for Vestriya, we don't even have horseball to cheer us. The Realm Chalice has been canceled.

19
River

All was quiet at the circus.

River knew this kind of silence well, though it had been years since she'd last heard its uniquely hollow quality—a yawning, eager emptiness, waiting to be filled up with music and spectators. For now, the performers sat in their closed tents, stretching out sore limbs and resting tired eyes before donning their costumes for another night of dazzling spectacle. The rides and food stalls stood unattended, looking much more worn down in daytime than they did under the evening's glowing magicked orbs.

River and Celine had landed inside the carousel. There was no ride attendant to make it spin. No other guests to sit on the paint-chipped benches or atop the backs of faded pastel figures of horses and dragons.

Celine's eyes were rimmed red from tears. A sleeve of her blouse had been scorched by her own flames.

"I knew we would be safe here," River said. "The last thing the performers want to do with their time off is walk around the grounds. And in all my years in the guild, I've never heard another assassin express an interest in seeing what a circus looks like during the day. Good thing is, if anyone does happen to find us, I suppose you can just blast them with fire, right?" She needed to address this as soon as possible, or she might let Celine do what she always did—fascinate her in some other way, discussing a book she'd read, or an idea she'd wanted to explore, or a memory she'd held on to in stunning completion. It had all been a distraction. Smoke and mirrors Celine had put up to hide behind.

Yes, the circus was the right place to go, indeed. Celine was just as much a performer as the rest of these people.

"You can recite conversations we had almost fifteen years ago like they just happened yesterday," River said. "You recall details about the people we meet like you're not a person but an encyclopedia. Yet just now you set those men on fire with your hands. That was magic, I know it was."

Celine said nothing, biting her lip to keep it from trembling.

"I've known for a while you had a secret," River continued. "I've been falling over myself trying to figure out what it could be. I never could've guessed this."

The silence pressed down on her. She wished for music or spectacle to distract her from the suffocating pain of this betrayal, but she had nothing but her own feelings, as she was finally forced to confront them in their entirety.

"Say something!" she shouted.

"I was born with the hand magic gift of fire." Celine's voice was so quiet that even the silence seemed to lean in to hear her. "I don't know how to control it. I can't conjure it at will, and I can't make it stop at will, either. I learned a very long time ago that the best way to prevent the fire from starting was to distract myself. I buried the threat of magic with curiosity and knowledge and obsessive attention to detail. For years, it's worked. But something in me broke inside that tunnel. The way they framed Galwell. The mimic killing those men. The guards harassing me. Knowing the harpies had made my volatile magic even stronger. I couldn't stop the fire from rising up."

Fresh tears fell down her cheeks. She wiped them away, but it was fruitless. New ones came just as fast.

River had the overwhelming urge to comfort her. She wanted to hold Celine until the tears stopped. Tell her everything was going to be okay. But that would be another lie.

And River was done with lies.

Instead, she dug her nails into her palms. The sensation was dissatisfying. Nothing distracted her from the hurt.

"I have never had everlasting memory," Celine continued. "At least not magically so."

"I see," River said.

"Whatever it is you think of me now, believe me, I've thought it of myself for far longer and with much more loathing. So go ahead and see me as the real dangerous one between us. I already knew it would happen this way. I've never wanted to be defined by this magic, but I suppose I can't stop that anymore."

"You thought I would reject you for this," River said. "But I don't care at all about your 'dangerous' fire power. When have you ever known me to fear danger?"

Celine said nothing, shoulders trembling as she leaned against a lavender carousel horse.

"Exactly. I know you didn't mean to kill those men, as evil as they seemed to be. Who would I be to judge you for that? I'm an assassin for a guild that might have been making me kill people far more innocent than those men anyway. I've gone along with countless assignments without questioning the validity of the accused's crimes. I might have killed a dozen Galwells and not even known it."

It was River's turn to fight back tears.

"I care that I shared with you things I've never told another soul," she continued, pushing past the dangerous quiver in her throat. "I care that I trusted you, despite myself. I've never lied to you about my nature. Yet all this time, you've been lying about what you can do. Not just here. But always. For as long as I've known you, you've lied. *That's* what hurts the most. Everything about my life has been a lie. The guild isn't what they used to be. Maybe they never were. And now this . . . this . . . *thing* with you and me—whatever it is—isn't real, either."

River shouldn't have said it, but she couldn't help herself. Why not suffer one last indignity by addressing the simmering tension that had existed between them since the very first moment they reunited in the Mythrian alleyway? What did it matter anymore if Celine didn't feel it, too? Let it be one last thing for Celine to burn.

But Celine still had another surprise up her charred sleeve.

She kissed River hard, pressing them together with such intensity that they leaned into the handle of the wheel at the center of the carousel. The ride began to lightly spin, with its accompanying music starting up in a gentle twinkle.

All of River's anger floated away, replaced with insatiable curiosity. The feeling of Celine's lips. The grip of her hand on River's neck. She was soft but determined. Shy yet commanding. It was a paradox of sensations, and River lost herself in it, wrapping her arms around Celine, reaching under the fabric of her untucked blouse to feel for her skin beneath. She wanted to know every last bit of her. Run her fingers through the muss of her curls.

"*This* is real," Celine whispered, her breath quick and hot. "And I've wanted it forever."

Words River had never even dreamed of hearing. Maybe to Celine, they were the truth. But to River, they were a fantasy.

All of this was.

River pushed Celine off her, wiping her mouth as if she could somehow erase the memory, the traitorous tingle of desire that still coursed through her. "We're done here."

Oh, how she wished she could laugh. Or even cry.

But she could do nothing.

"If you've wanted me forever, you should've told me the truth much sooner," she said. "I'm done playing pretend. I never want to see you again."

She leapt from the edge of the carousel to the ground.

"Where are you going?" Celine called out after her.

River didn't owe her an answer, but she gave one anyway. "No matter what happens, you and I will never work out, so why bother pretending we can? It's an insult to us both. I'm going after the guild. I'm taking them down before they can take me first, and I'm making sure they don't come after you, either. It's my final act for you. Don't bother to follow. Don't try to find me. Let me leave in peace."

It didn't matter if the guild itself no longer followed the rules. River still would. And she was done breaking the first one she'd ever made for herself—never surrender your heart.

She rounded the corner, leaving Celine and the carousel behind for good. This would be the start of the rest of her life. This would be how she fixed everything. As she walked, she forced herself to tilt her head toward the sun, hoping the brightness would expedite her healing process. It already hurt too much, and she knew this was only a fragment of the pain to come.

She paused, squeezing her eyes shut, the blinding midday light turning the inside of her eyelids a glowing red.

It wasn't much, but it was a start.

Until someone came up and sucker punched her in the face, and everything went dark.

20
Thessia

What a honeymoon.

Thessia had fought back tears for the past several hours over Galwell's safety and whatever remained of her relationship with Hugh—not to mention her political position in Vestriya.

All were utterly ruined. She was engaged to a man whom she did not love, who did not love her, and she was struggling to keep the realms from war.

Deep down, Thessia felt guilty. For once, she'd seized her own independence. For once, she'd flattered herself with the pretense of leading her own questing party.

Look where it had gotten them. What a queen she was. *Thessia the Thoughtless*, she deemed herself darkly. *Thessia the Terrible*.

She stood now in front of the guards preventing her from entering Ario's chambers in the Vestriyan palace. Guards she knew—guards with whom she'd drunk just the other night. It felt like years ago, her moments of inspired, inebriated liberation. When she was, if only for one night, gloriously free.

Thessia knew it was nothing short of miraculous that the guards were not throwing her out of the palace entirely. Instead, she would continue her residency under the royal roof, though she suspected the king and queen only permitted this in order to spy on her.

The peace with Vestriya was, put generously, tentative. Galwell had escaped without Thessia's help, fortunately. The Vestriyan crown could not blame Mythria for his misdeeds without outright war. However, if they found the formerly heroic fugitive, they would kill him.

Thessia hoped he was very, very far from here. Out of the city or even the realm, if possible. If *she* found him, she would have to marry him in hopes of reversing the king's rash, vengeful judgment and preventing war.

While Thessia's presence in the palace was for the moment entertained, her permissions, however, were unsurprisingly restricted. She'd ventured to Ario's chambers to investigate the only problem she could—the rumors of the other prince's injuries.

She had watched Ario leave with the fallen Ezio, panicked but entirely unharmed. None of the conjurations captured Ario clearly, however, and the scribes were reporting uniformly that the prince was bedridden.

"Please," Thessia implored the chamber guards. "I only wish to offer my support to the healing prince."

Remorse flickered over the guards' faces. "No one is to be admitted," one replied reluctantly. "King's orders."

Thessia chewed her lip. She did not want to push matters with the king, not with how precarious their relationship was right now.

Yet she needed to do *something*. Only the hope of helping, of furthering justice or protecting her silver-haired poetical friend, quieted the guilt pounding in her exhausted heart.

"He must be so lonely," she insisted. "I brought poetry to read to him."

She held up the book she'd found in her room—*Voluminous and Visionary Verses for the Vivification of Our Fair Realm*. The title did not inspire confidence, leaving Thessia wondering why they had not gone with *Fair Vestriya*, which seemed to be right there.

The guard hesitated, looking torn by the thoughtful gesture.

"Look." He dropped his voice. "He's not even here. He's been moved to the Pale Palace."

Thessia startled. The Pale Palace was renowned even in Mythria for employing unconventional methods to solve impossible medical problems. Some swore by the unimaginable gifts of its hand magicians, whose underground studies—for the purpose of concealing their practices—gave them the ghostly complexions for which their place of healing was named. Others found their methods . . . less commendable.

The other guard shifted uncomfortably. "The king doesn't want anyone to know how vulnerable the throne is right now," he offered.

"I hear he's recovering slowly. There's no need to worry," the first guard reassured Thessia, seeing her widened eyes.

Thessia respectfully disagreed. There was, she felt, very much reason to worry.

She knew she would get nowhere convincing these noble guards of the suspicions starting to form within the fog of doubt in her mind, however. Nor did she need the king knowing of her concern for Ario's condition, given her connection to his other son's alleged assassin. She smoothed her features. "Very well," she replied gently. "Thank you for your time. Please tell me if there is anything I can do to help the prince."

She started to leave, having meant the offer only in idle pretense of her generosity.

"Your Highness?" The man spoke hesitantly. "There is one thing . . ."

Thessia spun, inquisitive.

"Wait here," the guard requested.

He entered Ario's chambers quickly and shut the door. Thessia did what he asked, uncomprehending. She fought down the hope starting to speed her heart. Was it possible she'd gained their confidence enough for them to provide her more confidential information? More indication of Ario's safety, or his peril?

Instead, when the door reopened, the guard returned carrying a glass container. Inside, Thessia found Benjamin the snail.

Or, Benjamin's shell, really. While she could glimpse the chartreuse creature inside, Benjamin had withdrawn in fear, or discontent, or possibly—Thessia feared—mourning. Or perhaps he was hungry.

"Can you take care of him?" the guard implored. "The king has declined to make arrangements for him. Right now, me and the guys are taking turns sneaking in to feed and clean his habitat. But—if you don't mind, it would be less dangerous for us if—"

Thessia gently took the container from him. "Of course I will," she reassured him. She noticed Benjamin emerge just a little from his shell when he heard her voice. "I'll keep him safe until Ario returns," she promised.

At the mention of Ario's name, Benjamin's eye stalks extended. He twirled them excitedly. Thessia could not help smiling slightly.

"Thank you, Your Highness," the guards each replied.

Returning to her chambers, Thessia felt, improbably, how responsibility for the snail heartened her. *This* was something to do. Not perhaps for Galwell, or Mythria, or her friends, but for someone—someone slimy and horseball-sized, yes, but important nonetheless—who needed her help.

The fortified feeling lasted until Thessia opened her chamber doors.

Hugh's suitcases were half packed on the cushioned coverlet of their royal bed. He stood over them, calmly returning his clothing to his luggage. He said nothing when she entered.

The sight's wounding shock to Thessia's heart was instantaneous. Pretending to ignore him, and therefore her hurt, she continued into the bathing chamber, where she opened Benjamin's container, lifted out the compliant snail and placed him on the cool stone. She felt bad he'd probably spent much longer than usual cooped up. When she picked some flowers from the plants flourishing on the windowsill and placed them in the marble tub, Benjamin slimed over to them happily.

Forcing her steps, she returned to the bedchamber. Though the political situation demanded Thessia remain in the palace, she knew Hugh could not. Their precarious position, including Galwell's safety, relied on the painful truth they'd just told the king of Vestriya. They were, officially, no longer on their royal honeymoon.

Still.

While Thessia had made the sacrifice of her declaration willingly, she was not expecting how much it would hurt to see Hugh go. Heroism had its price, she found herself realizing. Galwell had long known this—Galwell, who had in their youth intended to marry her out of honor. Galwell, who had laid down his life to save his friends and his realm.

She'd never fully recognized everything he did for her, for Mythria, too wrapped up instead in her own frustration with being the one needing to be saved.

Now she understood. Now it was her turn.

Hugh packed slowly, still silent. His fingers folded his clothing, the well-stitched but unpretentious, unshowy garments Thessia knew he preferred. *His fingers*—the same ones she'd watched strum desire on his harp just the other night, pulling her heartstrings now.

Remembering that night, Thessia decided that while Galwell knew more than she of heroism's costs, she'd learned something the hero hadn't. Sometimes, she had to claim the small happiness she could *while* she could.

"Hugh," she said softly.

"I'll be out soon," he murmured. "I promise."

He would not meet her gaze. *Will he miss me? Is he feeling heartbroken like I am?* She dared not entertain the possibility. Likelier he was frustrated. He felt foolish, or scorned. Chances were, he would never forgive her.

Still.

"I know," Thessia persisted. "I just—I'm sorry things had to end this way for us."

When Hugh smiled sadly, it let the quickest sliver of hope into her heart. Perhaps he did not hate her for this.

"Me too," he replied simply.

The sliver opened wider, into a reckless rush. Hugh reached for the shirt folded next to his suitcase.

Thessia put her hand on his.

He did not look up. "We can't," he said with quiet urgency. "If they were to find out . . . Galwell would have nothing to protect him."

The rush was now a roar. For in Hugh's furtive declaration, Thessia heard everything felt but not said.

She stared, hoping to force him to meet the unwavering demand in her eyes.

"Can't what, Hugh?" she returned breathlessly.

Now he did meet her gaze.

Thessia saw what she felt raging within herself. She recognized the fire in his eyes. When he did not reply, she summoned her courage. Sometimes courage was for heroism. But sometimes, she determined, it could be for *her*.

"If we find Galwell, I'll have to marry him," she said.

Hugh's knuckles whitened as he squeezed his poor shirt. "I know."

"I'll be signing away any chance of passion I could have had—forever. He and I don't feel that way for each other. I'll never—" She swallowed. "I'll never know what it's like."

"Thess." Hugh's voice was stripped raw.

It nearly stripped her raw. *Thess*. Like in his carriage. More memories, rending her soul with miserable, unbearable need.

"I thought when we made our arrangement, I would be content with never knowing," she went on. Every word was a step over sharp crystals, but the queen of Mythria kept going. This conversation was its own quest, its own perilous journey to something Thessia could only begin to imagine. "But now . . ." she said, staring right into Hugh's glorious dark eyes. "Now I know what I'm losing."

She wanted to reach out. She wanted to touch him. She *wanted*. But she would not surrender to wanton impulses. She needed him to know she meant everything she said.

"You said you don't pursue physical relationships because you know you cannot give all of yourself," she went on. "Well, there's no danger of me asking for all of you, is there?"

His free hand rose to her elbow. Then rose higher, until he was caressing her arm. Something strained his gentle grip. Sympathy warring with want. "It wouldn't make this easier," he said.

"No." Thessia shook her head, not giving up. "Not easier. But we don't always do things because they're easier."

She stepped closer to him, his hand still on her.

"We do them because they're worth doing. Because one night can be . . . everything. Even if we're like doomed players in a Chestlewitt play."

The reference made Hugh smile his same sad smile.

Then his gaze met hers. Thessia watched the moment something in him changed.

His smile turned subtler, more slyly determined. This was the dauntless, world-ready Hugh Mavaris she knew. The man she was—*oh, fuck it, why deny it*—falling for, deeply. Irrevocably, she feared. Even if he didn't feel the same for her, even if he never could. He wanted her. That was enough. That was something to hold on to forever.

"One night," he repeated in a low rumble.

Thessia nodded.

Hugh's eyes dropped, then raked up her body on the way back to her face. Her waiting mouth.

Thessia practically shivered, for she no longer just felt want. She felt *wanted*. It lit her up like magic.

"Best make the most of it, then," Hugh said.

When Thessia threw herself at him, he caught her. He lifted her easily, pulling them close, consuming her with kisses.

"I thought," Hugh said when their lips parted for a fragile moment, "you said you didn't like being carried."

Thessia grinned into his mouth, remembering her foolish, futile words on their ship of passage.

"I liked it too much," she confessed. "Even then."

In wordless reply, Hugh tossed her onto the bed, then followed, climbing slowly up her body, trailing his nose up every one of her curves.

He kissed her passionately, hard, on the mouth. Now his caresses didn't fill only her with music. Now they were a duet.

Hugh clasped her thigh, pulling her knee upward while he clenched her ass. She plunged her hand down, feeling the hard length of him through the fabric of his pants. He moaned. She sighed into his mouth.

When she grabbed his hand, relocating it exactly where she wanted under her skirts, Hugh didn't miss a note. With the finesse she remembered from his fingers on his harp, he delved into her with perfect dexterous intensity.

Gasping, Thessia started to undress him.

She felt like a queen often. Until now, she'd never felt like a woman who had everything.

As she ripped off his shirt, Hugh returned the favor, peeling off her skirts, her corset, her underclothes, until she lay naked beneath him.

Exposed under his gaze, she felt as if her skin were pure moonlight. She heard sounds she hardly recognized, sobs of joy, waiting in her throat. Waiting for *him*.

His eyes roved over her like he was starving.

"Please," he managed, "permit me a moment just to look at you. It's been . . . years since I—"

Thessia sat up, shocked. Had he not been with a woman since Zaralie died? "I—didn't know," she said, fumbling for the right words. "I know you haven't loved since her, but I figured you had . . . other desires."

His eyes rose from her body to meet her gaze. Their intensity silenced every concern, indeed every thought in her head, entirely. The insistent rhythm of the pounding of her heart filled her ears.

"Not like this, Thess," he said quietly. "Nothing like this."

Nothing like this.

Nothing like this.

"With you, I—I feel like I'm out of my mind sometimes with how much I want you," he confessed. The words conjured deep, powerful magic in Thessia. Hugh hesitated, then spoke gently. "Have you ever . . . ?"

Thessia nodded. "Only fumbling one-night stands with visiting royals. Nothing that ever satisfied me," she said honestly. When Hugh's expression flickered, she looked at him more keenly. "Does it bother you I've been with others? I suppose you probably assumed—"

His laughter made her cheeks heat, but she knew not entirely why. Was it more embarrassing if he thought her too experienced or not experienced enough? Why was nothing ever uncomplicated?

THIS WILL BE INTERESTING

"Ghosts no," Hugh replied. "I just hope I live up to expectations. Satisfying a queen is tough work."

The tension left Thessia immediately. The rush—relief combined with sweet prelude—emboldened her. She rose to her knees to kiss him deeply, pressing her breasts into the hard plane of his chest, feeling the thrill in her stomach when her nipples met his unyielding musculature.

"Is it?" she whispered when she withdrew from the kiss. "I think satisfying royalty is fairly easy."

She lowered her lips to his neck and reached down slowly to grasp the length of him. He bowed his head with a shuddering exhale.

"Simply," Thessia instructed, "do as I say."

She felt Hugh's smirk. "You'd like to give me orders?"

"Only if you'd like to follow them," she replied.

Slowly, teasingly, he drew his hands up to her breasts, sparking rough pleasure in her with his calloused fingertips. His eyes were dark with desire. "I'm your willing subject, my queen," he promised.

It was everything—*everything*—Thessia wanted.

She wordlessly directed him to lie beneath her, repositioning them so she was on top. Straddling him, she sank down onto him so slowly that Hugh's breath escaped in a moan that sounded like a hum. Desire shot through her. Whether from his gift or simply from the sound itself, she would never know.

With Hugh deep inside her, she moved slowly, finding their new rhythm, pleasure mounting in her. Hugh's hands roamed over her incessantly like he was desperate to experience every part of her. Heroically, he held out until she'd found her crescendo, then lost himself within her.

In the darkness, everything vanished into the echo, the consuming embrace of their one night, ringing in her ears like whole symphonies of shattering joy.

* * *

When Thessia woke, he was gone.

Fighting the tears in her throat, Thessia reminded herself she knew this was coming. As with her sham marriage to Hugh, she knew the terms. She knew what *one night* would mean. It meant tomorrow would come without mercy.

On her pillowcase was a folded parchment. Opening the scrap, she found Hugh's handwriting.

You will always be the song of my heart I cannot sing.

Tears filled her eyes. Was it possible he felt more than desire for her? She would never know for certain, she supposed. Clamping her quivering lips together, Thessia held the note close, memorizing every facet of Hugh's handwriting. She knew she could not add the note to her box of keepsakes for fear of discovery, which would dash her entire plan and doom Galwell's life.

She went to her fireplace, waving her hand over a rune in the wall to conjure purple flames. When they leapt to life, she tossed the note in, then quenched the fire when Hugh's words were nothing but ashes.

Miserable, she continued into the bathing chambers. She checked on Benjamin, who did somewhat manage to ease her heartache. He'd consumed three of the flowers and was presently making vigorous work on the fourth. When Thessia opened her palm, he readily scooted on. She found herself smiling, starting to understand why Ario cherished the gastropod's silent, slimy company.

It was then, incidentally, that the queen realized something was very wrong.

Benjamin.

Why *was* the snail here in the royal palace? Why had Ario not requested him?

Even if he were injured—which he couldn't be—he would not forget his snail. If the prince were merely "recovering slowly," like the guards had reassured her, he would have demanded his pet immediately.

Unless he truly could not.

Cold possibilities presented themselves in the shadow of her reasoning. Was *Ario* dead, too? Had the mimic assassin, or whoever sent him, somehow managed to finish off the job? Were the royal family covering up the killings of their princes to maintain some semblance of strength? Or was he safe in the Pale Palace but cut off from the world? A poet silenced.

Thessia needed to know. If Ario was in danger, or worse, she needed to find him. For her own struggling heart, for Vestriya, and for Benjamin the snail.

21

Galwell

He woke with pounding in his head.

No, Galwell realized. It wasn't only in his head. The pounding was the rhythm of music echoing in the room, damning his efforts to doze. *Ugh.*

He groaned, righting himself on the uncomfortable booth where he'd curled up for fitful sleep. The revelry in Mona's club had only died down for several hours, and now the pummeling music was restarting?

Except he was in no position to complain. Mona was sheltering him from the entire Vestriyan royal guard, who were out for his head.

Well, they could have it if this headache carried on.

He rubbed his stinging eyes, preparing for a miserable day of hiding. Of cowardice. Should he get drunk? Would that improve matters? He'd never gotten drunk before, his large and muscular body seeming always to absorb the drink's effects faster than he could imbibe. Perhaps *that* could be his goal for the wayward day—drunkenness.

He waved down one of Mona's leather-clad servers. "Your . . . worst alcohol please," he demanded with heavy-tongued words.

The server eyed him pityingly. *One more new experience for Galwell the Great. Pity! How grand.*

He hunched in his seat while the server departed to retrieve his order. He wondered whether the staff recognized him. Whether they cared they were sheltering Vestriya's fugitive wanted for murdering their prince. Or had Mona's depravity, her entire lack of morals—

"Our *worst alcohol?*"

The amused voice repeating his order shook him from his condemnations. Mona stood over him, holding what he presumed was his drink.

She slid into the booth opposite him, not surrendering the glass. Her smirk was ruthless. "Look at you," she crowed. "What a villain you've become."

Galwell glared. He reached for his drink—his hope of salvation—which Mona deftly withdrew out of reach. Galwell glared harder.

"The entire royal guard is pursuing you, you know," Mona informed him. "They've even sent the shriekwings. I've never done something bad enough to warrant a search by shriekwing."

Galwell grimaced. So that was the sound he'd heard outside when the music quieted, like daggers on chalkstone.

"I'm impressed," she remarked, sounding genuine. "A little jealous, even."

"I'm innocent," Galwell grumbled.

Mona sipped from his drink, maddeningly. "Are you?" she returned. "And yet you're hiding while the real villains are out there. No guilt for that?"

Galwell clenched his jaw hard enough for his teeth to hurt. Mona knew exactly which insecurities in him she was playing on.

He repeated the rationale he'd found meager comfort in, like a one-log fire on a Northern Mountains night. "If I'm caught, it could mean war between Mythria and Vestriya," he explained. "Thessia believes marrying me would prevent it. I can't let it come to that. No matter if it means I'm reduced to getting drunk in your criminal lair."

Mona grinned. Once more, Galwell had the infuriating impression of having played right into her hands. Into her hands was not where he wanted to find himself.

Or—well, no, not like—

"Ah, so there remains a hero in there after all. I wasn't so sure," she commented coyly.

Galwell's gaze narrowed. She straightened, arching her back, her posture working unfairly to emphasize the swelling curves of her breasts. *Mona the Merciless, indeed.* Galwell diverted his gaze.

"What choice do I have? I cannot leave here. It's not safe," he reasoned.

"Curious you think it's safe here," Mona said, brows raised.

Of course. Didn't he learn yesterday not to make assumptions about Mona's regard for him? "I suppose it's not," he ground out. "You could hand me over directly to whoever wants to kill me like you always threatened."

Pondering his point, Mona nodded. "It's a shame the spymaster is unwell. I could have given him the city's most notorious villain. I am the second, of course," she conceded, looking like she very much enjoyed the concession.

Galwell snatched his drink from her distracted hand. Mona laughed, the delighted sound like shattering crystal, while he drank recklessly. He needed to get so drunk his thoughts would become unfocused. *Then* Mona could not read his incriminating mind.

"Drunk people reveal the most, actually," Mona said.

Galwell grunted.

"What is it you wish to hide from me, exactly?" she asked him, leaning forward, folding her now-empty hands calmly on the ebony tabletop.

No, Galwell would not have her intruding upon his mind. Whether with her magic *or* with prying conversation. He needed to shift the focus off him. Onto her. "Nothing. There's nothing to discuss. Just shelter me until you can collect whatever it is Clare promised you," he said.

Mona's sly gaze pinned him, completely aware of his motives. *Rather clumsy*, he could admit of the effort.

Of course it was, though. Galwell the Guileless had no need for evasion or subtlety in the usual particulars of his heroic life. Only Mona, with whom survival required gifts of deceit, demanded otherwise.

"Ario is the touchy subject, then?" she inquired.

Galwell dug his fingernails into his thigh, hoping the pain would consume his thoughts.

"You did seem very grouchy about him before the game," Mona mused. "Did he do something to you?"

"Of course not," Galwell replied readily. He welcomed the relief of an easy question. "He's a wonderful young man and I hope he makes a full recovery. I'm sorry you won't be able to continue your conversation with him. You seemed to get along so marvelously."

Mona blinked. Galwell gulped.

Slowly—victoriously—his counterpart smiled.

The former hero knew this was not good. In fact, he suspected this was how he would feel if the shriekwings got him, their murderous cries currently filling the Vestriyan sky.

"No, you're not," she replied.

Galwell was out of patience with her games. "Not what?"

"You're not sorry," she said. "You're . . . pleased."

He pushed his incredibly strong fingers into his leg, hoping to pierce his skin. Whatever was required to dispel the unheroic inclinations Mona was uncovering in him.

"Stop that." Mona reached under the table.

Her touch, improbably gentle, combined with the removal of his self-inflicted pain, was too much for Galwell. The relief made his thoughts explode from him. Not within his head—but straight from his mouth.

"Does what we shared the other night mean nothing to you?" he exclaimed.

Mona withdrew her hand from him in surprise, so startled she did not even gloat.

Small mercies, Galwell reckoned.

"What we shared?" she repeated.

He struggled to explain himself. "When you—when we—" Frustration was starting to consume him. The heat coloring his cheeks only worsened his plight. Indeed, were questing this difficult, Mythria would have fallen to the Fraternal Order and Galwell would have ventured no farther than his village marketplace.

Galwell suddenly understood his sister. Her agony when everyone teased her about Vandra. Perhaps it was better to be a withdrawn grump. What did emotional honesty earn you? Nothing but scoffs and pitying looks.

Mona scoured the pity from her face. "Our night together was a lot of fun, G. I'd happily pick up where we left off anytime," she promised him.

"But you wanted to flirt with another man," Galwell insisted, hoping to hide how perplexed her nonchalance left him. He did not succeed, for Mona's eyebrows shot up.

"Just because I want to fuck you doesn't mean there are any promises between us. We're not betrothed to each other," she clarified.

"Why not?" Galwell asked.

Mona laughed, not unkindly. She reclined in her seat, looking comfortable now. *At least one of them was, then*, Galwell thought.

"Galwell, surely you know the difference between lust and love," she started gently.

"I know people pretend there is a difference," he replied. "To me, I suspect there isn't."

Her eyes widened. For the second time today, he'd managed to surprise the mind reader. He would have congratulated himself on the feat were he not in the darkest mood of probably his entire life.

"I see," Mona said.

Her noncommittal reply managed to embarrass him even more. "Just leave me alone," he pleaded.

He drank deeply from the hard liquor in his black glass. *Alone.* It was his new destiny, he supposed. He did not have his old friends, whose lives in Mythria had continued on without him. He knew not where his new friends were. Probably hiding from peril themselves. Or—who knew—perhaps they genuinely suspected him of plotting the gruesome murder of the crown prince of Vestriya!

Even if they wanted to, they could not come for him. Not without endangering themselves or their Queendom. Or without being forced to wed him, apparently.

He would stay out of everyone's lives, he decided, and they could carry on like they had when he was dead. It would be better this way.

"That's not true," Mona said.

Her voice hummed with urgency, but her words did not affect Galwell the way she intended. "Get out of my head," he ordered her. He was getting angry now. It felt . . . good. Like scratching an itch to the point of painful relief. No wonder everyone he knew found comfort in the emotion's masochistic clutches.

Mona only shook her head. She stared him down, imperious. "You came here to hide, but this isn't you," she insisted. "You need to be out there, fighting. Being . . . heroic."

For once, she'd not made the notion sound offensive.

It offered Galwell no reassurance, however. "I'm hardly a hero anymore. Haven't you heard? I'm a wanted criminal now," he said sharply. "Besides, it's not like I can go gallivanting in the streets. I can't risk war. Or marriage to Thessia."

"You don't want to marry her?" Mona pressed him.

"I just explained my feelings on the subject of marriage, Mona," he said slowly, with undeniable indication. When he'd first made his vow to Thessia, he hadn't known what he was sacrificing. Now he did.

He held Mona's gaze, daring her to test him. She could use her magic to discern his meaning exactly. Fine. He wanted her to understand. To feel how deep the well of his desire was.

Instead, Mona stood. She met him confrontation for confrontation, with fire in her Grandhart-cerulean eyes.

"After the game, I managed to make contact with the mysterious figure who hired the guild to kill you," she informed Galwell. "We've brokered a meeting in the Evriel Mountains. If you could get out of the city, you could uncover the plot. I suspect it'll connect to framing you for Ezio's murder. It would bring justice to you and to Vestriya."

Galwell glanced down, frowning into his glass. He'd nearly finished the contents yet felt no drunkenness. Of course not. "What do you care for justice?" he challenged Mona.

Surprisingly, her crystal eyes flashed with hurt. "You think very little of me for proclaiming to love me," she remarked.

Impatient, Galwell set his glass down heavily on the table. "Why do you care, Mona?" he repeated stubbornly. "None of this involves you."

Mona hesitated. "I . . . I don't like seeing you this way," she finally confessed.

Hope flickered in him. The emotion had its own stubbornness, he found. He could never quite manage to stamp it from his soul, whether with drink, unfortunate flights from royal law enforcement, or dealing with this frustrating woman.

Perhaps part of her did care for him.

If Mona read his thoughts on that subject, she remained quiet.

"I have no crew," he replied, eyeing the table dejectedly. "A real hero knows how dependent he is on those who help him."

"Good thing you have me, then," Mona replied.

Galwell looked up. He would permit hope no further, however.

"I've been smuggling in and out of this city for years," Mona went on. "I can get you out, and we will go to this meeting, and you'll get the fuck out of this tavern and start acting like yourself again."

"You'd . . . do that for me?" Galwell asked. He did not hide his surprise. Nor could he have, with Mona's magic.

She looked uncomfortable. "Don't read into it. Just sober up and be ready to go at nightfall," she ordered him gruffly.

When she walked off, Galwell found himself grinning. Yes, perhaps she cared for him more than she pretended—or even more wonderful, perhaps Mona the Merciless was not merely the criminal she considered herself to be, the mercenary who thought only of her own interests. Perhaps she was good inside.

A hero, even.

22
River

River had been locked up for so long, restrained by magical ropes that prevented her ability to teleport, that she'd taken to listing aloud the things she missed.

Well, it was supposed to be things. That was how it started. She talked about how she longed for a cup of scalding brew. How she'd do anything to feel sunshine on her face in the late morning. All the ways she'd sell her soul to sit her aching muscles in a tub of hot water.

Eventually, her mind turned to what—no, *whom*—she really wanted. She started whispering her name like a prayer.

Celine.

Celine.

Celine.

It was water on parched lips. The only balm for this horrid situation.

If Celine could invent everlasting memory as a magical gift, so could River. But she had everlasting memory for one person, and one person only.

She thought of Celine at sixteen, gritting her teeth in determination as River helped her walk across a tightrope that was only two irons off the ground. Celine had squeezed River's hand with so much force that River started to lose circulation in her fingers. But she hadn't minded one bit. She couldn't believe she was the one Celine trusted enough to stop her from falling.

THIS WILL BE INTERESTING

She thought of Celine in the dimness of her childhood bedroom, whispering her hopes of someday writing grand tales of adventure. Tales she'd make up for River on the spot, spinning them into lullabies until River drifted off to sleep, lost to a land of dreams where she and Celine slayed dragons and danced on clouds together.

She thought of Celine as the woman she'd become, still full of the same grit and determination. Her firebird, fighting so hard to do what was right, keeping secrets in the name of protecting herself and others.

Oh, how River missed her.

River had never had regrets before. Not any she'd admit to, at least. She had more than she could count now. If only she hadn't pushed Celine away, ended their kiss. Told her she never wanted to see her again. If only she'd stopped trying to fix things before she even knew what was broken.

Dougal Farkenstomp opened the door of the squat, windowless cell where he'd been holding River captive. He'd survived his time in the boat on the Sweetwater Sea. Of course he had. You didn't become one of the guild's best assassins without a hardheaded resourcefulness that stretched beyond all logic and sense. River never should've let Thessia load his boat with supplies.

"Sorry it took so long," he said, smiling as his gloved hands sprinkled fresh leaves into the bag he'd been putting over River's head. "Couldn't find where I'd put the rest of my nightmares. But I see you've been keeping busy. Celine, eh? She works for the *Mythria Spectator*, right? A shoddy place for a scribe of her talent, but we all start somewhere, don't we?"

"*Don't say her name,*" River warned him through gritted teeth.

Dougal scoffed. "But *you* can? That hardly seems fair. You're the one who took everything from me. I think I have a right to some things that belong to you. I appreciate you finally talking about her out loud. I've been pretty sure she's the woman you fancy. It's nice to get confirmation. Sure took you long enough, but I knew you'd crack eventually. Everyone does, in the end."

River thrashed. These damned power-silencing ties.

They were—as Dougal hoped they would be—torture.

"These leaves are from a cursed forest in Mythria. Have you ever been to Featherbint?" Dougal continued. "It's a strange little town. I haven't visited, myself, but the nightmares I've had other guild members procure from there have saved me in more than one torture situation. They're a wonderful addition to any assassin's arsenal. They make you drift off to sleep, climb into your mind, and haunt you with your worst fears. It's great stuff."

"Sounds wonderful," River deadpanned.

"I agree. Now, do tell me, what do you think of the ropes that stop your powers? Aren't they impressive?"

"No," River said, even though she could think of a dozen situations she'd found herself in where magical ropes such as these would've been a great help. She'd never seen such a thing before.

"You want to know where I got them, don't you?" Dougal intuited. Though River said nothing, he still smiled. "They came from Myke Lycroft, the now-dead magical weaponeer from the Fraternal Order. He could take the powers of others and replicate them inside different implements."

"I know who Myke Lycroft is," River said. "He was one of the most prominent faces of the evil the guild used to fight against. Or so I thought."

"Enemies always come back," Dougal said ominously. "Todrick did. Myke is dead, but his power remained in these. You tried to send me away, but here I am. The guild won't be able to get rid of me, either. Since I was unceremoniously fired, I didn't see a reason to return them. I'm sure they are quite sad to lose such a rare magical weapon, and that warms my heart. I do wish I had my hands on more of the new poison they're making out here, though. Cinderflower. It's quite unique, and I've already used up my supply. Ah, well. What can you do?"

River wanted to scream. The Fraternal Order and the Deathrose Guild, two organizations supposedly on opposites sides, were working *together*.

"What do you want from me?" River asked for easily the hundredth time.

"You really haven't figured it out? I thought by now you'd get it. I want to break you." He said it so casually, as though placing an order at Harpy & Hind. Then he tugged the bag over River's head.

She plugged her nose and squeezed her lips together, knowing if she breathed in the scent of the leaves while they touched her skin, the nightmares would start.

She couldn't hold them off forever. Still, she fought for every last scrap of dignity she could maintain.

"Thanks to you, the career I've built no longer exists," Dougal said. "The guild thinks I failed the same way you did. Silly them, though. They had me come to Vestriya to build this holding cell months ago. No one ever told me I couldn't use it for my own activities. Really, no one said what it was for at all. I'm sure you can relate to how tedious the guild's secrecy can be. I got much less of it than you did, but even I wasn't immune."

River heard singing again. It was faint, and it had been happening on and off for a while, occurring somewhere above her. It was the only clue that she had about where she was being held. She'd started to believe she might be hallucinating, because the singing almost sounded like her favorite musical act, and that made no sense at all.

With every passing minute, hour, day—she had no idea how much time had gone by, no way to track it without light—retaining these kinds of details had become less important. No one could save her here, and without her teleportation gift, she could not save herself. Soon all the little clues she'd gathered about her location would cease to matter altogether. So she let herself believe the Brethren, a trio of musically gifted brothers, were indeed practicing their soulful tunes somewhere above her.

Dougal, as if reading her thoughts, pressed his lips against her ear. "This will be a suitable place for you to die. Dignified, really. We're so far underground, you're already buried."

River could wait no longer. She gasped for breath, and the nightmares strangled her thoughts until their darkness took hold.

In her mind, River was back on the carousel. Only this time, it was night, and everything was gray. The entire circus had been coated in ash.

River smelled it then. The stale remnant of a long-extinguished fire.

Though the circus felt deserted, the seats that lined the carousel were not empty. There was Hugh. Ario. Galwell. Mona. Thessia.

They'd all been burned to death.

River knew this the same way she'd known the guards in the stadium were dead, but still, she moved to search their bodies for signs of life. Only, her feet were glued to the ground. She could do nothing but look at their corpses.

"No," she cried out. "No!"

These were, she realized, her friends.

She had friends.

River spun hopelessly around the carousel, searching for a solution, a way to turn back time and save them. It didn't matter that she knew this was a figment of her imagination, an all-too-vivid rendering of her fears. That was the trick of nightmares. You knew they weren't actually happening, and still, you could not escape.

"Help!" a voice cried out.

THIS WILL BE INTERESTING

At the center of the carousel, in the booth where the ride operator usually spun the wheel, was Celine, tied up with ropes.

River knew then, too, the way you know things in dreams without reason or proof, that this fire was not Celine's fault, but that she would be the one blamed for it. She'd be burned herself as punishment for all the people they'd say she'd killed.

And River could not stop it.

The carousel spun faster and faster until it was moving at an impossible speed, and all the other people were gone, leaving River alone to die.

Her worst fear.

There was no way to squeeze her eyes shut. The dread could not be avoided, for this was a nightmare, and the dread was the point.

Suddenly, the smell of smoke evaporated as the bag was ripped from River's head. The scent of dank, rotting earth surrounded her, dragging her back to reality.

Dougal lay unconscious at her feet, and Vandra Ravenfall stood above him with her hands on her hips, smiling.

"Pretty impressive, right?" she said.

River struggled for breath, for words. For understanding. "How did you find me?" she stumbled out.

Vandra smiled her easy, eager grin. She had on some of her finest attire—a golden-yellow velvet tunic with matching blouse and high-heeled boots—but that was the least surprising part of this whole ordeal. "I'd tell you it was difficult, but that wouldn't be true. Once Thessia told me she'd set Dougal Farkenstomp to sea, I knew he'd survived."

Some semblance of sanity returned to River, if only so she could prickle at the fact that she'd thought the same thing. It was strange to hear her thought process echoed by Vandra. To know she hadn't been the only one after all.

"Before you and I got paired up, I worked with him once." Vandra leaned against the wall, sharing gossip like this was not a squat cell where River had been using an odious wooden bucket as a toilet but one of the many Deathrose Guild mixers they'd attended together. "He told me when he's not undercover, he still likes to use an alias— Sir Justyn Justynson. Only took a few well-placed conversations to discover Sir Justynson had been staying nearby."

River tried to laugh, but it came out choked. She was perilously close to crying. This was all so absurd. The kidnapping. The rescue. Dougal at her feet, easily sixty-five-years old, wishing to be called Justyn Justynson.

Was this another nightmare, and its shape was still forming?

"I know." Vandra laughed, too, as she bent over to pick Dougal's pocket for a knife to cut the ropes. She approached River, and all her playfulness was replaced with a somber stoicism. "I told you to quit the guild."

This was real, River assured herself. Because in nightmares, Vandra wouldn't be this forthcoming.

"And I told you to stop wearing jewel-toned velvet on secret missions," River said.

"I hope you don't think I'm doing this out of the kindness in my heart." Vandra untied her. "I'm being paid handsomely."

"Good for you," River said.

Vandra had to help her up. She'd been sitting for so long in such an uncomfortable position that her legs had fallen asleep.

"Don't you want to know who hired me?" Vandra asked.

"It's obviously the queen. You already work for her."

"It was not Thessia."

River could use her sleeping legs to explain away the halt in her step. But she could not account for the sudden jolt in her heart, pressing against her bruised rib cage.

THIS WILL BE INTERESTING

Vandra opened the heavy door she'd entered through. It was weighted to shut after each use and magicked to lock upon closing, but Vandra had lodged a hairpin in the jamb.

"I'm good, aren't I?" she said, taking her fluttering lightwing clip and pushing it back into her long black curls.

"Galwell hired you, then," River guessed. "You rescued him from wherever the Vestriyan guards took him, and he used his majestic Galwellian presence to manipulate you into saving me."

"We haven't seen him, though we believe it's highly likely he is with Mona Grandhart," Vandra replied. "Do you think Galwell and Mona have something going on? Elowen says there's no way, but you know me. I'm a romantic. I love the idea of Galwell with a woman like her. Perfect opposites." Vandra stopped, pressing a magimanicured hand to her mouth in realization, as if she'd told herself she couldn't do this very thing—chat excitedly with River about their mutual acquaintances. "I don't have any more time for this game where you pretend you don't know it was Celine. She begged me to rescue you. And I have. My work is done. You're out of the cell. You're safe. Go ahead and teleport to her."

River trained her face to stay calm. She *did* know it was Celine. But that didn't mean she believed it.

"You were right," River admitted. "About the guild."

"Of course I was." Vandra tossed her curls over her shoulder. She paused on an inhale, as if she was waiting for something. The silence stretched on, until finally she said, "Nothing more to say?"

"Not really," River told her.

"Then I need to be on my way. I have more important things to do. One of Elowen's favorite shadow play stars is here visiting ahead of Vestriya Now. She's requested I go secure an autograph."

River felt a pulse of excitement. *Vestriya Now*.

So she really had heard the Brethren rehearsing.

"Doesn't Elowen want to get it herself?" she asked.

"Oh, darling. She'd rather die than admit she's a fan of someone." Vandra laughed. "Stubborn people. I have a way of finding them."

She put a hand on River's chest. It was not a parting sentiment. It meant *Stop. Don't follow me.*

"Figure out what to do with Dougal," she said. "As you know, I'm not in the business of killing people anymore. I'll leave that decision to you."

Out Vandra went, down whatever tunnel had led her to River.

In the end, River decided to leave Dougal locked in the room. He'd already defied the odds once, surviving his time on the Sweetwater Sea. She did not expect he would defy them twice. But she didn't care. This was a fate of his own creation.

Maybe enemies did return. But River wasn't scared to face them.

She took her time exiting, memorizing the labyrinth of tunnels that led to her cell. When she emerged aboveground, she squinted so hard her eyes watered as she struggled to adjust to the brightness of day. When she tried to teleport, she failed. She was either too exhausted, or those ropes took a while to wear off.

If she wanted to get to Celine, she had to walk.

23
Thessia

What remained of Queen Thessia's noble questing party surrounded her in their carriage. She could not even find enthusiasm to try to properly name the group. Not with Celine sulking beside her, not with Hugh up front driving in determined silence.

No, they were not *quest-vengers* or *quest-panions*. They were miserable.

Having donned disguises to travel inconspicuously, they journeyed into the rolling hills of the Vestriyan countryside in their rented carriage. Not even the land's dappled green or high ridges of olivera plants could distract them from their discontent.

Thessia found herself unable to muster small talk. How exactly *did* one engage in casual conversation with the man you've realized you love, with whom you shared one perfect night but could now never be with ever again? Even the greatest of heart healers, potently powerful with gifts of emotional repair, would not know what to do with *them*.

For his part, Hugh offered none of his easy, jovial companionship. He lapsed instead into speaking to their horse about every minor detail of the scenery. "Have you ever seen hills this green?" he murmured to the chestnut creature. "Yes, of course you have," he chastened himself. "You're a horse. You live here. It is I who looks with wonder on what your worldly eyes have seen."

The carriage, not outfitted with the comforts of a royal chariot, hit every dip in the winding road with punishing emphasis. Not used to, well, discomfort, Thessia grimaced when her soon-to-be ex-husband's unapologetic driving caused her butt to knock painfully against the seat board.

Celine, usually equanimous, was uncommonly prickly, like the olivera spines on the hedges they rode past. Thessia suspected her withdrawnness had something to do with River's continued absence, despite Celine procuring the former assassin's rescue. Thessia could not explain why River hadn't teleported to them yet, but considering Celine's sour mood, she could only conclude more heart troubles plagued their crew.

Perhaps Galwell was right, she ruminated ruefully. Perhaps they should not have permitted romance in their questing party.

Of course, it was not romance that kept Galwell himself from joining them. No one had heard from Vestriya's most wanted man since the Realm Chalice. When Thessia tried to contact Mona, suspecting Galwell's difficult relationship with the law might lead him to Vestriya's crown princess of crime, Thessia was told she had left the city on personal matters.

She could only hope "personal matters" meant helping Galwell. Not only for his safety's sake—she was starting to suspect Mona personally mattered to Mythria's hero.

The possibility of Galwell finding refuge with Mona cheered Thessia, reminding her that despite the fractured state of their company, she was not alone.

It was something. A single note where she yearned for a symphony, yes. Nevertheless—it was something.

When Hugh started to slow the carriage, Thessia noticed the changes in the scenery. Gone were the green hills, the olivera plants. The sunlight here was searing. The ground and the rock formations were rugged white stone.

THIS WILL BE INTERESTING

Hugh rounded the corner past one such massive formation. The Pale Palace loomed ahead.

Thessia shivered. The structure was instantly unsettling. Yes, the formidable towers, sculpted spires, and hand-hewn columns with spiraling ornamentation were impressive. But Thessia could not shake the fearsome feeling of emptiness pervading the Palace. The marvelous walls were silent of kindness or cheer. Vacant of hope.

"I don't like this," Hugh said honestly.

While Thessia welcomed his candor in place of horse jokes, she fought to hold her courage where even her courageous husband—ex-husband?—could not. "We'll be okay," she reassured them. "What can they really do to a royal?"

Hugh frowned, halting the horses. "Isn't that what we're quite literally here to find out? If something sinister is happening with Ario, Vestriya's new crown prince, why would you expect to be safe? We should find another way."

"There is no other way," Celine said, seemingly unmoved by their procession toward the hushed Pale Palace. "I've tried for days to get access. I've talked to every scribe in the city, and none of them are even interested in investigating Ario's condition. It's strange."

"It's a warning, is what it is," Hugh told them.

His judgment sounded disturbingly convincing. Still—while Thessia could not change the misfortune of their position, she could change tactics. "You'd have us abandon our ally?" she asked Hugh.

Now Hugh looked uncomfortable. He turned to face her, their eyes meeting for—the first time since they were bared to each other.

"Of course not," he returned evenly. "But, Thess . . . ia—"

Oof. She heard his effortful denial of her nickname.

"You're nearly an enemy of the realm, and this sure fucking looks like a place to torture enemies."

Panic flared in Hugh's eyes. She understood its source well. Hugh had faced deep loss, the loss of someone he cared for. Someone he . . . loved.

Rogue hope followed that thought. Thessia wished she could hide the emotion in her keepsake box, out of sight.

Celine spoke up. Fortunate, given Thessia's words were caught in her throat. "I can keep her safe if it comes to that."

Her voice was low but seemed to echo loudly. When they'd returned to the villa after the Realm Chalice disaster, Celine had revealed everything to Hugh and Thessia. Her devastating power. Her concealment of her magic.

Thessia had not judged the other woman for her secrecy. She understood perfectly not wanting to be defined by something one could not control. What's more, the queen trusted Celine, which was why she'd asked her to undertake the day's dangerous quest.

"There," Thessia murmured to Hugh, intending to comfort. "If you see fire, you can charge in. But otherwise, it would be . . . better if no one saw us together."

Better. Ghosts, she'd just negotiated her realm right up to the edge of war—she'd stood down the imposing rulers of Vestriya with countless lives on the line without flinching. Yet commending her separation from the man who'd stolen her heart? Nearly impossible.

Hugh grumbled but did not protest further. He guided their horses up to the gates of the Pale Palace. When their carriage stopped, no one greeted them. Thessia stepped out into the silence, then turned back to her seat, where her only traveling companion who'd given her no cause for concern or consternation waited.

Benjamin the snail extended his eye stalks. He swirled them intently, which Thessia had learned meant he wanted something.

Of course, if the new crown prince was inside this fortress of solitude, Thessia would *not* deny him the chance to reunite with his precious pet. Upon Benjamin's eloquent request, she extended her hand, letting the snail scoot purposefully into her dress pocket.

* * *

Every footstep deeper into the Pale Palace unnerved Thessia. Something—she could not quite explain what—made the sanctuary the most unwelcoming place she'd ever found herself. This was saying something, for Queen Thessia had been kidnapped thrice in her life.

Perhaps the white stone of which everything was sculpted unsettled her. The only color found in the palace were the grand rooms' fountains of . . . Thessia knew not what substance flowed in them—a gleaming, iridescent white that shimmered hues of purple or blue when the cascading liquid met the surface.

Or perhaps the silence disquieted the queen. Other than their own footsteps, the only sound was of the rustling outside of dust-colored, spider-limbed plants Thessia did not recognize.

Thessia and Celine were guests of the palace's healers, who'd granted the visiting royal a tour as a result of Thessia's invented premise of considering expanding the Pale Palace into Mythria—an idea onto which the healers latched with hungry zeal. They were being shown the grounds by the head healer, introduced as Master Marko, and his apprentice. Marko was once part of the Collective of the Resurrected Ghosts—the zealots who believed the Ghosts, heroes of Mythria's past, lived once more. In Marko's unsuccessful proselytizing in Vestriya, curiosity had led him to disgraced healers whose hand and head magics promised impossible results. Eventually he gave up proselytizing and the Collective and changed vocations to develop his healing craft in the Palace.

As they walked, he extolled in a whisper the iridescent "healing pools" and promised introductions to the magicians who could ease patients' pain by immersing them in labyrinthine dream states.

Thessia feigned interest while Celine diligently jotted down notes for the scribesheet story she was pretending to write to commemorate the palace's impending Mythrian expansion. Meanwhile, down every corridor, past every open doorway, they searched for Ario—without success.

Marko moved ahead of them with reptilian deliberateness, his eyes keen with unreadable focus. Despite his wisps of hair, the smooth, sallow head of the septuagenarian rather resembled a skull.

This unsettled Thessia, too. She was rather tiring of the day's many unsettlements. Indeed, she would probably have preferred a straightforward kidnapping.

When he led them into the largest common square within the palace, where head magicians were conducting some sort of meditative hypnosis on patients—who, dismayingly, did not include the prince—Thessia felt their complimentary tour concluding.

She would need to force the matter.

"And what of your progress with the crown prince?" she interjected.

As if she'd just dropped a glass jar of red spicy dollpepper sauce on their pristine pale floor, the healers' faces fell.

Marko met her question evenly, his mouth a line. "The case is a challenging one, but he is in the best hands in Vestriya," he intoned.

Evasion. Dread rose in Thessia. It was a feeling she did not much like.

"I wish to see him," she replied, as charmingly as she could.

Marko's apprentice spoke up, flustered. "I'm afraid we cannot—"

"Then I'm afraid I rather cannot endorse your expansion into Mythria," Thessia interrupted, with full imperial loftiness. What good was queendom if one could not get what one wanted *some* of the time?

THIS WILL BE INTERESTING

When the healer began to protest, Thessia started to spin like she intended to show herself out.

Marko held up his hand, silencing his student and halting Thessia. "We . . . can arrange a meeting," he said in displeasure. "But the scribe must sit it out."

Thessia met Celine's gaze. The condition was dangerous. Thessia, isolated, in this place of warped, whispered magic, without the one person who could fight their way out if everything fell apart.

But . . . they needed to find Ario.

"Of course," Thessia conceded, keeping her composure.

Be careful, Celine mouthed when the healers led Thessia from the common room.

Thessia followed the healers up staircases their tour had passed by. If possible, the Pale Palace's hollow, echoing silence only deepened with the climb. They entered the highest tower, the elegant spire Thessia had seen from the carriage that looked like the palace's spine pointing skyward.

When they reached their destination, Thessia noticed the heightened security. They passed bars of whitened metal, guarded by unmoving hand magicians.

She felt herself start to sweat as the healers led her to the hall's farthest door. What would she find inside? Implements of morbid torture? Gruesome medical misdeeds? Or—the instruments of her own captivity, or worse?

The door swung open.

It was . . . nice inside.

Thessia exhaled. Strangely enough, the room resembled the comforts of the franchised inns springing up in Mythria. Without personality yet pleasant. The white stone gleamed cleanly in the daylight. The gauzy curtains over the small window were still. The plant in the corner, of the same kind growing outside, seemed to be flourishing.

That was good, Thessia reasoned. If the healers could keep plants healthy, perhaps they could keep princes healthy, too.

Upon this thought, Thessia found the object of her quest.

Ario lay in a clean bed by the window. While his eyes were open, gazing out toward the glimpse of daylight, they were . . . vacant. He did not move or respond when Thessia and her cohort entered the room.

Chills ran over Thessia's skin. She rushed to his side. When she clutched his hand, she found his palm clammy, his fingers ungrasping. His pallid unresponsiveness did not change.

No. No. Real fear hammered on the gates of Thessia's heart. How? What had happened? Ario looked genuinely physically uninjured. No head wound. No bruises or bloody bandages. Given how obviously unwell the prince was, she found only small comfort in the confirmation of the reliability of her own memory. What had thrust the emotional young man who'd fled the Realm Chalice into this state?

She was desperate to wake him. Inspiration struck her. "Ario, you do not look yourself. Put your worries . . ." She struggled. "Up on the shelf," she said, concluding the rhyme.

This poetry thing wasn't easy. She would stick to queendom and questing, she decided with new empathy for Ario's creative plight.

When her rhyme elicited no response—none whatsoever—Thessia knew the fault lay not with her poor lyricism. Or not entirely. She rounded on the healers, her panic mounting.

"What's wrong with him?" she demanded. "I see no injury."

Master Marko looked on with something like sadness. Feigned? Thessia wondered. "The crown doesn't wish for us to speak of it," he replied.

No. Cheap political excuses would not waylay her. Not while her friend suffered. "How am I to know that *you* haven't done this to him? He looks like he's under the effects of some curse."

Marko looked more impatient than indignant. "We would never, Your Highness."

Thessia strode right up to the healer. "Explain what's going on or I'll be forced to tell the scribe out there what's happening in this place of *healing*," she said, emphasizing the word with venom. "Mythria has a free press. She won't be stopped."

The master healer held her gaze with an impressively stony resolve. Then he gestured to his party.

"Leave us," he ordered.

While his cohort filed out, Thessia realized she was alone. Entirely alone, except for Ario. Without guards. Without witnesses.

The healer sat on the sole footstool in the room. He winced at the pressure on his knees.

"Please," he murmured. "Stay your quill. The crown gives us very few resources. We do what we can."

Master Marko's voice held raw despondency. Thessia covered her shock.

She studied him, seeing with sudden sympathy what his statuesque demeanor concealed. He was no skeleton, no reptile. He looked like a weary man with an impossible job.

In this kingdom, where Thessia was learning that nothing was what it seemed, she should not have been surprised.

"The crown would rather the people they send here be forgotten," Marko continued. "But we truly care for everyone who comes our way. People with inconvenient or difficult maladies deserve to be treated with respect. We . . . do what we can with what we have," he repeated. "With magic or medicine, we seek to stay pain or prolong life. But most patients we receive have been sent here to die."

He gestured to the crown prince.

"We suspect that Prince Ario has been poisoned," he explained gravely. "But nothing we do seems to help."

Thessia blinked. She struggled to accept this information. The healer was openly admitting that the king and queen . . . wanted Ario forgotten? While he succumbed to poisoning? Why hide his state unless . . . Could the royal couple have been the ones to poison him? Days after the death of their eldest son? She looked desperately for flaws in the plot, possibilities unaccounted for.

She found none. The scribesheet reports of Ario being injured were . . . lies, easily disseminated by the crown.

"What—" She gulped. "What poison could do this?"

Forlorn, Marko studied the prince. The man was not without compassion, Thessia recognized now. "We suspect cinderflower extract," he replied. "It's a newer creation, one produced only in Vestriya and with terrible costs. We've seen more and more cases of it. In small doses, it's a painkiller, harmless and undetectable. In larger ones . . . there is no treatment."

"Is it . . . fatal?" Thessia forced out.

Marko eyed the motionless prince.

"No patient has survived longer than a fortnight," he said.

Tears leapt into Thessia's eyes. *A fortnight.* The prince did not have long, then.

It struck Thessia how deeply this wounded her. She hardly knew Ario. Yet in every moment with the young prince, she'd felt the incandescence of his spirit. His frivolity was just passion by another name, his poetic indulgence only the embodiment of his confidence and zeal. He was joyful, and kind, and dying.

A stirring in her dress pocket pulled Thessia from these mournful ruminations.

Thinking of Ario's beloved snail having to lose him, she stifled a sob. When she lifted Benjamin from her pocket, the snail pointed his eye stalks with intent toward the prince.

Gently, Thessia lowered the colorful creature onto Ario's cold hand while Marko's wispy eyebrows rose. She'd hoped that Ario could say hello to his pet. Not that they would need to say goodbye.

The snail slimed with determination up Ario's arm to his chest, right over his heart. When Benjamin started twirling his stalks—his sign of want—Thessia could hardly watch. She knew the depth of the snail's emotions was profound. In his way, Benjamin was expressing his desire for Ario to return from his poisoned stupor, to—

The prince's eyelashes fluttered.

Thessia startled. Benjamin had elicited the only movement Thessia had yet seen from the convalescing prince. Was she imagining—

No. With Benjamin suctioned over his heart, Ario's breathing evened and deepened. His eyes moved to his snail with unmistakable clarity. Color started to return to his cheeks!

"How— What—" Marko had risen to his feet. "What is that—snail?" the old healer uttered.

"His name is—" Thessia started, offering the only explanation she could.

Ario sat suddenly upright.

"Benjamin!" the prince exclaimed. Thessia recognized the rapturous look that entered the young man's eyes. "*Oh, my joy, it knows no limits—* No," he interrupted himself, focusing with effort. "Wait. Yes! *Oh, my heart could never fail under the care of my precious snail!*"

It was then that Thessia knew the crown prince was going to be all right. She smiled.

"Remarkable," Marko exhaled in wonderment.

"He is," Ario replied fondly while the snail swirled his stalks.

"The snail's slime," Marko said. "It's miraculous. It's a natural antidote!"

"Slime?" Ario repeated. He looked up in indignation. "Don't be ridiculous. This is just like one of the great poems, where a slumbering prince is awoken by the power of true love!"

"My . . . prince," Marko managed. "I assure you, it's the slime."

"True love is not always romantic, my dear man," Ario pronounced with certainty. "Sometimes your soul mate is your pet, your snail, your Benjamin."

When he gazed down, Thessia really did see the height of poetic emotion in the prince's eyes.

The old healer cleared his throat. "Not to belittle your . . . feelings," he said, "but may we take a sample of that true-love slime before you go?"

* * *

Defying royal orders, the Pale Palace released Ario upon the prince's near-instant recovery, having no desire to hold someone against his will. The healers promised not to inform the Vestriyan crown of the prince's departure until forced to. This, Ario pointed out, would require his parents actually visiting him, which they would not do.

He remained weak, although he could speak and stand. Thessia held him up while they returned to the carriage where Celine waited. Upon seeing them, Hugh leapt out, his surprise unhidden.

"Good day, King Hugh." Ario greeted him enthusiastically. "My snail has saved my life!"

"I— What?" Hugh asked.

When Thessia passed off the prince to Hugh, their fingers brushed. She ignored the frisson of heat.

"Thessia and Benjamin saved me from death by cinderflower extract," Ario explained with a conspiratorial grandeur that was ill-fitting in describing one's own poisoning.

"Cinderflower?" Celine startled. "You're sure?"

"You were poisoned?" Hugh said.

"Yes and yes," Ario confirmed. "Unfortunately. Likely by my parents."

"Why would your parents want to poison you?" Celine asked.

Ario shrugged as if contemplating the realm's many wonders. "They had Ezio killed. They hired a Deathrose Guild assassin, who framed Galwell, but I knew it was them, because they hated how popular my brother was. He was planning a coup," he informed the group matter-of-factly. "While I mourned my brother, they prepared for me a very terrible soup. Poison, I now know."

"And after killing Ezio, they . . . wanted to kill you, too?" Celine asked.

"Yes, well, I said I would expose them. My brother deserves justice," Ario replied. He stroked his snail happily. "Hence the soup."

The questing party exchanged glances.

"That was . . . very heroic of you, Ario," Thessia said, speaking for everyone.

"Eating soup? I suppose in some circumstances soup can be rather heroic. When it's very hot, certainly, or—"

Thessia restrained her laughter. "No. Threatening to expose their crime."

"Hm? Oh, yes. I still plan to," the silver-haired prince replied. Hero or not, he looked preoccupied with his pet for the moment. "I just need proof."

Thessia considered this, for her own heroic heart had started to pound. "Maybe if we can follow the trail of the poison? Trace it back to its source," she ventured.

"I—" Celine began, a shadow flickering over her face. "I might know exactly where to look."

24
Galwell

Galwell had never known wonderment like this.

Oh, the snowy peaks of the Evriel Mountains were stunning, of course. Cloudlike snowbanks of lavender surrounded them on the winding road. The winter wind ruffled his enchanted coat, sewn of hand-magicked fur imitating the soft pelts of cloudfoxes. The sky overhead was deepening from purple into night.

Yet these natural splendors were not what captivated him. Instead, his focus was on the woman sitting in front of him in the massive sloping hroxen saddle.

Mona, wrapped in imitation furs herself, looked more carefree than he'd ever seen her. When snow tumbled from the purpling sky, she laughed with delight.

Galwell's heart swelled at the sound. The medical implications of this worried him, for he'd often heard himself deemed "bighearted" or said to possess the "largest heart in Mythria." In moments of Mona Grandhart's laughter, Galwell nervously hoped these characterizations were indeed figurative.

She lifted her head, catching the lavender snowflakes on her cheeks. Her eyes closed in pure bliss.

Galwell was certain *she* was the most beautiful wonder in the realms.

Mona startled. Galwell remembered.

She eyed him skeptically while snowflakes dusted her lashes. "You can't seriously think that."

"You are more beautiful than anything I've ever laid eyes on," Galwell replied.

Mona said nothing. She eyed him a moment longer, looking stunned—stunned that he'd just said exactly what she'd heard him think.

Why this puzzled her puzzled *him*. The hroxen lumbered forward, swaying over the snowbanks.

Finally, Mona faced forward without replying.

Galwell refocused on the snowy splendor. He breathed in deeply, welcoming the night scented with the sweetness he'd noticed on their daylong journey. Vestriyan snow was unique, nothing like the mercilessness of the Northern Mountains in Mythria. The gleaming landscape was idyllic, not isolated, glistening with crystalline cold. It was, he'd gathered from Mona, a place of peaceful refuge. When he'd inquired whether they need remain vigilant for snowsnakes, Mona had simply laughed.

The farther they got from the capital, the more his worries left him. Up here, the guards were not looking for the villain Galwell. No shriekwings menaced the purple sky. The mountainfolk had not seen the conjuration of his face assassinating their prince.

He was just another traveler. Another adventurer. For the first time in a long time—perhaps ever—Galwell the Great felt the peculiar sensation that he could be whoever he wanted.

* * *

They reached their destination too soon, in Galwell's humble opinion.

The mountainside village looked postparchment-perfect, the sort of snowy hamlet one might expect to see indulgently rendered in storybook scenes of the Winternight Festival. Dwellings sturdily fashioned of resinous redwood, smoke curling from chimneys that stood jauntily on roofs decked in pale purple pillows of snow. Overhead in the darkness, Vestriyan starjays with their shining tail tips flew, sending pinpricks of light streaming through the night.

The wind gusted over the idyll while they dismounted their hroxen. Galwell didn't feel the cold—he quite liked his coat, which Mona had provided him while they stole out of the city, hidden in a shipment of quarry stone.

He followed Mona into an inn. Every window overlooked the vast mountains with breathtaking views. While she consulted with the clerk, Galwell waited in the cozy lobby, admiring the fire. They had real cinderoak here, probably chopped down nearby, forfeiting none of its fresh potency. The crimson of the flames indicated how the fireplace's single log was producing enough cinnamon-scented heat to warm the entire floor.

Mona's smirk was doing some of the work, though, when she concluded her conversation with the innkeeper. She returned to him looking delighted, and very evil.

"Our meeting will be in the hot spring," she informed Galwell.

"That sounds lovely," he replied honestly.

Mona raised her eyebrows in coy innocence. "You packed your swimming clothes?"

Now he understood. The problem. The source of her delight. Reading him understanding her, Mona grinned gleefully.

"Did you really not know *where* you arranged a meeting with my would-be killer? Seems like leaving me vulnerable in a hot spring would be exactly what they want," he said.

"They don't know you're coming. And no." Mona wrinkled her

nose. "You really don't know how meetings between two evil undisclosed villains work. Follow me," she ordered him, without waiting for Galwell's objection.

He watched her swaying form proceed to the stairwell. What could he do except follow?

The stone staircase led them down to what Galwell gathered was the inn's spa, where stones like the quarry slabs they'd escaped the capital alongside were heated for massages and ever-warm baths. Their destination waited past these features, the centerpiece of the spa—the hot spring itself.

Off the main room, the hot spring's current flowed into private chambers. The spa's attendant led them into one.

The cozier dimensions of the private spa, half contoured of stone and half of the inn's same sturdy wood, concerned Galwell. Perfect for assassinations, or—

Worse. When the attendant departed, closing the door, Mona started immediately to undress.

"Shouldn't we wait for our contact?" Galwell managed. Did his voice sound pinched? Strangled? No doubt merely the lingering effect of the frost in his lungs.

Mona shrugged. "He's running late and my ass is killing me after that ride up the mountain," she informed him. "I could use the healing waters. Possibly a massage." Raising an eyebrow, she dropped her coat to the floor, then bent over slowly to unlace her snow boots.

Galwell found himself watching, mesmerized. Their hroxen could have crashed through the spa right now, and he suspected he would have continued to watch Mona.

With unhurried deliberation, she removed her riding wear, stripping down to only her underclothes. He'd never seen the skin of her shoulders, her stomach, her thighs. The warm, sun-dusted contours of her, seeming somehow to glow with her own untamable light. Perhaps she *did* want to kill him.

Well, he'd died in worse ways.

Mona slid into the hot water, moaning obscenely. Galwell was certain his cheeks had assumed the deep crimson of the firelight upstairs. Natural bubbles and foaming currents in the hot spring obscured her body within the sheer fabric of her underclothes—but Galwell's imagination had never had such cause to run wild before in his life.

It wouldn't do. He felt the rogue grip of passion pushing him in dangerous directions.

Controlling himself, he sat down heavily on the bench, far from the hot water.

"You're not joining me?" Mona inquired.

He wanted to. He desperately wanted to. On his bench, despite the steam warming the room to fireside temperatures, Galwell felt like he'd stepped outside onto the Evriel mountainside in nothing except *his* underclothes.

But he could not forget the deeper cold he'd felt with Mona. The last time she'd seduced him—the way he'd felt the next day when she revealed how little their passion meant to her.

"I want to," he said honestly. "I want to touch you in that water. To taste you. To have you taste me again. But I . . . want it to mean something to you, and I know it doesn't."

Mona's smirk slipped.

"You really just say what you're thinking all the time," she remarked.

He shrugged his enormous shoulders. "I have no reason for deception. Especially not with you."

Mona sank deeper in the water, the foaming opaque surface rising to the tops of her breasts. Wanting pierced Galwell. *Cold, desperate cold.*

"Curious. Most people feel the exact opposite," she said.

"I'm not most people," Galwell replied.

Her confident gaze faltered. Mona paused, eyeing him like—like she was realizing something.

"No," she concurred. "You're not."

He did not know what Mona found surprising in this revelation—Galwell the Great, hero of Mythria, villain of Vestriya, possessor of uncommon magic and presently living his second life, who preferred milkbrews *without* whipped candycream on top—was quite literally not like most people.

But he continued, offering Mona more of the honesty she evidently found uncanny. "It must be horrible, knowing exactly how much the people in your life conceal from you. How much they lie," he said. "I expect, even among my closest friends, they all have secrets, thoughts that could hurt me. I know people are not always their thoughts, but nevertheless, I'm grateful not to know every worst one. No wonder you carved out such an independent existence."

His companion's expression went Evriel-wind chilly. "You mean no wonder I'm such a villain," she snapped. "You think you've figured me out. *Mona turned to darkness because she saw the darkness in everyone around her.*" She scoffed.

With his magical strength, Galwell knew how to heap extra gentleness onto precarious gestures. And in the company of Mona's wisecracking sibling, he'd learned it sometimes felt easier to speak ill of oneself so that others would not indulge in the opportunity.

He kept his voice soft. "I think it would be very hard for anyone to endure knowing all that. It's remarkable that *despite* your knowledge, you're no villain," he said.

Real surprise shocked the disdain from Mona's features. "You—*can't* believe that," she pressed him.

"You know I don't lie."

Seeming conflicted, she considered his response. Finally concluding . . . something, she turned, concealing her face from his view.

"You think I'm not a villain, do you?" she murmured. "Ask me what it is my brother promised me in exchange for keeping you safe."

Despite the dark charge in her ominous invitation, Galwell didn't flinch. "Whatever it is, I won't think less of you for it," he promised her.

"Very well." Mona turned back to him, her upper half rising from the water, glistening in the steam. Galwell fought to concentrate despite the crystal-clear droplets clinging to her skin. "I propose a game, then," she declared. "You tell me lies, and I'll tell you truths I conceal from everyone. We will see which of the two of us is happier in the end."

"I love games," Galwell replied readily.

Mona raised an eyebrow.

He grinned. "Not bad for my first lie."

She laughed. "Let's begin, then." She paused, thinking. Water trickled down her skin. "I killed my first man when I was fifteen. Name of Kell," she announced. "He was a mentor to Clare. Sort of bandit father figure, even. Clare loved him. But on a con together, I learned from Kell's thoughts that he planned to leave Clare behind to take the blame. The people they were stealing from would have killed my brother."

She shrugged hollowly.

"Clare wouldn't listen to me when I warned him. He trusted Kell. He believed he could be reasoned with. Of course he did," she said. "My brother, the noblest thief there ever was. Because he gets to live a life where he can't hear the evil in people, clawing in their minds like rats in a cage," she went on viciously. "I do. So I did what Clare couldn't. I gutted Kell—I made him suffer."

Galwell knew Mona expected him to react to her bloody violence.

He did not. His mind—his legendary heart—lingered on Mona herself, young and trying to protect her older brother.

"He would have killed someone you love," Galwell replied without guile. "You saved Clare, even if he didn't thank you for it."

"He did more than *not thank me*. He said he never wanted to see me again," Mona spat. Her eyes flickered. "He called me merciless."

Mona the Merciless. Galwell imagined her then, as if in a conjuration. The young Mona, losing the love of her family, fleeing home with Clare's condemnation ringing in her ears. In Vestriya's underworld, she'd remade herself in the echo of the most painful word anyone had ever said of her.

"I'm sorry," he finally replied. "I'm sorry for what it cost you."

Mona scrutinized him, but she looked like his earnest, understanding response pleased her. "Now the lie," she prompted.

He sat upright on the bench. He would perform his disingenuousness in support of his words, he decided. His posture would seem . . . carefree. Sturdy. Confident. Everything he did not feel. "It is . . . easy to be a hero," he ventured. "I never doubted my sacrifices."

With heaviness in his throat, he found he—Galwell the Great, with inhuman strength—could not carry the confession's weight effortlessly.

Mona watched him, her gaze without judgment. It was . . . welcoming, and welcome. It was what he needed.

Finally, she nodded in satisfaction.

"After that first kill," she continued, "I was wanted for murder in Mythria. I fled my ungrateful family and came to Vestriya hoping for a fresh start, only to lose my friends, those who took me in, to a horrific accident. I have no one to blame for their deaths. If I did, maybe I'd feel better, because I'd have sought my revenge. Instead, I can only blame everyone and everything. Fate. The world. All I can do is take my vengeance daily."

Galwell's heart broke for her. Lost, unmoored, grasping onto the only family she could find, only for tragedy to rip from her everyone she cared for. No wonder she had hardened herself to everyone she knew. Her honesty emboldened him.

"I'm glad my friends erased my sacrifice and brought me back to life."

Mona's breath caught. "You wish you'd died?"

Galwell stared down the ugly feelings within him. He let himself acknowledge them fully. "No. I'm glad to be alive. But . . . they stripped me of my heroism. I do not know how to be the one saved."

Mona didn't flinch away from his feelings. "I think you can still be a hero even if you have to be saved from time to time."

Galwell considered this. He didn't know how to reply.

Wordlessly, Mona sank underwater, vanishing for moments before resurfacing, using her hands to slick her hair back perfectly. Her eyes opened, finding his with unreserved understanding.

The look pulled Galwell from his seat.

"I *don't* regret not getting in that pool with you," he lied in rasped syllables. Even while he spoke, he was shedding his coat, his riding clothes. He removed everything down to his underclothes.

Mona's severe expression never changed, yet her eyes danced with delight when he stepped into the wonderfully hot water. The scalding reminded him of truth itself. Pleasure extracted from pain. Raw relief on the edge of exposure.

"That's two lies now," Mona observed. "I owe you something good."

The note of promise in her voice made *good* sound like its opposite. He waited—on the edge of himself now—while Mona drifted closer, parting the water with even, rippling movements. When she neared him, he could glimpse the peaks of her breasts under the wet fabric of her underclothes.

"I flirted with Ario to make you jealous," she confessed.

Galwell felt himself grow hard at the admission. It demanded everything in him not to reach out and cup her curves.

"I *can't wait* to go home to Mythria," he murmured. He was delving deeper into his soul for these lies now. He knew he should want to return to his homeland, where he was revered, where heroism was uncomplicated. Yet the idea filled him with dread.

Mona swallowed. She was close, close enough that forbidden magic seemed to vibrate in the distance between them. "Being with you . . . scared me," she confessed. "I can't stop thinking about you. I'm afraid of what it means. What *you* could mean."

For once, Galwell wished he had her magic. He wanted to hear that thought resonate deep in her heart, not only on her lush lips. *I can't stop thinking about you. I can't stop thinking about you.* Instead, he had only this criminal's honesty to rely on.

But the desire in him cared nothing for criminality, or honesty, or lips deceiving hearts. Passion roared in him. He reached for her, chasing impulsiveness like he never had, and pulled her body close.

"I *hate* how wicked you are," he rumbled, then pressed his lips to her neck, hungry with need.

She moaned into him. "Which part of that is the lie, Galwell?" she got out, sounding like she was struggling with the syllables. "That I'm wicked? Or that you hate it?"

"I don't know anymore," Galwell said. His hands sunk lower, his powerful muscles going taut when he caressed her hips—when he clasped her ass—under the unwinding water.

It was another lie.

It severed his restraint, and Mona's. His lips crashed against hers the moment she lifted her face to his. In the hurtling rush, Galwell forgot everything of their snowy climb to this mountain of pure heat. He could not even remember what cold felt like. After forcing out noble lies, he realized how much he'd repressed his own desires—no longer.

He was pure selfishness now. He released his grip on Mona, letting his hands roam everywhere. Touching her everywhere. Delighting with how deeply she seemed to enjoy it. He reached up, following nothing except ferocious want, to grab her hair in his fist. Mona gasped.

"Is this what you like?" he demanded in a whisper.

"Yes," she responded, breathless. "Is it what you like?"

"*No*," he lied deliciously from deep in his chest. "*Not at all.*"

Mona laughed. The sound was like snowflakes, except they pinpricked him with quick fire. Or like starjays, flying on winter nights. Her laughter was dazzling light streaking through the darkness.

She reached under the water to stroke him while he groaned deeply into her neck, into the sweet night-floral scent of her skin, still steaming with hot water. She urged him closer, closer, while he lost himself in her . . . only stopping when she knew he was right on the edge. Then she withdrew to look directly into his eyes.

"Clare promised to tell me where our parents are," she said seriously. "He's stayed away from me for more than a decade so that I wouldn't read the answer in his mind. When I find out where our parents are, I'll seek them out, and I'll make them pay for the life they forced me into. For surrounding me and Clare with people like Kell. For leaving me to kill my brother's ruthless friend, breaking Clare's heart." Her voice was ice cold, mercilessly guttural. "I'll make them pay in every way I couldn't when I was a child."

The shock disoriented Galwell. He stilled, staring into her eyes, suddenly horrified. Galwell knew from Clare that his parents had been bandits. That his childhood had been full of uncertainty and fear. But Clare had seemed to move past it. While Mona . . . She couldn't possibly . . .

Yes, she could, he realized. It was why she'd negotiated her return to Mythria with Thessia. Not for criminal enterprise. For ruthless revenge.

In that moment, Mona heard everything he did not say. Her face crumpled, just for an instant. Then her indifferent, amused mask returned. "See? Told you I'm no good," she said. She moved past him to step out of the water. "I'm your villain, G. Not your . . ." She gestured. "Whatever this is."

Galwell's hand shot out. He grabbed her wrist, unyieldingly but gently.

"Revenge won't bring you happiness," he said urgently. "Don't do this to yourself."

Halfway out of the water, Mona stared down at him. She held his gaze without mercy.

"What if I do?" she asked slowly. "Will you hate my wickedness for real?"

"I . . ." He did not know. He felt, deep down, in some place in his heart that reason's light never reached, that he could never *hate* Mona the Merciless. Yet he did not know how he could ever fully understand someone who lost herself willingly, entirely, in such depths of gruesome vengeance.

He did not have to. Right then, their private room's door opened. Galwell had nearly forgotten they were here for the inconvenient problem of the recent attempts on his life. In strode Mona's contact—

"You," Galwell said, earnestly surprised.

The moment Sir Cheswick Chestlewitt laid eyes on Galwell, the raven-curled scribe shrieked. Having read his intentions, however, Mona was faster—she leapt out of the water to cut off Chestlewitt's path with a knife to the man's jawline. Where she'd hidden a knife beneath her flimsy underclothes, Galwell had no idea.

"You're the one who wants me dead?" Galwell marveled.

"You know this man?" Mona asked.

She did not get out to the theater much, the hero figured. "He's a playwright," Galwell explained. "He wrote a play about me and Thessia. It wasn't well received. And now you want to kill me for it?" he asked Chestlewitt, more out of wonderment than ire. "It wasn't *my* fault."

"Of course it was," the playwright hissed. "If you had just stayed dead, you would have been the perfect tragic figure. A real hero worthy of the stage. Alive, you're ... just a person," he finished in disgust.

The insult did not reach Galwell. *Just a person.* Neither hero nor villain. The notion met him with unsettling relief. He rose from the water, reaching for his enchanted coat to cover his enormous frame. He tossed Mona hers, which she deftly slipped on while keeping the knife to the playwright's neck. Chestlewitt's eyes darted between his captors.

"You hired the Deathrose Guild," Galwell said, piecing this together. "Why did they accept the contract? I don't fit the qualifications for their marks."

"I don't know," Chestlewitt responded, flustered.

Mona glanced over her shoulder, meeting Galwell's gaze. "Lie," she informed him. "The guild told him they too were frustrated with your return. Villainy was on the decline due to your resurrection, which was bad for the business of killing villains. So they were pleased to work with Chestlewitt for their own purposes."

The playwright's eyes rounded. "How did you—"

"Wait, there's more," Mona murmured. She studied Chestlewitt, concentrating with genuine concern now. "They've severed their ties with this man. They were offered a better deal—an easier deal. Someone else hired them to kill the prince. They framed you for the murder and destroyed your reputation, which they believe has crushed spirits in Mythria and will revive evil in the realm more effectively than your death."

Once more Galwell felt himself on that cold, cold mountainside. *They've destroyed your reputation.* They had, hadn't they? He was now the villain of Vestriya as part of the guild's greater plan.

"So much for their sacred oath to me!" Chestlewitt fumed, his frustration surmounting his curiosity over Mona's magical mind reading. "My greatest work—destroyed. Now you're no hero. You're a villain. Who would go to a play about a villain!"

Mona considered the playwright's premise. "I don't know. A story about a villain sounds compelling. Not a hero—an *anti*hero. It would be interesting, wouldn't it?" she mused.

"Don't be ridiculous," the scribe spat. "No one wants that!"

Ignoring Mona's dramaturgical contemplation—and her dagger—he looked directly at Galwell.

"Galwell," he implored. "You need to save my play."

The once-hero found himself growing furious. He understood the sacrifice of his *life* in the name of heroism, in the name of defending his realm. The guild had stolen something even more precious to him—his sense of who he was. His power to inspire. "I don't care about your play, you dithering dragonwart," he growled.

Chestlewitt drew back, looking—impressed. "Dithering dragonwart," he repeated. "Did you come up with that?" He nodded like he planned to pilfer the insult for himself. "Of course you want to save my play," he went on impatiently. "It means being a hero again. Clearing your name."

"And then *dying*!" Galwell reminded him.

Chestlewitt stayed silent.

"We're done here," Galwell said to Mona. "This man is a weak fool."

Desperation leaping into his eyes, Chestlewitt licked his lips. *Spare us your soliloquies*, Galwell nearly said, except he worried the man would latch onto this alliteration as well.

"The guild has new leadership," Chestlewitt offered. "Risen to the top when their business was weak. This new leader wants to go further. They want to ensure villainy *never* dies. Perhaps you'd like to know their plot. Save the day. Be a hero. One fit for the stage."

Galwell paused. "You're lying," he said to the playwright.

Gloating with the victory of an audience reengaged, Chestlewitt grinned. "Ask your beautiful mind reader." His eyes flitting to Mona. "I'd love to get your name before I go, by the way. The pages cry out for a . . . a *damsel of destruction*," he said with a flourish, inventing the coinage on the spot.

Mona did not respond to his request.

Her face paled. She looked to Galwell.

"He's telling the truth," she said urgently. "The guild plans . . . to kill Thessia and take over Mythria."

Fear clutched Galwell instantly. *Of course*. He'd known vicious leaders, oppressors intent on inspiring hopelessness, on crushing the realms under their control. They never stopped with mayhem. They wanted *everything*.

"It's horrible, right?" Chestlewitt said, grimacing. "Not even an original concept. I mean, taking over the realm? How trite and tawdry. Where's the drama? The emotion?"

Galwell ignored the poetical fool. He'd wanted a chance to be the hero since the moment he set foot in Vestriya. But not like this. Not when his dear friend was once more in danger. Not when he had no idea who he truly was.

"Who is the guild's new leader?" he demanded unevenly.

With genuine insouciance, Chestlewitt shrugged.

"I never saw their face. I don't know. But you're the only chance to stop them," he replied. "Save the day, Galwell. Save—my play!"

25
River

For over a day, River could not teleport. But she'd felt the effect of the magical ropes finally wear off—or rather, she'd felt the absence of effect, the same way a burn from the sun dulled into nothingness—and still, River had neglected her power, opting to move through Vestriya on foot.

Walking gave her time for all that thinking she hadn't yet done, without any sort of crisis occurring to distract her. She wasn't chasing Galwell, or fighting with guild members, or being kidnapped. She was making her way to Celine with patience and intent, gathering together a sufficient apology while building out a plan for her new life.

Only when her chest began to ache with longing did she realize she was using walking as an excuse. She was afraid that Celine might turn her away for taking so long. She was afraid Celine had only had her rescued out of standard kindness, not something more.

She was afraid of what her own feelings actually meant.

When River could avoid it no longer—worried she might keel over from all the longing—she finally closed her eyes and imagined Celine.

She ended up teleporting to a strange, run-down village called Arveto. There was a makeshift sign hammered into a tree stating the village's name, painted in an ominous red. Or maybe the threatening energy had to do with all the deterioration. Everywhere, spindly weeds with tiny specks of blackened berries sprouted in between broken pathways and up the walls of battered buildings. More windows were boarded up with wood than fitted with panes of glass. All the trees were leafless and gray.

For once, River's magic did not drop her directly in Celine's path. Instead, Celine was several paces ahead of River, carrying a basket packed with loaves of bread and chunks of fresh cheese. She passed them out to villagers as she walked by, offering a kind smile and squeezing many hands.

All the practicing River had done in her head seemed insufficient when presented with the fullness of Celine, observing her generosity of spirit. And the reality of her. Those lips she'd kissed only once. That body she'd barely held. There was so much she wanted to know about Celine's life, and so many things she hoped to be worthy of but didn't know if she ever could be again.

It was true that Celine had lied, but River no longer felt the pulsing heat of anger when she thought about it. She'd developed an understanding in their time apart. She too had told lies to protect herself, on more than one occasion. And the truth was, she missed Celine more than she cared about what she'd done.

In the distance, Celine held out a vial of dark liquid. "Do you recognize this?" she asked a wizened old woman seated in a rocking chair outside what looked to be the village's apothecary shop.

The old woman held the small green bottle up to the sunlight. "Of course I do. This is our cinderflower extract."

Celine nodded, like she already knew that much. "When I last visited, it was only being used as a painkiller. Can you tell me when it started being used as a poison?"

The old woman tensed. "Are you in trouble?" The concern with which she asked suggested a prior relationship between her and Celine.

"No, no." Celine pasted on the smile River had come to know as her false one. "Something happened to a friend of mine involving this. He was very nearly killed by it."

Intrigued, River checked again that her location was secure, wanting to continue watching without disruption or notice. She was tucked into the narrow alley between two buildings, and the passing villagers paid her no mind, far more interested in securing some of Celine's food or, perhaps more pressingly, her attention.

"It was discovered that in large doses, the cinderflower is deadly," the old woman said, her face wrinkling in regret. "A man came to our village with a bad headache. He took more than we recommended, and he fell dead within the hour. It was a horrible accident, and we tried to stop production altogether once we figured it out." The woman swirled the vial, watching the dark liquid swish around the bottle. "But the royal guard showed up not long after, telling us they'd be buying out our entire supply indefinitely. They didn't say why, but one can make an educated guess."

Celine pulled out her notebook and quill to scribble down this information.

"I'm sorry to hear what happened to your friend," the old woman said. "I'm glad he survived it. It's certainly not what our village wants to do with the extract, but it's the only way we can survive at all. We're the only ones who can make it, since it grows from our ruined soil. It's all we have."

Celine bit her lip, looking away for a moment before she said, "Thank you, Mariana."

Mariana.

So they did know each other.

"Of course, dear." Mariana rose slowly from her rocking chair to peek her head into the shop. "Loris, tell the children Celine is here."

A moment later, several children, all between the ages of three and six, rushed through the front door of the apothecary shop. They were dressed in clothing that was more patches than original fabric. Their faces brightened at the sight of Celine, and they hugged her, crying out her name in delight.

Once the greetings ended, Celine sat in the rocking chair beside Mariana's and pulled a children's book out of her basket. As if expecting this, the children took spots at her feet, sitting with their legs crisscrossed as Celine began to read. She gave a committed performance, putting on special voices and taking great care to make sure the children saw each illustration before turning the page.

When she finished, the children cried out for more.

"That's the only story I could fit into my basket," Celine told them regretfully. "But I will leave it with Mariana so you can revisit it as often as you'd like."

"More! More!" cried the children.

River knew what she had to do.

With a running start, she hurdled down the empty road that led to the apothecary shop, propelling herself into a roundoff back handspring. The ground wasn't very forgiving, but River had enough adrenaline to power herself through the maneuvers anyway. Out of her back handspring, she rebounded high, stretching as tall and straight as she could before rotating into a magnificent laid-out back somersault, even going so far as to open her legs into a split while upside down for extra flourish.

When she landed, the children erupted in rapturous applause.

"You're here," Celine managed to say, her voice barely rising above the din.

"I am," River said, looking long and deep into Celine's eyes.

There were entire conversations in this exchange. Words that would fill hundreds of pieces of parchment, running countless quills dry. At its simplest, this look was an apology. It was a question. It was an answer, too.

I am sorry. Will you take me back? You were all I thought about while kidnapped. You kept me alive.

"More, more!" the children cried, this time for River.

Knowing she and Celine could not yet reunite in full, River obliged the children, handspringing and cartwheeling and somersaulting until her shins stung and her neck ached. The children, so desperate for joy and so clearly lacking in chances to receive it, still wanted more. So River switched to doing for them what the acrobats of her family's circus had once done for her—she taught them how to tumble instead, and they put together their very own circus performance.

River could've spent the rest of daylight showing the children how to stand on their hands and work as a group to make their own spectacular show. But Mariana, wise as she was, summoned the children back into the shop to wash up for dinner.

"Thank you," Mariana said, squeezing Celine's hands and then River's.

Celine's eyes were filled with tears as she told Mariana, "It's the least I could do." She handed over the remaining contents of her basket. "For dinner."

Mariana kissed her forehead, then entered the apothecary shop, leaving River and Celine alone.

"You know, I'd been planning to yell at you," Celine said.

River laughed. Oh, it felt so good to do so, loosening up the tension and pain in her chest, freeing up space for all the hope that wanted so desperately to bloom inside her. "What did you want to say?" she asked. "I'm quite sure I deserve to hear it."

"Oh, I had grand plans," Celine told her. "I even wrote some things in my notebook. They were very harsh. But now that you're here, all I want to do is kiss you."

River took a step forward, using her impish grin as one final peace offering. "I'm pesky like that, aren't I?" They were nose to nose. If River had ever had a real place to call home, this was how she imagined it would feel. Comfortable, secure. Enveloping. "I was in a similar situation. I'd been quite upset with you for lying to me. But when I was held captive, none of that mattered very much anymore."

For a moment, they stilled, saying nothing, intertwining their fingers as they breathed in synchronicity.

"What is this place to you?" River finally asked.

"My magic," Celine said quietly, as tears filled her eyes. "The first time my family visited Vestriya, I burned this village to the ground."

River worked to make sense of this, adding this new information to everything she already knew. It fit like a key into the final locked barrier that stood between them. The voyage Celine took right before she met River. The lying about her gift. The reaction to receiving the harpies' amplification.

This was why.

"How did the fire happen?" River asked.

"It wasn't on purpose," Celine said softly, the tears beginning to fall. "My parents and I were in an argument. My emotions were out of control. I got so angry. I couldn't stop it from rising up in me. And then everything was burning. I never meant for this—"

"*I know, love.*" River moved her hands to stroke gentle circles on Celine's arms with her thumbs.

"I'm sorry I lied to you," Celine said. "I've been to Vestriya many times. I come to Arveto as often as I can to check on everyone who still lives here."

"I figured as much. Not that I don't think random children wouldn't fall at your feet for story time without knowing you. You have an arresting effect."

This made Celine smile—small, but there.

It was a start.

"It's not enough," Celine said, unraveling once more. "I came here again because Ario was poisoned, and it's my fault."

"How can that be your fault?" River asked, unconvinced. She implored Celine with her eyes. *Trust me*, she begged. *I can handle it.*

"I knew the poison they used was a product of my own destruction," Celine said. "When the soil in this area first mixed with the ash, the land never recovered. But then the cinderflower berries popped up, and the people realized they could be of use. Except now they are a weapon. Just like me." New tears stifled her words. "I cause so much pain. I'm a danger to everyone else."

River pulled her in, wrapping an arm around her waist and pressing the other to her cheek to wipe the tears away. "Love, you did this by accident," she said. "I've done bad things on purpose. Many, many times. I did a bad thing the moment I left you on the carousel, and I think—I *hope*—you've forgiven me anyway."

"I have," Celine said.

"Then why can't you do the same for yourself?"

They fell quiet again. It was nearly dark outside, and the air had a heavy static to it, a silence filled with grief and loss. Still, the villagers had made the best of the worst. They'd survived.

"Let's go somewhere," River suggested. "Just for us."

Celine gave her a permissive nod, and River closed her eyes.

When she opened them again, they were inside the Grotto. The cave was empty. It was just River, Celine, and that same strangely calming glow of the water that turned everything bluish-green.

"Ario had mentioned that no one is allowed inside after the sun goes down," River said. "Looks like it's true. Too bad no one else knows how to teleport."

Already River could see some liveliness returning to Celine's face, her eyes wide in wonder, just as they had been the last time they were here.

"It's quite fortunate," Celine said. She crouched down to run her fingers through the glowing stream. Her features began to relax, knots of tension unspooling with every gentle swirl and swish she made. "I'm still afraid of what the amplification to my powers will do," she whispered.

"I know," River said, squatting down to join her. The water was warm and somehow silky, like petting a soft animal. "Just because you're afraid doesn't mean you have to hide, though. We can figure it out together."

"Thank you for coming back to me," Celine whispered.

River caught the tremble in her voice, the threat of sadness waiting to crest once again.

"Hey," she whispered back. "It's okay. Come here."

She turned Celine's body toward hers, pressing them together.

And she kissed her.

She kissed her like they'd spent centuries apart. She kissed her like Celine was breath itself, and River would die without her. She kissed her with everything she had, until she felt *more* stirring inside her, a trembling ache of want that bloomed low in her belly.

River kissed Celine all the way over to a wall of rock. She kept kissing her until they reached another alcove not unlike the one they'd hidden in the last time they were inside the Grotto.

When River gasped for air, it was Celine who pulled her back, hungry in a way River understood. They kissed as they peeled off layers of clothing, tearing off blouses, tossing away skirts and leggings, still standing against the cool rock, enjoying its rough edges and unforgiving sturdiness.

Even skin to skin, they did not come up for air. River's hand wandered instead, sliding her fingers down until she found the slick, warm source of Celine's need.

Celine let out a throaty gasp of pleasure, and this was no time for cautious exploration. River's fingers worked as fast as they could, and Celine's cries grew louder with the effort—a ragged, echoing sound against the hollow emptiness of the cave. River craved more of it, panting with exertion, pressing and coaxing until Celine's desire crested.

Hot, orange flames licked the air around them both.

This was not the work of River's imagination, or a feeling that had become vivid through the fervor of their touch.

No. Celine had caught fire.

"*Shit*," they breathed in unison.

River closed her eyes, thinking of velvety warmth, and soon they were submerged in the Grotto's pool.

Though the water looked opaque on the surface, it was crystal clear beneath, and River saw Celine in full, the curves of her naked body flowing with the water, her wild brown curls ribboning around her. Ghosts, she was beautiful.

They shot up to the surface together.

"You sparked fire," River said in disbelief.

"You put it out," Celine replied, equally as stunned.

They stared at each other until the shock turned into laughter. And then they were delirious with it, gasping between bursts of joy, kissing and spinning each other in the silky water.

"Seems we make a good match," River couldn't help but say. "You catch fire, I bring us to water."

Rivulets ran into Celine's mouth as she smiled, but that now-familiar sadness was starting to creep back in. "I wish I didn't have fire at all. I thought with all my years away from my power, my age and wisdom had given me more restraint. But even now, I still can't contain it. Most people learn how to control their gifts. Clearly, I'm not worthy of that."

River kissed her forehead. "Of course you're worthy. How could you ever think anything else? You've made amends in Arveto the best you possibly could. Everyone in that village adores you. And look, even the harpies blessed you." She waved her hand around, secretly hoping said harpies might reappear, if only because it would make an already unforgettable night even more incredible.

"I don't want their blessing," Celine said, and River was glad the harpies did not heed her private wish, because it seemed the kind of thing the mercurial creatures might not like knowing. "The last thing I need is *more* power."

Hearing Celine say things about herself that were so obviously untrue sharpened River's mind in a way few other conversations ever had. She knew Celine was not defined by her magic . . . yet River constantly defined herself by her own.

If she believed Celine did not need to be, then couldn't she offer herself the same grace? Couldn't she want a different life after all?

26
Thessia

"Are you quite certain he cannot ride upon my shoulder outside the hood?"

Ario's plaintive inquiries on the subject of Benjamin's riding position had accompanied them for much of their stealthy walk through the seedy wharves of Vestriya's capital, where they had returned from the Pale Palace with the recovering prince.

"He's fine inside," Thessia promised Ario patiently while the prince fidgeted with the heavy garment covering his entire upper body. Peering into Ario's hood, Thessia could just discern the faintly glowing eye stalks of the snail. "He likes the dark," she reassured Ario.

"She is right," Hugh murmured. "If anyone sees you and your conspicuous pet, they'll recognize you."

Ario humphed. "What's so dreadful about that anyway? Then they would know my parents are deceiving their fair realm."

He was not incorrect. The Vestriyan king and queen continued to have their scribes report that Ario remained in the Pale Palace, his condition not improving. Worse, the gloomy reporting was gathering sympathy for the supposedly grieving royal couple, parents who might lose their second son on the heels of the death of their first. The positive press had silenced the indignant voices who would have joined Ezio's coup.

"Your parents would send assassins after you," Thessia reminded him. "Right now, the Pale Palace is covering for us all."

Ario frowned. "I'd wish danger on my tail over hiding my snail," he rhymed grumblingly.

Hugh led them up seawater-slickened stairs where one grimy dock ended, returning them into the narrow, shadow-cast streets of the city. Rumprats skittered across their path, fleeing under wooden doors darkened with soot and splintered from decades of overuse.

"Why did your brother want to depose your parents?" Hugh asked, as if to distract the prince.

It worked. Ario startled. In response, he gestured to their surroundings. "Look around you. See how hard the lives of these people are?" he inquired earnestly.

Thessia did look. Under the wharf's granite sky, she saw what ever-present danger and her own complicated situation had led her to ignore. Fishmongers huddling in the cold while they knifed open their catches with crooked fingers. Exhausted manor servants hustling from stall to stall under the weight of their woven satchels. Men wandering the docks without destination, their hungry eyes haunted.

"Crime runs rampant in much of our realm, hidden behind the gilded facades of the richer districts," Ario continued, quiet fury in his voice. "Our parents do not care that so many of their people suffer in poverty. Ezio did. He was going to change things. He would have looked out for our people the way he looked out for me. They only wanted me to be spymaster because I was a joke. Ezio was the one to make me look . . . dangerous. He protected me."

His voice broke, and tears sprang into his eyes. His grief was not like the poets depicted—he did not wail or tear at his hair or collapse to his knees.

Thessia knew it was because the wound was too deep. He'd had no proper chance to mourn his brother. Right now, he needed time, care, perspective. Not . . . questing.

Sympathy softened her. "We'll find proof," she reassured him. "You can win Ezio's people to your side."

This stopped Ario in the middle of the stone-walled street.

"Me?" he exclaimed. "You want *me* to be k—"

Hugh interrupted him urgently. "*Cook*, yes," he said, loudly cutting off the prince's exclamation for the fishermen passing them. "Cook for our party. Yes, you would make an excellent cook, wouldn't you?"

Ario reddened. "No, I would be awful!" he exclaimed. "My brother deserves justice, but someone else should be the . . . um, cook."

"Perhaps we can discuss this when we reach the safehouse Celine arranged," Hugh replied gravely, "because right now, I fear we are being followed."

Forgetting herself, Thessia whipped around very conspicuously to look for whomever Hugh had noticed. But Hugh was there, grabbing her hand, pulling her forward hard to stop her erratic surveillance.

He drew her around the next shadowy corner, his harp callouses rough against her soft skin.

Hastily, he released her, like he'd realized they needed to hold hands no longer. They shouldn't, in fact.

Hugh's abruptness—or perhaps the pink invading Thessia's face, embarrassment feuding with lingering heat—did not escape Ario's notice. "Using my former spymaster skills, I did overhear the healers gossiping that the pair of you broke up. Ezio would have been so proud of me." He sniffled. "Are you . . . doing okay?"

The young prince did not sound scandalized or—even more remarkable still—like he was looking for poetic inspiration in the depths of their lovelorn emotion. He was sincerely checking on them.

"We didn't break up," Hugh amended roughly. "We were never officially together—"

She cut him off. "Is now really the time?"

Ario scoffed grandly. "Time is no lord over love," he pronounced.

Thessia and Hugh's gazes found him. It was just that his poetical sentiment was . . . rather good.

Like he knew it, Ario proudly put his hands on his hips. "You'd really have me give up my poetry for . . . cooking?"

Thessia laughed. "Who's to say you cannot do both?"

"Sorry," Hugh cut in.

Was he grouchy about Ario's line of romantic questioning? Thessia wondered.

"We *must* flee," he insisted with unusually stern intensity. "We really are being followed."

When he glanced over Thessia's shoulder while directing them around the next street corner, Thessia was able to follow his gaze, glimpsing—okay, yes, there really was a hooded figure pursuing them.

Assassin? Spy for the king and queen? Whoever it was, she and Hugh needed to keep Ario safe and out of sight.

The small square into which they exited was thronged with people. Fishmongers hoarsely hawking the whitefish and pincerlings, the scuttlesnails and pestleshells they carried in wicker contraptions over their heads. Thessia moved quickly with her friends, and glancing once more over her shoulder, she saw no sign of their hooded pursuer. They stole nervously into the passageway on the square's opposite end, where open ocean waited on one side—

Rounding the corner, Thessia realized their mistake.

The hooded man stood in front of them, his grin visible from under his cloak.

They hadn't lost him. Of course not. He probably knew Vestriyan streets like he knew the map of scars on the hand holding the curved knife he drew from his robes. They were right where he wanted them.

THIS WILL BE INTERESTING

Thessia was so sick of being right where people wanted her.

Hugh felt the same, evidently.

In the very moment the hooded man rushed forward, Hugh pushed Thessia hard off the path. Flinging her hands out in front of her—finding nothing, no purchase, only empty sky—Thessia flew right into the ocean.

"Swim!" her husband shouted. "*Now!*"

Thessia wanted to. When the cold water hit her, shocking her senses, she went under. She resurfaced sputtering, struggling. Her waterlogged cloak was heavy, the dense fabric constricting her limbs like the grotesque tentacles of some monstrous depthwalker. Panic gripped her, the grimy salt water rising past her lips while she gasped, thrashing, fighting the soaking cloth—

Hugh was there. He dove in, perfectly, like a Mythria Games competitor, then an instant later emerged next to her.

"I've got you," he promised, his dark hair lashed to his face. "Just breathe." He ripped her cloak off, freeing her from the constraining fabric.

Just breathe. Thessia could only obey.

Hugh held her up above the surface, giving her the chance to fill her lungs, to calm her pounding heart. She searched the surface of the water frantically for the prince, but only the lurching shapes of the boats moored in the crowded harbor surrounded them.

Oh, Ghosts no. Without Hugh's strong embrace, Thessia herself would likely have drowned. Their charge, their objective—they couldn't possibly have let him . . .

Then she glimpsed the prince on the docks. The hooded man was close . . . but had not reached Ario. Instead, their pursuer was clutching his foot, yelping.

"You broke my foot!" he shrieked.

Ario covered his own ears, looking utterly mortified, while their pursuer hobbled off, weeping. Following Hugh, Thessia swam to the dock, where they heaved themselves up onto the wood. "What in the realms . . ." Thessia started to say.

Interrupting her, Ario, who looked rather seasick, vomited very suddenly into the ocean.

"For the record," he managed miserably when he'd finished, "I did *not* break his foot. Oh, how horrid. Unimaginable. I only broke his . . . his . . ." He gagged. Thessia hastened out of the way, fearing more princely puking. "His toe!" Ario wailed.

Hugh, visibly confused, patted Ario on the shoulder. Thessia understood the import of the confession, however. "You used your magic for us," she said.

Ario nodded, his color starting to return. "And it was as terrible as I remember it. Just ghastly. Disgusting. The poor man."

"He likely was paid to kill you," Hugh reminded him gravely.

"And now he'll never receive the money he needs to set his toe!" Ario replied. "How awful!"

Swallowing her laughter, Thessia put her hand comfortingly on the prince's other shoulder. He did not react to the seawater her wet hand seeped into his cloak. "Thank you for stopping him," she said earnestly. "I know how much you hate using your magic."

Her gratitude eased the prince's illness, which was fortunate—Thessia did not wish to get vomit on her remaining clothes, now soaked. The filthy ocean water of Vestriya's harbor was bad enough.

"Yes, well," Ario managed. "I owe you. You saved me."

Thessia started to smile.

Then she was wrenched backward, heavy hands pulling her hard onto one of the boats docked nearby. She opened her mouth to scream, certain the gruesome toe injury had in fact *not* waylaid the fearsome man with the curved knife who'd come to finish them off. Yet she could not scream, not when hands clamped down over her mouth.

She struggled, fighting to glimpse her captors—

Relief's wonderful wave hit her instantly. Not only did she recognize everyone surrounding her. No, what was more, they were perhaps the people whom she most wanted to see.

Beatrice and Clare, Elowen and Vandra of the newly minted Five faced her, looking utterly delighted. When Hugh and Ario followed her on board, Vandra removed the plank joining the doorway to the dock and closed the ship, sealing them within the gently rocking vessel.

Celine had promised them safe contacts who would shelter them while she went in search of a lead on their poison. Thessia hadn't known Celine meant her fondest friends in the realms.

With everything she'd faced in recent days, Thessia could not help herself. Tears leapt into her eyes, and she rushed into Beatrice's arms. Beatrice laughed with wet joy. Even Elowen joined their group hug.

"Sorry for grabbing you," Clare said sheepishly when Thessia withdrew. "We've been trying to wave for a while, but this fine young man's retching was distracting you. Clare Grandhart," he said to Ario, extending his hand to the prince.

"Ario Vestras," the prince returned, clasping Clare's hand readily. "And this—"

He whisked off his cloak. Gasps went up from the heroes of Mythria.

"Oh my," Elowen uttered.

"—is *Benjamin*," Ario finished grandly, displaying the chartreuse snail, whose eye stalks extended in vigorous introduction.

Clare lowered himself very earnestly to the snail's eye level. He missed his eagle, Thessia suspected. Like the crown prince of Vestriya, the elder Grandhart was very fond of his pet. "Hello, Benjamin," Clare greeted the creature. "You have a very magnificent shell."

Ario puffed his chest with pride. "Yes. Yes, he does," he concurred.

Clare moved past Ario, pulling Hugh into a hug of deep affection. "How . . . are you here?" Hugh wondered out loud.

"Your colleague Celine hired me for a rescue mission," Vandra answered. "Of course this lot wasn't going to let me sail to Vestriya alone. They all came along. Couldn't stop them, really."

Thessia found herself smiling—until something occurred to her. "Wait," she uttered. "If you're here . . . *who is running Mythria?*"

Beatrice and Clare, whom she'd left as her erstwhile rulers, exchanged guilty glances.

"Do you know our friend Cris?" Clare finally asked.

The bashfulness in his voice did not inspire confidence. Thessia's royal eyes rounded.

"Who," she demanded, "in the Ghost's Gate is *Cris?*"

"He's a Clare impersonator," Beatrice replied, mustering more nonchalant confidence than her partner.

The light of recognition flitted into Hugh's eyes. "Indeed!" He nudged Thessia, who was opening her mouth to speak but could not decide which of her questions would proceed first. "You know Cris! He formalized our *not*-wedding!"

Thessia rounded on him. While she did now remember the man, she did not understand Hugh's warm reception to the news that this eager impersonator was now de facto ruling the realm.

The objections died on her lips. Hugh was, of course, soaking wet. He'd shed his cloak, leaving him in only his *very* see-through ruffled white shirt. His black trousers were plastered to his thighs, leaving nothing to the imagination.

"About that," Clare interjected, audibly eager to change the subject from his and Beatrice's questionable governmental decisions. "We read it in the scribesheets. Your marriage isn't real? But you seemed so . . . in love."

Thessia pulled her gaze from her *not*-husband's drenched physique. "Hugh is a very skillful performer," she managed.

"I wouldn't say it required much skill on my part."

His words drew Thessia's eyes back to his. She found his stare hot on her.

Which was when she remembered she was as wet as he. Her own garb hung semi-opaque with seawater. Exactly how much of her curves did the water reveal? Suddenly self-conscious, she slicked her hair back with nervous hands.

Hugh emitted a strange sound within his throat.

Clare watched everything. "*Riiiight*," he responded, grinning.

"Excuse me," Elowen interjected, "but have you heard from Galwell?"

Thessia grasped onto the distraction. "He's safe with Mona," she rushed to reply.

Clare grunted. "That's the first time anyone's ever said that sentence."

"Thessia, how can we help?" Beatrice spoke gently. "Celine said you'd undertaken a rescue quest."

Her friend's query was what Thessia needed. She straightened, remembering herself. She was queen, yes. But here, in Vestriya, she'd started becoming something more—the *more* she'd promised herself when she set out. She was the leader of her own questing party, despite her difficulty finding the proper nomenclature for said group.

"Yes, Prince Ario here is in danger of assassination from his parents," she informed her friends. "They fear he will reveal incriminating information about them. We must get him out of the realm."

"No."

Thessia startled when the prince spoke up. She turned to Ario, finding him squaring his shoulders. Looking a little like his slain brother. Or trying.

"You're right that I should be a cook," he declared, then corrected himself. "I mean king! Celine said she would find proof of my parents' crimes. When she has it, I need to expose them to my people, and then I . . ."

He hesitated.

"I need to be a better ruler than they were," he said.

Elowen narrowed her eyes.

"This sounds suspiciously like a quest," she observed.

"Indeed," Beatrice concurred. "We did make it clear we're retired, right?"

Thessia met the prince's eyes. She smiled. "It's *our* quest," she reassured Beatrice. "We'll help you get word out to your people," she told Ario. "You four"—she spoke to the heroes of Mythria—"we just need you to keep Ario safe until we figure out how."

Clare nodded, intrigued. "A mini-quest, then!" He elbowed Beatrice encouragingly. "Surely we can handle that."

When Beatrice smiled, relenting, Thessia remembered the other versions of them she'd seen in her throne room. The Clare fighting for composure, encouraging his shattered friends to mend the pieces of themselves in the interest of helping her and saving Hugh. How far they'd come. How far every one of them had come.

Vandra smirked. "If only camping were involved," she said, seemingly to Elowen.

"Thank you. The friendship of Mythria and Vestriya depends on you keeping him safe," Thessia told her friends sincerely. "It perhaps also depends on you having some dry clothes we could change into. I fear Hugh and I will stand out on our journey back to the palace like this."

"Of course." Clare pulled fresh garments from their luggage. "How pleasant for you," he remarked with Grandhart sarcasm, "that you no longer have to pretend that the sight of each other in soaking clothes is enticing! What *relief* you must feel!" When he looked to Beatrice, she giggled into her hand.

"What a *slimy* feeling that would be," Elowen concurred, causing Beatrice's laughter to grow louder. Clare and Vandra joined in—the four of them obviously enjoying some secret joke.

Glowering, Hugh grabbed the dry clothing from Clare and stormed into the boat's narrow hallway.

"You're lucky I'm not the type of queen to declare jokes at my expense a crime," Thessia remarked. "I could have your *eyebrows* for that."

She issued this threat specifically to Clare, who reached in horror for his perfectly sculpted flaxen eyebrows. Thessia laughed, victorious, while she snatched the clothes he'd produced.

Following Hugh's exit, she continued into the hallway of the small vessel—where she stilled as the door shut behind her.

Hugh was there. He leaned against the wall, waiting.

For her.

His racked, desperate expression permitted no doubt of his intentions. He watched her like a starved man, and she was a feast.

Thessia knew then exactly how much of herself was visible in her wet clothing. Enough to drown him on dry land. Enough to consume him whole.

He pushed himself away from the wall. Deliberately, without hesitation, he closed the distance between them. Her face was in his hands before she could even suck in a breath.

Their mouths met in silent explosion, their hands fisting drenched fabric. Now Thessia felt herself go under, plunged beneath waves of pure longing.

What were they doing? Who were they to each other? Ex this. Fake that.

What did it matter, when he made her feel like this?

Hugh kissed her deeply, frenzied with feeling yet utterly determined, lips caressing hers in urgent chaos. His scent was . . . everywhere, unmistakable past the salted musk of seawater. They were closer than Thessia thought possible while still wearing their wet clothing, wrapped in each other like ocean currents swirling in uncharted depths.

Only when they heard voices nearing the door to the hallway did they suddenly split. Thessia darted into the nearest doorway with her change of clothing, her mouth stinging.

Surely quest leaders stole clandestine kisses in hallways from time to time. Didn't they?

27
Galwell

Galwell stared at his own face rendered in harsh charcoal. The likeness was impressive, even flattering. His heroic features were remade into rugged savvy under the cunning charcoal strokes. His long hair, ashen instead of auburn, looked windswept, like the portrait caught him in the midst of some daring escape.

What he found unwelcome were the words in heavy lettering underneath.

WANTED
GALWELL THE GRUESOME

His stomach knotted harder with every moment he studied his own wanted posters. Wanted posters! For *him*!

He remembered his discomfort with the statutes of Galwell the Great in Mythria, commemorating his heroism. If only he'd known how much worse matters would get. Mere weeks in Vestriya, and he'd exchanged songs celebrating his exploits and reverent depictions of his questing for wanted posters!

Yet despite Galwell's displeasure, someone else was enjoying his notoriety greatly.

Mona clapped her hands with glee, then passed Vestriyan sterling to the criminal who'd ripped down the poster from the walls of the capital city. The crook—the twenty-seventh man who'd conducted this particular deal with Mona in the past hour—nodded on his way out of Mona's club.

Presumably to collect more posters, Galwell reckoned glumly.

When they'd returned to the city from the Evriel Mountains and noticed the first poster, Mona, ignoring the minor existential episode the poster provoked in Galwell, delightedly put the request out in the underworld. *Payment in exchange for every poster delivered of Galwell the Gruesome.*

While they hid out in Mona's club, ever more posters were delivered. Mona was spending a small fortune on them, depositing each delivery—like the one they'd just received—onto an expanding pile next to the dance-floor dais where she was holding court.

"You can cease this, you know," Galwell grumbled. "You can't possibly purchase them all."

"Can't I?" Mona returned coyly.

"Everyone has already seen them," he complained. "What's the point?"

The darkness he heard in his voice echoed something resentful rattling within him. *What's the point?* What *was* the point? In Mythria, he was a pointless hero for a realm already saved. In Vestriya, a villain for a realm empty of honor.

"The *point*," she said, "is that these are exceptionally impressive. I mean, never in my many years of crime has Mona the Merciless gotten such a grand wanted poster. And for your criminal debut, no less." She shook her head. "Honestly, G, you're a natural."

"Hm," Galwell responded.

"Besides." Mona's voice went poison sweet. "I'm not stopping until I can wallpaper my entire bedroom in them." She winked.

Now *this* coaxed a small smile from Galwell. The insinuation she wanted his face near her while she slept . . . He supposed wanted posters were not the worst punishment in the realm. Indeed, where Mona was concerned, *wanted* was very much his hope.

"Galwell the Gruesome and Mona the Merciless make quite the pair," he conceded, warming up.

Mona elbowed him. "They do, at that."

He was forced to recognize that while her endorsement did not cure the pain of his disrepute, Mona had managed to ease the sting. Even if no one here considered him a hero—even if he did not know *what* he was these days, in these changeable lands—Mona seemed to like him. Which was something.

And Ghosts, he liked her. Quite a lot.

Her cheeks flushed. Undoubtedly hearing his thoughts, Mona opened her mouth like she intended to interrogate his devotion. Galwell was ready to meet her like a soldier of kindness on the field of her heart. *What of it?* he thought loudly, with his customary reckless generosity. *Why should Mona the Merciless have all the fun?*

Neither of them got the chance.

On the precipice of their clash, everyone Galwell yearned to see piled into the club. River trailing after Celine, Hugh near Thessia like he could not help himself. Mona had invited them here for their clandestine reunion.

Galwell sprung from his seat, rushing to greet them. He clasped Celine and River in a huge hug—Celine emitted a squeak, for Galwell had only half remembered to repress his magical strength—then clapped the grinning Hugh heartily on the back.

Lastly, he took Thessia's hands in his. "You doing okay?" he asked her softly.

Thessia squeezed his combat-calloused fingers, smiling with tears in her eyes.

"I'm glad to see you again," she whispered. "I've had quite enough of you disappearing on me for a lifetime."

In reply, Galwell swept her into an embrace.

When he released Thessia, he regarded his friends, feeling incomparable gratitude. "It is wonderful to see you all again," he said. "I cannot thank you enough for standing by my side at this time."

"I knew you'd never have done it," Hugh replied.

"Anyone who knows you knows that, Galwell," Celine agreed.

Galwell nodded, surprised to feel a lump in his throat. It was peculiar comfort, he supposed, the reassurance his friends did not suspect him of being a deadly assassin.

"You're a questing party I certainly don't deserve," he said. "How is Ario? Is he well?"

"Aside from hiding from assassination attempts by his parents? He's great. He and Benjamin," Thessia said. "We need to find a way to expose his parents' crimes and help him claim his throne. But first—Galwell, you aren't safe until we marry. We should make arrangements as swiftly as possible," she declared.

"No."

Galwell hardly recognized the immediate denial he heard pass his own lips. Feeling everyone's aghast stares on him—except Mona's—he cleared his throat, abashed. He did not wish to continue, not with Thessia eyeing him in open surprise. Especially when she was all queenlike in her focused leadership.

Yet continue he did.

"Thessia, I should have said this when we were betrothed ten years ago. I love you, but . . . not in that way," he explained. Heroism was hard, yes. Sometimes, he suspected, knowing oneself was harder. He muscled onward. "Maybe I could have learned to, once, but now . . ."

His eyes strayed to Mona. In her clear gaze, he found everything he himself was feeling.

"I do not think it's possible," he finished quietly.

Her surprise wearing off, Thessia did not look insulted. Indeed,

Galwell found, she looked—comforted. She smiled, bittersweet. Like she was . . . proud of him for drawing into the light what had once hidden in sad shadows. Like she was proud of herself for understanding.

"What in the realms do you mean?"

This exclamation came from Hugh, startling everyone. Hugh straightened, eyeing Galwell with something like indignation.

"How could you not love Thessia? Look at her!" he protested, flinging out a hand toward the queen. "She's . . . wondrous."

Thessia's eyebrows flew up. Her mouth fell open a little. Everyone else—once more, except Mona—assumed the delight of those in the presence of secrets shared.

Seeming to remember himself, Hugh flattened the confrontation out of his expression. "I just mean anyone would be lucky to marry her," he managed. "It's not a *burden*."

Galwell smiled. He did not need Elowen's magic to sense his friend's feelings. It only made him more confident in his decision not to wed Thessia.

"Isn't love unpredictable?" he asked Hugh. "I've learned that recently. I've also learned that virtue without honesty is no virtue at all. Sometimes we have to own the selfish sides of ourselves. Even if it's unheroic of me to admit it, I selfishly don't wish to marry Thessia. And I suspect she feels the same."

Thessia's eyes held only the same calm strength Galwell felt in his own heart. She nodded her confirmation.

"Wonderful!" Mona clapped her hands. "So no wedding. Besides," she went on cheerfully, looking to Hugh, "it appears you consummated your marriage after all, and divorce really is so tedious . . ."

The royal couple flushed deep pink. Hugh coughed. Celine gasped something that sounded rather like *Thugh*.

With the scribe's exclamation, Mona rounded on her in delight.

"Looks like double congratulations are in order. Everyone has had very erotic weekends, it seems."

It was River's turn to *humph*, toeing her boot into the club's floor, while Celine averted her eyes. There would be no escaping Mona the Mind Reader.

"How wonderful," Mona rattled on. "We'll just resolve Galwell's 'wanted' status another way—by helping Ario expose his parents, yes?"

No one spoke.

Galwell wondered whether they now regretted flouting his commandment of no romance in the questing party. "Don't be embarrassed," he encouraged his sexually active companions. "The physical side of love is extraordinary."

"Okay, then," River responded loudly while Mona laughed. "If we must protect Galwell by helping to remove the king and queen of Vestriya, then we need to give Ario a platform to speak to his people and reveal that he isn't hurt. He can expose his parents' corruption, completing the work Prince Ezio intended."

"It needs to be public," Celine elaborated, following River's intuition effortlessly. "Not subject to the propaganda his parents control."

"Vestriya Now," Thessia said, her cheeks still flushed pink.

Mona frowned. "The . . . talent contest?" she clarified. "You want to launch a coup at a talent contest?"

Thessia nodded vigorously, her eyes sharpening. "Yes," she replied. "I was asked to present the contestants alongside Nevo Yrillis. The whole realm attends. I can bring Ario onstage, and he can expose the corruption in front of his people."

Galwell was struck, watching her step more and more effortlessly into the role not only of a queen, but of a leader. He'd always recognized Thessia's intelligence, selflessness, and vivacity. This was different. His heart swelled, observing in her the commander their party needed, and the ruler Mythria did.

Yes, he did love this woman, in many, many ways. He was truly grateful his resurrection allowed them to be friends, allowed him the chance not to be the leader of this quest—but to follow *her*.

"The setting is perfect, of course," Hugh remarked, and under his soldierly strategizing, Galwell heard love of other kinds, and fear and devotion. "But I do note how odd it is for the king and queen to have allowed you the honor of hosting their realm's event while relations are so strained."

"I must agree with Hugh," Celine said. "They tried to kill Ario to cover up that they assassinated Ezio. We know they're working with the guild. But what is the guild's aim in all this? Why frame Galwell after trying to kill him?"

Galwell looked to Mona. "While in the Evriel Mountains, Mona and I met with the man who ordered my assassination. It was Cheswick Chestlewitt—"

"The playwright?" Thessia asked in surprise.

"Yes. Long story," Galwell replied.

"Without a happy ending," Mona said, pouting.

"*Hm*, yes." Galwell hastened on. "Chestlewitt said the guild has fallen under new nefarious directives in order to ensure villainy spreads in the realm, thus providing them good business for the assassination of evildoers. Ruining my reputation and aiding the king and queen of Vestriya was only part of the plan. The rest . . ." He hesitated. "Involves killing Thessia and taking over Mythria."

Thessia snorted.

"If I had a farthing every time I heard that one, I could buy this whole club drinks," she said.

"While your bravery is impressive, you should not ignore this warning," River replied. She was pale, a drawn, almost weary look on her face. "When I was held captive by Dougal, it was in a guild lair built in the ancient city. I heard the Brethren rehearsing."

"They're opening for Vestriya Now," Celine said.

Galwell nodded. Everything fit. "The guild plots to enact their plans there. We cannot doubt it. Knowing the guild is already conspiring with the king and queen, we must conclude that inviting you to host the event is a trap."

He had watched the queen's forces face down the Fraternal Order, men and women venturing onto fields of war from which they would never return. He had led his friends into realm-changing danger. He could recognize fear. He had *known* fear.

He saw none in Queen Thessia of Mythria.

"Then we shall enact our plots as well," she declared. "Galwell and Ario need us. What's more, Mythria and Vestriya need us. If they have planned a trap, we will just have to evade it while we save the realms."

She looked to her compatriots, each of them in turn. Galwell felt himself quietly surprised—it was just, he was usually the one making the speeches.

He did not resent someone else doing it, though. Just this once.

"I have faith in us. In all of us," Thessia promised them. "We will not fail in our quest."

Deep in his heart, Galwell knew she was right. He looked to his companions—his questmates. His friends. Most of them didn't even know one another weeks ago. Now . . . They were perhaps not a conventional group of heroes, but they were a group of heroes nonetheless. "I will do all I can," he said. "You have my strength, Thessia."

"You have my loyalty," Hugh vowed. "Forever, Thess," he said more quietly. His eyes locked with hers.

"I will stand for what the guild has abandoned," River joined in. "You have my blade."

"I offer something more powerful than the fire in my veins. My quill," Celine said.

Then—quiet.

Everyone looked to Mona. With guarded eyes, she returned their stares, and with no head magic of his own, Galwell suddenly, piercingly, felt he could hear everything she was thinking. Every defense she put up, every shadow she withdrew into. Every lie she lived within, every promise she repeated to herself. That she was no good. That she wasn't worth holding on to, or comforting, or cherishing, or believing in.

So Galwell the Great thought the loudest he'd ever thought.

We need you, Mona the Magnificent.

I need you.

Mona rolled her eyes, her smile unconquerable.

She stepped forward. "I'm not sure I have anything to contribute, unless you'd like a small mercenary army of criminals to pull a coup. We could install a dictatorship within the hour," she offered. "No? Not interested?"

When no one replied, Vestriya's princess of crime sighed.

"Very well, then. I suppose I can only offer myself," she conceded. "My magic and, of course, my exceptionally good looks."

Galwell nodded. "These are much appreciated. They will be useful in our heroic quest."

Yes, he supposed. Hero or villain, queen or criminal. Vestriyan or Mythrian. *I can only offer myself.*

He could not have said it better.

Vestriya Now Returns with Ceremony— and Caution; Not Enough Shell Flutes

by Sava Seville, *Voice of Vestriya* senior reporter

Vestriya Now returns! Every year since the ageless founding of Vestriya's most ancient city, our fair Vestriya has played host to the most wondrous talent competition in the realms. This year is no exception, carrying forth the greatest celebration of inter-realm music, comedy, art, magic, performance, and much, much more! Vestriyans and visitors may hope to marvel over acts as varied as sandwalker step-shoe dance and synchronized wing-dog jumping. One surprise omission was a pestleshell flute performance, despite recent auditions on the instrument and given the auditory delight the marvelous instrument would have supplied spectators.

The other stunning upset was the hosting choice of Mythrian queen Thessia, sharing presentation duties with horseballer Nevo Yrillis. Given present realm conflicts, the choice of Thessia is perplexing, verging on offensive, similar to the exclusion of pestleshell flutes from the competition. One can only wonder whether Vestriyans will stand for such distaste.

The Grand Theatre will once more play host to the famed competition. Constructed on the very ground where the first Vestriyan showmanship competitions were held when our ancient city was new, the theater, renovated last decade, holds every imaginable outfitting for spellbinding performances. The realms' finest magicians and craftspeople were consulted in engineering the enchanting lighting mechanisms surrounding the stage. The elegantly raftered ceiling is a geometric masterwork in itself, the design work of architect Theo Thorvald. Indeed, the theater is enough to inspire one to imagine playing one's pestleshell flute with incomparable harmoniousness in Vestriya Now since one was a young girl.

Of course, recent events mean spectacle cannot be the sole concentration of the Vestriyan mind, no matter the sensation or sparkle. Were the competition to include a Worst Deadly Fugitive category, the dishonor would surely go to GALWELL THE GRUESOME. The monstrous Mythrian who slew our crown prince and gravely injured his sibling has eluded captivity. The Vestriyan crown requests every Vestriyan's help in identifying this dangerous villain, who will be imprisoned on sight.

Finally, the crown requests we keep in constant prayers the health of their surviving son, Ario. He remains unconscious and under care in his palace chambers, the crown confirms mournfully.

May Vestriya Now provide much-needed entertainment to our fraught realm, and may the winner's contribution match the elegant strains of pestleshell flutes!

28
River

They arrived at the ancient city to find it blocked off, with a large crowd of people gathered at the gate requesting admission.

Just beyond the tall iron gates stood the Grand Theatre, where Vestriya Now was to be held. The theater had an unusually round shape, and where the stone exterior had once been white, it had turned a dingy gray. This was where the earliest Vestriyan entertainment had been provided, and now it was where they would hold their annual talent competition. The lucky winner would secure a fully funded touring performance that traveled not only through Vestriya, but also into other realms.

River had conjured the competition every single year since the spell service in Mythria made it possible to do so. Maybe she didn't actually like horseball, but she did love when a Vestriya Now contestant bared their soul through song or overcame great personal adversity to showcase their triumphant dancing. Regretfully, Mythria had no comparable talent shows.

River herself had gone to see last year's winners—the Brethren—perform in Mythria's Vermillion Vale. She found it very poignant the way their voices blended together, sounding as one as they sang of love lost and hearts in need of mending. They were worthy winners.

She allowed herself a single pinch of her wrist. Never in her wildest dreams could she imagine she'd be at the actual event.

"Did you just pinch yourself?" Celine whispered.

River said, "Perhaps."

"You love this, don't you?"

"Perhaps," River said again.

"I love that you love it." Celine's eyes sparkled with delight, and River had the peculiar wish that she could bottle the look somehow, so she could hold on to Celine when they weren't together.

"I wish I had a piece of you," River blurted out, no longer capable of stopping the red in her cheeks. Celine's own coloring flushed, and River forced herself to explain. "It's just, when Dougal held me captive, I spent so much of my time wishing for you, and I had nothing but my own thoughts. They weren't enough."

Ghosts, this was getting worse by the minute. River had never been so utterly foolish about anyone before.

Celine didn't seem to find it embarrassing. Instead, she reached her hand into her hair, the mess of curls she always kept fashioned into a pile on her head, and she pulled out the quill she stored there.

"Here," she said. "This is my favorite one. My father had it made for me when I was young. Long before the fire. I told him I always hoped to one day write a book, and he said I should use this quill to do it. I've never gotten around to the book, but this quill is the most sentimental thing I have."

River tried to brush her off, saying she could never take such a thing, but Celine insisted.

"I don't have anything comparable to give you in return," River said, marveling at the quill in her hands. She tucked it carefully into her satchel.

"Worry not," Celine said. "I carry you all up here." She tapped her head.

"Everlasting memory," they said in unison.

"The nonmagical kind." Celine winked.

"Only performers, scribes, or important public figures are allowed in," announced a guard. He said it in a bored monotone, as if it was the hundredth time he'd repeated the sentiment.

He stood on a platform that had been placed in front of the door. It had been fashioned into an informal stage of sorts. Though most of the contestants had already been selected, Vestriya Now still made room for last-minute additions to the show, so as to be sure they saw the best talent of every realm. Auditions were held in front of the waiting crowd, with decisions made instantly on whether the performer would be allowed into the event.

Thessia, ever the diplomat, reassured their group. "I will bring all of you into the city with me. Having a personal entourage is not any different than my royal guard, really."

They made their way through the bustling crowd of eager potential contestants. Some held instruments they intended to play. Others had juggling equipment, or arrows and targets.

Suddenly, a woman cried out in fear. "It's Galwell the Gruesome!" she yelled.

"And Mona the Merciless!" yelled another.

It took a matter of seconds for the crowd to redistribute themselves, forming their own blockade.

Celine, Thessia, Hugh, Ario, and River clustered together as Galwell and Mona stood back to back. There was something poignant about it. Virtuous Galwell on one side and dangerous Mona on the other, both of them with their chins held high and eyes fixed forward.

The Vestriyan guards shoved their way into the center of the action, crossbows trained on Galwell and Mona. The guards expected resistance, yet received none.

In fact, the arrest was so void of theatrics that the air hung heavy with empty anticipation, like the threat of a sneeze that never came to fruition.

With nothing to jeer at, no dramatic scene to enjoy, the prospective contestants scattered, allowing the group to continue toward the entrance once more.

"Excuse me," Thessia said to the Vestriyan guard who stood at the gate. "Would it be okay if I brought some friends in alongside me? They've all been longing to see the Grand Theatre."

"Only performers, scribes, or important public figures are allowed in," the guard repeated, not bothering to look down at who was speaking to him.

"Of course," Thessia said. "It's just, I assured them as queen of Mythria and co-host of this year's festivities that I could make it happen."

The guard's expression fell. "My apologies," he said, extending a hand to help Thessia up the small staircase that led to the stage. "You can come in right away. But I cannot let you bring in anyone who is not a performer, scribe, or important public figure."

Celine flashed the small parchment she carried in her skirt pocket to verify her credentials. "I'm with the *Mythria Spectator*," she said.

The guard waved her up.

Thessia and Celine hesitated at the gate.

"Go on, then," said the guard. "We can't have you up here all day. Auditions are about to start."

Celine and Thessia looked back with worry, but the guard urged them forward again. The tall gate closed behind them, leaving River, Ario, and Hugh to exchange their own looks of concern.

Hugh was technically still king, but everyone now knew their divorce was on the horizon and he was soon to be a commoner again. Ario was in disguise and could not declare himself the prince, since the realm believed him to be bedridden and gravely ill. River was a recently kidnapped Deathrose Guild defector with a constant target on her back.

"We . . ." Hugh started, tapering off with no real plan in sight.

"*Are going to teleport inside,*" River whispered into his ear, grabbing for his hand.

"No. We will have to be in hiding the entire time we're here. It's better if we have legitimate permission." He stepped forward, flashing the dazzling smile that all of Mythria had come to cherish. "We're performers!" he proclaimed to the guard.

"Indeed!" Ario confirmed.

Knowing the worst thing she could do was throw them both under the wagon, River forced herself to go along with it. "Correct," she muttered, fighting for composure.

The guard let out a long, laborious sigh. "And what are your talents?"

"I'm a *poet*," Ario announced.

"Go on, then," urged the guard. "Let's hear it."

Ario let himself up onto the stage. He cracked his neck in both directions, shook out his shoulders, and took a deep breath.

He turned to the crowd and began his performance.

> *Clouds in the sky,*
> *Way up high.*
> *Over us*
> *They lie in the sky.*
> *Why?*
> *I don't know.*
> *It looks like they fly*
> *But they don't.*

For a long while, the crowd stood silent, waiting for the catch. When they realized there was none, laughter broke out, loud and enthusiastic.

THIS WILL BE INTERESTING

Even the guard cracked a wide, toothy grin. "A gag act," he said, delighted. "My favorite kind."

River clocked Ario's disappointed brow scrunch. *Nice job*, she mouthed, tipping her head to him.

The guard let Ario through the gate, then quickly fixed his face back into its usual stoic stare. "Are the two of you performing a joke act, too? Because we can only take a few of that kind. They lose their appeal if we do too many."

"We're legitimate performers," Hugh assured him.

"And what's your talent?"

"I play the harp," Hugh told him.

"He's very good," River said, though she had no clue if it was true. She imagined it would be, though. Hugh was the kind of guy who seemed to be good at a lot of things.

He looked around and grabbed a harp from a passing musician who'd just been rejected. "May I borrow this? Thank you so much, good sir." He put his hands on the strings, and with only the first notes plucked, River knew she was, in fact, correct. He played the chorus of a popular Sir Noah Noble tune, putting past winner Noah himself to shame. Hugh's musicianship was impeccable and full of raw emotion. He'd have even given the Brethren a run for their farthings last year.

"You're *in*," said the guard. River swore he almost swooned.

"And she sings," Hugh said, pushing River to walk up the stairs alongside him.

"No," River said.

She could teleport inside, and all of this would be solved. There was no need for this charade to continue with just her left to secure entry.

But she didn't want to.

Instead, she stood on the platform's wooden ledge, letting her heels hang off the edge. There was no time to turn around and estimate how high up she was. She had only her instincts—and a healthy dose of adrenaline—to see her through.

With a precision she'd honed over decades, River swung her arms up as she pushed off her toes. As she rose into the air, she drove her shins over her head, tugging her arms tightly to her right shoulder so that her body would begin to spin as she flipped. The platform was high enough that she completed two full twists while upside down. She landed in a perfect squat, taking one step backward into a dramatic finishing lunge.

"I'm an *acrobat*," she proclaimed.

29
Thessia

Thessia paced the tent nervously.

The Vestriya Now preshow music echoed from the main theater, magically projected to fill the night, while conjurated beams of light shot high into the darkness. Outside the flaps of the preparation tents, pages, stagehands, and contestants rushed from place to place. The clamor was impossible to ignore.

Or impossible unless one was fretting about the fate of one's questmates.

"Don't worry," Celine consoled Thessia. "River will teleport them in soon." Celine's sympathetic gaze followed her panicked pacing.

"Why hasn't she yet?" Thessia replied.

"She's probably just waiting for the right moment," Celine reassured her gently.

When the tent opened, Thessia practically pounced on the page who entered with the scroll listing the night's contestants. She snatched the parchment, while the page, startled by the queen's haste, scurried out into the night.

Celine moved urgently to Thessia's side as Thessia unrolled the heavy, ornamented sheet. They read hastily, until a rush of relief hit Thessia when she reached one contestant's name.

Benjamin Slime—Poet.

"Ario's in," Thessia confirmed.

They kept reading until Thessia found the other name she wanted.

Sir Hugh—Harp. Thessia exhaled. "Oh, thank the Ghosts—" she started to say.

Celine shrieked.

Thessia sprang into defensive action, her eyes flying to the tent flaps to face whatever danger undoubtedly interceded—until Celine stabbed the scroll with her finger. "*River* has entered the competition?" she exclaimed.

Thessia followed to where she pointed to the name *Fearless Flyer—Acrobat.*

"I have to speak with her," Celine said. She rushed from Thessia's tent, leaving the bewildered queen to her scroll.

With the safety and position of the members of her party confirmed—if somewhat professionally surprising—Thessia found her gaze wandering to the tent numbers next to each contestant's name. *Vulgaris Brothers—Comedy, T.18* . . . *Erick Theo—Hamsterjay Juggling, T.47.* Thessia wondered briefly how such a feat was possible. *Lockwood Cheer—Hand Magic Insta-Sculpting, T.67* . . .

Sir Hugh—Harp, T.81.

Thessia had some spare time before facing down the Deathrose Guild, exposing Vestriyan corruption, and clearing Galwell's name, didn't she?

Without second-guessing herself, she strode from her tent into the night. Following the numbered signs, she navigated the muddy walkways of the ancient city's venerable ruins, the pathways running through enigmatic, half-destroyed stonework hinting inarticulately at the glories of lost eras.

Thessia found black tent 81 without difficulty. Hearing the notes of a harp within, she slipped inside.

Hugh did not notice her entrance. Thessia smiled, watching him as he was preoccupied with his music. Sitting on the room's low wooden

THIS WILL BE INTERESTING

stool, he strummed his harp, focused, picking out the shape of a new melody with experienced hands.

It was a shame. He could've made a marvelous songstar.

He hummed softly to the music his nimble fingers summoned from his harp. The song was melancholic. Full of yearning. The more Thessia listened, the more the wistful chords pulled at her emotions. She didn't want to interrupt him, yet she could not help herself.

"What are you writing about?" she asked softly. "Paramar Bay?"

Hugh startled. With her mention of his hometown, the tips of his ears reddened.

"Why do you think that?" he replied.

Thessia struggled to put into words what his music had conjured in her. "It sounds almost . . . homesick," she explained.

Hugh's eyes found hers. His gaze hummed with something soft and serious. Even with his harp silenced, Thessia felt she could hear the phantom strains of longing chords.

"Homesick is exactly right," he said.

He did not elaborate. Nor did he speak to the song's subject, Thessia noticed. Perhaps not Paramar Bay, then. One could, she knew, be homesick for memories. For a quality of light, or the sounds of a laugh. For feelings.

For people.

Her heart fluttered. Hugh dropped his gaze, clearing his throat. "The problem is, I'm shit at lyrics," he murmured.

He restarted his strumming, his voiceless melody sharpening with his new effort.

"You would sing again?" she asked, remembering the night he sang for only her in their carriage.

His gaze flitted back to hers. "I find myself inspired anew."

Wistfulness strained in her now, Hugh's magic coaxing her

exhausted heartstrings. She wanted to reach out and touch someone, to be touched. She wanted the feeling of home that comes with the right embrace. His magic entwined with his music in his inimitable caress.

"I'm not sure you need lyrics," she exhaled.

Hugh smirked. His style changed, his playing becoming lower, more urgent. Thessia felt the emotion in the darkened tent... shift. Her cheeks flushed, her heartbeat picking up. Fire grew low within her.

"That's hardly fair," she fought to say.

"Is it?" Hugh replied. His hands stilled on his harp. The silence offered Thessia no reprieve from the desire coursing through her. "It's how I feel when I'm around you."

Thessia had no reply. She wanted to be the conquering hero, yet she could not conquer the want consuming her now. Ghosts, how she had resisted. How hard she'd fought the feelings she'd started to have for him—on the *Sapphire Palace*, on their disastrous, wondrous honeymoon, on this quest.

With no more obstacles in their way, Thessia found that instead of winning the fight, the fight was winning her. With this extraordinary man playing his extraordinary music, she could only surrender.

"You're not marrying Galwell," Hugh said.

"I'm not," she whispered.

Hugh carefully set down his harp.

"I have to apologize," he said, "for breaking my promise to you."

Thessia paused, thrown. *His promise?* Did he mean his... wedding vows?

"You thought I would be a safe fake husband because I could never love again," Hugh continued. "But it turns out I'm a traitor. To Zaralie, and to you, to the word I gave you."

Thessia heard the emotion constricting his voice. The raw pain piercing his sturdy frame.

"Hugh," she managed. "What are you saying?"

"I'm saying I'm not the knight I should be. I'm . . . terrified. Because I already gave my heart to someone whose loss broke it," Hugh said. "I don't know if I could survive loss like that again."

Loss like that. Now Thessia understood.

Loss like Ezio's public assassination. Loss like the Deathrose Guild's shadowy promise to kill the queen of Mythria.

"And I'm . . . not a safe person to love," she completed quietly.

"No," he confirmed. "You're not."

Oh, how she wanted to rush to him. Wanted to hear the three words he'd avoided saying. With Hugh's scent surrounding her, his caress embracing her, his music filling her, she wanted to convince herself they would defy the odds together.

But courage was for heroes. Idealism was for lovers.

Queens, however, could not afford hope.

Thessia knew they could fail this night. If they failed, the guild would succeed. She would die. How could she *ever* contemplate surrendering to her passions? How dare she ever *imagine* freedom from everything facing them? How could she put Hugh through more tragedy? How horribly would it break him?

She loved Hugh. Finally, she understood the feeling wholly. Thessia had obeyed no ruler but herself in years, yet now love held merciless sovereignty over even her.

She knew what she needed to do. What love demanded.

"Don't, then," she uttered. Her commandment was clear and cold even while her heart cracked with her words.

Hugh's eyebrows furrowed with confusion until he realized what she meant.

Don't love me. Don't hope for us.

"That's what you want?" he replied.

Thessia nodded, only because she was certain she could not

manage to repeat herself. Her sobs would rebel, an insurrection of the heart.

She stepped back, wishing she had not come. But turning to flee, she nearly collided with someone entering the tent.

"Good, you're both here." Ario swept in with nervous preoccupation, oblivious to the wreckage he'd just entered. "I've written something for the competition and I—I think it might be good. It might be my best poem ever," he explained urgently.

Flustered, packing away the jagged pieces of her broken heart before they caused more harm, Thessia fought to understand. "You . . . you what? Ario, you're not really going to compete," she reminded him. "You'll use your time onstage for the plan."

The prince shrugged hopefully. "Surely the plan could incorporate some poetry, though? Just . . . look," he pleaded, thrusting the parchment toward Hugh.

Hugh's hand shook when he took Ario's poem, the only hint of the emotions waging open war within him.

When he started to read, however, his expression changed. His hand steadied. He mouthed words, his eyes widening.

While Ario practically vibrated with nervousness, Thessia watched Hugh with mounting incredulity. "Is it . . . good?" Ario finally ventured.

"It's not a poem," Hugh replied.

Ario wilted. "It's not?"

"No." Hugh looked up. His gaze found the prince's. "Now I know what I can sing onstage. Ario . . . you've written a great fucking song."

30
Galwell

His very first prison cell. How exciting.

Galwell found himself contemplating the many firsts he'd experienced in Mona's influential company. His first wanted poster. His first flight from royal guards. His first . . .

Yes, many interesting firsts indeed. Mona seemed to summon them when the two of them were together.

He inspected his carceral surroundings. Honestly, they were not as bad as he expected when they'd made this plan. A wooden bench suspended perpendicular to the stone walls with chainwork. Polished obsidian flagstone floor. Candlelight sconces. The room was windowless—they were several levels underground—yet even here, the echoes of the Brethren onstage drifted into their confines.

Yes, Galwell found the conditions entirely acceptable. Perhaps he'd adapted to his days of villainy, he concluded darkly. Or perhaps it had something to do with how hot-as-fuck Mona looked in shackles next to him.

Neither possibility was entirely comforting.

Fortunately, they were precisely where their plan demanded. While plotting the coup on Vestriya Now, the group had determined this would be the fastest way to secure an audience with the royal guard—whose support they would need if Ario's overthrow of his parents went the way the heroes hoped.

The problem was, the guardsmen escorting them seemed entirely uninterested in the famous fugitives' claims of an impending assassination of the queen of Mythria.

"In you go," their unaccommodating guard stated while he shoved Galwell over the threshold. Mona, shackles removed, strutted in willingly as the guard locked the heavy iron door.

Galwell spun and clasped onto the bars. "Just listen to me," he urged. "Please."

His jailer withdrew, pointing the metal key vehemently at Galwell. "You," he spat, "killed Ezio. I don't care what *you* have to say."

Galwell spoke from the heart. "Sometimes the stories we are told are just that," he said. "Stories. With the heroes and the villains of someone else's determining."

He remembered royal engagements no one had ever really understood. The unknowable challenges of escaping death, of the sacrifices heroes never shared. The hidden costs and complications under the narratives the realms willingly accepted.

"Don't let someone write you into a role you didn't choose. Ask yourself the questions you need to make your own choices," he urged their jailer. "Who was the dead man on the pitch if not an assassin? More assassins are here tonight. You should ask yourself who paid for them. Who benefited from Ezio's death? It certainly wasn't me."

He felt his words starting to work. What held the guard in place wasn't head or heart magic. It was stronger—the truth.

Galwell gestured to his cell. "Look where it's landed me."

He decided to withhold accusations of the king and queen's corruption, sensing they would not go over well.

Which would suffice. Sometimes change need not come in one decisive stroke. Sometimes hope need not roar into flame from the first spark.

His crew would conjure that fire, completing the rest of their plan. For now, Galwell needed something other than conquering force.

THIS WILL BE INTERESTING

Reading Galwell's mind, Mona interjected effortlessly.

"Ezio would have made a great king," she said quietly.

Her earnest calm surprised even him. She sounded . . . like she meant her praise. Like even Mona the Merciless once held something like hope for her realm's salvation under just and compassionate leadership.

Her words reached their guard. He nodded, visibly emotional now. Mona continued. "So would his brother."

The guard faltered, confused. "Ario? He's not likely to survive," he informed them, repeating the scribesheets' public line.

Mona shrugged. "Say he does. Say he were to come here tonight, completely healthy—I trust you would guard his life from all attempts against him, no matter from whom?"

"Of—of course," the guardsman responded. "Ario is a good man. Though, not sure he is king material like his brother."

"People can be capable of more than you think," Galwell replied.

The guard locked eyes with Galwell. Galwell hoped he saw courage in the man's gaze.

"Whatever you see tonight," Galwell continued, "decide for yourself what your part in the story will be."

He released the iron bars. As he retreated to the wooden bench, where he sat heavily, new guards rushed in to confer with their commander.

"Fights are breaking out," one reported. "We're needed in the audience."

After a long moment, the jail guard pulled his eyes from his convincing convicts. Hardening his features, he led his men from the cells.

Silence—broken only by the faint sounds of the Brethren's upbeat music—found Galwell and Mona.

"Think we planted the seed?" Galwell asked.

Mona—clearly comfortable behind bars—stretched languidly. "I read his mind," she replied, rolling her neck. "When he sees Ario, he'll know he's been lied to. He loved Ezio. He will want justice."

Galwell nodded, hoping Mona's confidence and their guardsman's courage were enough. Not on their own, obviously. Heroism was much like hardshoe sandwalker step-dancing, which, incidentally, Galwell had noticed on the castle-high scrolls advertising Vestriya Now's participants. It only worked if everyone—*everyone*—did their part.

With nothing to do except wait until River teleported in to remove them from their cell once everything else was in place, Galwell sat in silence. Mona, however, would not keep still. She stood, brushing her fingers thoughtfully over the bars of their prison.

"This reminds me of how we met. You behind bars. Me tormenting you," she reminded him.

"I remember vividly."

He did. He remembered the moment she first touched him, while he was confined in her club's cage. How the dark lightning in her fingertips had . . . changed something in him, in ways he could never have predicted or fully understood until now.

"Yes," Mona murmured, reading his thoughts. "Yes, you do."

"You said you wanted a man who could surprise you," Galwell recalled.

Mona eyed him, leaning her back against the bars. He knew her well enough to know the rakish nonchalance was put on. Pretended carelessness. From the opposite side of their prison cell, he could stare into Mona's eyes and feel the want rolling off her. Could feel what she was daring him to do.

He rose to his feet. In the flickering light, he prowled toward her.

"Well, Mona," he challenged. "Have I surprised you?"

Mona swallowed. He'd flattened her to the iron grate, forcing her chest up, her chin rising to hold his gaze.

"Constantly," she confessed, breathless.

"You've surprised me, too," he remarked. "Clare warned me you were horrible."

Like he expected, Mona smirked. She sought the upper hand in owning her underhandedness.

So Galwell went on. "He didn't warn me at all how utterly lovely you are."

Mona looked to the side to hide her shock, though she could not hide her bashful smile.

It wouldn't do. With gentle fingers, Galwell drew her chin up. He looked right into her cerulean eyes. "Don't hide from me just because I've said something you don't know how to face," he commanded softly.

"I—" Mona started. She fought the waver out of her voice. "No one has ever spoken to me like you do," she whispered.

Galwell knew the princess of lies was being entirely honest with him now. It wounded him, with real, physical pain. The ways this realm had made Mona Grandhart see herself were, he reckoned, perhaps the worst injustice he'd ever known.

Galwell the Great hated injustice, and when he encountered it, he fought it in every way he could.

"You're lovely," he murmured into Mona's ear while he stroked her hair.

He felt her fierce posture weaken.

"You're captivating," he went on. He kissed her cheek. "You're the bravest person I've ever known." He kissed her other cheek, then her forehead.

Mona trembled under his gentle efforts. He may have been the only virgin. But she had as little experience as he in this—in love.

"Kindness isn't usually my kind of foreplay," she managed.

"What's foreplay?" Galwell asked.

Mona did not laugh, though he intuited he'd exposed yet one more sexual shortcoming in his innocent repertoire. "Want me to show you?" she offered instead, smiling with a shy eagerness he found breathtakingly beautiful.

He nodded. "Yes."

The next moment, Mona was kissing him roughly. Galwell responded with pure instinct, pressing her hard up to the bars. Impulsive, he thrust his hand under her skirts, desperate to touch her.

Mona was there, guiding him. When he found slick warmth, she bit down softly on his lower lip.

"*There*," she urged.

He pressed harder, coaxing her, making her gasp into his shoulder. With deepening rhythm, he continued, until she was quivering under his fingers, her whole body tremoring with every exhale. Suddenly she was frenetically undoing the drawstring of his pants.

"Do you wish to have sex with me, Mona?" he inquired.

The question came out earnest, even polite. Mona laughed. She returned him the same simple certainty. "Yes."

"Good," Galwell replied. "Even though we are in the midst of a quest with very important stakes and this timing seems irresponsible and selfish, I would like to have sex with you, too."

"You don't have to be a hero *all* the time," Mona replied. With this, she untied her dress in one deft pull of the drawstring, letting the garment fall from her entirely.

She was . . . perfect. No underclothes hid Mona's soft, gorgeous skin from his hungry, devout eyes. The shadows of their cell seemed sculpted to her, their inky fingers caressing her everywhere he wished to.

"Aren't you afraid someone will come?" he whispered.

Mona shook her head, her dark hair sweeping slowly over her shoulders. "I'll hear their thoughts approaching."

He hardly grasped her explanation. How could he concentrate

given the sight in front of him? Need, scorching low in his stomach, compelled him. He reached up for Mona's bare breasts. When they filled his hands, he shuddered, his vision starting to constrict.

"Tell me what you want," Mona urged him. "You can't hide any of your fantasies from me, Galwell. Give me every wicked little thought."

"You," he replied. "You're my fantasy. Just you."

Mona stilled, her eyes finding his.

In them, he found not only lust. Not only need. Those were there, yes. But for once, Mona looked—fully herself. Stripped. Naked in skin, naked in soul.

He knew she could hear every way he wanted her. Every way he loved her. He was fiercely glad she could.

Withdrawing, he removed his cloak and laid it on the floor for them. When he helped Mona down—very chivalrously, of course—she chuckled. "You find this humorous," he observed without indignation.

"No, no," Mona responded. "I just . . . didn't expect this to be a first for me, too."

He needed no further explanation. With one careful hand, he opened Mona's legs. She guided him, her hand shaking with quiet eagerness, until he slid deep inside her.

Everything vanished except ecstasy. The unwelcoming walls of their prison—gone. They could have been on the Evriels' harsh slopes or the clouds of the Ghost's Gate. The wanted posters, the ignominy—gone. The plan, the quest—gone. Heroism, heartache, power, corruption, legacy—gone.

There was only Mona. He pressed deeper inside her with every stroke, finding the perfect combination of deliberate rhythm and drawn-out need. He wanted to feel every inch of her wet desire. He wanted ever deeper. He wanted forever.

Instead of losing himself to pure instinct, he paid attention to Mona. Her guidance was very helpful, and *very* vocal. Galwell clung to every word—not just her demands, or her promises, but how the syllables sounded in her mouth, husky and intoxicating.

"Slower," she commanded. "*There.*"

There. He caressed her thighs, imitating her when she clasped her hand on top of his, urging him to clench her ass. He listened to every sigh she made when he pushed into her, making her quake in delight.

Her gasps shallowed—her eyelids fluttering while her lips parted—and Galwell knew they were on the edge of the same precipice now. When his pleasure exploded, she held him close, looking into his eyes.

Galwell held her gaze. She wasn't only succumbing to the pummeling ecstasy shattering her body. She was facing the feelings between them head on.

Happy and spent, he collapsed onto her. *No wonder Clare sought sex the night before they entered the Grimauld Mines*, he recalled. No wonder Elowen and Vandra were always slipping off together.

Was it like this always? Or did Mona make it unforgettable?

He suspected the latter.

When he noticed her shivering, he reached immediately for his abandoned shirt to wrap around her shoulders. "You're cold," he observed.

Mona smiled. "I'm not."

Confusion combined quickly with dread. He frowned, fending off horrible, embarrassing conclusions. Feeling rather like he was stalking into the Grimauld Mines himself, he voiced his concerns. "Was I . . . not good?"

Mona smiled wide, every inch her old self. Ghosts, villainy looked good on her.

"Galwell the Great, indeed," she commended him slyly.

Relief rushed over him. "Is something wrong, then?" he ventured.

Mona shook her head, eyes full of feeling. "No, I just never thought I would—"

Right that instant, River teleported into their midst. If this were not sufficiently startling, nothing could prepare the contented postcoital couple for the figure River clasped by one elbow—Clare Grandhart.

Glimpsing Galwell with Mona, the roguish hero shrieked, clapping his hands over his eyes.

"River!" Galwell exclaimed, panic constricting his voice. "You're early! And—why do you have Clare?"

"Celine needs my help before I go onstage. Figured I would spring you two early," River explained. She regarded them with interest. "Didn't realize I would be . . . interrupting. Honestly, good for you, Galwell. We didn't know if you had it in you."

"No!" Clare protested. "Not good for you! Absolutely no congratulations are in order here! Commiserations! Lamentations! Condolences!"

Mona, who was not easy to embarrass, had flushed pronouncedly pink. She hurriedly pulled on Galwell's shirt. The hero himself was left to clumsily cover his privates with his cloak.

River went on cheerfully. "Spotted this guy about to get arrested from my tent. A fight broke out in the crowd. Lots of unrest in this city. When they saw Clare—" River gestured to the elder Grandhart, who remained covering his eyes.

"Apparently, I'm famous even abroad, and Vestriyans really don't like heroes—especially Mythrian heroes, given current interrealm relations. Not even strapping six-time Sexiest Man Alive winners," Clare grumbled, forgetting his mortification momentarily. "Someone threw a punch at me, and somehow *I* was the one the guards arrested. Or they would have, if River hadn't snatched me. Honestly, please take me back," he pleaded. "I'd take anything over this."

Visibly mustering his courage, he peeked out from behind his hands with one eye, observing the half-dressed Mona and—

"Galwell," he chastised his friend indignantly. "How could you? She's my sister!"

"I—I did not know you felt so protectively for her, Clare," Galwell replied.

Clare ignored him. "And *you*." He charged on, redirecting his ire at Mona. "How could *you*? You're evil and he's . . . a kind, gentlehearted king of a man."

"Why, thank you, Clare," Galwell interjected, genuinely touched.

"No." Clare cut his gaze back to his friend. "You're still in trouble. I'm deeply disappointed in you both. And in a *jail*?" Clare shook his head in utter and unmistakable dismay. "I fear the realms really will come to ruin."

"Okay, I'm going to go help Celine!" River interjected. "This seems like a family matter."

She vanished. The next instant, she was inside their cell. She grabbed the half-clothed couple by one elbow each. Galwell's head spun from the shocking momentum of River's magic. Then, suddenly, they were on the other side of the bars. Except—

"River! My pants!" Galwell reminded her desperately, for the garments remained in the cell, and not, regrettably, on Galwell's person.

"Shit. Sorry." River rematerialized lightning-quick in the cell. She collected his pants and tossed them through the bars to the chagrined Galwell. Then, with a cheerful wave, their companion—the only member of the present company not related to or sleeping with each other—teleported out, leaving Galwell and the Grandharts.

Galwell dressed himself hastily.

"Do you love each other or was this a . . . physical thing?" Clare demanded, muscling through the question. When Galwell opened his mouth to reply, Clare preempted him. "No. I don't want to know. Neither answer will comfort me."

"I love your sister very much, my friend," Galwell reassured him. Clare roared.

"I assure you I have the utmost respect for her," Galwell persisted. "I seek never to hurt her."

"Only when I ask him very nicely," Mona said, smirking.

Clare staggered to the wall. "I think I might be dying," he pronounced.

"To be fair"—Mona inspected her crimson-charmed fingernails—"you did send him to me for safekeeping . . . So really this is your fault. Speaking of . . ."

Mona's gaze hardened. Clare's eyes widened.

"You can't be serious," he replied.

"I kept him safe, did I not?" Mona returned humorlessly. "You didn't say 'keep him safe and don't give him the best sex of his life.' I believe you owe me what was promised."

Clare's dramatics disappeared. Everyone's sex lives were forgotten. Clare's somber seriousness was like none Galwell had ever seen on his friend.

Galwell rounded on Mona. *What was promised* . . . Surely she wouldn't . . . Not now. He'd hoped—foolishly—to calm her yearning for revenge. To show her how joy and love and *hope* could lead her out of darkness. Realizing nothing had changed . . . his heart hurt.

"Hunting them won't change the past," Clare pleaded. "It won't make all their wrongs right. It won't make yours right, either. They've changed, Mona."

"You fool," his sister snapped.

Even dauntless Clare winced.

"Your quests may have made you famous, brother, but they have not made you wise," Mona hissed. "Nobody *ever* changes. Not really. Not the worst things they've ever done. No one escapes their wrongs—the hurt they've inflicted. Or they shouldn't," she finished darkly.

"They do, Mona," Clare insisted. "Please, listen to me, for once—"

Mona's eyes hardened. "No. If I listened to you, you'd be dead. You only got to have your *perfect* life, beloved by all, because *I* made the real sacrifices for you."

Clare gripped the bars of the cell, his knuckles white. "I've survived on my own just fine without you. You left me behind and I made a new life. You could, too."

"I tried! *Your* friends live. Even when they die, they come back to life—" She threw a hand out toward Galwell. "Who do I have?"

"You have *me*." Clare's voice broke. "You apparently have Galwell. Don't act like you're the only one who has suffered tragedy. I lost my whole crew in the Grimauld Mines. I was prepared to let the Orb Weavers kill me. Galwell and Beatrice and Elowen gave me a reason to live again."

His eyes strayed to Galwell, who felt his heart ache with the pain he remembered in young Clare—hiding his grief, his hopelessness, under swaggering recklessness. Pain Galwell now saw reflected in Clare's younger sister.

"We're nothing alike," Mona said, cutting through his thoughts.

Clare sighed. Galwell heard his friend's extinguished hope. "Look, personal disgust aside, it's clear you've rubbed off on Galwell the Gruesome here. But I have to hope Galwell the Great has rubbed off on you, too, Mona," Clare said. "You can't do this. I can't let you."

Mona flipped her hair behind her shoulder.

"It doesn't matter what you can and can't do, brother," she said softly. "I've already stolen what I wanted from your mind."

31

River

"*It's showtime*," River whispered in disbelief.

Ghosts, it had been a very long while since River felt the heady, fizzy anxiety of an impending performance. That would've been more than enough. But there was an extra layer.

Many, really.

For one, she was inside the Grand Theatre. Where the outside still had the ruinous look of history long gone, the inside had been reinvigorated—ornate moldings all around the stage and a beautiful backdrop in the rear, easily forty irons high, with swordlike orbs of light jutting out around it.

River had to give it to the Vestriyans. They had an eye for theatrics.

But Mythria's representation in this affair was not to be overlooked. Queen Thessia was an excellent co-host, playing wonderfully against Vestriyan horseballer Nevo Yrillis. Thessia was as charming as she was effusive, complimenting each performer as they finished in a way that felt both personal and fair. She commanded the stage the same way she commanded their realm, her generosity of spirit as sparkly and vibrant as the crystal tiara on her head.

"Are you ready?" Celine asked, squeezing River's hand.

"No," River told her. "But no one ever is."

They stood in the very back of the theater where the elevated seats were the highest, providing them a clear view of all the action. It was not unlike the night they'd spent watching the Vestriyan Caravaners together.

River and Celine each held a stack of small, folded pamphlets, the contents of which contained every detail they needed to carry their plan to completion.

River had read the pamphlet over many times, amazed at each pass. It was informative, heartfelt, and entirely damning.

This pamphlet would change Vestriya forever.

Onstage, a dancer and musician—husband and wife, River recalled from rehearsals—finished their performance. The crowd began politely applauding.

"Shall we?" Celine asked, taking a step down the staircase that ran beside each row of seats, ready to begin passing out pamphlets.

Before she moved, River did what she'd been trained to do, something so second nature she did it without thought—she scanned the crowd for danger, just like the guild had taught her to do.

That was how she spotted Deathrose colleagues scattered throughout the audience. They were in groups of two or three, dressed to blend in with the rest of the crowd, but they were *everywhere*—at the very front of the stage and even all the way to the back, only a few seats to the right of where Celine and River stood, cloaked by darkness.

"They're already here," River whispered, her nerves taking on a new form.

"It doesn't matter." Celine gripped River's hand once more. "The truth must get out."

"But if we try to pass these pamphlets out, they'll stop us before we can get them into everyone's hands."

The two women fell quiet. Onstage, Thessia appeared again, commending the couple on the way they showcased their love through music and movement.

"I have a better idea." River snatched Celine's pamphlet stack from her hand.

"What is it?" Celine asked.

River kissed her on the lips, quick and hard. "You'll see."

At that, she hurried down the steps until she stood at the foot of the stage, just beneath Thessia, who was waiting for the judges to finish offering critiques of the latest performers.

Announce me next, River mouthed.

Thessia disappeared into the stage's cavernous wings, likely to let everyone know of the change, then emerged again, giving River a nod.

River had no time to prepare. She hadn't run through the routine in her mind or performed any of her usual rituals. She hadn't even stretched.

It didn't matter.

It was now or never.

Nevo moved to center stage, prepared to announce the next performer, but Thessia cleared her throat before he could speak, saying, "Up next, we have the dazzling, the *daring*, the one and only Fearless Flyer!"

River ran up the steps, building momentum for her opening tumble.

She'd chosen to wear all white. It was an idea she'd had ever since she was young, when she'd hoped to someday become a member of the Pricemark Family Circus. Back then, she wanted to wear white so she could be like the doves that flew out of the magician's hat made real. She wanted to be seen not just as beautiful but pure.

Wearing this costume now was more defiance than acceptance. She could be her complicated, complex self and still wear this. She could reclaim the performer she once hoped to be and fold her in with the person she actually was. She knew now that she did not need to be something fragile and ethereal to be worthy.

She could be anything.

And so, River tumbled. She flipped and spun with all her energy and all her heart. The aches that usually sprang up could not reach her. Only as she neared the end of her performance did it occur to her that moving in the lineup might change the logistics of her planned finale. She looked to the upper rafters of the stage, relieved to find her silk dangling there, with a stagehand waiting for her cue. She gave him a nod, and he let the long white silk fall.

Instead of climbing it, River knotted the silk around her waist and through her legs like a harness. She'd placed the pamphlets within her reach, and she grabbed a stack in each hand.

With a running start, she propelled herself over the crowd, flying above them like she really was a dove, releasing the pamphlets at the peak of her ascent so they rained down over everyone in the audience.

When the swing of the harness pulled her back to the stage, she grabbed another stack of pamphlets, and off she went to throw them in a new direction.

On her final pass, she directed herself toward where Celine stood stage left. Because each row of seats was higher than the last, her silk swing brought River closest to the people in the back rows.

River had released all her pamphlets by the time she reached Celine, so she stretched out her empty hand instead, and Celine caught it, their fingers gripping one another for a single electric moment.

When River swung back to the stage, she untied the rope and took her bow, unable to contain her joy. She'd done it. Flawlessly. The pamphlets reached more seats than they would have in their initial plan. Not only that, but River had made the most of her time onstage.

No matter what happened, she'd successfully performed for Vestriya Now.

Thessia returned to the stage with tears in her eyes. "Wonderful!" she exclaimed into the magical amplification wand that made her voice audible for all. "Just magnificent, Fearless Flyer. I know our judges will have much to say. Let's hear it."

"Fantastic work," her co-host Nevo offered. "Loved that little bit at the end."

"So romantic!" Thessia said with a wink.

Nevo cued the judges to offer their critiques. River wanted to listen, but she couldn't stop her eyes from wandering, wanting to see the audience reactions to the information in the pamphlet. She expected gasps of horror and shock. But when she looked into the crowd, she found no one was reading them. Most hadn't even picked up the pamphlets from wherever they'd fallen.

Disappointment weighed heavy on her heart. She felt her face frowning, even as the judges praised her, so she forced herself to smile. Inside, her mind raced. Celine had worked so hard on the pamphlet. The plan had been improvised quickly and executed as well as it could be. And still, it hadn't worked.

In fact, the guild members scattered throughout the audience were rising from their seats. But they weren't charging the stage. They were headed for the back row.

For Celine.

River had spotlighted her. She'd shown them exactly where to go.

She had no idea whether the judges had finished their critiques or not. She hadn't heard a word either way. She was too busy teleporting herself to the back row. But she was too late.

Gary and Mary held Celine on either side. Mary had a knife pressed to Celine's throat, and Gary had another near Celine's stomach.

Mary smiled at River, sickly sweet. "Once again, you've made our job easier."

"We really need to thank you some day," Gary said. "But we won't."

"What do you want with her?" River asked.

"She's too dangerous to be left alone," Gary said.

Mary nodded eagerly, adding, "She possesses a power we cannot fight against."

"I'll never join your guild." Celine kept her calm, holding her chin up as she said it. "I would rather *die*."

"Exactly," Gary said, but he was looking at River. "That's exactly what's going to happen. Unless you give us a good reason not to . . ." He moved to plunge his knife, forcing River to yell out a halting *stop*.

She knew what was really going on.

Their plan was not to kill Celine. Not really. They would, if necessary, but it wasn't the goal. Their goal was to use River. They wanted her connection to Thessia. Her teleportation abilities. All of it.

"I'll take you to Thessia," River said. "I'll teleport her into the prison you set up. I've been there. Dougal Farkenstomp showed it to me. Which I'm sure you know. You probably had to clear out his rotted corpse. It won't be difficult for me to get Thessia. She trusts me completely."

River could feel the determined force of Celine's stare, urging her to stop at once, but River didn't dare meet her eye.

Gary put his knife into the sheath around his waist. "Very smart," he said. "Very smart indeed."

"If I betray Thessia like this, you let Celine and I go forever when it's done," River said. "We will escape to another realm. You'll never hear from us again."

"Fine," said Mary.

"Great. You have my word." River spit on her hand and stuck it out for a shake. "Gary, Mary, let's shake on this."

Once the deal had been sealed with spit, River wiped her damp hand on her black leggings and said, "Oh, Mary, I need you to come with me. Galwell will be backstage, and he is our biggest obstacle.

THIS WILL BE INTERESTING

You can distract him with combat while I seize Thessia. Gary, you can stay on Celine."

The assassin siblings gave their nods of approval, and Mary moved to follow River.

Finally, River looked at Celine. "I was wrong, by the way," she said.

Celine's puzzled expression did not relent.

"I do have a weakness," River continued. "*You.*"

32

Galwell

Galwell concentrated on the quest.

Much too much would have occupied the hero's head otherwise. He feared he would lose himself irrevocably were he to spend even one moment recollecting, reliving, *re-glorying* in the wondrous memory of having sex with Mona.

Then there was the calamitous fallout with Clare, who'd stomped off, declaring he needed "the strongest ale in Vestriya" to contend with recent events. Galwell felt guilty. *Galwell the Guilty.* He hadn't planned on romance during his Vestriyan refuge. He certainly hadn't planned on romance with his closet friend's sister *ever*.

Yes, there was entirely overmuch going on in the hero's personal life.

Galwell focused on following Mona through the catacombs under the Grand Theatre. They were bound for backstage, where they would watch Thessia and keep the queen safe.

Mona guided them using her magic. Whenever she detected guards' thoughts, she pulled Galwell with her into the closest doorway or shadowy corner. The concealment inevitably drew Galwell close to Mona. Mona, whose scent of roselia petals opening on winter nights haunted him. Mona, whose soft skin enchanted him.

Mona, who'd rocked his realm with her—

The quest. I must focus on the Ghosts-damned quest.

Thank the Ghosts, they reached backstage. Galwell scouted their surroundings the same way he would enemy ramparts or nightwalker tunnels. Onstage, magicians were engaged in some manner of performance where they play-fought conjurated mythical beasts.

Galwell would have spectated were he not questing. Their dragon special effects were marvelous.

Unfortunately, he had surveillance to conduct. Dismayingly, backstage was crowded. Contestants waited in line for their turn in the spotlight. Magicians and engineers enhanced the performance, monitoring instruments of glass globes and colored currents corresponding to music and lighting. Conjurists enhanced the stage with projections of Vestriya Now's ubiquitous logo on the glittering curtains and painted theater ceiling.

The effects were stunning in composite. There was no question why this was the premiere performance competition in the realms.

Pity one sex-starved, danger-damning hero could not enjoy them.

Galwell was completing his reconnaissance when Mona waved cheerfully. "Best wishes saving the realm," she offered him. "Drop by when you're done sometime!"

She strode for the exit.

Galwell fought past his surprise. He leapt to her side. Grabbing Mona's wrist required withstanding the rush of contact with her skin, which he only just managed while retaining consciousness. "What?" he got out. "Where are you going?"

Mona looked up innocently, like her departure was the expected result of the day's proceedings. "To Mythria, apparently. Cloudcliff Village," she replied. "That's where Clare's thoughts said our parents are." She gave him a wry smile. "I'm off for some revenge!"

"Now?" Galwell asked, not releasing her hand. "It couldn't wait—oh, I don't know, one hour?"

Mona's coy cheer disappeared. Her eyes hardened. "I told you this would happen," she reminded him. Menace sharpened her every word. "I warned you that you wouldn't like the real me."

"*This isn't the real you*," Galwell ground out.

Mona ripped her wrist free. She drew nearer. "Imagine growing up miserable and poor among the very worst bandits in Mythria," she hissed. "Imagine hearing in your parents' heads how much of a burden your existence was every single day."

Despite their closeness, Galwell could only focus on the pain-drenched poison in Mona's voice.

"Imagine running away because you're desperate to stop ruining your family's lives. Imagine moving to a new realm, losing everyone you love," Mona went on.

Desperate. Yes, desperation was what he heard from her now. To escape her past? Or merely for him to understand how she never could?

"I'm not a hero. I'm not my happy, silly brother." Tears of rage filled her eyes. "I'm not you," she spat. "I'm not here to save the day for a realm that doesn't deserve it."

For several long moments, Galwell said nothing.

Mona's mind-reading magic was her gift and her curse. Galwell found himself possessed of his own damning gift now—understanding.

He understood Mona. He understood her wholly. Her unforgiving determination. Her vow of vengeance. Her wounds were permanent, so she'd sharpened her scars into weapons.

Worse, he understood the impossibility of what he was asking of her. Forgiveness? For what she'd endured? But heroism demanded his effort.

Yes, heroism meant fighting evil would-be rulers or vanquishing rampant monsters. Sometimes, though, it meant this. Facing down the darkness rising in the soul of someone he loved.

"Just wait," he pleaded. "Wait, and . . . We can talk about this. We need you, Mona. We need you now."

Her eyes widened. She'd heard the war raging in his heart. She knew what he was offering. Not condemnation, not rejection. Patience. Something more, even.

She sighed deeply. "Assassin approaching from your left," she announced.

Upon her warning, Galwell reached out with one massive hand, intercepting the black-booted woman rushing toward him—it was one of those twins, he remembered from their Grotto escape, the square-headed, sneering Mary—and knocking her unconscious with one heavy thump on the head. "See?" he implored Mona. "We make a good team. Stay. Help us. Help me."

His encouragement earned him an eye roll. "If I stay, it doesn't change anything," she informed him. "You're still going to have to accept that I am who I am."

"I know who you are, Mona," Galwell said, his voice low.

Mona shook her head sadly.

She doubted him. Well, what of it? Galwell the Great had contended with impossible odds. He'd endured the unendurable. He'd returned from death itself, hadn't he? He could prove to the woman he loved the goodness he saw in her.

His determination evidently distracted Mona, for he'd never seen her startle the way she did when Thessia greeted them. "Dear friends," the queen said, clasping their shoulders. She was heading into the catacombs, dressed in a robe like she was in between costume changes for the performance. "Everything going well, I trust?"

Galwell reprimanded himself. He should have focused on his surroundings. Reconnaissance. The quest! He should not have let Thessia surprise him. He was protecting her!

"Yes. We're here to watch your back," he replied confidently, hiding his chagrin.

Thessia smiled. The expression did not entirely reach her eyes. Galwell felt sudden sympathy for the queen. While the plan rested on every one of their shoulders, everything Thessia did, she did knowing the Deathrose Guild wanted her life.

Her composure was queenly. Her courage was heroic.

"Good. Good," she repeated nervously. "Perhaps you could go ahead of me to my dressing room and make sure it's empty?"

"Yes, of course," Galwell reassured her. "With the two of us"—he gestured to Mona—"we'll be able to find and remove anyone seeking to do you harm."

Thessia nodded, not looking entirely reassured.

Galwell led Mona in the direction Thessia gestured into the catacombs. He was, he recognized despite the direness of their circumstances, delighted Mona had not left. He could get through to her, he knew he could—

Contemplating these hopeful possibilities, Galwell nearly did not notice the assassin who stepped in front of them, long dagger in hand.

He whirled, only to find another knife-wielding cloaked figure closing off the corridor. They were ambushed.

Mona looked frustrated. Galwell felt guilty—had his thoughts preoccupied her, preventing her from hearing the assassin's mind nearby?

He thrust Mona protectively behind him, preparing himself for the first knifeman closing in. Galwell lashed out with one powerful kick—

Which did not connect. Galwell wobbled while his boot struck the oncoming man with meager force. The man stumbled, slowed but not injured.

Unnerved, Galwell punched his opponent in the face. The punch would have shattered other men's jaws. Galwell expected teeth to clatter on the catacomb floor.

Instead, the punch sent pain shooting into Galwell's knuckles. He gasped involuntarily—*did punching hurt everyone else like this?*—while the assassin only grunted.

Galwell withdrew, his movements clumsy. Weak.

The assassin swiped his long knife, slashing Galwell's shoulder. The hero's resistance to pain would have made the injury insignificant under ordinary circumstances. These were not, Galwell knew now, ordinary circumstances. The gash stung deeply, consuming his concentration.

He collapsed into Mona, who clung to his hulking, helpless form. She hunched, her eyes disoriented, her movements uncoordinated. Nothing like when he'd fought her. When she could predict his every move. Instead . . .

"You can't read their minds, can you?" he exhaled. "You didn't hear this ambush coming, either."

Pale, Mona shook her head. When the other assassin stabbed, she only just managed to dodge out of the way.

"Something is wrong," she uttered.

Oh, he knew.

They'd lost their magic. Somehow, something had stolen their power in the past . . . minutes? Hours? Mona had read his mind in their imprisoned liaison. When had he last possessed his inordinate strength? He could not remember.

He leaped out of the way of his assassin's next furious stroke. What did he have left? No magic. No realm. No reputation.

He was no hero here. Galwell the Gruesome. He was no hero to himself, either. Galwell the . . . nothing.

He was nothing.

What choices did he have? He could die nobly, defending Mona . . .

who would undoubtedly meet the same fate moments thereafter. Without her magic, she was uncoordinated and frightened, just like him. He could surrender, hoping for the guild's mercy. Or . . .

He rammed his knee up, right into his assassin's precious stones. The man yelped, folding inward over his crotch.

Or Galwell the Great could fight dirty.

Yes, Mona the Merciless had rubbed off on him, like Clare said. *Sometimes to do good, one has to be bad.*

The Deathrose man recovered. When the assassins lunged, Galwell let their knives slash his chest.

Oh, Ghosts, it hurt. He leaned into the feeling. Wailing dramatically, he stumbled into the wall. He found inspiration in the Chestlewitt play performer he'd watched mawkishly imitate his own death. Clutching his chest, Galwell pantomimed grievous injury.

The Deathrose Guild men paused. They neared their incapacitated mark, cautiously wondering if they'd completed their mission.

Galwell thought of his friends then, his questing companions who fought without magically enhanced power. Who fought with something stronger than strength—courage.

He recalled how Beatrice fended off enemies, vicious and determined. How his sister Elowen was careful and quick.

Knowing he had only one chance without his enormous strength, Galwell summoned courage and cunning into the most ferocious moment of his life. Rising from his slump, he mustered all his regular, ordinary, non-heroic strength into slamming the assassins' heads together.

In the echo of the loud crack, their assailants crumpled.

"Well done." Mona straightened, watching Galwell.

"Yes, well," he panted. "Good thing I've learned a thing or two about lying."

Hardly recognizing himself, he winked. Mona grinned, and Galwell extended his non-magical hands to help her up.

"Where the Ghosts has our magic gone?" he wondered out loud.

"I don't know," she replied. "For the first time . . . it's quiet. I don't know what you're thinking."

He heard panic humming in her voice. Once more, he understood her perfectly. Mona had considered herself cursed with her mind reading, yet without her magic, she was . . . terrified. Lost in the shadows everyone else confronted.

Galwell felt the same, contending with the same commonplace strength his companions possessed. What Mona needed, he knew, was comfort.

He clasped her hands, looking right into her eyes. Forcing her to meet his gaze. "You don't need your magic to know what I'm thinking," he reminded her firmly.

Mona's breathing evened. Her clenched grip relaxed.

"I—suppose you're right," she conceded, nearly smiling. "Still, I'd like it back. Have we been poisoned? It's the guild's style."

"Possibly. Thessia seemed off, too," he remembered. "I figured she was just nervous. But without magic of her own, perhaps the poison is making her sick?"

Or killing her, he realized. Fear coursed through him.

Immediately, he was running, Mona with him like she could read his mind even without magic. They needed to find the queen. Presumably she'd fled when the guild cornered them, but where was her dressing room? Mona on his heels, Galwell retraced their steps.

When they reached backstage, though, nothing was out of place. River had arrived, watching from the wings, distanced from the stage magicians. Thessia was onstage, having swapped her robe for a stunning crimson gown.

Galwell exchanged glances with Mona. Cautiously, they moved to join River.

"Our next guest is one you aren't expecting," Thessia promised. Her voice echoed over the crowd, magically enhanced while she stood in the circle Galwell saw faintly illuminated onstage. "You've been told he's unwell. That he has been in the Pale Palace after suffering an undisclosed injury."

The queen's manner was changed from their earlier meeting. Thessia presented with confident clarity.

He permitted himself some measure of relief. Either the poison no longer upset Thessia or the effects were mild enough for her to maintain her composure.

"I will let him tell his story for himself, but, Vestriyans, it is my honor to announce your prince," she declared. *"Ario Vestras."*

Every magician and engineer backstage faltered, while in the theater, the audience hushed. No one knew what was coming—no one except Galwell and his companions.

His heart pounded, for their plan had reached the precipice of success. The Vestriyan people needed more than heroism, more than justice. They needed the story of their realm returned to them.

From the crowd, Ario rose.

The theater fell completely silent as the prince strode slowly—protected from guild assassins by thousands of eyes—onto the stage. Thessia stepped out of the illuminated circle, ceding the enchanted projection to Ario.

"Vestriyans," Ario greeted his people. "I know you are confused. I promise I will answer every question you have. But to help, I must start at the beginning.

"My brother was born in spring," Ario announced fondly. "When the dewdrops hung from the olivera plants like harpies' tears."

Thessia rejoined Galwell and Mona offstage while Ario went on.

THIS WILL BE INTERESTING

"I do hope he gets to the point a little faster," Thessia remarked, watching Ario with nervous excitement. "Audiences can be so impatient."

"Backstory is necessary," Mona replied.

Thessia nodded. "He does look good, though," she conceded. "Kingly."

"But how are you?" Galwell inquired. He examined Thessia closely for paleness or disorientation. "Mona and I suspect we were poisoned. The corridor to your dressing room was an ambush."

Thessia pulled her gaze from the stage. Confusion clouded her expression.

"I don't have a dressing room," she said.

No one spoke for a moment.

"But you just pointed us to it," Mona reminded her.

Fear rose up in Galwell. "Are you all right?" he pressed her. "Perhaps the poison has affected your memory. Mona and I have lost our magic."

River had watched their conversation wordlessly, her expression unreadable. The mention of poison could not shake her guild-hardened demeanor. Galwell knew she preferred remaining vigilant and reserved in such situations, and he had hardly noticed her silent observance—

Until she reached out to grasp Thessia's shoulder.

"My magic works just fine," she said.

Galwell did not have time to intervene. In a flash, River and the queen were gone.

33
Thessia

Under Thessia waited—nothing.

Only empty space, vast distance. And then, far below, the Vestriya Now audience.

Thessia clung onto River, who had magicked them into the crossbeams high over the theater. Peering down from the perilous height made the queen feel sick. So did the questions exploding in her head like fireworks over the stage.

What is happening? Has the plan changed?

What the fuck is River doing?

"I need you to listen to me," River said, holding Thessia securely. "We don't have long."

"River," Thessia gasped out. "What—"

"The guild has demanded I kidnap you," River interrupted. "They threatened Celine. You understand?"

Thessia forced herself to focus. She fought to ignore the deadly drop to the theater below. To concentrate on River, who held Thessia's life in her fingertips, literally.

She had no choice. If she screamed, everyone would see, but River surely would teleport elsewhere. Thessia would fall. What good would being seen do while she plummeted to her death?

She wobbled on the beam. Her heart leapt into her throat—but River held her steady.

Thessia finally looked directly into River's eyes, finding desperation in her companion's gaze.

"Trust me," River pleaded. Gone from River's racked expression was the hardened, isolated assassin Thessia remembered.

Instead, Thessia saw her friend. Thessia saw someone who wasn't alone, and knew it. Someone who would fight for the woman she loved—and, Thessia knew, for her friends. River would not let harm come to Celine, which meant she would not let harm come to the rest of them, either.

"Trust me," River repeated.

"What do you need me to do?" Thessia whispered.

She could see the relief in River's posture, though the other woman held them skillfully balanced on the rafter beams. Releasing one hand from Thessia, River pulled a blindfold from her pocket.

"This is our chance to find out who is behind the guild's corruption. I'm going to bring you to them, and I need it to look convincing," River explained.

Thessia took the blindfold. "I think you'll find all my years of being kidnapped have prepared me for this," she remarked, wrapping the opaque cloth over her eyes.

She heard River chuckle. River's other hand found Thessia once more—

Then the beam underneath them disappeared.

Moments later, hard ground, stone, surfaced reassuringly under Thessia. She dropped to one knee, recovering her balance. Ghosts, she'd never get used to River's magic.

Blindfolded, Thessia measured her surroundings in the ways she could. The room was dank, cool, stale. Underground, Thessia concluded. Shuffling sounds of boot soles and metal weaponry indicated other people were in the room.

"Hello, colleagues." River greeted them formally.

Her voice was unrecognizable to Thessia. Cold, iron-edged. Was this how she sounded in the guild?

"I request an audience with the new leader. I will only deliver the queen to them personally," River declared.

Someone laughed gruffly. "You won't be making demands," the rough voice replied.

"Actually, I will," River returned with emotionless disdain. "I assume you've lost your leverage on me by now? Should have warned you that scribe is hard to hold on to. You know, I've been cast out of the guild long enough to have spent many hours talking with Celine. Gary's uncommon ticklishness may have come up. I imagine you found him on the floor in a fit of giggles. Isn't that right?"

Thessia fought back a smile, knowing humor would not help convince the guild of her captivity.

No one replied. Thessia heard more shuffling. Embarrassment, most likely.

"*I'm* the one with leverage. I will deliver the queen to the leader *only*," River said lethally. "I will reclaim my position in the guild."

Thessia tensed. Her humor disappeared. River . . . couldn't possibly intend to turn on Thessia, on all of them, and return to the guild, could she? When Thessia first met River Pricemark, River's only desire was ending her expulsion from the guild.

Now . . .

"You can't come back," the man crowed.

"No?" River returned. "Then I suppose I will teleport the queen all the way back to her throne right now. You'll never have another chance at her."

Once more, River's retort quieted the room.

Thessia held her breath. River was convincing. *Too* convincing? Her fear rising, Thessia started to struggle. But River's grip stayed firm.

THIS WILL BE INTERESTING

River had told Thessia to trust her, the queen reminded herself. Thessia would—not that she had much choice.

"I have no reason to give you what I want with nothing in return," River said. "The leader. Now."

Someone grunted in displeasure. The metal door of their room scraped open, and the Deathrose Guild lackeys seemed to exit.

For moments, Thessia heard nothing, until—footsteps.

The paces sounded confidently on the stone. Slow, purposeful. Predatory. The footsteps of someone utterly in control. The way Thessia wished she felt.

The room became colder somehow. Magic? Thessia wondered. Or merely the intimidating power of someone meant to lead?

The footsteps drew closer. Thessia felt River's grip on her tense nervously. River did not move otherwise, though. Her posture remained cautious, not combative.

Closer and closer strode the Deathrose Guild's leader.

Fabric rustled, like someone opening their cloak. Or removing their hood.

The next instant, several things happened. River gasped. In recognition, Thessia realized. Wind passed Thessia's face with the whoosh of fast movement. Something struck hard very close to Thessia—cutting River's gasp short.

River's grip on Thessia released, and Thessia heard her companion hit the ground.

Whoever stood in front of Thessia had knocked River out instantaneously, faster than she could teleport. Or Thessia *hoped* River was merely unconscious. Heart in her throat, Thessia waited for blood to pool under her knees—but felt none.

Still, without River's grasp on her, fear held Thessia captive. Whoever had entered the room was not just powerful. They were very, very dangerous.

Thessia permitted someone to grab her hands roughly and tie her wrists with rope. Queen or not, Thessia was in no position to resist.

Finally, the leader spoke. A woman's voice, unnervingly familiar. "Take Miss Pricemark out of here," she ordered. "Watch her."

"Someone should stay to guard you," a rough-voiced man replied.

"I'll be fine," the guild leader said. "I wish to speak to the queen alone."

Thessia trembled. Oh, how she yearned for courage.

No, she counseled herself furiously. She was the queen of Mythria. She need not *yearn*. She commanded. She could command herself now. She'd known evil. She'd known terror.

She remembered every horrible person who'd ever sought to threaten or control her. None of them had succeeded. Nor would this mysterious woman.

Over the sounds of the Deathrose man hauling River from the room, Thessia straightened her spine. She controlled her heartbeat. She summoned Galwell's strength, Hugh's self-control, River's hardened intensity, Celine's dauntless fire. She even summoned Ario's indomitable spirit. Why not, right?

When the leader's hand found the side of Thessia's face, she flinched violently. Then something strange happened—the gemstone on Thessia's wrist hummed, the talisman tying her to . . . No, it couldn't be.

Careful fingers grasped Thessia's blindfold, then removed the cloth, leaving Thessia face-to-face with—

Herself.

Thessia's head spun. She struggled for comprehension.

Finally, she grasped the devastating irony of her situation. Thessia had often considered herself her own worst enemy. Not her person—but her name, her image, her title. For much of her life, the queen of Mythria had held Thessia captive.

Now she literally did.

"*Tabitha*," Thessia exhaled.

Her body double stood before the captive queen. She wore shimmering golden robes, fit for the commander of the Deathrose Guild—or the hostess of Vestriya Now, or the queen of Mythria. Her smile shone like Thessia had never seen on the humble, considerate woman she'd known. It was wide, venomous, and utterly merciless.

Atop her golden hair sat Thessia's tiara.

"Well, well, well, Thessia. Damsel once again," Tabitha gloated. "But this time, no one is coming to rescue you."

"Tabitha, I—I never knew you were this unhappy," Thessia managed. She felt dazed.

Tabitha laughed in delight. "I'm not unhappy. You were the unhappy one, Thessia. I'm giving you what you've always wanted. Really, you should thank me," she remarked cheerfully. "You no longer have to live the life you hated. I will become the queen you so resented being."

Thessia's mouth worked, but nothing came out. She hated how deeply her double's words cut.

Instead of ruling her queendom, Thessia had let her role rule her. She'd become exasperated, stifled, resentful. In her resentment, Tabitha had found her opportunity.

Thessia had to do . . . something. Even now, her powerlessness overwhelmed her.

"How?" she asked, hopeless.

Tabitha preened. "I never got to have my own life, you know. I was always living the pale shadow of yours. When Galwell returned, I realized how I could not only reclaim my life, but claim yours as well. While I was filling in for you at a dinner for Mythrian arts, I was forced to listen to Chestlewitt's concerns for his upcoming premiere the entire night. I gave him the idea to commission the guild to save his play."

Thessia's breath caught. *The whole time.* Tabitha was behind *everything* while within arm's reach of Thessia the whole time.

"Did you know I'd been seeing an assassin in my off hours? Bertram. He was a clumsy lover, but his gifts were useful and ... similar to mine." She paused, shrugging. "Your friend River killed him at the Realm Chalice. Saved me having to break up with him, I must admit. He'd already served his purpose to me by then, giving me an in to approach the guild and explain exactly how much they stood to gain with Galwell's death. My vision impressed them so much, they put me in charge," she continued. "But I have to thank you, my dear Thessia, for bringing me to Vestriya. It was only when I filled your spot in the masquerade that I got to speak to the king and queen of Vestriya directly."

Thessia remembered it. How Tabitha had explained she'd already traded pleasantries with the king and queen. Thessia had been *grateful*. What a fool she'd been.

Tabitha trailed a finger down Thessia's cheek, gloating. "We came to a new agreement," she said. "I'd take care of their brewing coup with the use of my guild of assassins and they would recognize me in your place when the time came."

"You—you can't—" she got out.

"Let me stop you right there," Tabitha said sweetly. She halted her pacing in front of Thessia, holding her perfect posture above the humbled queen. "I can. I can do everything you can. Because I *am* you. This"—Tabitha gestured grandly to herself—"is you. No one will ever notice you're gone. Because this is all that matters of you, Thessia of Mythria. A face ... in a tiara ... on a throne."

Tabitha leaned down, her identical features level with Thessia's.

"Nothing more," she said.

Thessia's eyes welled with tears. Oh, she hated the feeling. The humiliation, the hopelessness. The realization that everything Tabitha was saying was . . . true.

"What then?" Thessia croaked out. "What will you do? Spread more villainy? Run the guild in secret?"

"That's the thing," Tabitha murmured in Thessia's face. "I'll do *whatever I want.*"

Whatever I want.

Thessia hardly recognized the rage mounting in her. She clung on to the feeling, for in the flames, she found the first flicker of power. Of strength.

No, Thessia would not surrender any part of herself to this impostor. She wanted her life. Tabitha sought to steal her throne, her power, her independence, her very self. Well, Thessia would steal something in return—her enemy's confidence, her conviction. In order to escape, to defend her throne, Thessia would copy her double. She would imitate her own imitation.

While Tabitha smiled, crowned in the glory of her plot, Thessia did the unimaginable. Something *royals* would not do.

She reared back and spat in Tabitha's face.

When Tabitha shrieked in disgust, flinging saliva everywhere, the tiara dropped to the floor.

Thessia pounced. In seconds, she seized the sharp metal ornament. She jabbed her wrists downward, using the glimmering crystal point of the crown to cut her ropes. It was *her* crown, after all. She knew well how sharp its edges were. She rose to her feet—

Tiara in hand, she swung upward, slicing the length of Tabitha's face with the crown's point.

Tabitha screamed while blood poured from the gash. The curtain of crimson descending over the impostor's features was the last Thessia saw of her double before dashing from the room clutching her tiara.

She hit the hallway—only to encounter familiar faces. Galwell and Mona were rushing in her direction. They stopped sharply, and Thessia felt Galwell's nervous gaze examine her for injuries. "We're here to save you," he stated with ever-so-Galwell certainty.

"I don't need saving," Thessia said honestly. "River does, though. She's captured down here somewhere. Find her while I return to the stage. Ario needs help. Tell them Tabitha is behind everything."

Without waiting for her companions' reply, she dashed past them, seeking the stage. For the first time, commanding her own quest felt . . . natural. It felt right. It felt like her.

Damsel? Fuck no.

Thessia would save herself.

A queen *and* a hero.

34
River

River returned to consciousness in the corner of a squat room, surrounded by four guild members playing an informal game of stackjack.

Her head throbbed as her mind tried to unspool what had led to this. She'd spent so much time being tortured by Dougal, she wondered if perhaps she'd never escaped. Maybe Vandra's rescue and all the subsequent action had been a dream.

She'd competed in Vestriya Now, after all.

But no, the smell told her it was real. Musty, earthy. Subterranean, yet not in the holding cell anymore. To her relief, she found there were no magical ropes on her wrists.

Enough of this, then.

She squeezed her eyes to teleport.

It didn't work.

Worse, the little grunt of disapproval she let out made the guild members aware that she'd awoken.

"Aww, she's wincing," said one, mockingly, tossing down a stack of coins and yelling, "All aboard!" the signal in stackjack that you were betting everything you had.

"You lose!" said another man with a row of golden teeth bright enough for River to make out even through her disorientation.

River strained to open her eyes all the way. It hurt too much.

The guild member who'd lost the game of stackjack shoved his chair back in frustration, rising and heading for River. Even through her blurred vision, she could make out the forming of his fist, preparing to knock her unconscious once more.

"Wait, wait," she forced out. "I'm one of you." She was pretty sure her words were slurred, but she pushed on. "I gave you Thessia. I followed orders. What's the problem?"

"Tabitha doesn't know if she can trust you yet," said the man.

Tabitha.

The leader of the Deathrose Guild was . . . Thessia's body double? River had only seen her for a moment before Tabitha had knocked her out cold, but she knew her face. She knew it because it was Thessia's face, more or less, with that damned shimmer effect.

It was all coming back now, the surreal events that had led to this moment.

Forget the scribesheets; this could be a plot in a shadow play, River thought, her mind searching for a comfortable distraction. Because this was not gossip or make-believe. It was real. And without teleportation, she was once again trapped underground with no escape.

"Of course Tabitha can trust me," River assured the man. "I gave up everything to help her."

"Yeah, but you've been spending all your time with Thessia," said Golden Teeth. "We don't know if you're going to be calm when we kill her."

"You should definitely kill Thessia." River's tongue felt swollen, like her own body was trying to choke her for even saying these words. "But . . . why, exactly? Won't killing the queen be . . . um . . . pretty bad?"

As her vision began to clear, she realized she did not know the guild members watching over her. These were the very top assassins, she figured, if they were allowed to be around Tabitha. Or perhaps they were the newest. The most ignorant. Because only a fool would let themselves get so close to someone as dangerous as Tabitha was, a woman wearing the face of the queen while actively stoking the flames of evil across two realms.

Either way, it didn't really matter. River could not show her true hand to them.

"So Tabby can take her place, of course," said Stackjack Loser. "From the throne, she can do anything."

"Sure, sure," River said, nodding. She wanted to vomit. Or scream. Perhaps both. "She can't already do that now?"

"You ask a lot of questions for someone who claims to be on our side." Stackjack Loser's face turned red again. He was quick to anger, dangerous in an unpredictable way. Definitely not the kind of assassin the guild would've once wanted. But that guild no longer existed. Maybe it never had. Maybe everything had always been a lie.

"Sorry, sorry. I'm not at my sharpest." River gestured to her aching head. "I'm loving everything you're saying, I really am." This was over-the-top, but these men were not bright. For one, they didn't have River secured. She could fight them if she wanted. Jump on their stackjack table and shove coins into their throats until they choked.

They weren't trained assassins. They couldn't be.

They had to be mindless henchmen, chosen because they would do Tabitha's bidding without question or complaint.

"You guys are just so clever," River continued, playing it up way too much, watching as all four of them cracked smiles. "I want to be sure I'm doing everything by the new honor code, you know? Which I assume you're all a part of creating."

They exchanged quick looks that told River they did not, in fact, have any part in developing the guild's new honor code. She pretended not to notice.

"I only want to know the Deathrose Guild's new goals, that's all," she said. "So I can reach them."

"You're probably not old enough to remember the good days, but we used to be a proper realm full of bad guys," said Golden Teeth.

"There was so Ghosts-damned much guild business back then," said the man who wore, for some reason, a red neck scarf. "So many people to kill."

"Todrick van Thorn went about it all wrong," said Stackjack Loser. "Sorry, do you know who that is?"

River was tired of this. Dougal had done it to her, too, assumed she didn't know details about the most famous evil organization in all of Mythria. The Fraternal Order's initial reign of terror was in full swing when River joined the guild over a decade ago. Of course she knew who Todrick van Thorn was—the Fraternal Order's leader. River had actually killed some of his low-level colleagues on her very first assignments with the guild.

But these men wanted her to seem young. Naive. She had to let them explain a history she'd lived through up close like it was their story to tell, not hers.

"I think I've heard of him," she said, nodding.

"He was way too showy," chimed in a third man with a braided beard. His first words since River awoke. "He understood we needed more villains to keep the realm in motion, but he didn't understand the most important part about it."

"Which is what?" River asked. She didn't have to pretend to be riveted. She was. Just not in the way they thought.

"We need the villains to look like our heroes," said Braided Beard. "That way, when they fall from grace, it stokes even more fear. Even the good guys can be bad. Maybe everyone is bad. The system feeds itself that way."

"With Tabitha ruling over the queendom as Thessia, we will never run out of work to do. People to kill. Chaos to chase," Stackjack Loser said.

"We'll become infinite," explained Red Scarf, grinning.

Outraged, River rose up to fight, but she was so lightheaded, she slumped down again, woozy. The guild wasn't fighting villains; they were *creating* them. All of this was nothing more than a sick game, designed to stoke flames of power and greed. River had played into it.

Not anymore.

The door flew open. Tabitha herself stormed into the room. A nasty gash across her face dripped blood onto the floor as she moved. "Thessia *escaped*!" she said, seething with rage. She picked up the stackjack table and threw it against the wall, narrowly missing River's head.

"How?" the henchmen asked in unison.

"She *spat* on me. Then she used the tiara to cut me! And the ropes to free herself! All because of you!"

River bit back her grin. Thessia, the queen of Mythria, had spat? On the leader of the Deathrose Guild?

She expected Tabitha's ire would be directed at her. But no, Tabitha was pointing a charmed fingernail at one of her henchmen, waving it toward his face, then moving on to the next one.

Each man backed away, genuinely afraid of her touch.

"I will silence all of your powers *right now*," Tabitha told the men. "And I'll do it as often as I please, until you've all learned your lesson!"

That was Tabitha's gift, then. She could touch people and take their magic from them. When she'd knocked River out, she'd taken her gift of teleportation.

The ropes, River realized. When River was being held captive, Dougal had said he was using magical ropes that had been a collaboration between Myke Lycroft and the new leader of the guild. It was Tabitha's magic inside them. And it was her magic that had rendered Galwell and Mona powerless.

The door flew open again. River knew that, despite her throbbing head and wobbly disposition, it was time to do her best to fight. Because this would surely be her end.

But more henchmen did not pour into the room.

Galwell and Mona did.

"Thessia sent us," said Galwell, the wind from the opened door wooshing through his hair, as it so often did.

He threw a punch at Red Scarf, and River's heart squeezed in relief. With Galwell's strength, taking out four henchmen would be child's play. She didn't need to do anything more than stay out of his way. But his punch turned out to be so pathetic—so shockingly weak and misplaced—that Red Scarf actually laughed.

Galwell's power was still silenced.

Mona followed up Galwell's failed punch with a roundhouse kick that had slightly more effect, knocking Red Scarf back a few steps.

"Mona the Merciless, here to join us?" asked Tabitha. She hadn't bothered to assume a fighting posture. In fact, she stood with her arms crossed and one eyebrow arched, so unlike the real Thessia, even while sharing her face and all her clothing.

Mona shoved Tabitha as hard as she could. "In your *dreams*."

River was surprised to find tears spring to her eyes. Galwell and Mona were both fighting. For River. Still standing by her side even though, for all they knew, she'd betrayed them.

It was very heroic. Perhaps the most heroic anyone could ever be.

Forget the wooziness. She had to join them.

Using an empty chair as a launch pad, she leapt up to reach for the pipes overhead, grabbing one with both hands and swinging like it was a playground bar. She caught Red Scarf's weapon sheath with her feet, one boot on either side of the dagger that poked out from his right hip.

"Galwell!" River yelled.

Understanding, he dashed over to meet her on the backswing, snatching the weapon out from between her ankles.

On her next forward swing, she let go of the first pipe and propelled herself to the next, catching it with her hands while shoving her feet square into Golden Teeth's chest. He fell back into the wall. Mona used the opportunity to swipe his weapon.

Now her friends were armed, capable of fighting the four henchmen in earnest, no magic necessary.

Pleased, River dismounted from the pipes with a back flip. It had the strange effect of righting her dizziness. Or perhaps knocking her so far off-kilter that she somehow felt normal again.

It also placed her in front of Tabitha, who ran out into the hallway, forcing River into a chase.

"You," River yelled out. "You destroyed everything I thought I knew! I gave everything to the guild! But all of it was a lie!"

Tabitha glanced over her shoulder before darting down a side tunnel. She thought she could escape, but River knew this underground labyrinth just as well as Tabitha did. She'd memorized it after being freed from Dougal's torture.

"What a coward!" she taunted. "Running away instead of showing up to this fight. A poor excuse for a leader in every way."

Tabitha halted, coming to such a startling stop that River nearly crashed into her. "You think you're so *clever*," she said. "But I wasn't the one fighting for a cause I didn't understand, was I? I wasn't the one following orders for years without question or concern. I wasn't the pawn. *You* were."

River should've armed herself with a weapon, too, but she wasn't thinking clearly. She only knew she wanted revenge. Justice. Something.

"You're right," River said. "I was a fool. But now I understand everything. Your lackeys laid it all out for me. And I know that *you're* the evil I was hired to eliminate. I know I have to kill *you*."

She realized as she finished her little speech that she was swaying. Heroic adrenaline had tricked her into thinking her dizziness had subsided. Standing still, it roared back to life, threatening to knock her to the ground again.

Still, she took a swipe at Tabitha, managing only to swat the air.

"Oh, dear, don't do this," Tabitha said. She used her queenly voice, playing the part of a benevolent ruler to sickly effect. "It only makes this more embarrassing for you. You're already going to die alone down here. Why not keep that dignity I hear you're so proud of?"

River may not have had her teleportation power. She may not have had her acrobatics, either. But for the first time in her life, River had real friends who cared for her, and a woman she loved. Yes, loved.

She loved Celine.

Celine, who had given her a quill.

River fumbled for where she'd tucked it away, wanting it with her at all times. She knew how this looked to Tabitha. Like she was grabbing for her heart, full of regrets. The desperate actions of a woman about to take her last breath.

Maybe she didn't have her full coordination, but she still had her wits.

"Make it quick," River told Tabitha in a raspy whisper.

Tabitha stepped closer, ready to comply.

River stabbed her in the throat.

"My last kill," she said as Tabitha crumpled to the ground.

She pulled the quill from Tabitha's neck, a fountain of blood spurting in its absence. River tucked the quill back into her pocket, blood staining her white costume.

It didn't take more than a few seconds for the light to go out in Tabitha's eyes. And as soon as she was dead, River felt a strange tingle down her spine.

Her magic, she suspected. It had come back.

She closed her eyes, thinking of Galwell and Mona. And there she was, back in the room, pleased to find her gift restored and all the henchmen unconscious. Shocked to find Galwell and Mona sharing a kiss.

"I thought you said no romance?" she joked, having regrettably seen up close that Galwell and Mona had done much more than kiss. But this was what friends did. They teased one another. Made harmless jabs that showed their camaraderie. "C'mon," she told them, smiling. "Tabitha's dead. But we're far from done."

She teleported the three of them to Celine, who watched the Vestriya Now performances from a new spot, standing in the open space behind the very last row.

"You're *alive*," Celine said, her eyes instantly welling with tears of relief.

River pretended to dust off her shoulders, but that dizziness reared its ugly head again and she nearly toppled sideways. "Not quite well, though. Don't worry—the blood on my costume isn't mine," she said with a sideways grin. "But I think I know what would fix it."

She gripped Celine's waist, hugging her close.

"What's that?" Celine breathed.

"A kiss from the woman I love."

With that, River pressed her lips to Celine's. All her concerns melted away. She was fire, indeed, warming River from the inside out, tingly and pleasant and perfect.

Abruptly, Celine pulled back. "Hold on a second. Did you say you love me?" She ran a finger over River's lips, and River nipped it playfully.

"I'd offer you your quill back so you could write it down, but I actually used it to kill the evil leader of the Deathrose Guild, who turned out to be Thessia's body double, Tabitha. I do still have it, but I haven't had a chance to wipe off all the blood." She enjoyed the way emotions ran across Celine's face in rapid succession—shock, horror, intrigue, amazement. "I think it's wiser if you just use your nonmagical everlasting memory for this." River kissed her again. "I love you. I love you. I love you."

"I love you too," Celine gasped out.

She could have stayed here forever, showering Celine with kisses, repeating that three-word phrase. It would have been perfect.

Except there was a sound around them. Booing, to be more exact.

Ario was *still* on the stage, flopping harder than ever.

35
Thessia

Nothing more. Nothing more.

Tabitha's words followed Thessia.

Nothing more. Nothing more.

She fought them like she'd fought her duplicitous double. She *was* more. She was a daughter. She was a fighter who'd survived kidnappings, conquerors, and questing of her own. She was a friend.

She rushed up winding corridors toward the stage. In defending herself against the Deathrose Guild, she'd found the strength to declare her independence from the pretty, perfect monarch she'd become. When she returned to Mythria, she would ensure more of *Thessia* occupied the throne.

But before that—she was going to save Vestriya.

She flew up the final stairwell. Reaching the shadowed wings, she gazed out onstage.

Dismay found her instantly. Ario remained under the lights, and . . . the plan was going poorly.

The prince did *not* look kingly. Vestriyans watched in confusion while Ario fumbled over his words. Sweat shimmered on his forehead, sticking his silver hair to his face. His speech veered from politics to poetry and vice versa . . . neither of which was engaging the audience.

It couldn't end here, panic screamed in her head. Her miserable gaze found the king and queen of Vestriya watching from their private box. The royal couple looked . . . delighted.

Of course they were. This was probably the shittiest coup she'd ever seen, honestly.

Not good. Not good.

She nibbled her fingernail furiously. Ario needed help. He needed support. *She* couldn't just go out there and join him, however. Why would Vestriyans ever trust her? In present political circumstances, they would think she sought to weaken the regime of their realm.

He needed . . .

Commotion in the wings distracted her. Stage pages were wrestling in frustration with someone who had left the line of people waiting for their turn on the stage. The contestant rushed for Thessia—

Hugh.

The solution came to her immediately. Ario needed *backup*.

Hugh's eyes roamed over her bloodstained gown, her bruised face. Pure, deep, soul-shattering fear drove him.

"I'm fine," she exhaled the moment he reached her.

She wanted to reach out for him. Hold him. Kiss him. Remembering how their last conversation ended, she only just managed to stop herself.

"You don't look it," Hugh exhaled. Frantic, he inspected every inch of her he could see for injuries. "What happened?"

"Tabitha," Thessia explained. "She's the leader of the guild. She wanted to take my life, literally. To kill me and step into my position on the throne, pretending she was me. But I escaped," Thessia went on, unable to help the pride in her voice despite the desperation consuming Hugh. "Galwell and Mona and River will handle her. What we need to do is help—"

Hugh's lips on hers cut her off.

This was *not* how their last conversation ended. Thessia cared not.

She collapsed into the kiss, passion and pride and independence combusting in unforgettable fire.

Hugh's harp fell to the floor while his hands wound in her hair. He kissed her with frenzied intensity, his mouth finding her neck, her cheeks, her temples. He kissed her everywhere he could.

"I don't care about all that," he uttered roughly. "You could have died."

Yes, she could have. Nothing would come of hiding from dangerous inevitabilities.

"I almost did," she whispered.

Hugh gripped her hard, like he hoped the force of his conviction could defend her forever. "I can't lose you, Thess," he insisted, every word wracked. "I can't."

Thessia pulled back to look into his eyes. She needed him to know she understood him fully. Whatever he needed, whatever he could or could not withstand, she had the strength to face.

"I know you pushed me away to try to spare me this fear. I know I let you. But it's too late," Hugh went on. "I'm already in love with you. I think I've been in love with you since I watched you sing 'My Home Is Mythria' to a bunch of drunk soldiers."

Thessia laughed, with tears in her eyes. Yes, she was so, *so* much more than her crown. She was loved. She was in love.

It felt like everything.

"I love you, too, Hugh," she said. "You're my best friend, you're who I think about when I wake up, who I dream about at night. And . . ."

She straightened. She was the queen of her heart now. The ruler of her fate.

"And I know we lead dangerous lives, but I saved myself tonight," she went on. "I'll keep saving myself. For the both of us."

Hugh grinned. Tears shone in his eyes, too.

"You'd better," he replied.

Thessia kissed him.

In their embrace, passion conquered panic. Hope overpowered fear. Her heart's quest, carried out under cover of royal obligation and clandestine yearning, culminated here, in the arms of the man she loved.

Abruptly remembering her objective, Thessia parted from him. Their reunion was very romantic, yes, very romantic, indeed. They had a realm to save, however.

"We need to help Ario," she announced.

If Hugh was thrown by the subject change, he didn't show it. He glanced past Thessia, grimacing while Ario pivoted to poetry on the subject of . . . horseball, it sounded like.

"I'd love to, but I'm not sure there's anything more we can do," Hugh remarked gravely.

Thessia reached for his hand. "There's something *you* can do," she insisted. "Vestriya needs courage. Ario needs courage. He needs *backup*."

Hugh's eyes widened in understanding.

Thessia picked up his harp and handed it to him. Hugh held her gaze, and in his smoldering stare, she could hear the potent music of promise.

"I will not fail you in this quest, my queen," he murmured, bowing deeply. Thessia's heart beat fast as she leaned forward, laying the softest of kisses on Hugh's cheek. Invigorated, Hugh fixed his focus on the illuminated stage.

While the prince spoke, Hugh strutted out under the enchanted lights.

Ghosts, he looks good. Thessia's mouth went dry. The spotlights shone on the sweep of Hugh's dark hair and sharpened the hard lines of his face. His eyes held roguish confidence, like he knew he commanded the crowd without having to try. He swaggered not like a soldier, or even a king. No, he could step right into the Songstar Hall of Fame looking the way he did.

Thessia smiled.

When Ario noticed Hugh, he looked pleasantly surprised to have company. Relief loosened the prince's shoulders. "Vestriyans!" he cried out enthusiastically, interrupting his oration. "I have a treat for you! Marvelous music for you to hear! A delight for soul and for ear!"

Thessia winced. *If Ario fucks this up with his rhymes . . .*

Then Hugh started playing. Thessia's doubt disappeared.

She recognized the low sweetness starting in her stomach, spreading to her limbs. The fearless feeling of Hugh's music captured her heart.

Yet Hugh's song was no ode to romance. Not exactly.

Hugh sang the words Ario had presented to him and Thessia in Hugh's tent. He sang of Vestriya, of home. Of first loves and second chances. Of family and honesty and a horizon free of storms. Words Ario himself had written.

Everyone in the audience hushed to listen. For too long, Vestriyans had been taken advantage of by those with no integrity. Hugh's song summoned in them the courage to yearn for more. The longing to love their realm and themselves.

Thessia shivered from happiness, feeling Hugh's emotion flowing into his playing. The love they shared, composed of compassion and dauntless hope. His magic coursed from him stronger than ever before.

In that moment, Thessia understood that love did not *require* courage. It didn't test courage. They were one and the same. Courage lived in every decision to love someone or somewhere or some fragile idea shimmering with promise—or even to love oneself. Every act of kindness or passion was an act of bravery. It made heroes of everyone, inspiring them to build a happier, fairer, wider future. To love was to dare the realms themselves.

As Hugh sang, Thessia's gaze moved to Ario. The enchanted music had worked on him, too. Hugh's magic stoked courage within the prince, who recognized the words Hugh was singing. Hearing his greatest opus seemed to focus him, reminding him of why he'd written it. He looked calmer, steadier. Proud and determined.

Hugh completed his chorus, his music subsiding to the soft refrain of the harp melody.

With the chords strengthening him, Prince Ario faced his people.

"Vestriyans, you deserve more than what those in power have given you," he declared. "You deserve truth. My parents have cared for nothing but their own wealth and well-being. Prince Ezio knew of their corruption. He knew of the villages my parents exploited. The unjust laws they've written in order to pad their pockets. The poisons they've spread in our own realm!"

He swept his hand out, evoking the imaginary Vestriya. The crowd started to respond. Indignant rustling and calls of encouragement interrupted the prince's speech.

"If you do not believe me, read the scribesheet at your feet!" Ario urged his people. "Ezio was killed to silence him. But *I will not be silenced.*"

He raised his hands skyward. Relief joined with awe in Thessia. He really did look kingly.

The Vestriya Now audience felt the same. The clamor intensified. Looking out over the crowd, Thessia watched more and more Vestriyans pick up the pamphlet. The one Celine had written.

She had documented firsthand what happened to a village beset by tragedy. How the king and queen had exploited the disaster for their own cunning ends. Discontented murmurs spread through the crowd.

The Vestriyan people rounded on the king and queen. Thessia watched them jeer, hurl garbage, and shout obscenities up at the velvet royal balcony. Hugh stopped playing, recognizing that the spark had been lit.

The royal couple stood. Though they remained stoic, Thessia saw fear in their eyes.

They were right to fear their subjects, she knew. They'd lost control of the narrative they'd written for their people. They'd sought to scribe the story of their Vestriya in corruption and carelessness, a realm where nobility meant nothing.

But stories could change. Damsels could become heroes. Heroes could become villains. Rulers could become despots, or fugitives. People, weary and frustrated, could rise up, becoming a realm unto themselves.

The king and queen fled their compartment. But their people followed, the mob's clamor growing. Thessia knew what would happen. She knew there would be no escape for the fallen rulers from their people.

For those who remained in the theater, righteous indignation changed into righteous joy. Over the cheering, Thessia heard one name, syllables gathering strength, chanted by the whole crowd...

"King Ario the Poet!" someone cried out.

Thessia knew her moment. While Hugh whistled in celebration, Thessia rushed onstage, where she placed her tiara upon Ario's head.

"King Ario the Poet!" she repeated.

Cheering, clapping, and stomping filled the theater. The very walls shook. Vestriya Now was no longer only a competition—it was a *coronation*.

Ario's cheeks were pink. The new king of Vestriya grinned,

flattered. "I shall lead with temperance and noblesse," King Ario the Poet promised his people, "and guide our righteous realm out of this fine mess!"

The cheering subsided. Thessia noticed an uncomfortable shuffling of feet in the wincing crowd.

Finally, a voice called out: "Just . . . King Ario, then!"

The Burning Truth About Arveto

by Celine Hazelton

Many years ago, a devastating fire ravaged the humble village of Arveto, where residents were once known to share weekly meals in the square, afterward singing folk songs and playing beautiful music together late into the night. Their homes were all destroyed by this fire, yet they were given no alternate living quarters or aid to help them recover.

Arveto's position in the lower region of Vestriya creates a uniquely arid climate, already known for producing strange flora and fauna. When that dry soil combined with ash from the fire, a rare flower began to bloom—the cinderflower. Ground into an extract, the cinderflower has properties that can offer pain relief in small doses. In large doses, it creates a scentless, flavorless, and, most important, *deadly* poison. The type of poison sought after by the most powerful figures in Vestriya. Figures with infinite resources at their disposal.

The king and queen of Vestriya.

The Vestriyan rulers have been forcing the Arvetans to continue to produce this cinderflower, preventing them from properly rebuilding their village. The royals have used this plant to dispose of countless enemies in the name of maintaining their positions within Vestriya. In fact, the king and queen used this very poison to incapacitate their younger son, Ario, so that he could never lay claim to the throne after the tragic loss of Prince Ezio, whose blood is also on his parents' hands.

Tired of the culture of silence his parents created, and the countless injustices they'd let stand throughout their rule, Prince Ezio planned to stage a coup. When the king and queen learned of this, they hired the Deathrose Guild to have Ezio assassinated, using both mimic magic and a charmed appearance to create the illusion that Mythrian hero Galwell True had killed him. In truth, the Vestras family was behind it all. Thanks to the help of his friends and the healing properties of snails, Prince Ario is now well enough to confirm that all of this information is true.

While it is often a scribe's duty to stay out of their stories, in this instance, it's not possible. Though the royals have profited greatly from this fire, it was not their doing. It was mine.

I, Celine Hazelton of the *Mythria Spectator*, destroyed Arveto.

I have the hand magic gift of fire, and I have never learned how to control it. While arguing with my parents on a voyage here to Vestriya as a young teen, my hands began to blaze, and the flames scorched a nearby building, leaping so quickly from one structure to the next that the fire could not be extinguished in time. This tragic accident remains the most painful mistake of my life. I have tried for years to aid the Arvetans, but I do not have enough resources on my own.

While this pamphlet contains many shocking admissions, it is most importantly a call to action—we must help Arveto. No longer should they suffer through such despairing conditions in the name of feeding the royals' thirst for power.

Together, this is possible. Together, we can restore not just the village of Arveto, but the kingdom of Vestriya.

36
Galwell

The questing party had gathered in the wings. Spirits were high.

They'd *succeeded*. Despite every challenge, they had won. Galwell's heart swelled as he watched Ario from the shadows offstage. His people had embraced him, chanting the young king's name. Ario greeted them with genuine devotion. With love.

When he left the stage, coronated and celebrated, he looked confident. The applause of his waiting friends undid him. Tears in his eyes, hand over his heart, he went right for his questing companions.

"Everyone!" he greeted them joyously. "I'm king!"

Needing no further encouragement, everyone—Galwell, Mona, River, Celine, Thessia, Hugh—surrounded Ario, sweeping the new king of Vestriya into their embrace.

"Group hug!" cried Hugh. "Group hug!"

It was indeed. Benjamin somehow slimed his way up Ario's back to perch on his shoulder, participating in the group hug by swirling his eye stalks with enthusiasm.

Only the commotion of the royal guard parted the celebrating party. When they separated, Galwell found himself face-to-face with the guardsman he'd spoken to earlier.

The grizzled man led a line of men and women dressed imposingly in Vestriyan royal livery, with swords and shields strapped to them. They looked ready for war. With hands on the hilts of their swords, the encroaching force waited for the command of their captain, whose stern eye met Benjamin's, then Ario's.

In front of Ario, the captain of the guard knelt on one knee and bowed.

"My king," he declared.

Galwell grinned.

"We await your command," he continued. "Should we pursue the kin— I mean your mother and father? As we stand here, they flee into the night."

"If they seek to return, we will have to deal with them. But I do not wish to start my reign with bloodshed," Ario replied. "Let us move into a future without assassinations and secrets."

His gentle pronouncement resonated with quiet strength. The guardsman nodded without hesitation.

Rising to his feet, however, he paused. His eyes flitted to the left of Galwell, where—*ah, how lovely*—GALWELL THE GRUESOME gazed out intimidatingly from the poster hung literally right next to him.

"This man has escaped our cells," the guardsman said, pointing to Galwell. "We apologize for our failure."

Ario held up his hands. "Let every prisoner of my parents be set free. Open the jails," he proclaimed grandly.

Now even Galwell straightened in surprise. He looked inquisitively at Ario, who put a reassuring hand on Galwell's shoulder.

"People need to be inspired to goodness. To caring for their companions, to loving their realm," he said. "Hope does not start with punishment. It starts with forgiveness. There was heroism in Vestriya once. There shall be again."

It was the uncommonest thing. With Ario's promise, the quiet knot Galwell had felt deep in his chest since his first day revived started to loosen.

Calm in his conviction, Ario faced Thessia next. "I hope our great

THIS WILL BE INTERESTING

realms can resume their close friendship, dear Queen Thessia." He spoke louder, sounding downright regal now.

Thessia smiled. "It never ended," she reassured him.

Ario clasped her hand vigorously, then returned his focus to his royal guard. *Not king material, hmm?* Galwell wanted to ask the man. Only with his massive magical strength did he restrain himself.

"Our work starts now. You serve the people, not the crown," he reminded his soldiers. "We must correct injustice wherever we see it. Where shall we begin? Take me to . . ." Only now did the poet king falter slightly, though he then found his course. "To the closest injustice!" he concluded.

The guards conferred. No doubt there were many nearby injustices, not to mention other more important yet less geographically proximate injustices. "Come with us, Your Highness," one guardswoman eventually said, gesturing in the direction of the audience waiting outside. Ario complied, giving his friends a thumbs-up on his way out.

Peace descended over the rallied questing party. The knot in Galwell unwound entirely, leaving him with only gratitude. Gratitude for Thessia and Hugh, who'd undertaken painful sacrifices for the sake of their realm, and gratitude for Celine and River, who'd dared conceive of new lives for themselves, and . . .

Mona. Where was Mona?

She wouldn't just leave to seek revenge on her parents immediately, would she? What of Ario's pronouncements about hope, punishment, and forgiveness?

He whirled, making himself a little dizzy, until he found her nearby, waiting apart from the group.

The sight unnerved him instantly.

Pale, with widening eyes, Mona held the pamphlet Celine and River had distributed. When Galwell moved closer, reaching out cautiously for her, she ignored him. Nay, she did not seem to know he was there. Instead, she seemed to read the lines of the pamphlet over and over, mesmerized, with vengeful concentration.

"You," she said.

She did not mean Galwell. When Mona looked up, he followed her gaze to the crowd of their companions. Crumpling the pamphlet in her hand, she strode with fury—

Right to Celine. In moments, she'd pinned the other woman to the wall, clutching Celine's throat without mercy.

Galwell rushed to the pair. Celine's eyes were wide with fear—yet not, it seemed, with surprise. Not restraining his magical strength, Galwell seized Mona's shoulder and pulled her off Celine. "What is the meaning of this?" he demanded.

"How?" Mona seethed. "How did you hide it? How did I never know?"

"It's not something I choose to think of very often," Celine replied.

Mona shook her head. "Your thoughts were . . . fragmented at times. Still, I never . . . No one's ever hidden something like this from me."

"I hide it from myself, too. How could I live otherwise?" Celine replied, quiet misery stealing into her voice. "I've had a lifetime of practice."

Deftly, Mona slipped out of Galwell's grip. She lunged for Celine, slamming her once more against the wall. "It was you," she said. "*You set the fire that killed my friends.* The only people I had."

Now Galwell did not rush for Mona. The revelation stunned him silent. His head spun.

"I didn't *set* the fire," Celine gasped from within Mona's choking grasp. "I *was* the fire. It was . . . an accident."

"It doesn't matter," Mona insisted. "You killed them all. Why have you hidden from justice?"

Celine struggled, prying at Mona's grip with frantic fingers. "I was just a child myself," Celine pleaded. "I didn't know cinderflower would grow out of the ashy remains of that village's soil. I didn't know they would be forced to sell the poison to the crown to survive. That the poison would be used to terrorize political enemies. *I didn't know.*"

Galwell saw Mona falter with the slightest hesitation. Or perhaps he only hoped he did.

"Now I do," Celine went on. "Which is why I shared everything in our pamphlet. *Everything.* Including my own involvement."

"It's—" Mona fought to keep the waver out of her voice. "It's not enough."

Celine's struggling weakened. In Mona's chokehold, defeat slackened her shoulders. "I know," she admitted.

Mona looked fraught. Galwell could practically feel her pain, could feel how Celine's revelations had ripped open the wounds from Mona's past. She'd thought her friends died by accident. But now she knew there was someone to blame. Someone she'd maybe started to call a friend. His heart broke for her.

Not only for Mona, though. Celine looked helpless, pinned to the theater wall. She wasn't just in Mona's punishing grip. She was in the unrelenting grasp of something even more damning—regret.

But the truth was, this wasn't something Celine had done to Mona. It was a tragedy they *both* had suffered.

He opened his mouth to explain exactly this. In the same moment, someone slammed hard into Mona.

Celine dropped from the wall to her knees, wheezing, as Mona and her attacker lay sprawled on the scuffed hardwood. Mona's assailant rose first.

"Lay one more hand on her," River warned, "and I'll kill you."

"Fine," Mona retorted. She stood, deftly pulling her long knife from her hip sheath. "Kill me, assassin."

Panic shot through Galwell. How could everything collapse *this fast*? He remembered what the other members of the Four had confessed to him, the way they had shattered in the wake of their victory. Was *this* what waited in the darkness after every quest? Pain, paranoia, infighting? Old grievances reopening and creating new wounds?

It couldn't be.

"Stop this." Galwell forced himself into their midst, separating the women with his magical strength. "We're on the same side," he insisted.

"No," Mona retorted. "We're not."

Her eyes never found Galwell. Her fury had refocused on River.

Celine rose to her feet. Rubbing her neck, she looked shaken. Hollow. "Mona has every right to revenge," she murmured.

"No," River replied fiercely. Her gaze found Celine's. "No, Celine. We are not every worst thing we've ever done."

With River's pronouncement, Galwell felt the fight ebbing from Mona. Her hesitation offered him the chance to push her farther from River.

While Mona's eyes stayed half frenzied, jumping between Celine and River, her shoulders slumped. Her long knife lowered limply to her side. With River moving defensively close to Celine, Galwell felt the situation safe enough that he could concentrate on Mona. He found her eyes—

Someone crashed sloppily into Galwell, jostling him sideways. Galwell caught raven curls and the shimmering threads of expensive clothing.

It was—*Chestlewitt?*

The playwright was visibly drunk. Unfortunately, he was also holding a sword. Fame and force had gotten him backstage, Galwell guessed.

"The story was nearly complete!" he hollered. He swung his sword with inebriated recklessness. He was dangerous, Galwell realized. "Just one more loose end to tie up. *You!*" he shouted at Galwell.

Ghosts, was he still wailing about his fucking play?

"Not now, Chestlewitt," Galwell growled, feeling rare impatience flare in his chest.

"You've ruined the ending!" Chestlewitt screamed, ignoring him. "This isn't how it's supposed to work. Heroes"—he pushed his insolent index finger into Galwell's chest—"live happily or sacrifice themselves for glory." He gestured to Mona next. "Villains die. *That's how it works.* You don't get to change the fucking ending!"

"It works however I say it works," Galwell replied, stepping forward to menace the scribe. "*It's my story.*"

Chestlewitt looked as if he were sincerely considering Galwell's words. He sized Galwell up, peering into the hero's face. Contemplation seemed to dull his drunken vengeance. He calmed, enough for Galwell to step back, until—

Without warning, Chestlewitt lunged.

He was close—too close. Galwell had underestimated Chestlewitt's wild-eyed vengeance and overestimated the playwright's judgment.

He had the strangest phantom memory of another blade hurtling straight for him, on the ramparts over Queendom, while the Fraternal Order's evil magic choked the sky. Was *this* where every quest ended? With the death of Galwell the Great? He couldn't possibly deflect or react quickly enough—

But the sword did not strike Galwell.

Having read the shift in Chestlewitt's mind, Mona had stepped in the way. Chestlewitt's sword went in cleanly. Straight into Mona's heart.

Galwell heard someone cry out in raw pain. Himself, he realized.

Mona dropped to her knees, looking dizzy. Galwell was there, moving on pure impulse, catching her as she collapsed. Past warping panic, he was vaguely aware of everyone else—his friends, their feud forgotten—rushing forward. Hugh subdued Chestlewitt, wrestling the playwright's sword from him. Thessia called for the guards . . .

None of it mattered to him now.

Mona wobbled in his embrace, her eyes going unfocused. He was already sobbing. He smoothed her hair out of her face, desperate to . . . He didn't know. He didn't know. He wanted to reach inside her somehow and hold on to the life he could feel ebbing from her.

"Mona . . ." he wailed.

He held her, crying her name in, he realized, wretched imitation of Chestlewitt's play. The scribe would have his dramatic ending. Galwell held his love despairingly, weeping. In the enchanted light cast into the wings from the stage, he had become the epitome of tragedy—

Mona coughed. She spat hot blood into his face.

This was no fucking performance. No tragic ending. It was real, and it was horrible, and it was happening too fast. Mona's skin went white. Her frantic grip clawed at his huge, helpless muscles. She reached out, grabbing his shirt, pulling him close—

"I love you, Mona," he sobbed. "I'll love you forever."

She could not speak. He wished he could read *her* mind. He needed to know what would help her most to hear before the end.

Instead, he felt hopeless. He could not save the girl. He could not be the hero. In the most important moment of his life, he was only who he'd always been—Galwell.

Finally, suddenly, far too soon, Mona stopped breathing.

The sight split him to his core. He could not breathe, either. Everything else had vanished, lost in this piercing moment. Time halted. Was this how Beatrice felt when she relived memory? Would he remain here forever? How could he not? He didn't want to move on from this horrible moment. He'd choose it forever over what would come next. A day without *her*.

He found himself fixated on Mona's empty eyes. He stared into them, determined to memorize their remarkable hue. They were vivid, stunningly cerulean. Even in death, they seemed to glow . . .

No, Galwell realized.

They *were* glowing.

He startled. Mona's eyes continued to sear brighter with enchanted light, blue fire emanating from her irises. The glow coursed slowly through her, setting her skin aflame. Slowly, she levitated up from his mournful embrace.

Galwell collapsed onto the floorboards. He looked around, searching for an explanation—which was when he saw Celine.

Her feet hovered off the ground as well. Blue light emanated from her skin, glowing from her feet and up her legs, engulfing her outstretched hands, to her face, where her eyes pulsated with the enchantment.

Surrounding her were the ghostly forms of the Grotto's harpies.

Slowly, Celine pointed one finger toward Mona. The song of the harpies filled the stage—or perhaps the haunting melody only invaded Galwell's head. The soundless notes of deep, mythical magic. While he watched, Mona's wounds began to *repair* themselves.

Color returned to her cheeks. Strength seemed to fill her slackened limbs. She revolved in midair, repositioned by magic, until she was upright, the soles of her feet returning gently to the ground—

Celine clenched her fist.

A gasp ripped through Mona's chest, and her eyes flamed with blue fire.

Halos of the harpies' magic shimmered in Galwell's vision as the enchantment receded. Gulping in shuddering breaths, Mona was no longer glowing but impossibly, unmistakably *alive*.

On his feet instantly, Galwell dove to Mona's side. He clasped her face in his hands, not daring to hope . . .

Mona's gaze started to refocus, the magic fading.

Celine floated to the floorboards, then walked to Mona without fear. "In the Grotto, the harpies' magic promised to enhance my power. I . . . don't want power, though," she said. "I don't want to burn and ruin. I want to help. To heal."

The magical light flared in one final flame through Mona's eyes—

Then she exhaled, and Mona, *his Mona*, stood before them.

"Good Ghosts," someone gasped. Thessia or River, Galwell didn't know.

Mona looked up, straight into Celine's waiting gaze.

"You . . . saved me," she murmured in disbelief.

Celine nodded.

"The moment you collapsed," she explained, "I called on the harpies. I saw them in my head, everywhere, surrounding me. Instead of enhancing my fire, I pleaded with them to grant me a new power. I needed something different. To *be* different."

Her gaze held Mona's.

"To change," Celine said.

Mona's eyes widened.

While Galwell watched, he felt Mona's convictions waver. *Nobody ever changes. Not really.* Without magic or enchanted light, he felt invisible wounds close in Mona. Celine had restored more than just her life.

THIS WILL BE INTERESTING

"The harpies would not change my power forever," Celine continued. "They granted me healing magic only this once. I still have to live with my devastating power, like I have to live with what I've done. I did a horrible thing to you, to your friends," she said solemnly. "But I know *I'm* not horrible. Our magic shapes us, but it doesn't define us. There's good and bad in all of us, isn't there? Mona the Merciless helped save the realm today. A man who can break bones with a thought can choose to be a poet or a king."

She faced Galwell, who had not left Mona's side. He continued to caress her cheek, not knowing how he would ever cease.

"A hero with surpassing strength can choose softness," Celine went on.

She looked to River.

"An assassin can be more than a killer."

Finally, her stare returned to Mona.

"Someone who hurt you can become your friend."

Mona's long dagger lay on the floorboards nearby. Close enough to seize.

But Mona did not move for the weapon. Instead, she stepped forward, closing the distance between her and Celine. Everyone tensed. In the corner of his vision, Galwell caught River reaching for Chestlewitt's fallen sword—

Flipping her hair behind her shoulder, Mona extended her hand to Celine in friendship.

Celine smiled in relief. She clasped Mona's hand. Behind them, guards hauled away Chestlewitt, while Thessia and Hugh applauded.

It took everyone several moments to realize more cheering was coming from onstage. Surprisingly enough, the realm's premiere talent competition had not paused after Ario's proclamation. No one in the audience knew Mona had literally died behind their show.

Instead, Nevo Yrillis strolled onto the stage. Thessia's co-host waved to the cheering audience, grinning his handsomest grin. In his hand he held an embossed parchment card, edges glinting gold under the stage lights.

When the clamor subsided, Nevo stepped into the projection circle.

"It's my enormous pleasure," the horseballer said to the crowd, "to announce that the winner of Vestriya Now is . . ."

He paused dramatically.

"*Fearless Flyer!*"

Everyone looked to River.

37

River

A shiny silver obelisk glistened against the cloudless afternoon sky. It stretched over one hundred irons high, with a dozen smaller obelisks in a semicircle around it, framing the glittering entrance to the Lightwing, Vermillion Vale's premier performance inn.

"And these"—the docent waved a hand toward the obelisks—"these are meant to replicate the great Pillars of Askavere."

"From Old Mythria?" River asked. She didn't know much about her homeland's earliest history, but she was pretty sure that the real Pillars of Askavere were much less . . . glossy.

"Precisely," said the docent. His lip quivered as he pushed his spectacles higher up the bridge of his nose.

Since returning to Mythria with great fanfare—yet another Mythrian winner of a Vestriyan talent show—River had been on a celebratory tour across her homeland, and this docent had been asked to provide River with a personalized walkthrough of Mythria's prolific Vale, explaining the meaning behind all the historical replicas that had been built throughout the nightlife-loving city.

Their time together was almost up, and the docent still had not made peace with the fact that River was an actual assassin.

"A *retired* assassin," she'd reminded him the first three times he'd flinched at her every movement.

"It seems some creative liberties have been taken here in the Vale," Celine murmured. She scribbled something in her notebook while the docent gave a long-winded speech on how hand magicians had spent years recreating the pillars to painstaking effect.

Celine nudged River's shoulder, pointing to where she'd drawn a few of the obelisks in a way that looked rather phallic, with the words *Shiny and foreboding. What are they overcompensating for?* written underneath.

River burst out laughing.

"That's enough outside," the docent said, eyes darting around nervously. "Let's continue on, then, shall we? Right this way."

Inside the glinting silver walls of the Lightwing, River was greeted by the sight of her own face.

COMING SOON!
FEARLESS FLYER AND THE BANDITS:
A KILLER ACROBATIC ACT

The gigantic hand-painted poster depicted River in her white bodysuit with a smatter of blood across her chest as she swung from silks, high above a group of indistinguishable fellow performers.

This was her prize for winning Vestriya Now—a touring show throughout Vestriya, and then a residency at the Lightwing in Mythria, where she'd perform her acrobatic act for the remainder of the year. It was also where she'd rehearse.

Celine squeezed her hand. "Look at you," she said in wonder, gazing at the poster.

But River was already looking at Celine. It didn't matter what sights she'd yet to see, or any of the places she could travel to with her magic. *This* was the best view in all the realms. Her curly-haired scribe, brave and determined and deliciously beautiful.

"Come on, then," said the docent. "This way."

He led them through rows of gambling tables until they reached doors labeled MAIN STAGE. Portraits of the Brethren, last year's Vestriya Now winners, still hung in frames outside the entrance.

"Your posters will be going up soon," the docent told her. "The singing brothers haven't finished their residency yet."

"Makes sense," said River. "Let those boys sing until the Ghosts carry us to the gates. Their voices are the real magic in this realm."

"Okay," said the docent.

River knew some people would only ever see her as deadly. That was no bother. What was stranger was the way some others celebrated her for what she'd done. Her Vestriya Now win would always be tied to the death of Tabitha and the downfall of the Deathrose Guild. As would all her life. She could never erase her past, and for all its faults and complexities, she didn't want to. Still, she'd worried that the Vestriya Now creators would revoke her title over it.

But the creators had thought the assassin aspect was brilliant. *Who wouldn't want to see a deadly acrobat perform?* they'd mused. *The blood on your costume? Electric!*

As River sat in long, exhausting meetings during which they'd discussed what the precise nature of her show should be, chiseling out the most appealing angle—Vestriya Now was very committed to finding the right performance package—inspiration struck.

River knew how to make her show stand out. It was yet another puzzle she could solve before anyone else could make sense of the pieces.

The docent opened the stage door. The theater was not as ornate as the Vestriyan one had been. It was very "of the Vale," as Mythrians were fond of saying, because it was sleek and dark and completely void of all sense of time and place. This was a place to get lost inside, enjoying drink and entertainment without another care in the realm.

The theater was not empty, as River had expected. Instead,

scattered throughout the orchestra seats were former Deathrose Guild members.

"Well, then, that concludes my time with you. I'll leave you to it," said the docent, skittering out.

"You're all here early," River said, stunned.

This was her troupe. Her bandits. Assassins, really, but the Vestriya Now creators found that word too off-putting. Not the blood, though. They were funny like that. They didn't want guests to believe they might be killed while watching River's show, but they wanted to maintain a sense of danger. They loved the idea of River gathering up a group of former assassins and turning them into acrobats alongside her.

River sought out the guild members who'd believed in the original honor code, the ones who stood for the true principles of the guild. At first, most were reluctant to sign on to this endeavor. It wasn't every day someone asked a layperson to join a traveling circus of sorts. But River sold them on the promise of a new life, and the guarantee that their unique skills would be put to good use. Even though the former Deathrose Guild members had never been considered outlaws, they were all willing to roll with their new title of bandits.

With their inclusion in this show, they were getting the same second chance River had gotten. The second chance they all deserved.

* * *

After River had spent sufficient time catching up with her troupe, Celine tugged on her blouse. "I have something for you," she said, handing River a letter.

River recognized the quillmanship right away. Long, dramatic cursive, with an abundance of swirling flourishes.

Vandra.

THIS WILL BE INTERESTING

River had mailed Vandra a letter on her last day in Vestriya, finally apologizing for failing to understand why Vandra had left the guild, and for not showing up for her in the aftermath. She hadn't been a good friend, and she knew it. Because they *were* friends. River had been wrong to dismiss that, too.

The Vestriyans were very fond of sending one another mail. River had come to appreciate that about their culture. It took patience and time to sit down and scribe a letter—two things River never had enough of, but she'd wanted to try it all the same. She felt Vandra deserved that much.

"It came in just before we left for the Vale, but I wanted to wait until we got here to give it to you," Celine explained.

River had provided Celine's address for return, partly because she didn't have one of her own, but mostly because she thought Vandra might not reply at all, and River couldn't miss a letter she wasn't checking for.

Riv,

I want to say I never thought I'd get a letter from the likes of someone such as you, but that would be a disservice to the generosity you have shown by writing me, and a discredit to all the work you've done to get here.

I accept your apology, and in turn, I want to offer you one of my own.

I am sorry for not helping you sooner. This excludes my dashing, daring rescue of you, of course, because I was paid well, and I looked fantastic doing it. But when you came to me the night you'd been given the assignment to kill Galwell, I turned you away. I was too stubborn, still set in my beliefs. I wanted you to learn the lesson for yourself.

I see now that you have. And I am very proud of you for that, but also, I should have known better. I was judging you for your circumstances, and you didn't deserve that. No one does.

You said in your letter that you miss me. I miss you right back. And I would very much like to reconnect.

But no, I will not join your traveling show.

At least not permanently . . .

I'd like to book myself for one night in Vermillion Vale, near the end of your residency. It must be a big, splashy affair. Tell the pubtenders to concoct special drinks in my honor. I want a portrait of me the size of one of those obelisks.

Vandra Ravenfall, featuring Fearless Flyer and the Bandits. Sounds nice, no?

It won't be like old times, but neither of us wants that.

It will be like new times. Something yet to be defined. I think we're both eager to discover what exactly that is.

Your friend,
Vandra

P.S. Tell your lover that if she's going to interview me for her book, I want at least one full chapter dedicated to me. Maybe even two.

"What a lovely note," Celine said. "Sorry, I read it over your shoulder."

River's chest flooded with the kind of warm, gooey hope she used to mock in others. She understood now how precious love was, how fragile and rare. And how you could feel it in so many different forms. She had so much of it now, it overflowed. For Celine. But also for Vandra. Her friend.

Celine had that look in her eye River recognized—the scribely determination one. "If Vandra's agreeing to two chapters in my book about the rise and fall of the Deathrose Guild, does that mean I can get you to commit to an official interview with me, too?" she asked, tilting her chin down to bat her long lashes.

"Come here." River grabbed Celine's hand and ran, dashing down the center aisle, then leaping up onto the stage so they could gaze out into the audience together.

"One day soon, you'll be the main attraction here," Celine said.

River almost said something cheesy about Celine being the real main attraction anywhere, but one of the guild members interrupted before she could, shouting out, "When do I learn how to do a back flip?"

This got the whole group laughing.

"Soon, Frank. Very soon," River said. "I have something else I have to do first."

She turned her focus to Celine, clasping her hands and squeezing tight. "When we saw each other again, it felt like no time had passed between us. And a lot of that was because you remembered the good in me. Good I hadn't had anyone recognize in a very long time. Maybe ever."

"What are you doing?" Celine interrupted, her eyes already wet with tears.

"*Shh*," River said. "Let me continue, love. I've spent a long time practicing this."

Celine nodded.

"You remembered my true passion for performance, and all you wanted was to see me realize it. It was so generous, and so very like you, always pushing everyone around you to be the best version of themselves that they can be. Now I have my very own show, the kind of show only I can do. The show of my dreams. Because of you."

"You did this," Celine protested.

"*Love*," River said in a hushed tone. "Please." She took a deep breath, trying to remember where she'd left off. "The stage is my happy place, but it isn't my home. I've never had one. Until you. You're my home, Celine Hazelton. And I wanted to know if you would come with me and the bandits on our Vestriyan tour, so I can have that home with me wherever I go? The quill just isn't enough. I need the real thing."

Celine said nothing, staring at River with a perplexed expression that made River's blood run cold, afraid that somehow, some way, she'd misunderstood what was between them.

River rushed to explain. "I thought you could use the tour to interview the other guild members for your book. I figured it was perfect. And since you're done at the *Mythria Spectator*, too, you'll have the time. But if you'd rather stay in Mythria, I understand."

She was failing in front of her troupe. Maybe that was good. They needed to see it was okay to fall on your face. They'd all be doing quite a lot of that as they learned their routine.

"Well?" River finally prompted. "Don't leave me hanging. Even an acrobat can't do that forever."

"Yes. Yes, of course I will come with you," Celine said softly. She let her answer linger before she added, "On one condition."

"Anything," River said, not quite ready to let out a breath of relief or embrace the excitement she wanted to feel about this.

"You let me interview you about your time in the guild," Celine said, her grin made of pure satisfaction.

River couldn't help but smile in return. Yes, this was her Celine, all right. The woman she loved with all her heart, and if she had one, her soul, too.

"You drive a hard bargain. But fine," River agreed with a playful nudge. "We will discuss the specifics of that later. For now, I should probably make the most of my troupe being here early and start teaching them the ropes." She moved to step off the stage, but Celine seized her wrist.

"Not so fast," Celine said. "I'd like to ask my first question."

"Love, I just told you, we have to negotiate some of my terms. There are things I don't want to discuss, no matter what, and I know if—"

"Will you marry me?" Celine blurted, dropping to one knee.

River lost her train of thought. Her sense of place. Her composure.

She lowered herself to the ground with Celine, staring blankly into the limitless pool of Celine's brown eyes.

"I thought that's what you were going to ask me, and I was so upset," Celine continued. "I wanted to be the one to ask it first. You know how much I love the hard-hitting questions."

Even through the fog of shock, River did not struggle to answer. It was as easy as breathing.

"Yes," she said. "Of course I will marry you."

The bandits erupted in whistles and applause.

"Let's do it right now," River yelled over the noise. "Here in the Vale!"

This got Celine to crack, her face awash with the same shock that had just taken hold of River. River suspected the two of them would never stop surprising each other. It wasn't possible.

"No," Celine said evenly, kissing River as she spoke. "We need to negotiate our terms first."

River laughed against Celine's soft mouth. "Fine, but soon," she said.

"Very soon," Celine promised.

Oh how River loved her soon-to-be wife.

With Celine, life was always interesting.

With Celine, River was never alone.

38
Galwell

None of his friends knew Galwell the Great was questing again.

Questing he was, however. On his own. Understandably, this would concern his companions. But it was important he complete his present errand personally.

The month since everyone had returned from Vestriya had been joyous for Mythria. It had not been pleasant for Galwell, however. Mona was gone. Having forgiven Celine, she'd explained to Galwell, she needed time to reflect upon who she was. She'd requested Galwell go home without her.

The decision frightened the hero. He would've volunteered to venture into the Grimauld Mines rather than wonder if Mona would decide she was someone who did not care for him.

But he would hold on to every moment they'd shared, would hold on to his wonderment and gratitude that she had survived Chestlewitt's killing sword stroke. The realm with her in it was more important than her loving him.

He walked a winding road, surveying his surroundings. The village was carved entirely into the enormous cliffs over the Southern Sea, which churned and rolled endlessly to the horizon. White-stone homes were nestled up against the contoured roads winding up, down, and even into the cliffs themselves. The perilous conditions made this village one of Mythria's most secluded municipalities. None of Galwell's quests had ever carried him to the quiet region.

THIS WILL BE INTERESTING

Until now, when reports of a dangerous Vestriyan criminal in Mythria had required Galwell's immediate attention.

He was giving said criminal's perfect curves his attention right now, very avidly. She walked ahead of him, wearing a dark hood, but he would recognize her swaying steps, her perfect ass anywhere.

Especially here, in Cloudcliff Village.

Where the Grandharts lived, Mona had said, after reading Clare's mind. Their parents sought seclusion from their old lives on the unforgiving cliffs. Knowing of Mona's vow, Clare had made the difficult decision to cut off communication with his sister to protect them.

Galwell had hoped that forgiving Celine meant Mona would relinquish her obsession with revenge upon her parents. Finding her here was . . . worrisome.

Mona reached her destination. The simple wooden door of the small home, sculpted of white stone, was no different from the surrounding cliffside houses. Except, Galwell suspected, in one very important way—the occupants.

Mona reached for her hip, where, Galwell remembered, she often kept her favorite knife. How many times had he seen her draw her devastating weapon of choice? Never idly. Did she intend to storm into her parents' home and torture or kidnap them? Or worse?

Legends never wait, Galwell reminded himself.

Nor, he decided, did very concerned ex-lovers.

He rushed past the wandering roadside merchants whose high-piled wares had provided him cover. He was close to Mona now, poised to halt her—

Mona spun, pressing her knife to his throat. The blade looked less sharp than her grin.

"You can't sneak up on a mind reader, Galwell the Guileless," she chided. "And thank you for the compliments to my ass. I enjoyed them very much."

Neither the knife nor the mocking troubled Galwell. Not while he stared into Mona's eyes for the first time since Vestriya. They overwhelmed him. Perfectly, marvelously blue. He doubted he could ever gaze into them without remembering the reviving flame of harpy enchantment, the source of his greatest gratitude.

Yet the truth was, for Galwell, that life-changing magic had shone like fire in Mona's eyes since the moment he met her.

He pressed forward, letting her knife dig into his throat and not caring. He needed to be closer to her.

Mona's eyes widened. "How reckless of you."

"If I'm to be killed, I'd choose your blade," Galwell said.

"You flatter me," Mona replied.

"As long as I draw breath," he promised.

Mona rolled her eyes. The pink in her cheeks betrayed her, however. Galwell smiled. He knew Mona the Merciless well enough to know that his sentimentality worked on the oh-so-hardened criminal.

She did not protest. Indeed, she even lowered her knife.

Mona's demeanor changed, weary wariness raising her defenses. "So you've come to stop my crimes?" she inquired.

"Please, Mona," Galwell returned immediately. He'd rehearsed this part on the wagon ride over. "You can't exact revenge on your parents. Please. Give *yourself* the second chance you deserve. Move on from this."

Mona did not look convinced. She did not laugh, though, or sneer or spit vitriol in his face. She sheathed her knife.

"You know, I thought you'd write," she said.

The unhidden emotion in her voice startled Galwell. No petulant playfulness or ironic indignation.

"I—I didn't know—I thought you wanted—" he managed. He *wished* he'd rehearsed this in the wagon.

Fortunately, Mona interrupted him. "If not to propose undying love for me after our night of extraordinary physical intimacy, then at least for *sacrificing myself* to save your life."

Galwell laughed, which only earned a beautiful scowl from Mona.

"No, I'm not laughing at you," he hastened to say. "You are right. You know I resented my friends for always saving me. I didn't know how to be the one in need of rescue. I thought it made me less of a hero."

He thought of his first days in Mythria after being revived, how much guilt and confusion he felt while his friends disrupted their lives to try to make him happy.

"What a fool I was," he continued. "When you sacrificed yourself for me—I was horrified. Not because of your act but because of the cost. But when you came back to life, I didn't resent you for what you'd done. Not one bit. Knowing you wanted to save me doesn't make me weak or worthless. It makes me stronger. It makes me a better hero. I am merely grateful someone like you could care for someone like me."

"Galwell the Grateful," she mused, her eyes soft.

Galwell laughed once more, and this time Mona smiled. He recalled when he doubtfully gave himself the honorific while watching the dramatization of his own death in Farmount.

Now, hearing the nickname in Mona's voice, the moniker rang true.

"And for the record," he continued playfully, "I am also grateful for the unforgettable physical intimacy, and I love you with everything I am and ever will be."

Waves slammed the Cloudcliff cliffside, sending spray skyward. Mona went even pinker. "It's nice to hear out loud. One doesn't always want to rely on what's in someone's mind." She stepped closer, holding his gaze. "Actions and thoughts can be so very different, after all."

Insinuation hummed in her voice. She was—

Was she flirting with him?

Galwell suppressed his smile. He wanted to look composed despite his enormous, incredulous relief. Mona was here, in Mythria, in her parents' hometown, and she was spending time flirting with *him*!

It had to mean something. The opposite of ominous.

The Galwell who escaped death would not have known how to contend with this situation. Neither would the Galwell who fled to Vestriya. Nor the Galwell who found himself caged in the club of the realm's most notorious criminal.

Galwell the Great had learned many things on his latest, greatest quest, however. Including flirting!

Leaning against the white stone, he struck his cockiest pose.

"Is that so? Well, Mona, I certainly *only* have your actions and none of your words to judge by. Shall we go over them? Indeed, you were enthusiastic—vigorous, even—in the bedchamber," he praised her. "Or shall I say jail cell. *Insatiable* could even be employed."

Mona grinned. She made no objection to his commentary.

"And then, of course, you chose to stay, to help us when threats closed in. That could have been for me. Or it could have been out of the heroism in your heart," he contended.

Now Mona grimaced.

Galwell forged ahead. "And we simply cannot forget you stepping in front of a sword for me. Romantically or heroically motivated? I cannot really know," he mused, enjoying his performance. "In some other life, I myself stepped in front of a sword meant for someone else, and I certainly held no romantic notions for her. It was simply . . . the right thing to do."

Mona pantomimed gagging.

"Cease this insistence on heroism and goodness. I did those things for the same reason I do everything," she insisted. "*Self-interest.*"

"Self-interest?" he repeated. *Legends never wait.* "Why was it self-interest to save *me*?"

Galwell's heart rate picked up. Her blade was to his throat once more—she just didn't know it. Her next words, he felt, could kill or save him. He leaned forward, closing in, pressing her up against the wall.

"Because I love you, you gryphon!" Mona shouted.

She clapped her hands over her mouth, eyes widening in mortification.

Galwell laughed. He didn't hesitate. He swept Mona to him, hugging her in the embrace he'd dreamed of for weeks. She smelled wonderful, Cloudcliff sea spray clinging to her perfect skin, enlivening her inimitable floral scent with the cold, clear depth of the waters.

"I love you, too," he murmured into her shoulder.

Mona laughed, the sound one of pure joy.

"I missed you," she confessed.

"I missed you, too, Mona the Mooning," he teased.

More laughter was on her lips when he crushed his mouth to hers. He kissed her with every hope and every straining fiber of longing in him. He clutched her tight, indulging in every feel and taste and smell of her. He wanted never to stop.

He did, though. Long before he wished to, he ended the kiss.

"But, Mona," he forced himself to say, "I cannot let you kill, torture, maim, kidnap, extort, or otherwise wreak any manner of revenge on your parents."

Mona pouted, then smirked. She did not look frustrated by his pronouncement. "Is that so?" she returned.

Giving him no opportunity to reply, she knocked on the door of the home they were pressed against. While they waited, Mona threaded her fingers through his.

The woman who opened the door had eyes of sapphire. She was in her sixties, like the man peering out past her. Silver streaked his dusty blond hair. His nose was crooked.

Neither of them looked surprised to see Mona, Galwell realized. In confusion, he tensed, fearing some cunning machination of Mona's—

Which was when he noticed *four* place settings on the Grandharts' humble wooden table.

"Mother, Father," Mona greeted them, her demeanor stiff. Yet Galwell felt something straining under her curt politeness, something like longing. "You received my letter, I take it?"

"Oh, Mona," Mrs. Grandhart replied. Tears sprang to her eyes. "You can't know how much it means to see you again. Please, *please* come in."

Mona shifted uncomfortably but did not withdraw. When she focused on the other woman, Galwell sensed her reading her mother's mind. Whatever she found there . . . *oh, thank Ghosts*, seemed to soften her. Clare was right. They had changed. People in their very worst of circumstances were rarely their best selves. With the farthings Clare had sent them over the years, they'd had the chance to lead different lives.

Galwell realized that this meeting would not be the one he'd expected. Mona *had* forgiven her parents. Or she was on her way, which was enough. Forgiveness was a journey, not unlike a quest.

He felt relief down to the core of his soul, not much different from when Mona had recovered from Chestlewitt's sword. Galwell the Great, who'd escaped death himself, knew somebody could return to life in more ways than one.

He was inexpressibly glad Mona had chosen to return to a life surrounded by those who loved her. The new king of Vestriya's words entered his head. *Hope does not start with punishment. It starts with forgiveness.*

THIS WILL BE INTERESTING

Mona stopped in the doorway. Instead of entering her parents' home, she pulled Galwell forward.

"And this," she announced, "is who I wrote to you of. I promised I would bring the man I love to meet you."

The Grandharts' gazes moved in unison to the enormous hero. When Mona locked eyes with Galwell, he startled.

Would bring the man—

He stifled delighted laughter. This meeting . . . rumors of Mona in Mythria . . . his ease in finding her in Cloudcliff Village . . . Mona had planned all of it. Her devious plot. Him ensnared. He'd never been so happy to be foiled by a villain in all his life.

He looked to the Grandharts. "It is my pleasure to meet you," he greeted.

He wondered whether they knew who he was, or perhaps, out here on their cliffside, they did not. He should explain he was also their son's dear friend. Instead, he decided he would commence with something simple. Something true.

"I'm Galwell," he said.

It was, he felt, the perfect place to begin.

39
Thessia

The portrait captured Benjamin's likeness handsomely, Thessia thought. The tapestry depicted him just as Thessia remembered, on the epauletted shoulder of Vestriya's new king.

His eye stalks extended enthusiastically. His chartreuse color was perfect.

Ario himself stood majestically in the portrait, decorated in kingly all black, no doubt inspired by River. The depiction found him in front of Vestriyan canals, his pale hair windswept. The Poet King—he insisted upon the moniker—held a quill and parchment.

"I think it's magnificent," Galwell volunteered, no hint of irony or insinuation in his voice. "How lucky you are to have such a lovely portrait to display."

River examined the likeness more closely. "I believe one of his horrible poems is actually written on the scroll," she observed.

"He's improved a little," Hugh mused, his hand on the small of Thessia's back.

River winced, scrutinizing the scroll. "He used *pulchritudinous*."

Thessia had no defense for *pulchritudinous*. "Well, he's making a wonderful king," she replied. "We received official missives from him, informing us of Vestriya's progress. He's happy, and Vestriya is rebuilding. He sent this portrait as a sign of the enduring friendship between our realms."

Galwell *hmm*ed.

THIS WILL BE INTERESTING

Thessia rounded on him. "What?"

The hero shrugged. "I'm afraid that means you'll have to send one back."

The queen's face fell. She'd never liked official portraits.

"Or you could send him the Wiglaf portrait! It's nearly finished!" Clare volunteered this idea from the other end of the dining room.

Thessia clapped her hands together. "Excellent suggestion, Sir Clare!" she enthused. In fairness, the Poet King would perhaps prefer the portrait of Grandhart's eagle.

Vandra and Elowen rolled their eyes, while Celine, standing with them, smiled. Everyone had gathered for the intimate banquet the queen was hosting in the royal dining hall. Nearby, Mona, whom Galwell had brought to Queendom yestereve, was engaged in illicit gossip with Beatrice—presumably on the subject of Sir Clare himself.

The Queendom palace had, in the month since Thessia's return from Vestriya, undergone some important changes. Thessia invited her companions to visit whenever they wished. Not only her friends, either. She'd opened large portions of the palace for the use of painters and philosophers, scientists and shadow play stars, musicians and magicians. Even poets.

Instead of lonely hallways choked with ceremony and quietly haunted with memories of her parents, they were filled once more with life.

Seeing everyone together, celebrating their triumphant return, filled Thessia's heart. *This* was victory, the queen knew. Friendship. Companionship. Loyalty. Love. Questing meant reaching one's destination. Victory meant coming home.

"I cannot believe," Mona interrupted Thessia's contented reverie, pausing her gossip with Beatrice, "you left my brother in charge of the realm."

"He wasn't solely in charge—fear not," Beatrice promised her.

Clare welcomed his sister's teasing and his lady's reassuring interjection. The rogue hero grinned.

"Like in all things, Beatrice is my ruler," he confirmed. Then he leaned closer, eyes on Thessia, and lowered his voice conspiratorially. "But seriously, Thessia. If you ever need someone to take over the realm, we're here for you."

Thessia smiled. Her hand found the sharp points of her tiara.

In accomplishing her very own quest, Thessia had not merely found her way home. She'd saved herself using the crown on her head. She would love every part of the life she'd defended.

"No," she said. "I'm ready to rule."

Clare nodded. She caught quiet pride in her courageous friend's gaze.

"This is why I've gathered you here," Thessia continued, moving to the head of the banquet table. She guided Hugh to take his place at her right hand. "In my life, I have found myself frustrated with how little purpose I have in my role as queen. I do not sit on any of Mythria's councils. I do not make decisions that impact anyone. I am a symbol of good and justice," she conceded. "But I do not wish to be only a symbol."

Celine reached for her quill, sensing a scoop. "Will you participate in the royal councils?" she inquired with poised eagerness. "While I don't work for the *Spectator* anymore, I'd love to cover this story."

Thessia shook her head. "I do not wish to disrupt the government we have. Nor do I wish to set an example for future rulers who might use my involvement as precedent to rule absolutely," she explained. "I will leave governing to those who have studied and prepared for it all their lives."

Celine nodded. She wrote nothing down. Her quill lowered while Thessia looked at her expectant friends.

"However," Thessia said.

Up went the quill.

"While I do not wish to join any of my councils, I think it would be fair if I were to *start* one," she declared. "I call now to order . . . the Council of Quests."

Everyone exchanged glances. *Council of Quests*, Celine wrote on her napkin.

Excitement hummed in Thessia. She'd envisioned every aspect of her new council on the journey home—including sharing her innovation with her closest companions. "This new royal council," she continued, "will be in charge of commissioning quests to spread good throughout the realm. I would sit on it along with all of you. The greatest heroes of Mythria."

Of course, Galwell the Great spoke first. "I heartily accept."

Clare's smile became lazier. "Now *that* would be fun," he commented. He exchanged conspiratorial looks that Thessia did not entirely understand with Beatrice, Vandra, and Elowen.

River shifted in her seat, appearing conflicted. "Celine and I have some traveling to do," she said.

Thessia waved a hand in reassurance. "I don't intend to chain you all to our capital. Go into the world. Live your lives. Find quests and report back when you can," she encouraged them.

River nodded, content.

"You all enjoy. I'm not sure I'm ready to publicly declare myself a hero," Mona announced.

Galwell did not hesitate. He pulled her warmly to his side. "Yes, you are," he chided gently. "You already told your criminal underlings to only steal from those with too much."

Mona flushed. "I told you that in private."

"You're one of us, Mona," Celine commented more softly.

Mona met the other woman's eyes. Even before they left Vestriya,

Thessia noticed the tension between them lightening every day. She had even caught them bonding earlier over their love of handmade crumbiellos from western Vestriya.

Mona's club's culinary front was, it turned out, not merely a cover. Mona shyly confessed to considering turning the crumbiello shop into her empire's first legitimate enterprise.

"*Fine*," Mona conceded. "I'll join your preposterous do-gooder council. You'll regret it, though."

"I know *I* will," Clare joked. "Don't kill any of my friends this time." He went to shove his sister playfully—but Mona, reading his intentions, ducked neatly out of the way, leaving Clare shoving his hand into Galwell's colossal chest. The men humphed in confusion.

"This will be fun indeed," Beatrice remarked.

"Worry not, brother," Mona reassured Clare. "None of these friends would kill you. They all adore you. I would know—I've read their minds."

"I should like to quest with you again," Galwell said to his old friends. "I was your leader once, but I think, should we go out to face evil once more, I would like to follow."

Beside him, Mona beamed, proud, then tried to hide it when Clare caught her expression.

"Perhaps we'll take turns leading," Elowen suggested practically. "We can play stackjack for the role before every quest."

"Or drinking swords," Clare suggested. "You're far too good at stackjack."

"May I suggest truth or dare?" Beatrice contributed.

"Perhaps something more straightforward, like a foot race!" Galwell supplied.

Hugh held up his hands to silence them. "How about a toast to our new venture, and to our queen." He took Thessia's hand. "To my wife."

THIS WILL BE INTERESTING

Thessia warmed at Hugh's words—honest now, luminous with earnest devotion. Life was not the only victory Thessia had wrested from the challenges of her quest. In finding their way home, Thessa had found love that felt like home whenever she and Hugh were together.

"Oh, thank the Ghosts we're done with the charade that your marriage was a sham," Elowen murmured.

"I have to work *very* hard to stay out of their minds," Mona commented. "Their honeymoon has no end in sight. Every other thought of theirs is impressively dirty."

Hugh grinned. Thessia laughed. She could not contradict Mona on this point.

"Who can blame me?" Hugh returned. "I am not ashamed to have consummated my marriage many times over!"

"Consummation of emotional love is wondrous, my friend, is it not?" Galwell commented. "One could even say . . . *magnificent*."

He winked at Mona. Thessia felt like she was watching hroxen fly. Galwell the Great making flirtatious innuendo?

Clare had a different reaction. He cleared his throat loudly. "You were mentioning a toast!" he prompted Hugh. Now Mona was the one to shove her sibling while Clare's ears pinkened.

Hugh raised his goblet. Everyone followed except Beatrice, whom Thessia noticed had not drunk wine all evening, oddly enough. Beatrice loved wine.

"To the heroes of Mythria!" Hugh cried out.

Everyone cheered. Everyone but Beatrice drank.

Thessia felt the most uncommon contentment. The kind, she suspected, no quest or throne or lover could ever provide solely. There was magic called life in the shimmering strands connecting each of them.

Thessia was so proud of what she'd built for herself. Her friends, her husband, her purpose. Herself.

Mona gasped suddenly. Thessia found every one of her companions staring at—her.

"Darling, your... hair," Hugh said.

Glancing to her shoulders, Thessia found her golden hair had returned to her natural chestnut shade. She shrugged. She'd had fun as a blonde, but she was ready to return to brunette. "The color spell must have worn off," she explained.

"I've spelled my hair before. It never changes that suddenly," Vandra replied.

Now her friends were examining Thessia like *she* was the flying hroxen. River stepped closer, intrigued. "Try changing something else," she prompted. "Your nails or your eye color."

Thessia laughed. "What an odd suggestion, River." She lifted her hand. "As if I could just wish for my nails to be red—"

She blinked. Impossibly, her nails had colored the most passionate of crimson reds.

"Interesting," River murmured, sounding more vindicated than surprised. "Interesting indeed."

"What, my love?" Celine asked.

No one's eyes left Queen Thessia. She was used to the experience, but never had it felt quite like this.

"Tabitha had the magic to silence others' powers with her touch," River elaborated. "The effects lasted longer depending on the type of contact. When I was held prisoner, I was tied up with a magically enhanced rope that Dougal indicated came from Myke before Hugh slayed him. Myke must have used his magic to imbue it with powers, and when Tabitha joined the guild, she got her hands on it. I couldn't teleport for some time even after the rope was removed because it had touched my skin for so long."

Thessia could not follow River's commentary. What relevance had River's confinement to the color of Thessia's fingernails—

Until she understood.

"You mean to say Tabitha silenced *my* magic?" she asked. "But I don't have magic."

"Not that you know of," River returned.

"You've been close to Tabitha since you were a child," Galwell mused. "It's very possible over all these years she muted your abilities."

The idea was . . . head-spinning. Thessia nearly sat down from dizziness.

Instead, contemplating a life rewritten, she giggled nervously. She was used to being the one who wasn't special without her crown. She'd lived that story for decades. The ordinary queen, powerful and powerless.

But stories could change.

"All your powers came back when she died," she pointed out. "Why would mine take until now?"

"Because you did not know your magic was there to tap into," Hugh replied. "What were you thinking of during the toast?"

"I was . . ." Thessia recalled. Her eyes widened. "I was thinking that I was happy to be me."

Surprise changed to joy on the faces of her friends. It was perfect. She'd found her magic, this wondrous gift, because she was appreciating the many other gifts of her non-magical life.

"Oh, you have to try something more fun than nails and hair," Mona interjected.

Exhilaration coursed through Thessia. "All right," she agreed. Grinning playfully, she looked at her friends, choosing one. She concentrated hard—

She felt a rush of enchantment through her. When the effervescence faded, everyone cheered, for the perfect replica of Clare Grandhart stood in Thessia's stead.

Clare whooped exuberantly. "Two of me! A gift to us all! Right, Beatrice?"

"It's quite warm in here, isn't it?" Beatrice replied.

"To think," Thessia said in Clare's voice, "I could have been anyone I wanted all along."

Anyone she wanted. Assassin, scribe, criminal. Commoner, like the disguises she'd once donned to wander Queendom's morning streets in peace. Prince or poet. Hero or villain. She could have escaped herself, like she'd yearned to do in her life of queendom.

But Thessia knew who she wanted to be.

With her dearest companions surrounding her, she returned to herself.

"You're perfect as is," Hugh said softly.

Thessia kissed him without restraint. She felt like herself, perfectly home. She would enjoy having magic, but with Hugh, she did not need it. She couldn't wait to bare herself, just herself, to him tonight—

"Oh, please, do get a room," Mona called out.

While everyone whistled, the royal couple separated from each other. Thessia cleared her throat and her embarrassment.

"I recall mentioning," she said, her demeanor queenly, "you all were invited here under *royal* auspices."

River dropped into her seat, grinning. Galwell nodded, duly chastened. "Very right, Your Majesty."

"My newfound magic will undoubtedly help us in our endeavors. Which is fortunate, for we have much to discuss," Thessia continued. "The Council of Quests is hereby called to order. Our first meeting," the queen said, "starts now."

Acknowledgments

We are so thrilled to have been given the chance to not just return to our beloved realm of Mythria, but also set sail across the Sweetwater Sea and explore the realm of Vestriya with a new cast of heroes and villains. Thank you to our agents, Taylor Haggerty and Katie Shea Boutillier, for continuing to champion E. B. Asher and making these books possible for us. You are our Council of Quests, and we cherish everything you do.

To our editor, Priyanka Krishnan, we are so grateful for your keen eye and your warm embrace of our humor and style, not to mention helping us tackle the daunting task of featuring three romances in one book! Thank you to you and the rest of our fantastic team at Avon, including Samantha Larrabee and DJ DeSmyter in marketing and publicity, production editor Jeanie Lee, editorial assistant Grace Vainisi, copyeditor Kathleen Cook, and proofreader Sarah Strowbridge. You deserve all the Vestriyan crumbiellos your hearts desire.

Our illustrator, Kate Forrester, and cover designer, Ploy Siripant, you have once again created hand magic with this cover, expertly capturing the wonder and whimsy we envisioned when putting this story together.

We are deeply indebted to the friends, family, and fellow authors who have quested with us through the release of many books since the three of us started publishing. It means the world to have you all by our side on this topsy-turvy journey. We thank the Ghosts for your loyalty and support.

And finally, we once again kneel in gratitude to the real heroes—the readers, librarians, and booksellers who read and champion our books. To put it plainly, we love you.

About the Authors

E. B. Asher is the author of *USA Today* bestseller *This Will Be Fun* and the pen name for Bridget Morrissey, Emily Wibberley, and Austin Siegemund-Broka. Bridget is the author of several novels, including *That Summer Feeling* and *Anywhere You Go*. She lives in Los Angeles with her two cats. Emily Wibberley and Austin Siegemund-Broka are the authors of novels including *The Roughest Draft* and Reese's Book Club pick *Heiress Takes All*. Married, they live in Los Angeles, where they continue to take daily inspiration from their own love story.

Check out E. B. Asher's *USA Today* Bestseller

Ten years ago, they saved the realm—and it ruined their lives. Now, four former heroes must reunite, and hopefully live to tell the tale, in this charming romantasy about friendship and redemption, perfect for readers of *Legends & Lattes* and lovers of *Shrek*.

"Witty, romantic, and addictively fun!"
—Sarah Beth Durst,
New York Times bestselling author of *The Spellshop*

DISCOVER GREAT AUTHORS, EXCLUSIVE OFFERS, AND MORE AT HC.COM.